THE
FURIES

Also by Mark Alpert

Final Theory
The Omega Theory
Extinction

THE
FURIES

MARK ALPERT

THOMAS DUNNE BOOKS • ST. MARTIN'S PRESS • NEW YORK

THOMAS DUNNE BOOKS.
An imprint of St. Martin's Press.

THE FURIES. Copyright © 2014 by Mark Alpert. All rights reserved. Printed in the United States of America. For information, address St. Martin's Press, 175 Fifth Avenue, New York, N.Y. 10010.

www.thomasdunnebooks.com
www.stmartins.com

Library of Congress Cataloging-in-Publication Data

Alpert, Mark, 1961–
    The furies: a thriller / Mark Alpert.—First Edition.
        Pages cm
ISBN 978-1-250-02135-9 (hardcover)
ISBN 978-1-250-02277-6 (e-book)
1. Artificial intelligence—Fiction.   I. Title
    PS3601.L67F87 2014
    813'.6—dc23

                    2013031726

St. Martin's Press books may be purchased for educational, business, or promotional use. For information on bulk purchases, please contact Macmillan Corporate and Premium Sales Department at 1-800-221-7945, extension 5442, or write special markets@macmillan.com.

First Edition: April 2014

10 9 8 7 6 5 4 3 2 1

For my in-laws,
By and Laura West,
who introduced me to the mysteries
of northern Michigan

Any sufficiently advanced technology
is indistinguishable from magic.
—Arthur C. Clarke

PROLOGUE

Essex, England
September 1645

Dressed only in her nightgown, Goodwife Elizabeth Fury hid behind a haystack in the midnight darkness. Inside her cottage, just a stone's throw away, the men from the village of Manningtree were torturing her husband. His screams echoed across the farm's pasture.

"Please, sirs! I speak the truth! I—"

Arthur let out a shriek, high and hideous. Elizabeth couldn't see what the villagers were doing to him inside the cottage, but she'd glimpsed the knives in their hands a minute ago when the men came marching down the road. As her husband howled in pain, she tightened her hold on Lily, their daughter. The four-year-old buried her face between her mother's breasts.

Arthur's howls subsided. There was a long, dreadful silence, and then one of the villagers in the cottage shouted, "Where is she?"

Elizabeth recognized the voice. It belonged to Manningtree's blacksmith, Tom Bellamy, a man she'd known for twenty years. She'd never heard him raise his voice before, but now he was bellowing at the top of his lungs. "By God, tell us where thy wretched woman is!"

"I speak the truth! I know not—"

"Lying cur! Where is she hiding?"

Arthur screamed. The sound was as sharp and horrible as a knife, and it tore into Elizabeth's soul. He'd been a good husband to her, loving and loyal. Although she knew she couldn't save him, she couldn't abandon him, either. She peeked around the edge of the haystack and saw shafts of light pouring out of the smashed doorway of their cottage. The villagers inside held torches. Arthur, a lifelong insomniac, had been awake and smoking his pipe outside the cottage when the torches had appeared on the horizon, approaching their farm. He'd ordered Elizabeth to carry Lily to safety while he tried to appease their neighbors.

Then, as Arthur's screams faded, she heard other voices coming from the cottage.

"He won't last long. He's bleeding like a pig."

"A fitting end for him. He was just as wicked as her."

"But how will we find the witch? Her satyr can't tell us now."

"She won't get far." Bellamy's voice drowned out the others. "You two, go to the barn and look for her there."

A moment later a pair of villagers rushed out of the cottage, each carrying a torch. Elizabeth ducked behind the haystack, but she'd already recognized the two men in the firelight: Simon Pearson, Manningtree's carpenter, and Guy Harris, the baker. Now she knew why the villagers had come. A wave of illness had swept through Manningtree that summer. Pearson's son and Harris's daughter had died of fever. Bellamy had lost all three of his children. The men were convinced that someone had used black magic against them, and they'd focused their anger on Elizabeth, who'd been a target of suspicion ever since she and her sisters came to the county of Essex twenty years ago.

She sat in the dirt, very still, while Pearson and Harris tromped toward the barn. The haystack was less than thirty feet away from the barn door. Elizabeth's plan was to wait for the men to go inside, then sneak through the darkness to the woods on the other side of the pasture. But as the footsteps grew louder Lily squirmed in her mother's arms and whimpered.

The footsteps stopped. Elizabeth clapped her palm over her daughter's mouth, but Lily kept squirming.

"Did you hear that?" It was Pearson's voice, low and gruff.

"It came from the barn," Harris whispered.

"Nay, it was outside. The witch is somewhere over there."

She heard a soft tentative step, crushing the loose bits of hay scattered across the dirt. Then another step. Pearson was coming closer. Elizabeth tensed her leg muscles, ready to sprint from the haystack to the shelter of the woods, but she knew it was hopeless. Even if she were alone, she couldn't outrun Pearson. With a squirming four-year-old in her arms, she had no chance at all. She heard a third step, then a fourth and a fifth, each a little louder. He was just a few yards away. At any moment he would see her. In agony, Elizabeth closed her eyes. Her lips moved soundlessly, mouthing a prayer.

Oh, Mother of Creation! Help me in my time of need!

Then she heard a different sound, a high-pitched bleating. One of the lambs in the barn had woken up. The noise awakened several other lambs, and they began to bleat, too.

"She's in the barn, cuz!" Harris whispered.

"Nay, the witch is—"

"I'm going inside. You can do what you will."

She heard footsteps again, but now the men were moving away. First Harris strode toward the barn, and after a couple of seconds Pearson followed. Elizabeth waited until the barn door creaked open and the men went inside, which triggered another chorus of bleating. Then she crept away from the haystack and ran barefoot across the pasture.

Clutching her daughter to her chest, she dashed to the far end of the farm and dove into the woods. She felt a burst of relief as she passed the first line of trees, but she kept on running. She hurtled over roots and stones and puddles, sobbing as she ran. She was thinking of Arthur. The poor man had sacrificed everything for her.

She didn't stop running until she reached the top of Clary's Hill. She dropped to her knees on the hilltop and let go of Lily, laying her down at the foot of an oak tree. The girl was quiet now and breathing deeply, as if she were asleep, but her eyes were wide open. She seemed to understand what was happening. Lily was a precocious girl, the wisest four-year-old Elizabeth had ever known. She'd probably remember this night for the rest of her life.

Rising to her feet, Elizabeth turned eastward. Clary's Hill was the highest point in the area, and from its top she could see her farm, more than a mile away. She spotted three torches near the barn and another three moving across the pasture. The villagers were still looking for her. Then she turned north and saw a much larger fire in the distance, an inferno the size of a house. It rose from the cottage where her sister Margaret lived with her husband and children. And to the southwest another giant blaze climbed toward the night sky, on the farm where her cousin Grace had started her own family.

Elizabeth was dry-eyed as she stared at the flames. It was all her fault. She should've seen the danger coming. She and her family should've left this place years ago, as soon as the villagers started gossiping about them. But this wasn't the time for second-guessing. The first thing to do was find out if anyone else had survived. Long ago she'd told her sisters and cousins that if they came under attack and had to leave their homes, they should meet at an appointed spot near the town of Colchester, about seven miles to the southwest. That's where she would go now. If she and Lily made steady progress across the countryside, they'd reach the meeting place by dawn.

Before they set off, though, she had to retrieve her Treasure. Squinting, Elizabeth searched the ground near the base of the oak until she spotted a big gray stone shaped like a turtle. She slid her fingers under the stone and heaved it aside, then began digging in the cool, dry soil. Lily propped herself on her elbows to watch. The girl's eyes shone in the light of the crescent moon, which had just cleared the eastern horizon.

"Mama," she whispered. "Where are we going?"

Elizabeth kept digging. She fixed her attention on the ground. "We're going on a journey, child. A long journey to a faraway place."

"Why do we have to leave?"

The question made Elizabeth's eyes sting. She shut them tight. She wasn't going to cry now. "Because our neighbors don't like us. They know we're different, and it frightens them."

"They shouldn't be frightened. We wouldn't do anything bad."

The child was so calm. So calm and so beautiful. Elizabeth shook her head as she scooped out another handful of dirt. Lily had enough goodness in her to save the world. "That's true, dearest. We would never hurt them. But they can't see that. They have too much fear in their hearts."

"Will it be better in the faraway place? Will the people there like us?"

"We're going to the wilderness. There won't be anyone else there. We can live in peace."

"What about Papa? Will he come with us?"

Elizabeth opened her eyes and stared at her daughter. The girl's face was full of sorrow. Lily already knew the answer to her question. She'd heard her father screaming.

"Nay, child. Thy father is dead. Remember him always, for he loved thee well."

The girl nodded. Then she fell silent. Elizabeth waited, ready to console her, but Lily simply stared at the rising moon.

Elizabeth turned back to the hole she was digging. Soon her fingernails scraped the lid of the iron box that was buried there. After another minute she unearthed the box and opened its rusty latches. Inside were a dozen gold sovereigns, enough to buy new clothes and cover the expenses of the journey. But Elizabeth's Treasure wasn't the pile of gold coins. It was the leather-bound manuscript lying beneath them.

She opened the book and was relieved to see that the pages hadn't been damaged by dampness or insects. The parchment was velvety and covered with runes. The language was so ancient that no one spoke it aloud anymore, not even Elizabeth or her sisters. But they still used it to record their secrets. They wrote their dreams for the future in the runes of the past, which marched across the parchment like footprints.

Satisfied, Elizabeth closed the book, latched the box, and hefted it under her arm. Then she stood up and stretched her other arm toward Lily. "Come, child. Let's start walking."

The girl took her mother's hand. They headed southwest toward Colchester, but their ultimate goal was the port of Southampton. There they would book passage on one of the ships sailing for America.

PART I
THE PARAMOUR

ONE

New York City
September 2014

She was smart and sexy and beautiful, but all that didn't matter. John Rogers fell for her because of what she said about God.

He met her in a bar on West Fourth Street in Greenwich Village, near the New York University campus. He was slumped on a stool at the end of the bar when she came into the place, laughing as she stepped through the doorway. Her laughter, that's the first thing he noticed. It was high and sweet, a chord of delight. He looked up from his half-empty glass of Budweiser and saw a petite redhead, most likely in her midtwenties, wearing a short spangly skirt and a low-cut blouse.

Two brawny young men stood on either side of her. Both were much taller than her and more casually dressed, in jeans and sneakers and T-shirts. She walked between them, her arms linked with theirs and her face turned toward the young man on her right. He was the one who'd just made her laugh.

The trio halted a few feet past the door and took a moment to scan the room. It was early in the evening, a little before seven, so the place was pretty empty. Only one of the tables was occupied, and John was the only person sitting at the bar. After several seconds of indecision the redhead and her companions chose a table about fifteen feet away from him. The girl sat in the chair closest to the bar and crossed her legs. They were nice legs, tanned and muscular.

John sipped his beer and watched her out of the corner of his eye. Her long fiery hair draped her shoulders and ran down her back. She had long eyelashes, too, and big green eyes. She tilted her chin up when the waitress came to their table to take their orders, and when she smiled at the other woman John felt an ache in his chest, a pang of longing and regret. She was so pretty it hurt to look at her.

But he kept looking anyway. He had the feeling he'd seen her before, although he couldn't imagine where or when. He wasn't a New Yorker. He'd lived his whole life in Philadelphia. He'd arrived in Manhattan that morning and spent the day in an NYU conference center where they held a job fair for unemployed social workers. Which turned out to be a bust, unfortunately. Jobs were just as scarce in New York as they were in Pennsylvania. John didn't have a master's degree in social work or any of the other qualifications that employers were looking for. All he had was a bachelor's degree from the Community College of Philadelphia and a résumé that listed a few off-the-books construction jobs and some part-time work at his local church. Now he felt like an idiot for coming to New York, but he was too tired and depressed to start the long drive back to Philly. So he'd headed for the nearest bar. He had less than twenty dollars left in his wallet, so there was no danger of getting too drunk to drive.

He took another sip of beer, a small one, trying to make it last. Over the next half hour the bar filled up. Most of the customers appeared to be NYU students—gangly boys with odd patches of facial hair and manic girls in tank tops and cutoff shorts. Some of the girls were good-looking but John couldn't take them seriously. They were silly, privileged kids who knew nothing about the real world, who wouldn't last a single day in the part of Philly where he grew up. Also, they were barely old enough to drink, and John was a divorced thirty-three-year-old. They belonged to a different generation. Maybe even a different species.

But he didn't feel that way about the redhead. Although she wasn't much older than the NYU girls, she seemed more sensible, less naïve.

Holding a glass of white wine, she spoke in a low voice to her companions, who smiled and nodded. The two young men looked alike—both had square jaws and strong cheekbones and auburn crew cuts—and it occurred to John that they might be her brothers. Although he couldn't overhear what they were saying, the three of them seemed very much at ease with one another. The only incongruous thing was the redhead's choice of clothes, the short glittery skirt and the revealing blouse. It seemed a little too sexy for a family get-together.

Then he realized why she looked familiar. He'd seen her just a few hours before, at the job fair for social workers. They'd both stood at the edge of a crowd that had gathered around a man handing out applications for jobs at the Children's Aid Society. The demand was so great, he ran out of applications; John didn't get one, and neither did the redhead. Looking more resigned than disappointed, the girl had sighed, "Oh well," to no one in particular and then headed for the other end of the conference center. She'd worn a gray pantsuit at the time, a sober, businesslike outfit that was the polar opposite of what she wore now. That's why John didn't recognize her when she walked into the bar. She must've changed clothes sometime in the past couple of hours.

He stared at her for a few extra seconds, wondering what her story was. Then she turned his way and caught him staring at her, and after a moment she smiled. Now *she* recognized *him*. She was probably remembering the same scene at the conference center. She raised her wineglass and waved hello.

It wasn't much, just a friendly gesture, but it triggered a burst of adrenaline in John's gut. He sat a little straighter on his bar stool. Luckily, he was wearing his best suit and it wasn't too rumpled. He smiled back at her and raised his own glass, which was almost empty.

She said something to the two men at her table. Then she rose to her feet and came toward him. He felt another burst of adrenaline, stronger this time. She was so damn gorgeous. Way out of his league, to tell the truth. John wasn't successful or fashionable. He was just a bruiser from North Philly who'd wasted his youth on the streets and washed out of the army and whose greatest accomplishment in life had been simply staying out of jail. The only thing he had going for him was his size—he was a big guy, six foot three, and still in pretty good shape. His ex-wife used to say he looked like Derek Jeter of the Yankees, and on John's good days he could see the resemblance when he looked in the mirror. Like Jeter, he had a white mom and a black dad, and his own skin color was exactly in-between. But Jeter was a happy guy, always smiling when John saw him on television, even when he struck out. John didn't have as much to be happy about.

The redhead stopped three feet away from him, behind the neighboring bar stool. He noticed she'd brought her wineglass with her, which was a good sign. She cocked her head and gave him a mock-suspicious look. "So was your luck any better than mine?" she asked. "Did you get any interviews?"

He liked her directness. This was a girl who got right to the point. He shook his head. "None whatsoever. It was a complete waste of time."

"I'm starting to think I picked the wrong profession. I should've listened to my mother and gone to dental school." She smiled again, revealing her perfectly white teeth. Then she held out her hand. "My name's Ariel."

Interesting name. Half-rising from his stool, he grasped her hand, which was slender and warm. "I'm John," he said. "John Rogers. Nice to meet you." He pointed at the bar stool next to his. "Would you like a seat?"

She glanced over her shoulder at her table. Her companions were ordering another round of drinks from the waitress and flirting with her. Ariel rolled her eyes and turned back to him. "Sure, why not. My friends are busy."

"I thought they were your brothers. They look like twins, almost."

"They're brothers, but not mine. I went to high school with them in Connecticut. They both work on Wall Street now. I called them this morning when I got into town and they promised to buy me a drink." She moved a bit closer and lowered her voice. "They feel sorry for me. They're making tons of money, and I'm still living at home with my parents."

John pulled out the stool for her. She sat down, crossing her legs again, and set her wineglass on the bar. He couldn't take his eyes off her. It took all his strength to stop himself from gawking at her cleavage. "So, uh, you still live in Connecticut?"

She nodded. "Yeah, and it's boring as hell. I moved back home after I got my bachelor's in social work. I thought I'd be there for just a month or two, but it's taking forever to find a job."

"Welcome to the club. I've been looking for almost a year. I work construction to pay the bills."

"I'm going to another job fair tomorrow. Luckily, I found a cheap hotel in Brooklyn to stay tonight." She leaned toward him, resting an elbow on the edge of the bar. "What about you? You live in New York?"

A beam from one of the overhead track lights illuminated the right side of her face, and John noticed a thin faded scar on her temple. Looking closer, he saw another faint scar just below her left ear and a tracery of lines on the side of her neck. He wondered how she'd been injured, wincing as he viewed all her scars. She must've been in a car accident, he thought, a pretty bad one. But judging from the faintness of the marks, he guessed it had happened a long time ago, when she was very young.

He was studying her so carefully he almost forgot to answer her question. "No, I'm from Philly," he said. "I came to New York just for the day."

"What part of Philadelphia? I have some friends there."

"They probably don't live where I do. It's a rough neighborhood."

"What, North Philly?"

"Yeah, Kensington."

She nodded. "I've never been there, but I've heard of it. Lots of drugs and gangs, right?"

He wasn't surprised that Ariel knew about the place. Kensington was such a notorious slum, it was mentioned in most of the social-work textbooks. John had seen some of those books himself, back when he was taking classes at the community college, and when he read the descriptions of Kensington he wanted to tear out the pages. They weren't even close to the truth. The neighborhood was a hundred times worse.

But he didn't want to talk about Kensington or its gangs right now. The last thing he wanted to do was scare Ariel away by telling her he was once a soldier with the Somerset Street Disciples. He tried to change the subject. "Yeah, there's gangs, but there's good people, too. And if you stick with the good people, you can stay out of trouble."

She cupped her chin in her palm as she stared at him. Her index finger stroked the faint scar below her ear. "So who kept *you* out of trouble?"

There was that directness again. She didn't waste any time. He couldn't think of a way to dodge the question, so instead he was honest with her. "Well, first it was the army, but that didn't last long. I didn't take well to the discipline, so they kicked me out. And then I got some help from a priest, believe it or not. Father Reginald Murphy of Saint Anne's Church. He was the oldest, toughest priest in Philadelphia. All the gangs were terrified of him."

"You belonged to his church?"

"Nah, I'm not even Catholic. But he saw me running around the neighborhood with all the other thugs, and for some reason he made it his business to save me. I'm still not sure why. He never told me." John winced. It still hurt to think about the old man. "And now I'm just trying to return the favor, you know? Trying to get a job where I can do something good. Maybe point a few kids in the right direction. Do the same thing for them that Father Murphy did for me."

"You're talking about him in the past tense. Is he dead?"

John nodded. He opened his mouth, ready to tell Ariel that Father Murphy had died in his sleep. But that was a lie, and after a moment John realized he couldn't tell it. He couldn't tell her the truth either, so he just sat there with his mouth open, trying to think of something to say.

Then Ariel surprised him. She leaned closer and rested her right hand on his forearm. "Let me ask you something, John. Do you believe in God?"

He narrowed his eyes and stared at her. *Oh, shit. Is this gorgeous girl a Jesus freak?* His heart sank as he considered the possibility. Maybe she was trying to proselytize him. But a bar was an odd place to look for converts.

"No, I don't believe." He frowned. "Do you?"

She shook her head. "No. It doesn't make any sense, does it?"

"What do you mean?"

"The world's a mess." She lifted her hand from his forearm and waved it in a circle. "I mean, look around. There's no way that a loving God would create such a screwed-up world. God and heaven, it's all just a fairy tale. It's amazing that anyone still believes it."

Now John was even more surprised. The girl wasn't a Jesus freak—she was a philosopher. He stopped frowning. This was the kind of conversation he enjoyed. "You know what else doesn't make sense?" he said. "When something bad happens, the church always says there's some mysterious reason for it. They say you have to accept all the shit that happens in life because it's part of God's divine plan."

"Yes, exactly." She nodded and took a sip of wine. "I hate that, too. It's like saying, 'You're not smart enough to understand God, so don't even try to make sense of things.' It's so condescending."

"It's worse than that." John raised his voice. "If someone did that to me for real? If someone fucked me over and tried to apologize by saying, 'It's all part of my mysterious plan'? I'd be pretty damn pissed." He wanted to say something stronger, something about shooting the motherfucker in the head, but he restrained himself.

"I'm with you, John." Ariel raised her wineglass and took a bigger sip this time. Then she set down her glass, which was nearly empty, and rested her hand on his forearm again. "We agree that God doesn't exist in the universe right now. But here's what gives me hope: there's a chance that God will exist in the future."

"What?" He assumed this was a joke. Ariel was playing with him. "What are you talking about?"

She looked straight at him, locking her eyes with his. "It's simple. I believe we can change the world. We can make it a better place. And then God will be born."

"Uh, I think I lost you."

"We can make it happen. We can turn ourselves into angels and turn the earth into heaven, a *real* heaven. That's our purpose in life—to bring God into the world."

Ariel was so close, only inches away. He could see the reflections of the track lights in her green irises. She wasn't joking. Her face was absolutely serious. John couldn't help but marvel at how serious she was. "So it's like the Christmas story? We're all headed for Bethlehem, waiting for Baby Jesus to be born?"

She considered the idea for a moment, skewing her eyebrows in thought. Then she smiled. "Yes, that's right. You're a clever man, John Rogers." She raised her glass once again and finished off her wine. "And you deserve a reward for your cleverness. I'm going to buy you a drink."

His throat tightened as Ariel turned around to get the bartender's attention. Even though they'd just agreed that God didn't exist—at least not yet—John directed a silent plea toward heaven. *Her phone number, Lord. I need her number.*

And the Lord, in His infinite wisdom, answered John's prayer.

He and Ariel spent the next three hours talking. At some point during the second hour, Ariel's Wall Street friends got tired of flirting with the waitress; they shook hands with John and kissed Ariel goodbye before heading for another watering hole. Then someone turned up the volume of the bar's loudspeakers and the room reverberated with the din of Lady Gaga. There was nothing to eat except the baskets of popcorn that the bartender placed in front of them, but John didn't care. He was having the time of his life. He'd never met a girl like Ariel before. It was so easy to talk to her, so effortless. He told her stories about his mom and growing up in Kensington. He even told her a little about Carol, his ex-wife, which was a subject he usually avoided. Ariel was a great listener, always asking questions and making smart observations. It was amazing, he thought, that such a young woman could be so wise.

Finally, at 11:00 P.M., she looked at her watch and said she had to go. Her hotel was in Bushwick—a dicey part of Brooklyn, especially late at night—and she was planning to take the subway. John immediately offered to drive her there instead. It was only a half hour out of his way, he said. After dropping her off at the hotel, he could take the Verrazano Bridge and I-95 to get back to Philly. And because he'd had only two drinks all night, he added, he was perfectly sober. Ariel thought it over for a few seconds. Then she leaned toward him, slow and sexy, bringing her lips close to his ear. "That would be nice," she whispered.

As they left the bar, arm in arm, and strolled down West Fourth Street toward where his car was parked, John should've realized that it had all happened too easily. But the thought never occurred to him. He was too damn happy.

TWO

The hotel was shabbier than John expected. Bushwick was a neighborhood in transition, with trendy restaurants and clubs at the western end and seedy tenements to the east. The Evergreen Inn was closer to the eastern section. As John drove down Evergreen Avenue he saw dark, vacant lots and boarded-up storefronts sprayed with graffiti. It wasn't as bad as North Philly, but it didn't look too safe. The hotel itself was an old, weather-beaten row house with a small neon sign over the entrance and a bunch of shifty teenagers loitering on the sidewalk outside. The kids stared at John's car, a battered 2003 Kia, as he pulled up to the curb. It's a good thing he drove a shit heap, he thought. The car was hardly worth stealing.

John shut off the engine and turned to Ariel. "All right if I walk you inside?"

She didn't say anything. Instead, she just smiled and reached for his hand. John's heart pounded against his breastbone. He knew what was going to happen next.

Eager as a schoolboy, he escorted her to the hotel's entrance. One of the teenagers whistled at Ariel as she and John walked by. They stepped into the Evergreen Inn and rushed past the night clerk, a scruffy, bearded dude who was reading the *New York Post* behind his desk. He looked up from his paper and grunted, "Good night," and then they bolted up the narrow staircase. Ariel was still holding John's hand. When they reached the third floor she let go of him and reached into her purse for the key to room 302. Then she opened the door and they stepped inside. They were in each other's arms as soon as the door closed behind them.

John had to lower his head to kiss her, and though he stayed on his feet he felt like he was falling. Ariel's lips tasted of salt and white wine. She shivered in his arms, her shoulder muscles trembling under the thin silk of her blouse. The only sound in the room was the whisper of her breath, which mingled with his own.

After a minute or so they pulled apart. Ariel reached behind her and hit the light switch, and John surveyed the room. It was small but clean. A queen-size bed took up most of the floor space, and behind it was a window with dark gray curtains. There was a night table next to the bed and a big ceramic lamp with a yellow shade, but no chairs and no TV. Ariel took his hand again and led him to the bed, which had a cheery blue cover and two large pillows. There was nowhere else to go, nothing else to do.

She slipped off her shoes as they sat on the edge of the bed. Then she looked John in the eye and squeezed his hand. "Are you okay with this?" she asked.

Amazing, he thought. She was ten years younger than him, and she was asking if *he* was okay. "Oh, I'm more than okay with it. I'm freakin' ecstatic. You're wonderful, you know that?" He lifted her hand and kissed her smooth knuckles. "But what about you? How do *you* feel?"

"I don't do this very often. Almost never, in fact. I guess you made a big impression on me." She reached for the lapels of his jacket and peeled them over his shoulders. John wriggled his arms out of the sleeves and let the thing drop to the carpet.

"I feel the same way," he said. "I was bowled over the minute I saw you. I didn't think I had a chance."

"Why not?" She grasped the knot of his tie and loosened it.

"You're so beautiful. And smart. I'm just a regular guy."

"Don't sell yourself short, John Rogers." She undid his tie and threw it across the room. Then she started unbuttoning his shirt. "You're special. Don't ever forget that. You're one in a million."

He kissed her again as she took his shirt off. Then he gripped the fabric near the bottom of her blouse and eased it out of the waistband of her skirt. She helped him pull the blouse over her head, and then he reached both hands around her and unhooked her bra. The lacy cups slid from her breasts, which were a wonder to behold. He stared at them for so long that Ariel had to tap his nose to get his attention.

"Come on, you," she said. "Take off my skirt."

She lay down on her back, sinking into the soft mattress. John's hands trembled as he reached for the clasp on her skirt and undid it. He couldn't believe this was happening, couldn't get over how lucky he was. He wasn't drunk, but he still got a little dizzy as she lifted her butt off the mattress to make it easier for him to slide her skirt down her legs. Her eagerness was inexplicable, but it was also a turn-on. Without pausing he hooked his fingers beneath the waistband of her panty hose. He yanked the nylon down her legs along with her panties, which were damp at the crotch. Then he started fumbling with his belt and kicking off his shoes, in a mad rush to get naked and lie down beside her. As he struggled with his zipper, though, he belatedly realized he didn't have a condom. He froze, awkwardly perched on the edge of the bed. Noticing his hesitation, Ariel looked up at him and smiled.

"Don't worry," she whispered. "I'm on the pill." She sat up and helped him take off his pants and boxer shorts. Then she lay back down on the bed and pulled him on top of her.

Her skin was so warm. John grasped her shoulders and kissed her breasts. He felt like he was falling again, diving from a great height into a deep, warm pool. Ariel clutched his back and murmured, "Oh, sweetness." Then she spread her legs and reached for his erection, gripping it firmly. John felt the wetness between her legs as she started to guide him inside her.

Then he heard the gunshot. It came from the corridor outside the door to their room. The noise was muffled by some kind of silencer; it sounded more like a snap than a boom, but it was still unmistakable. John's reaction to the sound was automatic: he pushed Ariel off the bed and they both hit the floor.

Another shot echoed in the corridor. Keeping his head low, John picked up his boxer shorts from the carpet and pulled them back on. He'd heard lots of gunfire when he was a soldier for the Disciples, but silencers were unusual. The only people who used them were the Italian guys in the South Philly gangs, the mafia types. As he scrambled into his pants and grabbed his shoes, he noticed that Ariel was putting on her panties. The girl wasn't screaming or crying. She moved quickly and silently, staying low as she slipped into her blouse and skirt. Then she opened her purse, which was also on the floor, and pulled out a Glock semiautomatic pistol.

That sight was even more startling than the gunshots. John felt a jolt of alarm. For a second he thought Ariel was going to shoot him. But instead she took cover behind the night table and aimed her Glock at the door. "Stay down," she whispered. "I'll take care of this."

"Jesus, what's going on?"

"I'm sorry, John. I've put you in danger."

"Are you a cop? Is that it?"

"No, I'm not. Just be quiet now, okay?"

While he struggled to make sense of things—if Ariel wasn't a cop, what the hell was she?—three more gunshots sounded in the corridor. Then the door burst open, its flimsy frame splintering, and a man holding a pistol staggered into the room. But he didn't fire at them. He stayed close to the doorway and flattened himself against the wall, as if taking cover from a shooter in the hallway. A moment later he reached around the broken door frame to fire at his pursuer. He carried a Glock too and held it expertly, keeping the gun steady as he pulled the trigger.

John recognized the man—he was one of the two brawny guys who'd accompanied Ariel at the bar in Greenwich Village. Judging from the way he handled his Glock, John guessed that he didn't really work on Wall Street. He moved like a Special Forces soldier or a paramilitary bodyguard, someone with plenty of training in firearms. But why would Ariel need a bodyguard?

The man fired again down the hall. Then he swung his head toward Ariel and pointed at the window behind the bed. "You can go out the fire escape," he whispered. "I'll hold them off here."

"Who are they?" Ariel asked. Her voice was calm, which was pretty remarkable considering the circumstances.

"Sullivan's men. At least a dozen."

John had seen enough. He reached into his pocket, pulled out his cell phone, and started to dial 911. "I'm calling the cops," he said. "I don't know who you are or what you're—"

Ariel snatched the phone out of his hands and flung it against the wall. The look on her face was pure ferocity. "The police won't get here in time. Do you want to stay alive?"

Another barrage of gunfire erupted in the corridor, and the bullets slammed into the door frame. Ariel's bodyguard lurched to the side, raising his arms to shield himself from the flying splinters. John realized in that instant that he was in the middle of a gang war. These gangs were different from the ones he knew—the Disciples, the Bloods, the Latin Kings—but the violence and viciousness were the same.

Ariel dashed toward the window behind the bed and parted the curtains. She unlatched the window and gripped the handle to slide it open, but the thing wouldn't budge. Her face reddened as she strained against it. "It's stuck!"

John lifted the ceramic lamp from the night table. He had some experience making quick escapes from row houses. "Get out of the way!" he shouted, and as Ariel stepped backward he swung the lamp against the window. The glass broke into a thousand pieces that clattered on the rusty bars of the fire escape. John used the lamp's heavy base to pulverize the shards remaining in the window frame, then poked his head outside. He heard some distant, scuffling noises, but the dark alley behind the row house was deserted. He glanced over his shoulder at Ariel. "It's clear! Let's go!"

At the same moment, the gunfire in the corridor intensified. Several shooters in the other gang were firing at once, and some of the bullets whizzed through the doorway. The bodyguard clutched his stomach and crumpled to the floor. Ariel shouted, "Richard!" and took a step toward him, but after half a second she stopped herself. Keeping her Glock pointed at the doorway, she went to her purse instead and pulled something out, a small notebook with a frayed leather cover. She tucked it into the waistband of her skirt, then draped the hem of her blouse over the thing to hide it. Then she raced toward John, who'd already stepped onto the fire escape.

He reached for Ariel and helped her clamber through the window frame, praying that she wouldn't cut her bare feet on the broken glass. As soon as she was on the fire escape, he pushed her toward the rusty steps that went upward. It was always better to go up than down, John had learned. If you made it to the roof, you could cross over to any of the neighboring row houses, giving you dozens of possible escape routes and hiding places. That was a lot safer than descending to the street, where you'd be an easy target for anyone shooting from the window.

They came under fire from below just as they reached the fifth floor. Luckily, their pursuers had to shoot upward, which was awkward, and the bars of the fire escape deflected their shots. A moment later, though,

John heard footsteps echoing in the alley behind the row house. The other gang was surrounding the building. Their soldiers might be on the roof already. He and Ariel pounded up the steps of the fire escape as fast as they could, but when they reached the top they saw the silhouette of a tall figure looming over them. Ariel aimed her Glock at the edge of the roof, but the tall man jumped backward. "Don't shoot!" he called. "It's me!"

"Hal?" Ariel dashed up to the roof, and John followed right behind. The tall man, he saw, was the other brawny guy from the bar. Ariel's second bodyguard. This man carried an assault rifle, an M4 carbine. And it wasn't a civilian copycat of the gun either—it was the fully automatic military version. John had seen plenty of them during his brief stint in the army.

The bodyguard lowered his rifle as Ariel came toward him. "Where's Richard?" he asked.

Ariel shook her head. "Lost."

Hal said nothing in response, but after a second he returned to the edge of the roof and crouched behind the low wall there. Pointing the barrel of his rifle over the wall, he took careful aim and pulled the trigger. Then he chose another target and pulled the trigger again. His rifle had a silencer attached to the muzzle. The gun was quiet enough that they could hear his victims falling to the pavement.

He fired six shots into the alley behind the row house, then four more at the soldiers climbing the fire escape. His face was blank as he sighted his targets through the rifle's scope. He was a professional, cold and efficient. John was familiar with the type; every gang in North Philly had at least a couple of seasoned killers in its ranks. They were scary as hell, even when they were on your side.

Meanwhile, Ariel took cover behind one of the rooftop vents, a rectangular steel unit about four feet tall. Holding her Glock in both hands, she scanned the roofs of the neighboring buildings, obviously searching for the best escape route. John, who was crouched behind a similar vent on the other side of the roof, did the same. There were nearly a dozen row houses running down the length of the block, and each roof had an emergency-exit door that led to the building's stairwell. Most of the doors were probably locked, but John was willing to bet that one or two had been propped open by the locals. The best strategy, he decided, was to cross over to the other buildings and start trying all the doors.

He was going to suggest this idea to Ariel but before he could stand up and scurry to her position, the door to the nearest stairwell flew open.

Three men with their own assault rifles rushed outside and sprayed bullets across the rooftop.

Hal spun around as soon as he heard the noise, but he was completely exposed to the barrage. One bullet hit him in the thigh, another in the stomach, another in the chest. Before he collapsed, he managed to point his rifle at one of the attackers and blast off the top of his skull. And in that same instant Ariel rose from her hiding place behind the vent and fired her Glock at another gunman, stopping him with a shot that ripped through his neck.

The third guy, though, was fast and aggressive, a thug with a shaved head and a spiderweb tattoo on his face. He ran toward Ariel, firing his rifle like mad, and one of the bullets clipped her right shoulder before she could duck. She dropped her Glock and fell on her side, sprawling a couple of yards behind the vent. The thug raced toward her, coming in for the kill, but now John was in motion too, leaving his own hiding place and charging across the rooftop at high speed. Although John didn't have a gun, he had the advantage of surprise. The thug didn't see him coming from the other side of the roof, and he couldn't hear anything either because he was still blasting away with his rifle. When the bastard reached the vent he fired another burst at Ariel, hitting her bare legs and making her scream. But as he pointed the gun at her torso, ready to finish her off, John tackled him from behind. He knocked the thug down and shoved his face into the tar and grit of the rooftop.

The assault rifle was trapped underneath the guy's torso, and John didn't give him a chance to use it. He knelt on the thug's back and pounded his head, over and over, pummeling him into unconsciousness. John hadn't beaten anyone like this in almost ten years, but it all came back to him in a second. This was his specialty when he ran with the Disciples, giving beatdowns to anyone who stole from the gang's drug crews. It never bothered him back then, but now he felt sick as he hammered the thug's skull. His stomach roiled and his knuckles ached.

Once he was sure the bastard was out cold, he rushed over to Ariel. Her shoulder wasn't so bad—the bullet had just grazed her there—but her legs were bleeding from deep wounds in her calves and thighs. He needed to get her to an emergency room, *fast*. Bending over, he slid one arm under her back and the other under her blood-spattered knees. Ariel let out a gasp as he lifted her, and she writhed in his arms as he carried her across the roof. The old frayed notebook slipped out of the waistband of her skirt, but despite the pain she grabbed the thing and clutched it against her chest.

Although the door to the row house's stairwell stood wide open, John ran past it. More thugs might still be in the building. It would be safer to try one of the other row houses on the block. He lugged Ariel to the roof of the neighboring building, but the emergency-exit door there was locked, and so was the door on the roof of the next row house. On the roof of the third building, though, the door was ajar. John dashed inside and went down the steps, trying not to joggle Ariel too much.

This row house was an ordinary apartment building rather than a hotel. Once John reached the ground floor he peered through a small glass square near the top of the building's front door. The sidewalk in front of the Evergreen Inn was empty now. The loitering teenagers must've run off when they heard the gunfire. John's Kia was parked just twenty yards away, sitting in a circle of darkness under a broken streetlight.

He looked up and down Evergreen Avenue, searching for signs of movement. Although he didn't see anyone, he was still plenty worried. One of the soldiers from the other gang could be hiding in a doorway or behind one of the parked cars. And if the asshole had a gun, he could pop them in a second. But John had no choice. He had to make a run for it. He prepared himself by taking his car keys out of his pocket and tightening his grip on Ariel, whose eyes were closed now. Then he threw his shoulder against the door and hurtled outside.

He bent low, keeping his head down as he raced toward his car. Twenty yards, just twenty yards. He was halfway there in a couple of seconds. He pressed the UNLOCK button on his car keys and the Kia's hazard lights flashed yellow in the darkness.

He was diving for the back door on the driver's side when he heard the first gunshots. The bullets ripped through the air just above his head, but he didn't stop, didn't hesitate for a moment. He opened the door and threw Ariel into the backseat. She might've yelped, she might've screamed, but he couldn't hear her because he'd already slammed the door shut and jumped into the driver's seat. As he started the engine another barrage smashed into the back of the car, the bullets thunking into the trunk and the rear fender, but an instant later he was barreling down Evergreen Avenue, his foot stomping the accelerator, zero to sixty in seven seconds. He made a sharp shrieking left turn on Halsey Street, then blew through three red lights and made a right on Howard Avenue.

John drove like a madman, making left and right turns every couple of blocks. He didn't slow down until they were miles away from Bushwick and he was certain that no one was following. They were in an industrial part of Brooklyn now, surrounded by warehouses. John was hopelessly lost, but up ahead he saw a square blue sign with an H on it and an arrow pointing left. They were close to a hospital.

He looked in the rearview mirror. Ariel lay on her side, half on and half off the backseat. She was motionless and her face was very pale. John couldn't tell if she was breathing. "Ariel!" he shouted. *"Ariel!"*

He glanced at her legs but couldn't bear to look at them. The Kia's backseat was slick with her blood. John considered trying to bandage the bullet wounds, but he knew nothing about first aid. Better to get her to the hospital as quickly as possible. He turned left at the sign and hit the gas.

"Just hang on," he shouted at the backseat. "I'm taking you to the emergency room. We'll be there in two minutes."

John wasn't really expecting a response, but Ariel opened her eyes and spoke in a loud, commanding voice: "Stop the car."

His chest tightened. She was alive! "No, look, we're going to the—"

"I said *stop the car!*" Ariel sat upright. Grimacing in pain, she lifted her right arm and pointed at him. "Stop *right now* or I'll throw myself out the door!"

Bewildered, John hit the brake. He looked over his shoulder as the car lurched to a halt. "Ariel, this is crazy. We have to—"

"You saw . . . what they tried to do." Gasping, she struggled to get the words out. "They're determined . . . to kill me. If we go to the hospital . . . they'll find us there. They'll finish me off."

"Then let's call the cops. We'll tell them what happened and they'll come to the emergency room. No one's gonna hurt you if there's cops in the room."

She grimaced again, squeezing her eyes shut. John was amazed she could stay conscious, much less talk to him. She still clutched her old brown notebook against her chest. "No . . . that won't work. I can't explain right now . . . but you have to believe me."

John shook his head. "Well, what do you want me to do? I can't let you bleed to death."

"Then get back here . . . and help me stop the bleeding."

"I'm not a doctor! I don't know how to help you!"

Ariel's eyelids fluttered, and for a moment it looked like she was going to pass out again. But she bit her lower lip and managed to hang on. "Don't worry. I'll tell you what to do."

THREE

Two hours later John drove across the Betsy Ross Bridge. The Delaware River was coal black under the 2:00 A.M. sky. The skyscrapers of downtown Philly stood on the horizon, about six miles to the southwest, still glittering even at this hour of the night. But John didn't plan to go that far. Kensington was two miles closer, a patchwork of dark streets between downtown and the river.

He looked in the rearview mirror for what must've been the hundredth time. Ariel was still asleep. If he listened carefully he could hear her breathing. She'd drifted off soon after they left Brooklyn, after John bandaged her legs using strips of fabric torn from her blouse. But it was a fitful sleep, because she was in terrible pain. She moaned and whimpered and occasionally spoke a few delirious words. She cried out, "Mother, help me!" a couple of times, and once she mumbled a sentence that sounded like poetry. It was pretty strange stuff. But everything about Ariel was strange.

The most likely explanation, John thought, was that she was connected to the mafia. She was the daughter of some powerful mob boss, maybe. Or maybe she was the boss's young wife, but she was fooling around on the side. Maybe she'd decided to go out and have some fun tonight, so she took her bodyguards to the bar in Greenwich Village and started looking for a playmate. But her husband figured out what was going on and sent his soldiers to the hotel in Bushwick to punish her and the bodyguards. That would explain the viciousness of the attack. And also why Ariel refused to go to the police or the hospital.

But it didn't explain her behavior during the assault, her coolness under fire. Could your average mob wife handle a Glock as well as Ariel could? Or give instructions on how to bandage a bullet wound? And what about the notebook she still clutched against her chest while she slept? What was that all about?

John let out a long, tired breath. It didn't make sense. If he were acting rationally, he'd deliver Ariel to the nearest emergency room, whether she liked it or not. But John wasn't rational. All his life he'd made choices with his heart, not his head. Although he'd just met Ariel, he was powerfully attracted to her. Part of it was sexual attraction, sure, but the sexiest thing about her was that she'd made him feel good about himself. She seemed to see something admirable in him, something rare and fine. And her regard for him, her belief in his goodness, had an enormous effect. Even though Ariel had nearly gotten him killed, he was ready to do anything for her. He wanted to justify her faith in him.

After crossing the bridge and driving three miles south along the Delaware River, John got off the highway at the Girard Avenue exit. It was a wide street lined with fast-food joints and car-repair shops, but as he drove closer to Kensington the commercial establishments grew scarce. By the time he turned right on Front Street, which ran under the tracks of the elevated train line, the only activity he saw was drug dealing. It was late, even for the dealers, but the cars were still coming in from the suburbs and stopping at the street corners.

The customers were mostly teenagers, white kids with money, hoping to score some coke or pot and then get the hell out of Philadelphia. The corner crews were also teenagers, but mostly black or Latino or some mix of the two. Swiftly and efficiently, they kept the line of cars moving along. One kid took the money, another ran to the stash house, another delivered the drugs and another kept a lookout for the cops. Every ten minutes or so, an older kid—in his late teens or early twenties—would come around the corner and observe the whole operation, making sure that no one in the crew was slipping any cash into his pockets. That had been John's job when he ran with the Disciples. The thug, the enforcer.

He got into the business the same way all the other kids did. At the age of nine he started hanging out at the corners and getting to know the people who worked there. Then he did a few odd jobs for them, getting paid twenty dollars a night to work as a lookout or a decoy. All his friends were doing the same thing, so he didn't take it too seriously. It was just an easy way to make some money. His real ambition in life was to become a pitcher for the Phillies. He had a pretty good throwing arm.

His mom knew what he did at night, but she couldn't stop him. Although her intentions were good, her life had been full of disappointment. She'd had bad luck with men, starting with John's father, who'd walked out on her as soon as she got pregnant. She'd had bad luck at work, too, drifting from one shitty waitressing job to another. And when John was thirteen she got hit by the shittiest piece of luck yet, a fist-sized tumor in her abdomen. The doctors cut it out and put her on chemotherapy, but she died a year later and John got sent to a foster home. He didn't stay there long, though. Within a few months he was working full time for the Disciples.

His corner was Front Street and Somerset. He started dealing there at the age of fourteen and didn't leave until he was twenty-three. For the drug business, that was a spectacularly long run. Most kids got killed or sent to prison long before they reached the five-year mark. But John was good at the job. He had a knack for sensing things ahead of time: when the cops were going to crack down on Kensington, when the soldiers from the Latin Kings were coming to visit his corner. Or maybe he was just lucky. He seemed to have just as much good luck as his mother had bad.

His best piece of luck was meeting Father Murphy. The priest ran a baseball league for the neighborhood kids, and sometimes John would watch the games in the vacant lot behind St. Anne's Church. Murphy knew John was in the Disciples, but the old man would talk baseball with him anyway. The guy was tremendously knowledgeable about the game—and the Phillies in particular—and over time they started talking about other things as well. By this point, John was one of the Disciples' captains, in charge of running several corners, and that was a dangerous position. He was in a winner-take-all situation, competing with the three other captains in Kensington. One of them, a ruthless prick named Salazar, wanted to take over John's corners and was already threatening to kill him. Father Murphy knew all this, and one day he offered John some valuable advice. "Get out of town, son," he said. "Go join the army."

John dismissed the idea at first, but he took it more seriously after Salazar's boys fired a warning shot at him. The army was desperate for soldiers at the time—the war in Iraq was in full swing—and the recruiters were delighted to sign him up. Once John started basic training, though, he quickly learned that he hated army life. The rules drove him crazy, and his drill sergeant was a sadist. After enduring the full ten weeks of basic, John got into a fistfight with his sergeant, who busted him out of the service. But when he returned to Philly and told Father Murphy what had happened, the old priest just laughed. Then, after he stopped chuckling, he offered John another chance. St. Anne's Church had just won a grant to start the Anti-Gang Project to convince the neighborhood kids to stay away from the drug crews. Father Murphy told John he'd be perfect for the job. He could get paid for steering kids away from the bad choices he'd made.

John was skeptical about this idea too, but it worked. Although the new job was part time and didn't pay as well as the drug business—he had to take landscaping and construction jobs to make ends meet—it didn't chew up his insides either, or make him jump every time he heard a noise behind him. After a few months he started to adjust to the regular world, the normal innocent life of paychecks and taxes. He bought a cheap suit and started a bank account. For the next seven years he was a happy, law-abiding citizen. He went to community college and met a great woman named Carol DeSantis. They got married and had a daughter.

Then his luck changed and everything went to hell.

Now John turned left on Somerset Street. He drove a few blocks and approached a two-story row house with peeling red paint. Since Carol left him three years ago, he'd lived alone in an apartment on the building's second floor. It was a small, dingy place, not so different from the apartment where he'd grown up. Despite all the bad memories, this neighborhood was still his home. He'd have a hard time living anywhere else.

He slowed down and scanned the street in front of his house. The sidewalk was empty except for a crumpled Budweiser can and a heap of broken glass that reflected the streetlights. But he didn't park in his usual spot by the corner. Instead he drove another three blocks and made a right on Hancock Street. He was going to see Gabriel Rodriguez, who'd also grown up in the neighborhood. Gabe was a thief and a junkie, but there was a chance he could do something for Ariel.

Gabe's house stood alone in the middle of the block. It was a brick row house whose neighbors had been demolished, leaving vacant lots on either side. For extra security, Gabe had put up a chain-link fence around the house and topped it with coils of concertina wire. Gabe's pit bulls, Maurice and Malaga, started barking when John parked by the curb. He stepped out of the Kia, opened its back door, and scooped up Ariel, who squirmed and grimaced but didn't open her eyes. Then he carried her to the gate at the center of the fence. The dogs hurled themselves against the other side of the chain link, snarling and growling. They usually calmed down once they recognized John, but the smell of blood must've disturbed them.

"Gabe!" John yelled. "Get your ass out here!"

A light came on inside the house, and a few seconds later Gabe appeared at the front door, wearing boxer shorts and a tattered bathrobe. Like most junkies, he looked like a scarecrow, a really pathetic scarecrow with greasy black hair. His face was so emaciated you could see the shape of his skull underneath his blotchy skin. He stared at John with sunken, red-rimmed eyes. "What's going on? Is that a girl?"

"Open the gate, goddamn it!"

Gabe stepped forward and removed a set of keys from the pocket of his bathrobe. The pit bulls slunk backward as he approached the gate. "I don't get it," he said, squinting at the wounds on Ariel's legs. "Why don't you take her to the emergency—"

"She's not a bystander. She's wanted."

"What? The crews are using girls now? Who—"

"Jesus Christ, hurry up!"

Gabe unlocked the gate and pushed it open. While he shushed the dogs, John carried Ariel into the house and down the steps to the basement. Gabe used this part of the house as his operating room. There was a padded table in the center of the room and bright fluorescent lights on the ceiling. Along the walls were various pieces of medical equipment that Gabe had stolen from Temple University Hospital before he was booted off the hospital's staff: a ventilator, a couple of defibrillators, a whole refrigerator full of antibiotics. Although the state of Pennsylvania had taken away Gabriel's medical license, he had a lucrative practice catering to the gangs of Kensington. He treated their injured soldiers, extracting the bullets from their bodies and stitching up their wounds, but unlike the doctors in the city's emergency rooms he didn't report the gun violence and stabbings to the police. In return for his services, the gang bosses paid him in dime bags of heroin.

John carefully placed Ariel on the padded table. As he let go of her he noticed that her skin was clammy. He pressed his fingers against the side of her neck, checking her pulse. It was there, but very faint and thready. "She's in shock," he said, turning to Gabe. "I can barely feel a pulse."

"Relax, Johnny boy." Gabe went to a stainless-steel sink in the corner of the room and washed his hands and emaciated arms. Then he ripped open a plastic bag containing an intravenous kit. "So you're telling me this redhead's a gangster?"

"Just get to work, okay?"

Holding a syringe and the intravenous tubing, Gabe approached the table and scrutinized Ariel. He grabbed her limp right arm and began hunting for a vein. "Well, she's got good muscle tone, I'll say that for her."

He plunged the syringe into the crook of her arm. Then he went to his refrigerator and removed a plastic bag full of blood. He hooked the bag to the intravenous tubing and hung it from an IV pole so the blood could drain into Ariel. The label on the bag said O NEGATIVE, the universal donor blood type. Gabe's refrigerator was full of the stuff.

He pointed at Ariel's bandages, the strips of black silk tied around her legs. "This is very creative. You did a nice job." Grinning, he looked at John over his shoulder. But his grin disappeared when he started untying the bandages. "Man, that's ugly. When was she shot?"

"Around midnight," John replied. He had to turn away from the operating table. "Two hours ago."

"What caliber? Jesus, these look like rifle shots."

"Yeah, the asshole used an assault rifle. An M4 carbine."

"What?" He looked over his shoulder again and raised an eyebrow. "Where did this happen? Afghanistan?"

"Look, is she gonna make it or not?"

Gabe didn't answer right away. He studied Ariel's bullet wounds, using a sponge to wipe the dried blood from her legs. "It doesn't look good. The bullets fragmented inside her. They cracked the fibula in her left leg and the tibia in her right. Tore up a lot of blood vessels, too." He shook his head. "Honestly? I'm surprised she's still breathing. She should've bled out a couple of hours ago."

John's stomach churned. He forced himself to look at Ariel, and for a moment he pictured someone else lying there on the table. A child's body, blood-soaked and torn. *Ivy's body.*

Clenching his jaw, he pushed the memory out of his mind. "Answer the question, Gabe. Does she have a chance?"

"Let me work on her. We'll see what happens." He went to his supply cabinet and collected the surgical tools he needed—scalpel, forceps, suction tubes. "You can go upstairs if you want. There's a coffee machine in the kitchen."

John would've loved a cup of coffee, but he didn't leave the operating room. Instead, he leaned against the wall and watched Gabe work. For a junkie, he had surprisingly steady hands. But this was no accident—Gabe timed his heroin usage according to a rigid schedule. He shot up at 10:00 P.M., which made him drowsy for two hours and then restless. He was alert and able to work from midnight till dawn, the prime hours for carnage in Kensington. Once the sun came up, though, he'd start sweating and shaking and going through withdrawal. Gabe would be completely useless a few hours from now, but for the moment he was as skillful as any surgeon in Philly.

John felt sorry for him, but also a little disgusted. He'd known Gabe since they were in kindergarten. The guy was fantastically smart and phenomenally stupid, all at the same time. In high school he aced all the tests but got suspended for throwing a firecracker into the girls' bathroom. He was accepted into the University of Pennsylvania, but then the campus police caught him selling pot to his roommates. Somehow or other, he made it into medical school, and for the next seven years it looked like he'd cleaned up his act. He became a success story, a Kensington boy who grew up to be an emergency-room doctor at Temple University Hospital. He'd managed to beat the odds and climb above all the shit. But it didn't last. He got addicted to codeine while working at the hospital. He stole the painkillers he was supposed to prescribe to his patients. After Temple fired him, he switched from codeine to heroin. It was an expensive habit, and he didn't have a salary anymore, so he started offering his surgical expertise to the local drug crews.

There was a clock on the opposite wall of the operating room. After an hour Gabe was still hard at work, cutting and cleaning and splinting and stitching, but John was too tired to stay on his feet a minute longer. So he slumped to the floor and closed his eyes. Maybe he could catch a little sleep.

He was luckier than Gabe, he thought. He didn't have to work for the crews anymore. But as long as you lived in Kensington, you couldn't really escape the business. It was always there. You were at its mercy.

When he opened his eyes it was almost 6:00 A.M. Gabe was at the sink again, washing the blood from his hands. Full of confusion and alarm, John staggered to his feet and rushed over to the operating table. Ariel's face was still pale, but now her legs were professionally bandaged and splinted. Gabe had covered her chest with a thin, white blanket, which rose up and down with each breath.

"Is she okay?" John asked. "She looks better."

Gabe dried his hands and nodded. "The lady gangster will live. I stitched the bullet wounds and set her broken legs. She'll be able to walk again in eight or nine weeks."

John felt a surge of relief so strong he almost lost his balance. He didn't understand it: in just twelve hours Ariel had become the most important person in the world to him. And he didn't even know her last name.

"So where the hell did you find her?" Gabe asked. "Here in town?"

"I met her in a bar. In New York."

"In a bar, huh? And this was before she got shot?"

"They followed us to Brooklyn. The assholes with the rifles, I mean. I think they were mafia."

"Mafia?" Gabe walked over to the other side of the table. "So what's this?" He picked up the small brown leather-bound notebook, which had slipped out of Ariel's grasp. "You think it's Italian?"

He opened the notebook and showed John one of the pages. It was inscribed with line after line of unfamiliar symbols. Some of them looked like backwards B's and P's and R's. Others resembled tree trunks and lightning bolts.

"Shit," John whispered. "What the fuck?"

"Crazy, right? It's like something out of *Lord of the Rings*."

"What are you—"

"*Lord of the Rings* has this kind of writing in it. To show the language of the elves and all those other weird fuckers."

John had to laugh. It was too ridiculous. "Well, can you read the language?" He pointed at the page. "Do you know what it means?"

"No, man. I don't have a clue. But it's pretty freaky, don't you think?"

Squinting, John took a closer look at the symbols. They were drawn in black ink by a skillful hand. Someone had obviously lavished a lot of time and effort on the notebook, sketching each character with great care, like Chinese calligraphy. Gabe was right: it was pretty weird. Did Ariel write those symbols in the notebook, or was she carrying around someone else's strange jottings? And were they part of a code?

"There's something else," Gabe said, putting down the notebook. He lifted the thin blanket to show Ariel's uninjured left arm. "This girl has scars all over her body. They're old and faint, but they're everywhere."

He pointed at several thin, jagged lines between her elbow and shoulder. They were similar to the scars John had seen on her face and neck when he met her. "Yeah, I noticed that, too. She must've been in an accident when she was a kid. A car wreck, probably."

"No, that would look different. Some of her scars are fainter than others." Gabe stared at her arm for several seconds, then examined the other arm. "It looks like she was in a lot of accidents. Some big and some small. But all her injuries healed nicely."

"So she's accident-prone. That's not so unusual."

"Hold on. There's more." Gabe let go of the blanket and pointed at Ariel's mouth. There was a bit of dried blood on the left side of her lower lip. He gingerly pressed his index finger to the lip, pushing it down to expose her teeth. One of her molars was missing. "I noticed this while I was cleaning her up."

John winced when he saw the gap. He remembered that Ariel had fallen on her side after she was shot. "She hit the ground during the firefight. I guess it knocked her tooth out."

"I don't think so. I found the tooth still in her mouth, under her tongue. I think it came out afterward, while you were driving her here. She was probably grinding her teeth together because of the pain."

"Jesus," John muttered, wincing again. This was even worse. "I didn't know you could lose a tooth that way."

Without letting go of Ariel's lip, Gabe stuck his other hand into his pocket. When he pulled it out, there was a tooth in his palm, but it looked oddly small. It was just the top half of a molar, with none of the roots at the bottom. "It came out because it's a baby tooth. Take a good look at the gap in her mouth."

John bent over the table and peered into the space between Ariel's teeth. He saw a gleam of white emerging from the pink gum. A new molar was growing into the gap. "That's the adult tooth? The permanent one?"

"Yeah, and it's coming in about ten years too late. Except for the wisdom teeth in the back of the mouth, all the permanent teeth are supposed to appear by the time you're thirteen."

John shrugged. He couldn't see what the big deal was. "Okay, she has dental problems. What's your point?"

"Do you know how many people I examined when I worked in the emergency room at Temple? Dozens every day, hundreds every week. And I never saw anything like this."

"You never saw scars or funny teeth?"

Gabe gave him an exasperated look. "It's more than that. The weirdest thing of all is that she's still alive. She should've died, John. You just can't survive after losing that much blood. The cells die, the organs fail, the whole body shuts down. But it didn't happen with her. You see what I'm saying?"

He was getting agitated. His voice rose in pitch and volume as he spoke, and beads of sweat trickled down his forehead. John wondered if Gabe was starting to feel the withdrawal pains already. His sunken eyes veered from left to right, as if searching for his next fix.

John placed his hand on Gabe's back, trying to nudge him away from Ariel. "All right, settle down. Maybe you should take a break."

"What? You think I'm imagining things?" He picked up Ariel's notebook again and waved it in the air, as if threatening to hit him with it. "I know what I'm talking about! I'm a doctor, remember?"

John took a deep breath. He hated this. He hated the fact that his oldest friend was a junkie. "I know, you're a doctor. Listen, you want me to get you something to eat? I can—"

"I'll tell you what you can do. You can pay me now. I've been working on your weird-ass redhead for four hours, and that means you owe me four hundred dollars."

"Okay, no problem. I'll go home and get it."

"You don't have the money, do you?" Gabe held the notebook above the operating table, still brandishing it like a stick. "I can tell. You're gonna stiff me. You think you can—"

He was interrupted by a sudden movement, a hand darting up from the operating table. Ariel grasped the brown-leather notebook and pulled it out of Gabe's hands. She held it against her chest and narrowed her eyes. "That's mine."

Startled, Gabe backed away from the table. "Fuck! What's going on? I gave her a sedative!"

"I'm a light sleeper." She stared at the junkie, her brow creased. "And you were very loud."

Gabe took another step backward. His hands were shaking. He was clearly afraid of her.

After a couple of seconds she turned to John. Her face softened and the creases vanished. "Thank you. For believing me. I see we're not in a hospital."

He smiled. "You're better off here. The health care system sucks."

She smiled too, then tried to sit up. Scowling in pain, she propped herself on her elbows. Then she turned back to Gabriel and pointed at her legs. "They're both broken?"

Gabriel nodded but kept his distance. "Yeah, compound fractures."

"Could you get me a piece of paper, please? And a pen?"

It was an odd request. Confused, Gabriel glanced at John, who gave him a "Why not?" look. So the junkie went in search of some writing materials.

He came back half a minute later and handed Ariel a Post-it note and a pencil. She held the notebook in her other hand and flipped through its pages till she found the one she wanted. After scrutinizing the strange symbols on the page, she wrote a couple of words on the Post-it note. Then she studied the page again and wrote a few more words. John watched her, fascinated. She was translating the symbols.

When she was done, she gave him the Post-it note. Written on it were five items:

> *Periwinkle, 10 grams*
> *Cat's Claw (Uña de Gato), 5 grams*
> *Horsetail, 10 grams*
> *Milk Thistle, 15 grams*
> *Purple Coneflower, 10 grams*

"What's this?" John asked her.

"It's your shopping list. Some of the herbs may be hard to find. Where are we exactly?"

"In Philly. Kensington."

"That's good. There should be health-food stores in the city. If you can't find the herbs there, go to the *botánicas* in the Latino neighborhoods."

Gabe let out a snort. "Herbal medicine? That's what you're looking for?" He shook his head. "It's good for treating a cold. Not so good for bullet wounds."

Ariel ignored him. She kept her eyes on John. "Will you do this for me?"

She needed his help. Again. And he had every right to say no. But as he gazed into those green eyes, he knew he couldn't refuse her. He was hooked. Bad.

John folded the note and stuffed it into his pocket. "I'll come back as soon as I can."

The shopping took longer than he expected. It was still early in the morning, and most of the health-food stores weren't open yet. He had better luck at the *botánicas*, most of which were run by elderly Mexican women. The shops were tiny and dimly lit, but on their dusty shelves were dozens of sacks containing crushed leaves and roots and powders. By 10:00 A.M. he had collected all the items on Ariel's list and headed back to Kensington.

John planned to stop at his apartment on Somerset Street to pick up some cash for Gabriel, but when he was two blocks away he saw a crowd outside his row house. Wary, he pulled over to the curb. There were lots of gangbangers in the crowd, from the crews that ran the corners on Somerset Street and Fairhill Square and Lehigh Avenue. That was a bit strange— the drug crews were usually fast asleep at this time of day. Then John saw something even stranger: a pile of familiar-looking furniture on the sidewalk. *His* furniture. The gangbangers had broken into his apartment, removed his couch and chairs and television and bookcase, and tossed them all outside.

His first instinct was to rush over there and kick some ass. Why were they messing with his stuff? What the hell were they thinking? But instead he stayed in his Kia, furious and fearful, and tried to figure out what was going on. Although the antigang project no longer existed—St. Anne's Church had cut its funding after Father Murphy died—John had continued doing outreach work on an informal basis. Over the past few years he'd made a deal with the local drug crews: they let him talk to the younger kids in the neighborhood, but not the older ones. He could reach out to the preteens, urging them to stay away from the crews, but he couldn't say a word to the teenagers who were already working the corners. This was the compromise they'd reached after the disaster three years ago. But now it looked like someone had broken the truce.

John slumped lower in the driver's seat and peered through the wind-shield. Some of the gangbangers were stomping on his furniture, break-ing the chair legs and ripping the couch cushions. Others picked through his books and DVDs, taking whatever they wanted. Several drunks and junkies wandered at the edge of the crowd, curious and amused, but a few of the older folks on Somerset Street shook their heads in disgust. The old-timers in the neighborhood hated the gangs, and sometimes they were brave enough to make their feelings known. One elderly man in the crowd seemed particularly incensed. He shouted something in Spanish at the gangbangers, then spat on the ground. After a few seconds John recognized the man—it was Victor Garcia, a silver-haired retiree who'd been a friend of Father Murphy. His face was pink with anger.

Victor turned away from the crowd and headed east on Somerset. As luck would have it, the old man was going to walk right past the Kia. As he drew close, John rolled down the car's window. "Hey, Victor," he called. "What's all the fuss about?"

The old man's eyes widened. He looked around nervously, then ap-proached the car. "You better get out of here, John," he whispered. "They're looking for you."

"Who's looking? Which crew?"

"All of them. Every punk on the street is trying to find you. What the hell did you do?"

John held out his hands, palms up. "Nothing. I was in New York yester-day."

"Well, you must've pissed off somebody. You should go back to New York. For your own safety." He glanced at the crowd down the street, then slapped the Kia's door. "Get going, boy. Head for the interstate."

Victor walked away quickly, looking over his shoulder. John stepped on the gas and made a left on Hope Street, but he didn't drive toward I-95. Instead, he returned to Gabe's house, taking a roundabout route that avoided Somerset.

He parked his car by the chain-link fence again and called for Gabe. As he stood in front of the gate, waiting for his friend, he pondered Victor's question, "What the hell did you do?" The only thing he'd done was run into Ariel. And maybe that was it. Maybe the gangs in Philly were coming after him because of what had happened in New York.

He had to yell for two whole minutes before Gabe came out of the house. As soon as he emerged, it was clear why it had taken him so long. His mouth hung open and his eyes were glassy. He wore only his boxer shorts now, and on his left arm was the reddish imprint of the belt he'd tied around his bicep not so long ago. Without a word, he opened the gate and led John into the house. This time, though, they didn't go to the operating room in the basement. Gabe stumbled into a dark, stuffy room on the ground floor and sprawled on a filthy brown sofa. Scattered on the floor were the works he'd just used to shoot up: the belt, the syringe, the spoon, the cigarette lighter.

John frowned. He'd seen this kind of thing a million times before, but he still couldn't understand it. He had to remind himself that this skeletal junkie on the sofa was his old friend Gabriel, the smartest kid in the class, the boy who used to love to play with firecrackers. John waited a moment for his eyes to adjust to the dark, and then he stepped toward the couch. The smell was horrible.

"How's your patient?" John asked. He had to breathe through his mouth. "When was the last time you checked on her?"

Gabe was silent and motionless. Then he nodded drowsily. He moved as if he were underwater. "She's fine. Don't worry."

"Great. Glad you're on the case." John turned away and faced the wall. He couldn't bear to look at the guy.

The room went silent again. Then Gabe slowly extended his arm and held out his hand. "You got it?"

"Got what?"

"The money. My money." His eyes darted. He seemed to be shaking off his stupor. "You owe me. Remember? Four hundred dollars."

"I couldn't get into my house. Some assholes from the corner crews were there, waiting for me."

This got Gabe's attention. He sat up on the sofa. "What did they want?"

"No idea. I didn't stick around to talk."

"Why not?"

"They were already trashing my apartment."

"That's weird, don't you think? The bad boys showing up at your place all of a sudden?" He craned his neck, trying to look John in the eye. It was amazing how quickly he'd sobered up. "You think it has something to do with the girl?"

Gabe was good at guessing things. He had a talent for ferreting out secrets. It was a useful skill for a junkie to have. Desperate people needed all the help they could get.

John shook his head. "I don't see the connection," he lied.

"Well, I do." Gabe scratched his bare chest and leaned back on the sofa cushions. "The girl has enemies, right? After you left New York they could've figured out who you are. Maybe they saw your car's license plate and ran the number. It's easy to do if you have the connections. And once they found out your name and address, they made a call to the drug bosses in Kensington, offering them big money to grab someone named John Rogers. And the girl too, of course." He grinned. "That would explain it, wouldn't it?"

It certainly would, but John wasn't going to agree with him. This was a dangerous subject. "Look, I'll get your money. You know I always pay my bills. In the meantime, I'm going downstairs to see how she's doing."

"Sure, go ahead." Gabe kept grinning. "Take your time."

John didn't like the look on his face. There was a threat behind it. He could feel Gabe's eyes on his back as he went down the steps to the basement. The guy was his oldest friend, but first and foremost he was a junkie. And now he had a chance to make some serious money, maybe enough to buy a month's supply of heroin. If the payoff was big enough, Gabe would betray him in a second.

Ariel was awake when John marched into the operating room. She seemed happy to see him. "Did you find the herbs? I was worried you might—"

"Shh." He raised his index finger to his lips. "We gotta go. I'll carry you back to the car."

"Why?" she whispered. "What happened?"

"Gabe's gonna turn us in. He's probably on the phone right now."

John slipped one arm under Ariel's back and the other under her splinted legs. She winced as he picked her up, but didn't make a sound. Holding her as gently as he could, John headed up the stairs. She held her notebook against her chest, just like she did last night.

Gabe wasn't on the sofa anymore. He'd probably gone to another room to make the phone call. John burst out the front door with Ariel and ran to his car. As he dashed through the gate he looked down Hancock Street, expecting to see all of Kensington's gangbangers swarming toward them. But the street was empty.

John rested Ariel in the Kia's bloodstained backseat. "We got a two-minute head start," he said. "Have any ideas about where to go?"

He didn't expect an answer but Ariel nodded. "Go west, young man," she said. "Take the Roosevelt Expressway to I-76."

"You have a destination in mind?"

"I do. But I have to warn you. It's a long drive."

FOUR

Agent Larson heard the motorcycle coming long before he saw it. The noise of its engine echoed against the concrete pillars that supported the New Jersey Turnpike above the Meadowlands. Although hundreds of cars and trucks sped along the turnpike every minute, the parking lots and rail yards below the causeway were almost always deserted. Larson had been standing beside his SUV for half an hour before he heard the rumble of the Harley-Davidson. A minute later Van came in sight, slaloming his bike between the pillars.

Larson hated this part of his job. Six years ago he'd transferred to the FBI's field office in New York, where he'd hoped to rise through the ranks of the counterterrorism division. Instead, he got assigned to the Violent Gangs Task Force, specifically the squad that monitored motorcycle gangs in New York and New Jersey. Although the biker gangs were involved in drug dealing and gun trafficking, the assignment was a lot less prestigious than tracking down terrorists. Larson spent most of his time looking for informants who were willing to rat out their friends. He couldn't stand dealing with the scumbags. They were, for the most part, outrageous bullshit artists.

Van, though, was an exception to the rule. A few weeks ago he told Larson about an upcoming heroin shipment, and that tip resulted in one of the biggest drug busts of the year. So when Van called the field office this morning, saying he had information about the shootings in Brooklyn last night, Larson was willing to listen. He agreed to meet the biker in the Meadowlands.

Van coasted to a stop but stayed on his Harley. He was tall and solid, in his late forties or early fifties but still in good shape. He had a face like a drill sergeant's, hard and lined and angular, but it was topped with long, messy hair that had turned dirty gray. His clothes were a mess too: ripped jeans, scuffed boots, and a grease-stained bomber jacket. All in all, he looked like an aging veteran who'd decided to spend his retirement on a long, debauched joyride. And for all Larson knew, that's exactly who Van was. The biker had refused to reveal his last name or any other particulars. He belonged to a gang called the Riflemen, which was a new club, much smaller than the established ones—the Hell's Angels, the Pagans, the Outlaws, and so on. Still, he had a lot of connections in the other gangs and seemed to know everything that was going on.

Larson stepped away from his SUV and cautiously approached the motorcycle. He'd met Van in person before and knew that he carried an old pistol in a shoulder holster. To defuse the tension, Larson grinned and put a jaunty tone in his voice.

"You're late," he said. "You get stuck in traffic?"

Van didn't smile back at him. "What are the cops saying about Bushwick?"

He was all business today. And that was all right with Larson. No sense in dragging it out. "They found six dead at the scene. One was the night clerk at the hotel, the other five are John Does. But there's evidence of more casualties. It looks like whoever attacked the place pulled out their wounded." For a moment he pictured the scene on Evergreen Avenue, which he'd visited earlier that morning at the request of the New York police, who'd discovered motorcycle tracks on the streets near the hotel. Blood and gore were spattered all over the hotel's roof and in the alley below. "The crime-scene techs collected a shitload of shells. There was a hell of a lot of shooting, that's all they know for sure."

"That's because it's a war. This was the first battle."

Larson waited for more, but Van fell silent. He looked up and stared at the concrete underside of the turnpike.

"You want to explain that?" Larson asked. "Who's fighting this war?"

The biker didn't answer right away. He seemed to be lost in some profound meditation. Finally he stopped staring at the highway and lowered his head. "They're connected to methamphetamine dealers in the Midwest. One gang is based in Michigan, the other in Ohio. Both of them are branching out, trying to sell their shit farther east. They already got operations in Philadelphia, and now they're coming to New York."

"So this is a turf war?"

He nodded. "Yeah, and both sides have plenty of soldiers. Some are gangbangers from Philly, but most are white dudes from the sticks. For the past year or so, they've been loading up on weapons. They got some military hardware, M16s, M4s."

Larson perked up when he heard this. Most of the shells collected at the scene were from 5.56-millimeter M4 cartridges. This fact hadn't been revealed to the news media, so Van couldn't have learned it from watching TV or reading the paper. "How do you know about these guys?"

"The gang from Michigan did some business with the Pagans in upstate New York. They bought a few dozen assault rifles that the Pagans had smuggled out of Fort Drum. Ammunition, too. If you check the headstamp codes on those shells you found, I bet you'll find they came from Drum."

By this point Larson was *very* interested. This kind of activity went way beyond the usual gang crimes. If midwestern drug cartels were stealing M4s from U.S. Army bases, that was pretty damn close to domestic terrorism. And if Agent Larson uncovered a terrorist plot, it could definitely resuscitate his career. "Well, that's interesting," he said, trying to sound casual. "So who won the battle last night?"

Van shrugged. "Hey, I don't know everything. I'm just telling you what I heard on the street. What people are saying."

"Do you know how they got out of Bushwick so quickly? By the time the NYPD got to the scene, only the corpses were still there."

"Well, a lot of these fuckers are ex-army. So they have some training." He raised his eyebrows, which were as gray as his hair. "But the word on the street is that one of them screwed up. He parked his car right in front of the hotel, then took off once the shooting stopped. He was in a beat-up old Kia with Pennsylvania plates. Some neighborhood kid saw the license plate and remembered the number."

"Did he tell the police about it?"

"Are you kidding?" Van looked askance. "The kids in Bushwick aren't big fans of the cops. But he told his friends, and it spread from there."

Larson felt a rush of adrenaline. "Do you know the plate number?"

The biker reached into the pocket of his bomber jacket and pulled out a folded slip of paper. "It wasn't easy to get. I had to talk to a lot of people. Ask a lot of questions. It was a fair amount of work."

"So I guess you're looking for some compensation?" Larson had to be careful. If he sounded too eager, the price would go up. "What do you want?"

Van thought it over. He looked up again and scrutinized the underside of the highway. It looked like he was doing some arithmetic in his head. "Five hundred," he finally replied.

The price was steep but not prohibitive. Larson went to his SUV, opened the passenger-side door and reached into the glove compartment. That's where he kept his petty cash envelope, which held a stack of twenty-dollar bills. Larson removed twenty-five of them, then returned to Van. "Here you go."

The biker handed him the slip of paper and took the money. "They're vanity plates," he added. "That's what made it easy for the kid to remember the number."

As Van turned his bike around and gunned the engine, Agent Larson unfolded the paper. The plate number was written in pencil: **IVY4EVR**

FIVE

The first thing Ariel did in the car was prepare her dose of herbal medicine. While John drove across North Philly toward the Roosevelt Expressway, she mixed the crushed leaves and powders in a half-full bottle of Poland Spring water she'd found in the backseat. He watched her in the rearview mirror as she raised the bottle to her lips and drank the concoction. She made a face, closing her eyes and twisting her mouth in disgust, but she downed the whole thing. Then she looked at him in the mirror.

"I owe you an explanation," she said. "But I'm afraid you won't like it."

She got right to the point, as always. John liked her directness. It was one of the first things he'd noticed about her. And now it convinced him to give her the benefit of the doubt, even though she'd led him into a shitload of trouble. He should've been fuming at Ariel—he was on the run because of this girl, his apartment had been trashed—but he couldn't get angry at her. Despite everything that had happened, he sensed she was innocent. "Give it a shot," he said. "Go ahead and try me."

Ariel shifted to a more comfortable position, stretching her injured legs across the backseat. "Meeting you in the bar last night wasn't an accident.

I chose you two months ago. Then I came up with a plan for introducing myself to you."

"Chose me? For what?"

"To father my child. I want to have a child."

John was so startled, he almost missed the on-ramp for the expressway. The Kia fishtailed as he made the turn. "What?" he shouted. "Father your—?"

"Let me explain. The truth is, I'm not from Connecticut. Not even close. I come from an isolated community in northern Michigan, a place called Haven. You know about the Amish communities? Or the Mennonites?"

He stared at her in the rearview mirror. "You're Amish?"

"No, no. We're not a Christian community. But like the Amish, we have different customs from the rest of the society. And we have very strict rules. Most important, we're not allowed to marry and have children in the usual way. When a woman in our community wants to have a child, she has to seek permission from our Council of Elders."

John was thoroughly confused. "Elders?"

"They're our leaders. If they give the woman permission, she has to go outside our community to find her paramour, which is our name for the man she chooses. But she can't stay with the man after he impregnates her. She has to come back to Haven to raise the child. She can never see the father again."

He heard what she said but didn't understand a word of it. His hands trembled as he steered the car onto the expressway, which luckily wasn't too busy at that hour. He was more afraid now than he'd been during the shootout last night. "A cult? Is that what you're talking about? You belong to a cult?"

Ariel shook her head. "I wouldn't use that term. Yes, we operate in secrecy, but really we're a family. A very large extended family."

John remembered her bodyguards, the brawny guys with auburn crew cuts. When he saw them in the bar for the first time he'd assumed they were her brothers. "Hal and Richard, they were part of this family, too?"

"They were my cousins." She bit her lower lip. "Their job was to keep me safe during my encounter with you. They gave their lives to protect me."

It was a real struggle just to keep the Kia in its lane. John wanted to stop the car on the side of the highway, but instead he tightened his grip on the steering wheel. "So you planned the whole thing ahead of time? Meeting me at the bar, wearing sexy clothes?"

She nodded. "It took some preparation. I knew you might get suspicious if I approached you from out of the blue. So I went to the job fair and made sure you saw me there." Ariel reddened and turned away from the mirror. "I apologize for lying to you. I never went to college or studied social work. And I lied about the birth-control pills. I'm obviously not using any contraceptives."

This was too much. John was finally getting angry at her. "You were going to get pregnant and then disappear? And never even tell me about my own child?"

"We have good reasons for our rules. We have to protect our community."

"Protect you from what? I don't get this at all. How many people have you tricked this way?"

Ariel looked at him in the mirror again. Her eyes were wet. "I'm sorry, John. In most cases it isn't this painful. We carefully plan these encounters to ensure that they're casual and quick. The contact with the paramours is brief, so they usually don't become too emotionally attached."

"But something went wrong in *my* case, didn't it? Who the hell were the people shooting at us?"

She raised her hand and wiped her eyes. When she looked at him again, her face was composed and businesslike. "They were once members of our community, but they turned against us. They left Haven and formed a new group, with its own rules and goals. Over the past year they've instigated several violent confrontations. But I promise you, we weren't expecting an attack last night."

John remembered a name he'd heard during the gunfight. "And the leader of this group is someone named Sullivan?"

She frowned. The name seemed to make her uncomfortable. "That's enough. We shouldn't talk about this any further."

"Why not? I need to know what's going on. What are you fighting over?"

"Trust me, John. I'd be putting you in danger if I said too much."

"Really? I don't see how my situation could get any worse."

"You still have a chance of surviving. I'm trying to keep you alive. You need to drive me to Michigan as quickly as possible. Once I've returned to Haven, the men who attacked us in Brooklyn will no longer have any interest in pursuing you."

John let out an exasperated grunt. "So you expect me to drive you across the country, but you won't tell me who's chasing us? Or why?"

"If you don't like it, stop the car and let me out." Her eyes narrowed and her voice turned harsh. "I'll find another way to get home."

"Come on, that's ridiculous. You have two broken legs. How will you—"

"I'll crawl if I have to. Just stop the car."

John had reached the part of the expressway where it crossed over the Schuylkill River. There was no shoulder on the side of the road here. He couldn't have stopped even if he'd wanted to. Instead he followed the signs to I-76 West. "All right, have it your way. I'll shut up and drive. Can I ask for directions at least?"

She gave him a smile. A very small, fleeting smile, but still lovely. "Stay on the interstate until you get to exit 328A. Then take Route 422 to Valley Forge. We need to pick up some supplies before we head for Michigan."

"I don't have any cash left. I spent my last thirteen dollars on your herbs."

"Don't worry. I know where to get some money."

John wanted to ask her about this—she didn't have a wallet or a purse or a bank card, so how the hell could she get cash?—but he stopped himself. He had a more important question for her. "I just need to know one thing," he said. "Why did you choose me?"

She didn't respond for several seconds, and John started to think she wasn't going to. But then Ariel leaned forward, moving as close as possible to him. "I chose you because of a news story I saw on the Internet. The story of what happened to you three years ago."

John's throat tightened. He couldn't say a word. So they drove silently out of Philadelphia, toward the green hills of Chester County.

Ariel's directions led them to the entrance of Valley Forge National Historical Park. They passed a visitor's center and a couple of parking lots, but luckily the place didn't charge an entrance fee. John followed a road that looped through a wide field dotted with monuments. Along the side of the road he saw several wooden huts, which—according to the signs— were reconstructions of the shelters that General Washington's army used during the Revolutionary War. John had never visited this park before, and he had to admit it was a pretty interesting place. But he couldn't understand what they were doing here.

He looked at Ariel in the rearview mirror. "You said we were going to pick up supplies?"

She nodded. "We need cash, that's the most important thing. And a few other essentials."

"Well, I don't see any banks or cash machines here, do you?"

"We can't go to a bank. Sullivan has spies who monitor the financial-transaction networks. He knows all my aliases and account numbers, so if I try to make a withdrawal he'll see where we are. And by this point he probably knows all of your information, too."

Her voice was calm and matter-of-fact, but John was alarmed. "So what are we going to do?"

"We have other options. Our community has a long tradition of preparing for emergencies." She pointed at the road up ahead. "Take the next right."

John turned onto Valley Creek Road and left the wide field behind. Soon he drove across a covered bridge that spanned a swiftly running stream. The creek flowed between two tree-covered hills that rose about three hundred feet above the road.

"The hill on the right is Mount Joy," Ariel pointed out. "And the one on the left is Mount Misery. Washington camped here because of the hills, they protected his flank. We're heading for Misery. Slow down, there's the trailhead."

He pulled into a small parking area at the base of the hill. There were no other cars, but he saw a sign that said Mount Misery Trail. It was a narrow dirt path that climbed up the steep wooded hillside. John shut off the Kia's engine, then turned around to face Ariel. "Okay, what now?"

She opened her leather-bound notebook. "I'll get the directions." After flipping through the yellowed pages for several seconds, she rested her index finger on a line of bewildering symbols. "Here it is. Walk up the trail about a quarter mile, till you see an oak tree with the name Mary carved into the trunk. Then turn toward the creek and go twenty paces down the slope. Then look for a large gray stone that's shaped like a teardrop. Lift the stone and start digging underneath."

"What is this, a treasure hunt?"

Ariel smiled. "Yes, that's exactly what it is. You're going to dig up an iron box. The money will be inside. Plus, a few other items."

"Did you put it there?"

"No, someone else in our family is in charge of this cache. There are dozens like it all over the country. Every twenty years we dig up the boxes and add new currency to them. Otherwise the cash would get outdated."

John shook his head in disbelief. "Every twenty years? How long has your family been doing this?"

"A long time. That's why we put our caches in national parks. The land there will never be disturbed or developed. On private land, there's always a chance the owner will excavate the property to build a house or business." She closed the notebook. "So you remember the directions?"

"Yeah, oak tree named Mary, then twenty paces toward the creek. Rock shaped like a teardrop." He opened the driver-side door but paused before stepping out of the car. He was worried about leaving Ariel alone. "You gonna be okay by yourself?"

She rolled her eyes. "Go on, get the box. You'll have to dig with your fingers, but it won't be buried too deep."

John was a city boy. Although there were lots of parks and hiking trails near Philadelphia, he never visited them. Walking through the woods wasn't fun or relaxing for him; it made him nervous. He stayed alert as he climbed the dirt trail up Mount Misery, his eyes flicking from tree to tree. He imagined soldiers hiding behind the tree trunks, taking aim at him with their carbines.

After about ten minutes he found the oak tree. It was tall and massive, with a gnarled trunk at least three feet wide. The name Mary was at eye level, written in old-fashioned letters, each four inches high. The person who'd carved it into the trunk had probably died a hundred years ago. John turned east and looked down at the creek, which was two hundred feet below him. The eastern slope of Mount Misery was so steep that the trees on the hillside were curved near the ground, their trunks bent like the letter J. Going twenty paces in that direction was going to be harder than he thought. If he wasn't careful, he'd tumble all the way down.

He left the trail and cautiously stepped down the slope, leaning backward to keep his balance. The ground was covered with dead leaves, which made the footing treacherous. He moved slowly and grabbed any handhold within reach—low branches, saplings, roots protruding from the dirt. Then his right foot slipped and he fell backward and his butt hit something hard. It was a smooth gray rock, about two feet across, shaped like a teardrop.

John crouched next to the rock and got a good grip on its rounded edge. With a grunt he flipped it over, exposing a bowl of dark dry soil. Fortunately, the dirt wasn't hard-packed; he could sink his fingers into it and scoop out big handfuls. The digging was so easy, in fact, that it made John suspicious. If no one had touched this cache in twenty years, the dirt under the rock wouldn't be so loose and powdery. He concluded that someone else had been digging here recently, maybe in the past few weeks. There was a good chance that the iron box was gone, already taken.

But no, it was there. After excavating about ten inches of soil, John felt the box's cold lid. He dug faster, widening the hole until he could slide his fingers around the box and lift it out of the earth. It was the size of a shoe box and weighed at least thirty pounds. The lid was decorated with the same symbols he'd seen in Ariel's notebook, the lightning bolts and tee-pees and backwards B's and P's and R's. There were two rusty latches securing the lid, and after a bit of effort John managed to unclasp one of them. He was working on the other when he heard someone above him yell, *"Hey!"*

Startled, he looked up. A National Park Service ranger in a gray-and-green uniform stood at the edge of the dirt trail, peering down the slope. He was tall and thin and red-faced, with a long nose and big ears under the brim of his ranger hat. And he carried a semiautomatic pistol in his belt holster. "What are you doing?" he shouted. "Did you dig that up?"

John couldn't deny it. The hole was right there and the box was smeared with dirt. But he gave it a try anyway. "No, this is mine," he said, putting a defensive tone in his voice.

"It's a federal crime to take artifacts from a national park." The ranger's right hand hovered near the pistol in his holster. "Now put that thing on the ground and come up here."

John glanced down the hillside. There was another trail at the bottom of the slope, running parallel to the creek. He could take that trail back to the Kia, assuming he could get down the hill in one piece.

"Sorry," he said. "Gotta run." Holding the box under his arm, he scrab-bled down the slope, his shoes kicking up the dead leaves.

"Hey! Stop!"

John surrendered to gravity. He hurtled downhill, swerving between the trees and leaping over the stones. After a few seconds he heard crashing noises behind him. The park ranger was chasing him down the slope, but John had been chased by police officers many times before, so he knew the rules. The ranger wouldn't take a shot at him just for stealing an old box. And because the park was fairly big, it would take at least a couple of minutes for a backup unit to arrive. So simply running away was a pretty good option.

But twenty feet from the bottom of the slope, John lost his balance. He fell on his side and slid the rest of the way down. The box slipped out of his grasp and tumbled end over end, hitting the dirt trail next to the creek at the same time John did. The fall knocked the wind out of him, and for a couple of seconds he couldn't breathe. The woods whirled around him in a green blur.

Frantic, he drew in an aching breath. He looked up, expecting to see the park ranger standing over him, but instead he heard a cry from half-way up the slope. The ranger had fallen too, and it sounded like he was in pain. "Shit!" the guy moaned. "Shit, shit, shit!"

John checked himself for injuries. His back was sore but nothing seemed to be broken. Dizzy with relief, he struggled to his feet and found the box, which had landed a couple of yards away. The lid had popped open, spill-ing a pile of coins and bills across the trail. The coins were silver dollars, dull and dirty with age, and the bills were a collection of old and new currencies, wrinkled greenbacks mixed with stacks of crisp cash. Under the pile of money were a pair of Michigan license plates and a clean, new Glock semiautomatic. But the thing that caught John's eye was a small glass jar, cylindrical and stubby, like a jar for baby food. It was filled with a cloudy, yellowish liquid. He was surprised that the glass hadn't broken when the box tumbled down the hill. He looked a little closer and real-ized it was a specimen jar. Then he saw what was floating inside.

It made him so sick he almost fell down again. He stood there on the trail, trembling, while the wind blew through the trees and the water rushed down the creek and the park ranger yelled, "Fucking hell!" from the hillside. Then he picked up the jar and threw it as far as he could. It splashed in the creek about fifty yards away.

He couldn't think. All he could do was get out of there. Bending over, he swept up everything from the trail—the money, the gun, the license plates—and stuffed it all back into the box. Then he ran down the trail with the box under his arm, heading for the trailhead where he'd parked his Kia.

Ariel gaped at him from the backseat as soon as he approached the car. She clearly recognized that something was wrong, but she remained silent as John stormed into the Kia and threw the box on the passenger seat and took off down Yellow Springs Road. Within a minute they were out of the park and racing across the Pennsylvania countryside. John waited until they were a couple of miles away from Valley Forge before looking at her in the rearview mirror.

"Tell me what's going on," he ordered. "If you don't, I'm taking you straight to the police."

"John, what—"

"There was something else in the box. A specimen jar."

Ariel's mouth opened. She took a deep breath. "That wasn't us. That was Sullivan. His men must be using that cache."

"What the hell are they doing? What . . ."

His voice trailed off. He couldn't say the words, couldn't bring himself to describe the thing. But he could see it, in his mind's eye, almost as clearly as when it was in front of him: a brown spidery object floating in the yellowish liquid. The liquid, he realized now, was formaldehyde. The brown thing was a tiny, severed hand.

SIX

Life sucks. That was the one thing Gabe Rodriguez knew for certain. It was the reason why he'd become a junkie. He just wanted to forget how shitty life was for a few fucking minutes.

He lifted his head from the couch cushion and looked around his shitty room. He stared at the shitty carpet and the shitty walls, the shitty bars on the shitty windows. He'd once been so proud of this house. He'd bought it for a song when he still worked at the hospital. At the time he thought he'd gotten the deal of the century. But there was an obvious reason why the price was so low: *because the house was in fucking Kensington.* It was surrounded by vacant lots and crack dens and gangbangers. Maybe other parts of the city were gentrifying, but this neighborhood was still a bad investment.

Gabe let his head fall back to the cushion. His mouth was dry and his stomach was empty, but he was too weak to get up from the couch. So he lay there and listened to his dogs barking. Maurice and Malaga were making a racket because the boys from the Somerset Street crew stood outside the fence, waiting for John Rogers to return. Gabe had told them that John would come back soon, although he knew damn well that the guy was gone for good. It was yet another fuckup, one more in a long line of them. He'd missed his chance to make some money and build some good-will with his suppliers. And once the gangbangers realized they were waiting for nothing, they'd take it out on him. He didn't even want to think about what they were going to do.

He closed his eyes. For a moment he thought of John and felt a twinge of regret. The poor bastard had already suffered his fair share of tragedy, and Gabe wasn't proud of ratting him out. On the other hand, they weren't really friends anymore. Ever since John got out of the drug business he'd had a holier-than-thou attitude. He should've kept his head down like everyone else.

Gabe tried to sleep but he knew it was hopeless. His mind was racing, already thinking ahead to his next fix. After a while he noticed that the dogs had stopped barking. That's good, he thought. Maybe the gang-bangers went home.

Then he heard a crash. He opened his eyes and saw someone burst through his front door. Gabe could tell right away that it wasn't anyone from the local drug crews. First of all, the man was white. Second, he was old, maybe fifty or fifty-five, although he looked pretty tough for an old guy. He was at least six foot three, and he had broad shoulders and a thick, muscled neck.

The man strode to the couch. He wore boots and leather gloves and a bomber jacket. "You Gabriel Rodriguez?"

Gabe tried to sit up but his whole body was shaking. He felt a sudden warmth in his boxer shorts. He'd pissed himself.

Reaching down with a big gloved hand, the guy grabbed Gabe by the throat and pulled him upright. "You the one who said he saw John Rog-ers?"

Gabe couldn't answer, couldn't breathe, but he managed a spastic nod. In response, the man let go of him and stepped back from the couch. In his other hand he held a knife, its blade smeared with blood and short hairs. Dog hairs.

"What?" Gabe croaked. "What did you—"

"You're going to tell me everything. From start to finish."

Gabe's eyes watered. He'd loved those dogs. "You didn't have to kill them."

"My apologies. Your curs got in my way."

The man's voice had changed abruptly. Now he was speaking with a British accent. For some reason this change was more terrifying than the knife. Gabe sensed that the man had just dropped a disguise because it was no longer necessary.

"What's going on?" Gabe screamed. "Who the fuck are you?"

The man smiled. "I've been using the name Van of late. Because it's short and sweet." He raised the knife and pointed it at Gabe's face. The bloody tip was just an inch from his nose. "But I'll let you in on a secret, friend. My real name is Sullivan."

SEVEN

John stopped at an Exxon station in Chester Springs. The area was farm country, green and peaceful, and there were no other cars on Yellow Springs Road. The Kia's gas tank was almost empty, but instead of heading for the pumps he parked behind the station's convenience store, next to a couple of Dumpsters. He needed a secluded spot for this talk with Ariel, because he knew he was going to yell.

But he never got the chance. As soon as he shut off the engine he heard a ripping noise behind him. When he turned around he saw Ariel tearing the bandages off her left thigh. Her face was grim. "I need to show you this."

"Shit! Stop!"

"You won't believe me unless I show you." She peeled off the tape that held the bandages in place, exposing layers of red-splotched gauze. "You have to see for yourself."

John averted his eyes. "I've already seen it! I bandaged you, remember?"

"Just look, damn it!"

Bracing himself, he looked at her thigh. For a second he thought he was staring at the wrong leg. He'd expected to see a jagged, red wound, but instead it was pink and smooth. The stitched flesh had already knitted together. It looked like it had been healing for several days. "Whoa. What happened?"

"It was the medicine. The herbs." She picked up the water bottle in which she'd dissolved the crushed leaves and powders. "They contain chemicals that promote rapid cell division and growth. They also fight infections and reduce inflammation."

John shook his head. "This is crazy. When did you drink that stuff? It couldn't have been more than two hours ago."

"The chemicals are drawn to the injured tissue. They accelerate the production of squamous cells, repairing the skin and blood vessels. The bones will take longer to heal, but I'll be able to walk in less than a week."

"No, no way. There's no way it could work that fast."

She pointed at her thigh. "But it did. You don't believe your eyes?"

He didn't. He kept thinking there had to be another explanation. Maybe the wound hadn't been so bad in the first place. But he remembered the gruesome sight so clearly.

Ariel put down the water bottle and began to rebandage her leg. "Most of those herbs come from tropical ecosystems, where there's an incredible variety of plant life. Scientists are just starting to discover the medicinal benefits of tropical plants, especially when they're taken in combination." She put the gauze back in place and rewrapped the tape around her thigh. "But the native peoples of Africa and South America have known about the benefits for thousands of years. And our community is devoted to collecting and preserving that knowledge. We've done a lot of work in the Congo and Amazon rain forests."

John stared at her. "I thought you said you came from Michigan."

"Yes, Haven is in Michigan, that's our headquarters. But we have outposts around the world. Most of the outposts are small and temporary— our researchers move from place to place. Because our community needs to keep its existence secret, we can't have too many people in one location."

He didn't know what to make of all this. Ariel's "community" still sounded like a cult. "Why do you have to keep everything secret? If all you care about is finding medicines, why not do it in the open?"

"It's complicated." She finished working on her leg and reclined on the backseat. "We have a long history. Four hundred years ago our family lived in Europe. We were in France and Germany, and then we fled to England. We had to keep moving because we were persecuted everywhere."

"Why?"

"Well, we weren't Christian, for one thing. Our traditions are older, they go back to the time before Christ. And there was so much suspicion and hysteria then. People hounded us because we were different. They burned our homes and farms. There were massacres, too. Sometimes they put us on trial before hanging us. They'd accuse us of poisoning their wells or murdering their children."

Although her face remained grim, John found it hard to take her seriously. Ariel's story was strange as hell, and yet it was also familiar. He looked at the water bottle lying on the backseat, noticing the clumps of wet herbs clinging to the inside of the plastic. *It's a potion*, he thought. *Like something out of a fairy tale.* "I'm sorry, but all of this sounds a little wacky. Are you saying you come from a family of witches?"

Her reaction was instantaneous. She leaned forward at the waist, nearly coming off the backseat, and pointed at him. Her face reddened and her jaw muscles quivered. "Don't use that word. Don't *ever* say that word."

"What? Witches?"

"I'm serious, John. It's like saying the word *nigger*. You know what it feels like to hear that, don't you?"

He nodded. Technically, he was multiracial, but he knew where he stood. He'd been called a nigger his whole life. Philadelphia had its share of racists, and his skin color was dark enough to make him a nigger in their eyes. But he didn't see the connection with witches. "I don't get it. What—"

"It was genocide. Tens of thousands of people killed in the sixteenth and seventeenth centuries. Most of them women." She grasped a lock of her hair and held it out for John to see. "Red hair and green eyes run in our family, so the churchmen told their congregations to look for people with those signs, the signs of the Devil. But once the killing started, it went out of control. Most of the victims had nothing to do with our family. The churchmen and the mobs, they killed anyone who was different— hermits, foreigners, simpletons." She let go of her hair. "That's why we adopted our rules, why we all swear an oath of secrecy. We came to America so we could hide from our enemies. We separated ourselves from the rest of the world."

When she was done talking, Ariel lowered her head. She pressed her lips together and stared at her lap, and the look on her face was so desperately sad that John knew she wasn't kidding around. She was telling the truth, or at least what she thought was the truth.

"So how does it work now?" he asked. "I mean, how do you stay hidden? Don't you have neighbors in Michigan?"

"Haven is way up north, in Michigan's Upper Peninsula. It's still a remote part of the country, mostly state forests. We own a nine-hundred-acre farm that grows corn and sunflowers, and our closest neighbors are miles away. Since the nineteenth century we've told the state and county officials that we're an Amish community. We dress like the Amish, in plain old-fashioned clothing without buttons or zippers. We run our farm in the old-order, traditional way. And like the Amish, we don't mingle with outsiders."

"Except when you want to have children, right?"

Ariel nodded. "That's the only time we have contact with the outside world. And the contact is brief."

This last statement infuriated him. John wanted to ask her what the hell was wrong with her family, why they chose to fuck strangers when they wanted to have kids. But something else bothered him even more. "You still haven't explained the jar. What was inside the specimen jar."

She grimaced. Her expression changed in an instant—when she looked up at him, all her sadness was gone, replaced by a keen, green-eyed fury. "What kind of body part was it?" she asked.

He felt sick again. "A hand."

"It's a perversion. They've broken our laws and corrupted our traditions."

"You're talking about Sullivan's men?"

"They weren't happy with the progress we were making. We were trying to develop a new kind of medicine, something that would help certain members of our family. But Sullivan convinced his followers that we weren't working fast enough. So they rebelled against us and started their own faction. Our Elders tried to stop them, but by that point Sullivan had dozens of men behind him. And hundreds of guns."

John thought of the men who'd attacked them in Bushwick. He pictured the one who shot Ariel, the bald guy with the spiderweb tattoo on his face. John realized that if you took away the asshole's tattoo, he wouldn't look so different from Hal or Richard, Ariel's cousins and bodyguards. The bald guy was related to her, too. "So this whole war started because of a medicine?"

"Sullivan thought he could make the drug on his own. But the main ingredient is a protein that's found only in human fetuses."

John had guessed where the severed hand had come from—how else could it be so tiny?—but it was still a shock to hear his suspicions confirmed. He couldn't imagine anything worse. "Jesus." He swallowed hard, tamping down the bile rising from his stomach. "How do they get the . . . the fetuses?"

"We think Sullivan made a black-market deal with someone who works for a medical-waste company. All we know for certain is that they've collected hundreds of tissue samples. They figured out a way to preserve the body parts without freezing them, and they hide the specimen jars wherever they can." She shook her head. "Now it looks like they're using our old caches. The specimen you saw was probably just an extra, a leftover piece of tissue that one of Sullivan's men needed to hide quickly. We think they've stored most of the fetuses in the really remote caches, in the big national forests and wilderness areas."

He closed his eyes while she was talking. It was easier to fight the nausea this way. When he opened them a few seconds later, he felt a little steadier. "What kind of medicine are they trying to make? What the hell does it do?"

She started to answer, then stopped herself. "I'm sorry, I can't tell you. I've said too much already."

"Oh, come on—"

"John, listen. If both my legs weren't broken, I'd go to Michigan by myself. I'd hot-wire a car or get on a bus or just start walking. But I can't do any of those things. I need your help."

"And I want to help you! But you have to be straight with me."

"You don't understand. Your situation is more dangerous than you realize."

"I know it's dangerous!" He raised his voice in exasperation. "Those assholes already tried to kill me!"

"That's not the only thing you need to worry about. Even if we outrun Sullivan's men and arrive at Haven, you'll still be in danger. Our Council of Elders will interrogate you. They'll find out what you know."

"Your Elders? Aren't they on your side?"

"Yes, and they'll be grateful that you helped me get home. But as I said, we have very strict rules. If you know too much, they'll have no choice but to kill you."

John opened his mouth, but no words came out. He was dumbfounded.

"I know it's harsh," Ariel added. "But we learned a terrible lesson from the genocide. Although the world is more tolerant now, people will still fear and hate us if they discover our secrets. Rather than risk another massacre, our Elders will eliminate any outsider who could endanger us. So please don't ask me to tell you anything else."

Her voice was calm and reasonable, but the sound of it enraged him. He couldn't remember the last time he'd been this angry. "And you'd just sit there and watch while your Elders execute me?"

"Of course not. But there's only so much I could do. Our oath requires—"

She abruptly stopped arguing and raised her head. She'd heard something, and in the sudden silence John heard it, too. It was a deep, guttural rumble, the sound of a pack of motorcycles. It came from the east, from Valley Forge National Park, roaring down Yellow Springs Road.

"The gun!" Ariel cried, pointing at the iron box that John had tossed on the passenger seat. "There's a gun in the cache, right?"

Without hesitation, he reached inside the box, pulled out the Glock and handed it to her. "Who is it? Cops?"

She ejected the Glock's magazine, checking to see if it was loaded. Then she slammed it back into the gun and chambered a round. "Sullivan's men ride Harleys. Instead of disguising themselves as Amish, they pretend they're a biker gang called the Riflemen."

There was no time to escape. The motorcycles were just a few hundred yards away. They'd reach the gas station before John could drive the Kia past the pumps. Ariel leaned against the rear door on the right side of the car and rolled down the back window on the left. Then, holding the Glock with both hands, she pointed it out the window. She might be able to pick off a rider or two as they turned into the station. But once the men aimed their assault rifles at the Kia, the show would be over.

John just sat there in the driver's seat. He was amazed at how calm he felt. He didn't even try to take cover. *At least it'll be quick*, he thought. *A storm of bullets, then lights out. And then I'll be with Ivy. I'll be with my daughter.*

When the motorcycles came down the road, though, he noticed they weren't Harleys. They were big luxurious touring bikes, Hondas and Yamahas in neon-bright colors. The riders were overweight couples wearing matching silver jackets that said PHILADELPHIA PHREAKS on the back. They rumbled right past the Exxon station.

Ariel lowered the Glock and let out a long breath. John thought she might smile, but she didn't. Instead she pointed at the box again. "Any license plates in there?"

He had to think for a second. "Yeah. A couple of Michigan plates."

"Take your Pennsylvania plates off the car and put on those. Just in case the police are looking for us." She removed the Glock's magazine and pulled back the slide, ejecting the bullet from the chamber. "Then we'll gas up and get the hell out of here."

John drove through the afternoon and into the night. He crossed the rugged hills of Pennsylvania, sticking to the back roads. Although he'd changed the Kia's license plates, he didn't want to take any chances with the state troopers on the turnpike. He stopped at a roadside convenience store to buy dinner—trail mix, Slim Jims, microwaved burritos—and then they cruised through the flat Ohio countryside. Taking the secondary roads slowed them down considerably, so it was almost midnight by the time they reached the Michigan state line. John was dead tired but he kept going north, driving for another two hours on an empty Route 52 until he reached the woodlands of central Michigan. Then Ariel leaned forward from the backseat and said, "In a couple of minutes you're gonna make a left turn. I know a place where we can stop for a few hours."

John was surprised. He'd assumed she wanted to get home as fast as possible. "I don't have to stop. I'm fine."

"We can't make it to Haven tonight."

"How far away is it? Seriously, I'm not tired, I can keep driving till—"

"Haven's in Michigan's Upper Peninsula, John. It's separated from the Lower Peninsula by the Straits of Mackinac, which connect Lake Michigan with Lake Huron. To get from the Lower Peninsula to the U.P., you have to cross the Mackinac Bridge."

"So what's the problem? The bridge doesn't shut down at night, does it?"

"There's probably a roadblock on the bridge by now. Sullivan has contacts in the FBI and the Michigan state police. He's used them before to pursue our people when they're on assignment outside Haven."

"On assignment?"

"Sometimes our Elders ask us to perform certain tasks. For instance, every year they assign our botanical experts to go to the Amazon to collect rare medicinal plants. The experts travel with forged documents, so no one can trace them back to our community." Ariel shifted in the backseat, grunting as she repositioned her legs. "Sullivan gives false information to the authorities, telling them that our people are drug dealers or terrorists. Over the past year three people from Haven have been killed in gun battles with the police, and two more died in prison after they were arrested. Sullivan was behind all those deaths."

"But we changed the license plates on the car. How will the police know to stop us?"

"I'm sure Sullivan told them what to look for. A tall man driving a beat-up Kia, a redhead with injured legs."

John slowed the car. He was wondering if they should turn around. "Is there another route we can take?"

"We could go through Wisconsin and take one of the highways running across the Upper Peninsula, but Sullivan has an outpost near Seney. His Riflemen keep watch over all the roads in that part of the U.P."

"So what are we gonna do?"

Ariel extended her right arm, pointing at the road ahead. "There's the left turn. We're going to rest for a few hours, and then we'll figure something out."

She spoke in a firm, commanding voice, and John was too tired to resist. He turned left onto a country lane that rambled through pitch-black woods. Then Ariel pointed to another left turn, which put them on a narrow, rutted dirt road. After jouncing on this trail for a couple of miles they reached a clearing in the woods, a thirty-foot-wide space overhung by pine branches. "This is the place," Ariel said. "We'll be all right here. Even if someone comes down the trail, they won't see the car."

John maneuvered the Kia into the clearing. Then he shut off the engine and headlights, and utter darkness descended upon them. "Whoa. That's spooky." He reached for the switch on the car's dome light and flicked it on. "I'll turn this off when we're ready to go to sleep."

"I'm ready right now." She pulled off her new sweatshirt—a simple gray thing John had purchased at the convenience store—and folded it to make a pillow, which she placed at one end of the backseat. Then she lay down and made herself as comfortable as possible.

John sneaked a look at her. She wore a T-shirt and gym shorts, also bought at the convenience store, and her legs were wrapped in bandages, but she still looked great. He remembered, with sudden vividness, how she kissed him in the hotel room in Brooklyn last night, how she shivered in his arms and led him toward the bed. Although sex was out of the question now, for a million good reasons, he still wished he could climb into the backseat with her. With great reluctance he turned away from her and focused on the lever for the driver's seat, tilting it as far back as it would go. This would be his bed for the night. Then he reached over his head to turn off the dome light. As he flicked the switch he glanced at the passenger seat, where he'd put the Pennsylvania license plates he'd taken off the Kia. The last thing he saw before the light went out was IVY4EVR.

"Thank you, John." Ariel's voice was softer now, a whisper in the darkness. "Thank you for everything."

He should've just said "You're welcome" and left it at that, but he was too agitated. Over the past twenty-four hours he'd been tricked, seduced, and ambushed. He'd nearly been killed by assassins carrying assault rifles, and now he was fleeing across the country with a modern-day witch whose family might execute him to protect their secrets. But oddly enough, his greatest worry wasn't Sullivan or the Elders of Haven. His thoughts kept circling back to what Ariel had told him this morning: *Meeting you wasn't an accident. I chose you.*

"Can I ask you a question?" He turned toward the backseat, even though he couldn't see a thing. "About the news story you saw on the Internet? The story about me?"

"Certainly. What do you want to know?"

"Was it the article that ran in *The Philadelphia Inquirer*?"

"Yes, it was."

John took a deep breath. Several newspapers had published articles about the shootings on Kensington Avenue, but the *Inquirer* story was the worst. "It wasn't true. None of it."

"What do you mean?"

"All those things they said about me? All that saintly turn-the-other-cheek crap? It didn't happen that way." He clenched his hands. "I was ready to kill them. I was going to shoot every last one of those bastards."

Ariel didn't say anything at first, but he could hear her moving in the backseat, propping herself up to a sitting position. He stared hard into the darkness, and after a moment he thought he could make out her silhouette.

"Do you want to talk about it?" she finally asked.

He wanted to. Very badly. But he'd promised never to tell. He'd sworn an oath on his daughter's grave, just fifteen minutes after he'd lowered her coffin into the ground.

"No, I can't," he said. "I just want you to know I'm not a saint. I would've killed them. I was going to."

She fell silent again. For the next ten seconds all he could hear was her breathing. Then he felt a caress on his cheek. She'd reached out and touched his face.

"It's all right, John. I never thought you were a saint. Now go to sleep, okay?"

He closed his eyes. Her hand was so warm. "Okay," he said.

She kept her hand on his cheek for another few seconds. He leaned toward her, pressing his face against her palm, luxuriating in her touch. By the time she withdrew her hand and lay down in the backseat again, he was calmer. He kicked off his shoes and reclined in the driver's seat. Within moments he was asleep.

EIGHT

She was close. Sullivan could sense it.

He and Marlowe were riding their Harleys up I-75, about ten miles north of Bay City, Michigan. To the east was the dark expanse of Saginaw Bay and to the west was Gladwin State Forest, which looked equally dark at four o'clock in the morning. The forest was a good place to hide, and the girl was an expert at hiding. She'd spent more time outside Haven than anyone else in the community, and she knew all of Michigan's secret places. Sullivan knew them too, but he doubted he could find her now. Not in the dark, not in that vast tract of woods. No, he'd have a better chance of catching her tomorrow. The state police were already checking each car that crossed the Mackinac Bridge. Sullivan and his Riflemen would cover the other routes to Haven.

He gunned the Harley's engine as the highway sloped upward. The night was cold for early September, and the frigid wind slapped his face. But at least it blew away the stink of the junkie. After interrogating Rodriguez, Sullivan had slit the wretch's throat, and some of the blood had splashed on his jeans. Although Rodriguez told him plenty about John

Rogers and the young redhead who'd been shot in the legs, the junkie didn't know which way they'd fled. Sullivan dispatched his men to the Pennsylvania Turnpike and the other interstate highways, and though they spotted many old, dented Kias, none of them was the car they were looking for. They had no choice but to regroup in Michigan and wait for their targets to approach Haven.

Still, the visit to Philadelphia hadn't been a total waste. Before leaving Rodriguez's house, Sullivan had placed the bloody knife on the floor next to the junkie's corpse. He'd acquired this knife from one of the gang members he'd hired to ransack Rogers's apartment. Its handle was greasy and covered with Rogers's fingerprints, and Sullivan had been careful to use gloves while holding it. Afterwards, he called 911 and gave the Philadelphia police an anonymous tip. John Rogers, he told them, had just killed Gabriel Rodriguez, a North Philly junkie, because of a drug deal gone bad. And now Rogers, he added, was heading for Michigan's Upper Peninsula in a 2003 Kia.

Sullivan got a call from Agent Larson two hours later. As expected, the Philadelphia cops had gone to the junkie's house and found the corpse and bloody knife. Then they'd gone to Rogers's apartment and discovered the fifteen pounds of methamphetamine that Sullivan had planted there. And then, after learning that Rogers was wanted by the FBI in connection with the shootings in New York, the cops had called Larson and told him what they'd found. Larson, in turn, contacted Sullivan to find out why Rogers would go to the Upper Peninsula. Sullivan acted cagey at first, pretending not to know anything. Then he said he'd heard a rumor that everyone in Rogers's gang was making a run for the Canadian border. His words had their intended effect: after another two hours, Sullivan's men in the U.P. reported that the state police had set up a checkpoint on the Mackinac Bridge.

Now, after riding his Harley halfway across the Midwest, Sullivan was less than two hundred miles from his destination. He glanced at Marlowe, who rode in the adjacent lane just a couple of yards to his right. Each man wore a backpack that held an M4 carbine and two hundred rounds of ammunition. Marlowe's face was a mess, so bloodied and bruised from the beating John Rogers had given him that his spiderweb tattoo was barely visible. But he rode his Harley as steadily as ever, his eyes full of hatred. Sullivan had promised him a chance to get his revenge on Rogers if they captured the man alive.

In addition to his M4, Sullivan carried a Mauser HSc, a vintage German pistol. Ever since he'd started the rebellion against the Council of Elders, he'd been collecting Nazi-era weapons and regalia. At first he did it as part of his effort to disguise his men, to make the Riflemen look like the other motorcycle gangs that roamed across the country. Over the past year, though, he'd come to identify with Hitler's Third Reich. Although the Nazis had committed some terrible crimes, at least you couldn't accuse them of underreaching. Their goal was to change the very nature of humanity. And this was Sullivan's goal as well. He was going to create a new race of men.

He kept his Mauser in a shoulder holster under his jacket. As he raced down the dark highway, the Harley roaring in his ears, he felt the pistol's handle against his ribs. In just a few hours this gun would make history. He was going to use it to kill the Chief Elder's daughter, the woman who'd opposed him more than any of the others, the woman he hated more than anyone in the world.

Ariel Fury. His sister.

NINE

The temperature dropped below freezing that morning—unseasonably cold, even for northern Michigan. They ate another meal of trail mix and Slim Jims, and then Ariel told John to drive to the nearest Walmart. He found one in the town of Alpena, and she gave him a list of items to purchase: a down coat, a scarf, a pair of slacks, a pair of sunglasses, and a makeup kit. Ariel waited in the car while he shopped, and then they drove across town to a medical supply store, where John bought an inexpensive wheelchair. Afterwards, while they were driving north on Route 65, Ariel explained her plan.

"It's a disguise," she said. "I'm going to bundle up and make myself look like an old lady."

John couldn't picture it. "You? An old lady?"

"I've done it before. When I'm wearing the scarf and sunglasses, only the lower half of my face is visible. That's where I apply the makeup. Lots of lipstick and rouge."

He gave her a skeptical look. "And you think this disguise will get us through the roadblock on the Mackinac Bridge?"

"No, the cops are checking the cars pretty carefully. And they'd be especially suspicious of anyone in a Kia. But we're not going across the bridge."

"How will we get to the Upper Peninsula then? By boat?"

"Exactly. We'll take the ferry to Mackinac Island. Ever heard of the place?"

John shook his head. He was baffled.

"It's Michigan's biggest tourist attraction," Ariel said. "Located in Lake Huron, between the Lower and Upper Peninsulas. It's famous for its fudge shops. People come from hundreds of miles away just to buy a slice of fudge there."

"I don't see—"

"There are two ferries that go to the island, one from Mackinaw City on the Lower Peninsula and one from the town of St. Ignace in the U.P. We'll take the Mackinaw City ferry to the island, then get on one of the boats that's going back to St. Ignace."

Now he began to understand. "So it's like a detour? A way to get to the Upper Peninsula without crossing the bridge?"

She nodded. "There are no car ferries to the island, because they don't allow automobiles on Mackinac, so we'll have to take the passenger ferry and leave the Kia behind. But once we get to the U.P., I'll find a car to hot-wire. And from there, it's only a forty-mile drive to Haven."

John thought it over, searching for flaws in the plan. "But what if the cops are watching the ferries, too?"

"It's still better than going across the bridge. The ferries are busy this time of year, so we can blend in with the crowd."

"Blend in? I don't know about that. You can't walk, for one thing."

"I'll be in the wheelchair. You'll pretend you're taking your poor old mother on a day trip to Mackinac Island. Perfectly ordinary."

He was still skeptical but didn't want to argue anymore. Instead, he focused on the road ahead, which ran straight as an arrow toward the lakeshore. Meanwhile, Ariel opened the makeup kit and started slathering rouge on her face.

After another half hour they approached Mackinaw City. John was amazed to see the calm, blue surface of Lake Huron stretching for miles and miles to the east and north. He'd never visited this part of the country before, never imagined that the Great Lakes could be so huge. In the distance he saw the Mackinac Bridge arching toward the wooded shore of the Upper Peninsula. Squinting, he glimpsed flashing lights at the far end of the bridge. This was the roadblock, obviously. Then he glanced to the right and spotted a smallish, green island about ten miles away. A ferry-boat was scudding across the lake about halfway between the island and the docks of Mackinaw City.

"Make a right," Ariel said. Without lifting her head from her makeup kit, she pointed at a parking lot next to one of the motels on the lakeshore.

"We're still pretty far from the docks."

"If the troopers are at the ferry, they'll be looking for an old Kia. So we should park as far away from there as possible."

John made the right turn and parked at the far end of the lot. He gathered all their remaining cash and stuffed it in his pockets. Then he looked at Ariel again and did a double take. Her face was caked with beige makeup. She'd already wrapped the scarf around her head and zipped up the down coat. When she put on the sunglasses she looked like an old woman, an ailing, shriveled, sallow biddy dressed against the cold.

"Wow," he marveled. "You look terrible."

"Thanks, sonny," she said in a quavering voice. "You don't look so hot yourself."

Shaking his head, John retrieved the just-purchased wheelchair from the trunk and helped Ariel into its seat. Baggy pink slacks covered her bandaged legs, and a pair of cheap Walmart tennis shoes completed the outfit. She thrust her hands into the deep pockets of her coat, as if she were freezing, but John knew she was hiding her Glock in the right pocket and could draw it out at a moment's notice. In the left pocket she hid the small, leather-bound notebook.

He locked the car and spent the next twenty minutes pushing the wheelchair toward the docks of the White Star Ferry Line. As Ariel had predicted, the place was busy. John didn't see any state troopers as he headed for the ticket booth, but hundreds of tourists were lined up at the wharf, most of them shivering and stamping their feet to keep warm. He bought two tickets, then parked the wheelchair at the end of the line.

He bent over so he could whisper in Ariel's ear. "So far, so good."

She nodded. "Just keep your eyes open."

Five minutes later the tourists started boarding the ferry. The name *OJIBWAY* was painted in big black letters on the boat's hull. The ferry was maybe thirty yards long, with a dozen rows of hard plastic seats on the lower deck and another hundred seats behind the pilothouse on the upper deck. As John pushed Ariel toward the gangplank he saw two people shepherding the crowd: a pudgy woman taking the tickets and a man in a green uniform eyeballing the passengers. He wasn't a state trooper— the uniform was the wrong color—but he was clearly an authority of some kind, maybe an officer with the Harbor Patrol. He had salt-and-pepper hair, cut short and neat, and his eyes were cold blue. He looked like a real hardass.

John tried to act natural, but he could tell that the officer was scrutinizing him. The hardass narrowed his eyes as John handed his tickets to the pudgy woman. Then the man stepped forward and moved in front of Ariel's wheelchair, blocking their way. John braced himself, getting ready to tackle the guy. But Ariel calmly kept her hands in her pockets and looked up at him. "Can I help you, young man?"

To John's surprise, the officer smiled. "No, ma'am, I'm here to help *you*," he said. He pointed at the nubbly steel of the gangplank, which was wet in some spots and icy in others. "It's a little slippery here, and I don't want you to go sliding. Is it all right if I grab the front of your chair and help you across?"

"Why, certainly." Ariel didn't miss a beat. "That's very kind of you." She twisted around in her seat and looked at John. "Isn't that kind, sonny?"

His pulse was still racing. "Yeah, definitely," he managed to say. "Thank you, sir."

As the officer guided the wheelchair across the gangplank, John got a closer look at his uniform. The stitching on the left side of his shirt said CAPT. BURT DUNN, WHITE STAR FERRY. The guy didn't work for the Harbor Patrol after all. He was the captain of the *Ojibway*.

"There you go, ma'am," he said once Ariel was safely aboard. Then he turned to John and pointed at the left side of the lower deck. "You should park your mom's wheelchair next to that window. You'll get a good view of the island from there."

John thanked him again and pushed Ariel toward the window. He wasn't accustomed to all this Midwestern friendliness. It made him nervous.

After another five minutes the boat was fully loaded and ready to go. It backed away from the wharf and slowly cruised out of Mackinaw City's harbor. Once it reached the open water, though, the engines revved, the bow tilted upward and the boat accelerated. Soon they were speeding across Lake Huron, going at least forty miles per hour.

John bent over the wheelchair again. "Hey, this isn't bad," he whispered. "We're really moving."

"It's a hydrojet ferry," Ariel whispered back. "Very fast and maneuverable. The boat has pump-jets that suck in water and spew it out at high speed." She pointed out the window. "Look, you can see the water jetting out of the stern."

He turned toward the back of the *Ojibway* and saw a high rooster-tail of water leaping into the air and crashing down on the boat's wake. They were already a couple of miles from shore and rushing past the Mackinac Bridge. John glimpsed the flashing blue lights of the police roadblock again, and this time he felt a surge of satisfaction at the sight. *Suckers! We're going right past you!*

After a while he turned to the front of the boat and stared at Mackinac Island, which was growing larger by the second as they zoomed toward it. Just past the island's wharves was an old-fashioned Main Street lined with two-story wooden buildings. A steep bluff loomed behind the street, rising about a hundred feet above the harbor. Perched atop the bluff was a cluster of buildings with a wall around them and a tall flagpole.

"That's Fort Mackinac," Ariel said, pointing at the island. "Built in the eighteenth century by the British, then taken over by the American army. It was a very strategic location in those days. A cannon positioned on that bluff could fire at any ship passing between the Lower Peninsula and the U.P."

"Is the army still there?"

"No, it's a state park now."

Within minutes they reached the wharves in the island's harbor. The *Ojibway* sidled up to a long wooden pier, where a crew of White Star Ferry employees fastened the boat's lines to a pair of bollards on the dock. As the passengers rose from their seats, anxious to disembark, John peered through the window at another wooden pier about a hundred yards away. A boat that looked very similar to the *Ojibway* was docked at the end of that pier, and a line of people stretched down the wharf, waiting to board the vessel.

Ariel noticed it too. "That's the ferry going to the U.P. As soon as we get off this boat, you'll push me down Main Street to the other wharf."

"Then we'll buy our tickets and get in line?"

"If we hurry, we can be in Haven in a couple of hours." She pointed at the gangplank, where the other passengers were already swarming ashore. "Go on, sonny. No time to lose."

Burt Dunn, the *Ojibway*'s captain, stood at the gangplank again, this time saying goodbye to everyone. He smiled when he saw Ariel. Without hesitation, he helped maneuver the wheelchair onto the wharf. Then John started pushing Ariel down the pier, heading for Main Street. The other passengers rushed past them, eager to hit the town.

As John maneuvered the wheelchair through the crowd, he gazed down the length of the pier and surveyed the traffic on Main Street. Although there were no cars on the island, dozens of cyclists cruised down the street and hundreds of pedestrians crowded the sidewalks. Several horse carriages clopped down the street as well, carrying tourists and their luggage to the island's hotels. Another carriage was parked halfway down the pier, waiting for passengers. The carriage's driver was nowhere in sight, but the horse was so tame it just stood there, untied, on the dock's wooden boards, its nose pointed toward Main Street. It was a big, brown horse, like one of the Clydesdales in the Budweiser ads. John admired the animal as he pushed the wheelchair past it, then faced forward and focused again on the Main Street end of the pier. Up ahead, the ferry passengers branched off to the left and right, heading for the island's fudge shops.

Then John spotted a tall, young man in a black leather jacket. Even from two hundred feet away, John could tell that the guy was trouble. He was eying each of the disembarking passengers, craning his neck to make sure he didn't miss anyone, and checking their faces against a photograph he held in his left hand. He wasn't a cop, though—he was too unkempt, too sketchy. And his hair was bright red, the same shade as Ariel's.

John slowed to a crawl. Ariel looked up at him, and he could tell from her expression that she'd spotted the Rifleman, too. "Shit," John whispered. "We're screwed."

An instant later the guy saw them. He stared directly at John, then at the photo in his hand. Then he stepped forward to get a better look, dodging the tourists moving in the opposite direction. He seemed puzzled at first by Ariel's old-lady disguise, but after a couple of seconds he saw through it. He started barreling through the crowd, knocking aside everyone who got in his way.

They were trapped on the pier. There was nothing behind them but Lake Huron. John glanced at Ariel, expecting her to draw her Glock from her coat pocket, but she shook her head. "I can't shoot. I might hit someone in the crowd." She looked over her shoulder, scanning the pier. Then she pointed at the horse carriage. "Turn around and get behind that thing."

"What? What are you—"

"Just do it!"

John spun the wheelchair around and ran back to the carriage. He heard footsteps and shouts behind him, the sound of the Rifleman barging through the crowd of tourists, but he didn't look back. Dashing past the horse, he pushed Ariel behind the carriage's back end, which shielded them from view. But by peering under the carriage and looking past the wheels and the horse's legs, John could see the Rifleman. He'd broken through the crowd and now stood less than a hundred feet away, with no one on the pier between him and the carriage horse. The man reached inside his jacket and pulled out a Glock that was identical to Ariel's.

At the same time, Ariel ripped off her scarf and sunglasses and drew her own gun. But she didn't aim it at the Rifleman. Instead, she pointed it straight up and fired into the air.

The noise was enormous. The carriage horse reared back on its hind legs, whinnying. Then it fell back on all fours and galloped down the pier toward the Rifleman, its hooves pounding the wooden boards.

The man stopped in his tracks. He raised his Glock and fired at the horse, but the shot went high and hit the carriage's awning. Then the terrified animal charged into him, knocking him to the side. He collapsed on the pier and the carriage's wheels ran over his legs. The horse kept galloping until it neared the crowd of tourists, who'd started running toward Main Street when they'd heard the gunshots. Then the animal pulled up short, frightened by the crowd's noise. Meanwhile, the Rifleman lay facedown on the boards, motionless. He was either dead or unconscious, it was impossible to tell.

Ariel had already put her gun back in the pocket of her down coat. Although everyone on the wharf had heard the shot, John doubted that anyone but him saw her pull the trigger. The panicked White Star Ferry employees fled right past John and Ariel, running away from the *Ojibway* and following the crowd to Main Street. John gazed down the pier and felt a pang of guilt when he saw Captain Dunn dashing toward the island. The poor man was probably scared out of his mind.

Within seconds the wharf was nearly deserted. Then John saw movement on the other wharf, the one with the line of tourists waiting to board the ferryboat going to St. Ignace. Another man in a black leather jacket ran down the pier, shouting into a handheld radio as he headed for Main Street. Two more Riflemen were already on the street, sprinting toward the White Star Ferry's wharf from the other side of town. Worst of all, John saw movement on the lake as well. He glimpsed a pair of sleek, neon-yellow speedboats about a mile to the southeast, racing toward Mackinac Island's harbor. He couldn't see the boats' pilots or passengers, but he was willing to bet they were Riflemen. The guy with the radio must've alerted them.

"More of them are coming," he said, pointing them out to Ariel. "What do we do?"

For a moment she just stared at the speedboats. Then she twisted around in her wheelchair and focused on the *Ojibway*, now abandoned by the White Star Ferry crew. "I know about hydrojets," she said. "I think I can pilot her."

"Wait a second. You're talking about the ferryboat?"

"Just carry me up to the pilothouse, okay? I'll figure it out."

"This is insane. You can't—"

"If you have a better plan, I'm all ears."

In seconds they were back at the gangplank. John pushed the wheelchair onto the *Ojibway*, then lifted Ariel out of the chair, and carried her up the stairs to the upper deck. Then they rushed into the pilothouse, a simple room with a big, curved window looking out the front of the boat. A wooden ship's wheel stood in the center of the room, and next to it was a control board with lots of switches and throttles. It looked pretty damn complex, but Ariel wasn't fazed. She pointed at the padded chair behind the ship's wheel. "Set me down," she ordered.

John lowered her into the chair. "Just one question. Have you ever driven a ferryboat before?"

"No." She narrowed her eyes and studied the control board. "But I piloted a freighter once. That ship was twice as big as this one." Leaning forward, she flicked a switch and pulled one of the throttles up. The deck rumbled as the *Ojibway*'s engines roared to life. Ariel grinned. "There, that was easy. Now all we have to do is cast off. Go back down to the pier and untie the ropes from the bollards."

He stared at her while she wiped the old-lady makeup from her face. *What's with this girl? How does she know so much?* The question bothered the hell out of him, but there was no time to think about it. He bolted out of the pilothouse and down the stairs to the gangplank.

The wharf was still deserted but Main Street was in an uproar. The tourists had stampeded away from the White Star Ferry and gathered in hysterical crowds at the north and south ends of the street. John saw no signs of the Mackinac Island police as he dashed across the gangplank. He assumed they were busy trying to control the crowds and hadn't figured out what was going on yet. For the first time he considered the consequences of what he was doing, how much trouble he'd get into if he hijacked the ferryboat. They'd probably throw him into state prison, ten years at the least. But right now he was more worried about Sullivan's men than the cops. He caught a glimpse of the three Riflemen at the Main Street end of the pier, where they'd stopped to regroup. They slowly approached their downed comrade, who'd started moaning and squirming on the dock. The men were cautious because they didn't understand what had happened to their friend, but John knew that any second now they'd go on the attack and rush down the pier. Meanwhile, he could hear the whine of the speedboats approaching the harbor.

John headed for one of the two bollards that the *Ojibway* was fastened to. It was a thick iron post at the edge of the pier, and the ferryboat's rope coiled around it in crisscrossing loops. He found the knotted end of the rope and started to unravel the loops, but it wasn't easy—his fingers grew numb as he tried to untangle the line, which was wet and cold. After struggling for several seconds, he managed to unwind the rope and toss it onto the deck of the ferryboat. But as he ran to the other bollard he knew he was out of time. The three Riflemen had stepped past their injured friend. They chose that moment to sprint down the pier, with their guns raised and pointed straight at John.

The first bullet whistled past his head as he dove for cover behind the bollard. The second hit the thick iron post, which rang with the impact. John fumbled at the coiled rope, but it was no use. The men kept shooting at him as they ran down the pier. Even if he managed to unfasten the line, he'd never make it across the gangplank. He was pinned down.

But John didn't panic. He kept working at the rope, loosening and unwinding it. He knew he wouldn't make it, but maybe Ariel could. He realized at that moment why she'd made such a big impression on him, why he'd sacrificed so much to help her get home. He'd fallen for Ariel because he had nothing else. He had no family anymore, no friends, no job. His life—his *real* life—had ended three years ago, when Ivy died. That's why he could stay so calm with all the bullets buzzing past.

The Riflemen were halfway down the pier by the time he freed the rope. He tossed the line over to the *Ojibway* and yelled, *"Go, Ariel!"* as loud as he could. While he gazed at the boat's upper deck, hoping she'd heard him, one of the Riflemen fired at the pilothouse. The bullet shattered the big, curved window at the front, spraying glass everywhere.

John's stomach lurched. All the strength seemed to drain from his limbs as he stared at the gaping hole where the window had been. Then he heard more gunshots, five of them in quick succession, but these shots came from the pilothouse, not the pier. One of the Riflemen tumbled backward and lay still. The other two stopped running and scrambled for cover, retreating toward the Main Street end of the wharf. Ariel had returned fire. There were no more tourists in the vicinity, so she was free to shoot at Sullivan's men.

And John was free to make a run for it. While the Riflemen retreated, he popped up from behind the bollard and charged toward the *Ojibway*. In no time at all he leaped across the gangplank, reaching the safety of the lower deck just as the bullets started flying again. Ariel must've been watching him from the pilothouse, because an instant later the ferryboat pulled away from the wharf. John retracted the boat's gangplank, manhandling it onto the deck, and then the *Ojibway* set out for the open waters of Lake Huron.

They headed northeast, with the pair of neon-yellow speedboats about a quarter mile behind them. Ariel throttled up the engines, pushing the pump-jets as far as they could go. John stood in the pilothouse behind Ariel's seat, looking over her shoulder at the control board. The needle on the speedometer pointed at 45 knots. He didn't know how many miles per hour that was, but judging from the way the boat was bouncing on the surface of the lake, he guessed it was pretty fast. The wind and spray blew into the pilothouse through the broken front window, coating their faces with cold droplets.

The speedboats were faster, though. After a few minutes they were less than a hundred yards behind the *Ojibway*, one on the left side of the ferry's wake and the other on the right, both clearly visible through the still-intact window at the back of the pilothouse. They were close enough now that John could see who was inside them. Sitting in each boat were two red-haired Riflemen, a pilot and a passenger, and each of the passengers carried an M4. As John stared at the men, they raised their carbines and aimed at the ferryboat.

In one swift motion he grabbed Ariel by the waist and pulled her off the pilot's chair, covering her body with his as they hit the floor. The bullets crashed through the back window of the pilothouse and shattered the glass, but luckily none of the shards hit them. After a brief pause the Riflemen fired a second barrage that struck the steel wall of the pilothouse below the window. Although some of the bullets dented the metal, they couldn't penetrate the wall. John breathed a sigh of relief. As long as he and Ariel stayed low, they'd be safe. "You okay?" he asked as he slid off her.

She nodded. Sitting up on the floor, she gripped the ship's wheel and straightened out the *Ojibway*, which had skewed to the left. "You'll be my eyes," she said. "Go take a peek out the front and see if we're still going in the right direction."

"Uh, it would help if I knew where we're headed."

"They're called Les Cheneaux, a bunch of small islands off the shoreline of the U.P. I know the area, it's treacherous for boaters. Lots of shoals and shallow spots."

John crept to the front of the pilothouse and peeked out the gaping window. The wooded shore of the Upper Peninsula stretched across the northern horizon. To the northeast, the shoreline turned jagged, pocked with dozens of islands and inlets. The nearest island was nothing but a long ridge of sand and shrubs. "Yeah, the islands are up ahead. Most of them are still pretty far off, but it looks like the closest one is only a couple of miles away."

"That's Goose Island. And there should be a shoal in front of it, about—"

Another barrage from one of the M4s hammered the boat. Again, John heard the sound of glass breaking. The noise came from the left side of the boat, probably the windows on the lower deck. "Jesus!" he cried. "Are they trying to hit the engines?"

Ariel shook her head. "The pump-jets are deep within the hull. And so are the gas tanks. Don't worry, the M4s can't hurt us."

As if in response, the Riflemen fired their carbines yet again. This time the bullets smashed the windows on the right side of the lower deck.

John had a bad feeling about this. He suspected that the Riflemen weren't shooting randomly. Their targeting was too deliberate, always focused on the *Ojibway*'s windows. They had a strategy, and he needed to figure it out. Creeping past Ariel, he went to the broken window at the back of the pilothouse and cautiously raised his head. The speedboats were only thirty yards away now, one on each side of the ferry. In the boat on the left, the passenger put down his M4 and reached inside a long black case. The Rifleman seemed to be assembling something, taking pieces out of the case and putting them together. It was probably another weapon, John guessed, but he didn't know for sure until he glanced at the boat on the right. The passenger there had completed the assembly process and propped the weapon on his shoulder. John recognized the thing from TV news programs he'd seen, footage of the wars in Iraq and Afghanistan. It was a rocket-propelled grenade launcher.

"Shit!" He looked over his shoulder at Ariel. "They got RPGs! They're gonna shoot a grenade through the broken windows!"

Her reaction was instantaneous. She spun the ship's wheel, and the *Ojibway* swung to the left. At the same moment, the Rifleman fired his RPG. As John lurched to the side, trying to stay on his feet, he saw the grenade rocketing over the lake, propelled by a long tail of flame. It looked like it was heading straight for him, and it was moving so fast he didn't even have time to duck. But the ferryboat's sudden turn shifted the pilothouse by a few crucial yards, and the grenade sailed past them, arcing over the upper deck. It dove into the lake instead, on the other side of the ferry, and the explosion lifted a plume of water twenty feet into the air.

John stood there, breathless. The boat rocked under his feet as he stared at the plume. He turned to Ariel and saw that she'd climbed back into the pilot's seat. She was jerking the ship's wheel back and forth, performing evasive maneuvers. The *Ojibway* zigzagged as it sped across the lake.

"Are you crazy?" he shouted. "Get down from the chair!"

"I have to see where we're going. I'm looking for a buoy." She pointed at the broken window at the front of the pilothouse. "Get over there and help me look."

"They can see you when you're sitting there! And if they can see you, they can shoot you!"

"The RPGs are the bigger problem now. The next one could sink us." She spun the ship's wheel clockwise, then counter, making the boat tilt like a carnival ride. "Come on, look for the buoy. It's red and black and shaped like a cone."

John grunted, "Jesus!" in exasperation, but he made his way to the front of the pilothouse. With the boat rocking so violently, it was difficult to see anything at all through the window. He felt dizzy as he stared at the horizon, which skewed up and down with every turn of the ship's wheel. After a few seconds, though, he spotted a flash of color on the gray surface of Lake Huron. The buoy looked like a dunce's cap, red at the tip and black below. "Off to the right!" he shouted, pointing in that direction. "About half a mile away. See it?"

"Yeah, perfect." Ariel turned the wheel again, aiming for the buoy. Then she reached into the pocket of her down coat and pulled out the Glock. "Here, take this. There's nine bullets left."

She held out the pistol, keeping the muzzle pointed at the floor. John stepped toward her, but he was reluctant to take it. He knew how to handle a Glock—he'd trained with semiautomatics during his brief time in the army, and even before then he'd done some target shooting when he was with the Disciples—but he'd never actually fired a gun in anger. "I have to warn you, I'm not a great shot," he said as Ariel handed him the pistol. "I don't know if I can hit those speedboats."

"You don't have to hit them. Just make them back off."

He stumbled to the back window of the pilothouse, keeping his head low. Glancing at the speedboats, he saw that the Rifleman on the right was busy loading another grenade into his launcher but the one on the left had already hoisted his weapon to his shoulder. So that's where John aimed the Glock. He cocked the pistol and gripped its handle with both hands to keep it steady. Then he took a deep breath and pulled the trigger.

The gun bucked in his hands and the bullet didn't go anywhere near the speedboat, but the Rifleman took cover anyway, ducking behind the boat's windscreen. John fired again and the bullet hit the water in front of the boat, which slowed down and fell behind the *Ojibway*. Before he could try a third shot, though, the Rifleman dropped his grenade launcher and picked up his M4. John knew he was outgunned, so he crouched below the window. A moment later the return fire battered the pilothouse.

Some of the bullets zinged inside and ricocheted off the ceiling, but Ariel stayed in the pilot's seat, steering the *Ojibway* toward the buoy. She passed to the left of it, then spun the ship's wheel to the right, turning the ferryboat so sharply it felt like they were going to tip over. This maneuver moved them away from the Rifleman with the M4, but it put the *Ojibway* directly in the path of the other speedboat. John dared a look out the back window and saw the speedboat's pilot change course, steering to the right to stay abreast of the ferry. By this point the Rifleman beside the pilot had reloaded his grenade launcher, and now he pointed the tube at the *Ojibway*'s pilothouse. John raised his Glock, but he was too late. The Rifleman had already aimed the RPG and was ready to fire. He had an easy shot.

Then the speedboat's bow suddenly tilted upward. The front of the boat rose high and fast, as if it had been jerked toward heaven by an invisible string. The bow kept climbing until it pointed at the sky and the boat came out of the water completely, its screw propellers spinning in midair. Then the speedboat flipped over and came crashing down, breaking into pieces of fiberglass as it scudded across the lake.

"Mother of Creation!" Ariel shouted. "It worked!"

John stared at the wreckage. Amid the broken sections of the boat's hull, he saw one of the Riflemen floating facedown. "What worked?"

"They hit the shoal, the Goose Island shoal. That's why the buoy's there, to mark the hazard, but they weren't paying attention."

She kept turning the *Ojibway* to the right, steering the ferryboat in a circle around a patch of dark water. This area looked different from the rest of the lake because there were rocks just below the surface. It was so shallow that several pieces of the wrecked speedboat lay on the rocks and poked out of the water. Another corpse was there too, bloody and twisted. Ariel shook her head at the sight.

Meanwhile, the other speedboat came to a stop just a few yards shy of the buoy. As the pilot turned the boat away from the shoal, the passenger picked up his RPG launcher. John pointed the Glock at him and fired, but this time the Rifleman didn't duck. Unflinching, he propped the launch tube on his shoulder while the bullet streaked into the water nearby. John fired again and again, almost hitting the boat, but the guy calmly aimed his weapon at the *Ojibway*, which was coming around the other side of the shoal and heading straight for him.

John turned to Ariel. "What the hell are you doing?"

"No more running." Her face was grim. She furrowed her brow and pressed her lips together. "It's time to end this."

"You're giving him a clear shot!"

In response, she throttled up the engines and the ferryboat leaped forward. Looking through the front window they saw the Rifleman point his grenade launcher at them. John pulled the trigger of his Glock one more time, praying for a miracle, and in the same instant the Rifleman fired his RPG.

The explosion knocked John off his feet. He fell sideways to the steel floor, which thumped and trembled. But he was alive, still alive. He wasn't even bleeding. The grenade hadn't entered the pilothouse. Ariel had thrown off the Rifleman's aim by pointing the *Ojibway* right at him. Instead of blasting them to bits, the grenade had hurtled through the broken windows on the lower deck and exploded there.

Even more remarkable, Ariel still sat in the pilot's chair. Hanging on to the ship's wheel for dear life, she kept the ferryboat on course as it shuddered from the blast. Then John felt another thump from below, a massive jolt accompanied by the sound of breaking fiberglass. The ferry's bow jumped into the air and splashed back down to the water.

John waited a moment for the rocking to subside, then pulled himself to his feet. He looked out the front window of the pilothouse but couldn't find the speedboat. Then he looked out the back window and saw more wreckage floating in the lake. The prow of the *Ojibway* had smashed the speedboat, splitting it in two. The bodies of the Riflemen bobbed in the ferry's wake.

Stunned, he turned back to Ariel, who was still gripping the ship's wheel. Her face was blank now. She didn't look triumphant, not by a long shot. Head bowed, she stared at the floor. Although Sullivan's men were her enemies, they were also her cousins. And she'd just killed four of them.

The *Ojibway* was still speeding across Lake Huron, but after a few seconds the ferryboat shuddered again. The walls of the pilothouse vibrated and the floor rumbled. Snapping out of her trance, Ariel lifted her head and throttled down the engines, slowing the ferry to a crawl. In the sudden silence, they heard bangs and clanks coming from the lower deck.

She bit her lower lip. "That doesn't sound good. You better get down there and see what's going on."

John nodded, then left the pilothouse. He walked past the rows of empty seats on the upper deck and headed for the stairs at the boat's stern. Halfway down the steps, he noticed the first signs of damage to the lower deck: gaping windows, charred walls, hard-plastic seats scattered everywhere. As he stepped farther down, he saw the jagged hole in the deck that marked the place where the grenade had exploded. The force of the blast had punched through the rivet joints in the floor, and black oily smoke rose from the gaps between the steel plates. The engine room had clearly been damaged, but John couldn't tell how serious the problem was. He noticed, though, that the ferryboat was listing to one side. They were taking on water.

He raced back to Ariel, who'd turned the boat toward an inlet between two of the small islands off the Upper Peninsula. The *Ojibway* was moving like an old man, making slow, halting progress. "How bad is it?" she asked.

"There's smoke coming from the engines. And I think there's water coming through the hull."

"But we're not swamped yet, right?"

"No, but the ship's going down. We have to take one of the lifeboats."

She shook her head. "The lifeboats are too slow. Sullivan has more men out there, on the lake and on the land. And they're communicating by radio, so they know where we are. If we take a lifeboat, they'll catch us before we get to shore."

"Maybe you didn't hear me. This ferry's going to sink."

"Well, let's get a little closer to home before that happens, okay?" With a grin, she reached for the control board and pulled up the throttles.

The engines clanked and sputtered, but after a moment the *Ojibway* shot forward. A breeze whipped through the broken windows as they rushed toward the islands, which were thick with trees but had no houses or docks. The inlet between the islands was less than fifty yards wide, but Ariel expertly guided the boat into the channel. John was impressed. "You've done this before?"

"I told you, I know the area. Haven is only ten miles north of here. I've canoed every inch of Les Cheneaux." She gave him another grin, then pointed at the Glock that lay on the floor of the pilothouse. John had dropped it when the RPG hit the boat. "Can you check the gun's magazine? I want to know how many bullets are left."

He picked up the pistol and ejected the magazine. It was empty. "Uh, it looks like I shot them all."

She frowned. "Okay, here's what we'll do. Once we get ashore, we'll go a couple of miles inland to a hiding place I know about. Then we'll wait till nightfall and hike the rest of the way to Haven."

Although this plan sounded reasonable, John felt uneasy. He tried to think of other options, turning away from the window so he could concentrate. As he stared at the side wall of the pilothouse he noticed a small cabinet with a glass door. Inside the cabinet was an odd-looking pistol with an oversized barrel, colored fire-engine red. He opened the glass door and removed the gun. "Hey, maybe we could use this. It looks like it fires shotgun shells."

Ariel chuckled. "That's a flare gun. You shoot it in the air if there's an emergency and you want someone to rescue you."

He felt embarrassed for a moment, but as he stared at the gun he still thought it could be useful. "The shell lights up and burns, right? So you can see it from miles away?"

"I know what you're thinking, but it won't work. A flare gun isn't a good weapon. The flare doesn't move as fast as a bullet, so it just bounces off whatever it hits. The only way it can hurt you is if it gets caught in your clothes and sets them on fire."

"It's better than nothing." He tucked the gun in the back of his pants and covered it with the tail of his shirt.

Soon they traversed the inlet and entered a calm bay between the islands and the Upper Peninsula. The shoreline of the U.P. was less than a mile ahead, but the *Ojibway*'s engines were coughing and whining now. As they reached the halfway point across the bay, a tremendous bang shook the ferryboat. When John looked out the back window of the pilothouse he saw flames rising from the boat's stern.

"Christ!" he yelled. "We gotta get off this thing!"

"Not yet." Ariel was grinning again. "We can make it to shore."

"The boat's on fire!"

"That just makes it interesting. Come on, where's your sense of adventure?"

She was actually enjoying herself. Her eyes shone with pleasure as the engines shrieked and the decks groaned and the wind fanned the flames at the back of the boat, hurling sparks on the water. Another bang rocked the *Ojibway* as Ariel steered the ferry toward a marshy cove. The shore was coming up fast.

John grabbed the edge of the control board, bracing himself for impact. "You're crazy!" he shouted.

"Thank you!" she shouted back at him.

Twenty yards from the cove, Ariel shut down the engines. The *Ojibway* glided into the shallow marsh, splashing silt and water everywhere as the boat's prow dug into the muddy bottom. The deceleration was relatively gentle. The ferry slowed and came to rest among the reeds and cattails, its hull tilting slightly to the left. The boat's stern was no longer burning; the deluge of muddy water had quenched the flames.

John unclenched his fingers from the control board. He didn't know whether he should be relieved or furious. "So was that good for you?"

"The best." She grinned once more, and for a second he remembered the look she'd given him after they'd rushed into her hotel room in Brooklyn. Then her face turned serious. She let go of the ship's wheel and checked the pockets of her down coat, making sure that her leather-bound notebook was still there. "All right, we better get moving. If the men on the speedboats radioed the other Riflemen, they'll be looking for us along the shoreline. We're going to hike through the woods, so you'll have to carry me."

He felt a sudden urge to kiss her, but he suppressed it. Instead, he leaned over the pilot's seat and picked her up, slipping one arm under her shoulders and the other under her fractured legs. Then he carried her out of the pilothouse and down the stairs to the lower deck.

The *Ojibway* had wedged itself into the mud at the edge of the marsh, and John was able to slide the ferryboat's gangplank onto a hummock of dry land several feet from the boat. After carrying Ariel to shore, he followed a dirt path that led from the bay to the woods. Just in front of the woods, about thirty yards ahead, was a two-lane state highway that roughly paralleled the shoreline of Lake Huron.

"That's M-134," Ariel said, pointing at the highway. "We'll cross the road and take the trail through the state forest to—"

Then they heard it, the same deep, guttural rumble they'd heard the day before, back in Chester County, Pennsylvania. To the west, a dozen motorcycles came cruising down M-134. The bikes were Harleys and the riders wore leather boots and black jackets. At the head of the pack was an older, gray-haired man in a bomber jacket. Ariel stiffened in John's arms when she saw him.

"Sullivan," she whispered.

TEN

The most disturbing thing about Sullivan was that he reminded John of Father Murphy. Although Sullivan wasn't as old as the late priest—he looked like he was about fifty—he had the same body type, tall and broad and muscular. Father Murphy had been famous in Kensington for his feats of strength; he used to impress the neighborhood kids by doing one-handed push-ups, sometimes with a youngster or two sitting on his back, all in an effort to win the kids over and lure them away from the gangs. Judging from the breadth of Sullivan's chest and the thickness of his neck, John guessed he could perform plenty of feats of his own, but his intentions clearly weren't as good. He had small eyes set deep and close together in a hard, weathered face. As he slowed his motorcycle and came to a stop on the highway's shoulder, his lips curled into a smile. His Harley blocked the path to the woods. John and Ariel were trapped between the highway and the bay.

Sullivan's men stopped too and dismounted from their bikes. Some were young guys with bright red hair, and others were graying. They fanned out, spreading across the marshy ground along the waterfront. As they stepped through the high grass they pulled out their weapons—Glocks, M4s, a couple of submachine guns. A few of the men headed for the bay and angled behind John and Ariel, surrounding them. Sullivan, though, stayed on his motorcycle. He seemed to be enjoying the show.

John looked in all directions. There was no escape. He could run back to the *Ojibway* but the boat was stuck in the marsh. Ariel squirmed in his arms, craning her neck to glance at each of the approaching Riflemen. Then she whispered, "Put me down."

She said it so emphatically that John felt a burst of hope. As he lowered her to the ground, he put his lips close to her ear. "Do you have a plan?"

"No." She sounded disappointed in herself. "I just don't want to look weak."

Then John remembered the flare gun. He pulled the thing from the back of his pants and pointed it at Sullivan. "Everyone, *freeze!*" he yelled. "Don't take another step!"

The Riflemen paused, staring at the gun. Once they recognized what it was, though, they continued moving in. Sullivan shook his head, still smiling.

John lowered his aim a bit. Maybe he could hit Sullivan's motorcycle. And if the flare got caught in the engine or the wheels, maybe it would set the bike on fire. But as he lined up the shot and started to squeeze the trigger, someone behind him grabbed his arm and yanked it upward. The flare shot straight up, a red fireball climbing into the blue sky, and as the gun's report rang in John's ears he saw the face of the Rifleman who'd just ambushed him from behind. He had some nasty cuts on his shaved head and a big purple bruise that almost hid his spiderweb tattoo. It was the bastard who'd shot Ariel, the one John had pummeled on the rooftop in Brooklyn.

The Rifleman gave him just enough time to make the connection. Then he rammed his fist into John's forehead.

The blow didn't knock him out cold, but he was only semiconscious for the next few minutes. His body went limp and his eyes closed. He could still hear the footsteps of the Riflemen, though, and feel their hands gripping his wrists and ankles. A moment later he was swinging in the air, suspended from his arms and legs. Sullivan's men were carrying him somewhere. He managed to open one eye while they crossed the highway. The Riflemen were hiding their motorcycles in the woods on the other side of the road. Then they fell in behind the men who were carrying John, all of them marching into the thick, shadowy pine forest. He couldn't understand why they were doing this. Why didn't they just kill him?

He didn't fully wake up until they dropped him on the ground. He lay on his back in the dirt under a massive pine tree that rose almost a hundred feet above him. The men who'd carried him there stepped backward and stood in a circle. The one with the bruised face stared at John and cracked his knuckles, clearly eager to take another shot at him. But the other Riflemen focused on Ariel, who sat in the dirt a couple of yards to his right. Even in her down coat and pink old-lady slacks, she looked proud and defiant. She stared back at Sullivan's men, her chin tilted upward.

After a moment some of the men stepped aside, making way for Sullivan to join the circle. He wasn't smiling anymore. His lips twitched as he stared at Ariel, exposing yellowed teeth. He locked eyes with her, and for the next several seconds they glared at each other, neither saying a word. Then he let out a deep breath and turned to John. "So you're the lucky paramour we've heard so much about?"

John said nothing. He was still woozy.

Sullivan pointed at him. "You're an attractive specimen. But a little duskier than what our women normally choose." He stepped closer, scrutinizing him. "Your father was Negro, is that not so?"

Although Sullivan looked like an aging biker, his accent was all wrong. He sounded like an old-fashioned Englishman, like an actor in *Hamlet* or some other goddamn play. John sat upright, grimacing as he lifted his head from the dirt. His anger was reviving him, clearing his mind. "Fuck you."

"Aye, you're scrappy. That's an admirable trait. Your DNA would've made a nice addition to the gene pool at Haven. I can see why the Elders approved the match."

"Enough!" Ariel interrupted. Her voice was sharp, commanding. "He doesn't know anything."

Sullivan raised an eyebrow. "Really? You've spent the past two days with the fellow. He must've demanded an explanation by now."

"Aye, he did. But I was careful. I didn't reveal any knowledge that's forbidden to outsiders." She was starting to sound more like Sullivan as she talked with him. Now John heard the same English accent in her voice, too. "I remember my oath. And so should you."

"But the oath doesn't apply in his case. This outsider will never get a chance to share his knowledge. He's living his last hour."

Ariel shook her head. "Nay, he's not your enemy. Do what you want with me, but don't murder an innocent."

"Innocent? I think not. Look what he did to Marlowe." Sullivan pointed at the Rifleman with the battered face. "And what about my men who were pursuing you on the lake? We lost radio contact with them a while ago. Did he help you kill them?"

"He was trying to protect me. That's his nature. It would be cruel to condemn him for it."

Sullivan stared at Ariel for several seconds, studying her. Then his eyes widened. "You wanton bitch. You care for him, don't you? That's why you're pleading for his life."

She scowled. "It's true, I care for him. More than I care for you, at least."

"Oh, no, it's more serious than that. You've fallen for the boy." He took a step toward her, clenching his hands again. "How quaint. The golden girl is in love."

The look in Sullivan's eyes was murderous. He took another step toward Ariel and towered over her, brandishing his fists. Alarmed, John rose to his feet, but he was still so wobbly he could barely stand up straight. Sullivan gave him a disdainful look, then turned to the Rifleman with the bruised face. "Marlowe, please restrain our guest. We can't allow his ill humor to spoil our festivities."

In an instant the Rifleman grabbed John by the wrists and pinned him facedown in the dirt. John's shoulders burned as Marlowe twisted his arms behind his back. At the same time, Ariel cried out in pain. John turned his head to the side and saw Sullivan kneeling on her chest. The bastard reached into the pocket of her down coat and pulled out the small, leather-bound notebook.

"I suspected you'd have one of these." He held the notebook in the air, just out of Ariel's reach. "We were observing you in New York the day before you seduced your paramour. When you arranged your meeting with Mariela's courier." He opened the notebook and flipped through its pages until he reached the most recent entries. "And lo and behold, it looks like you inscribed some new runes in your Treasure. Could this be the information you received from our cousins in Caño Dorado?"

Ariel panted through clenched teeth. Sullivan's knee pressed down on her breastbone, making it hard for her to breathe. Her hands were free, so she beat her fists against Sullivan's thigh and crotch, but her blows had no strength behind them. He laughed at her efforts, then turned to John, waving the notebook to get his attention. "Have you seen the runes? It's a devilishly complex language. I never learned to read it, but some of my men can." He closed the book and showed John its elaborately decorated cover. Then, with a vicious swipe, he slammed the notebook into Ariel's face.

John flailed on the ground, struggling to rise, but Marlowe twisted his arms and held him down. Meanwhile, Sullivan gazed with satisfaction at the blood streaming from Ariel's nose. The left side of her face started to swell and turn purple, but John could tell she was still conscious. Although her left eye was half-closed because of the swelling, it stayed focused on Sullivan, tracking his every move.

He slipped the notebook into the pocket of his bomber jacket. "Now that I have what I want, it's time for the entertainment to begin." He bent a little lower, smiling at her battered face. "How shall we do this, Sister? How can we make this experience as painful as possible for you?"

Ariel curled her blood-smeared lip. "You can't hurt me." She held out her hands. On her palms and fingers and thumbs were the thin, faded scars John had noticed before, the scars that seemed to cover her whole body. "I've been hurt too much already. I won't even feel it."

"But I'm not going to hurt *you*. I'm going to hurt *him*." He pointed at John. "Marlowe, let's start with something simple. Break his nose."

Nodding, Marlowe turned John over, flipping him onto his back. Then, before John could raise his arms to defend himself, Marlowe's fist smashed into his face. The pain exploded from his eyebrows down to his mouth.

"Nay!" Ariel screamed. "Stop it!"

"But we're just getting started, Sister. Let's break a few of his ribs now."

Marlowe stood up, drew back his foot, and kicked John in the left side of his chest. The toe of Marlowe's boot cracked at least two of John's ribs. The crunch of bone was so loud it echoed against the pine trees. John felt like his lungs had caught fire. He closed his eyes and doubled up, unable to breathe.

Ariel screamed again and Marlowe laughed. John convulsed in the dirt until his chest muscles finally relaxed, allowing him to gulp an excruciating breath. When he opened his eyes he saw Sullivan grasp Ariel's chin and turn her face toward him, forcing her to look. "There's your paramour, Sister. What do you think of him now?"

"You . . . filthy . . . *cocksucker!*"

"Good, very good. I like seeing you angry." He let go of her chin and tore off her down coat. Then he grabbed the front of her T-shirt, balled it in his fist, and lifted her off the ground. "Don't you remember what I told you? After you said you wouldn't have me? I said I'd kill any man who came near you." He shook her from side to side, tossing her around like a rag doll. "I keep my promises, Sister. I'm going to break every bone in his body."

Flecks of saliva sprayed from Sullivan's mouth as he shouted at her. He twined Ariel's shirt around his right hand, pulling it above her waist, and with his left hand he reached under her shirt and ripped off her bra. John felt a surge of adrenaline that suppressed the pain in his face and chest. He had to get up, he had to do something! The bastard was going to rape her! With a roar, he leaped past Marlowe and threw himself at Sullivan. John clenched his right hand into a fist and drew back his arm, ready to pound the motherfucker's face in, but before he could throw the punch he felt a sharp blow to the back of his head.

The whole world disappeared for a moment, replaced by a flash of white light. Then John lay on his back again. When he opened his eyes he saw the pine forest spinning overhead and Marlowe's purple face whirling above him like a planet. The asshole was rubbing the knuckles of the hand he'd just smacked into John's skull. Ariel lay on her side a few feet away, curled into the fetal position. Sullivan crouched next to her, gripping a hank of her red hair with one hand and pointing at John with the other.

"He's gallant, I'll say that for him. But also a bit thickheaded. Don't you agree?" He shook Ariel by the hair, trying to get her to answer. "Come on, join the conversation, Sister."

She winced. "Stop calling me that."

Sullivan cocked his head. "What's wrong? You think your paramour will think less of you if he knows how we're related?"

Ariel said nothing. Sullivan stared at her for a few seconds, narrowing his eyes. "Oh, I see what's troubling you." Grinning, he turned to John. "You'll have to forgive my sister. She's a little embarrassed. I suppose she didn't tell you that I'm her half brother?"

John struggled to concentrate. He took an aching breath and tried to stop the forest from spinning around him.

Sullivan waited a moment, clearly enjoying himself. He was having such a good time, he didn't seem to mind that John couldn't respond. "It's true, we're siblings. But what she doesn't want you to know is the exact nature of our relationship. Because I look so much older than her, you probably assume we have the same father, but different mothers. But that's not the case."

"Stop!" Ariel screamed. "You swore an oath!" She twisted and swiped her hand at Sullivan, curling her fingers like claws and reaching for his eyes, but he yanked her by the hair again and shoved her face into the dirt.

"In fact, the opposite is true," he continued. "We have the same mother, but different fathers. And her father died long before mine was born."

John focused on Sullivan. He wasn't making any sense. John stared at him hard, throwing all his remaining strength into the effort. Miraculously, everything stopped spinning and froze in place. "What?" he blurted. "What are you—"

"Think about it, good fellow. You haven't known my sister for very long, but you must've noticed a few odd things about her. Doesn't she seem a little wiser than her years? Doesn't she have more knowledge and skills than a typical woman of twenty or twenty-five?"

Ariel screamed "Stop!" again, but Sullivan ignored her. He grabbed her left arm and held it up to the light. "And you must've noticed how many scars she has. Didn't you wonder where they all came from? How do you think she accumulated all those marks?"

John shook his head. Everything came unglued and started to spin again, but after a couple of seconds he managed to regain control. "I don't . . . understand."

"Don't fear, there's nothing supernatural about it. Every member of our family has an extra gene. This gene is sex-linked, carried on the X chromosome, which means it has different effects for the different genders." Sullivan's voice took on a professorial tone. He seemed to enjoy giving this explanation. "For the sons in our family, who have one X chromosome and one Y chromosome, the extra gene gives them red hair and green eyes. It also makes us infertile. That's why our women have to be impregnated by outsiders."

Ariel had stopped screaming by this point. She was sobbing now.

Sullivan still held her left arm. He turned it slowly, examining it from every angle. "The women in our family also have red hair and green eyes, but the extra gene has a more dramatic effect on them because they have two X chromosomes and no Y. In short, it helps repair the long-term damage to their cells. This means their skin and muscles and bones and nerves don't deteriorate as time goes on. Their bodies develop normally when they're girls, but once they're fully grown they neither wane nor weaken." He pinched the skin just below Ariel's elbow, holding it between his thumb and forefinger. "She's not immortal, of course. You can still cut and bruise and burn her, which explains how she got all those scars over the years. But she doesn't age. She'll never grow old."

John took another painful breath and stared at Ariel. The tears leaked from the corners of her eyes. They mixed with the dirt that clung to her cheeks and the blood that still trickled from her nose. There was no more pride in her face, no more defiance. She was bloodied and beaten.

Sullivan dropped her arm and let go of her hair. He wiped his hands on his pants, obviously satisfied. Then, he grunted and stood up. "I know what you're thinking, John. You're wondering how old she is. A hundred years? Two hundred? Would you care to take a guess?"

John shook his head. He didn't believe it. Sullivan was talking nonsense, telling ridiculous lies. But why was Ariel crying? Why did all the fight suddenly go out of her?

"I'll give you a hint. She's older than the state of Michigan. Older than the entire United States, in fact."

He turned away from Sullivan. He didn't want to listen anymore. But the idea was in his head and he couldn't stop thinking about it, couldn't stop making connections. He remembered what Ariel had told him about Valley Forge and why General Washington decided to base his army there. And what she'd said about the cannons on Mackinac Island. Now that he thought about it, she seemed to know an unusual number of facts about the distant past.

"Give up? All right, I'll tell you. She was born in England three hundred and seventy-three years ago."

The number branded itself into John's brain. Three hundred and seventy-three. *Three hundred and seventy-three.*

"That must sound very old to you, but it's actually quite young compared with some of the women in our family. All our Elders are over six hundred years old. My mother—Chief Elder Elizabeth Fury—was already seven hundred years old when she gave birth to Lily."

John was bewildered. "Lily? Who's Lily?"

"Our family has a curious tradition regarding names. We all share the same last name—Fury—but each of us has two first names. We use our birth names when we're in Haven, but whenever we go outside the community we're required to assume a different identity. Lily is Ariel's birth name. Our mother named all her children after flowers and herbs."

Sullivan spoke in a matter-of-fact tone, as if everything he said was common knowledge. John looked again at Ariel, who still lay prostrate in the dirt, and wondered if it could be true. It was hard to imagine that she could be four centuries old, but he'd noticed that she hadn't denied it. She'd reacted instead with horror and grief, and now John realized why. She was devastated because he'd just learned her family's secret. And that meant he was doomed.

As he stared at her, Ariel sat upright and wiped her eyes. She'd stopped crying and her face had hardened. She glowered at Sullivan, her lips trembling with fury. "Why don't you tell him *your* birth name?" She turned to John. "When this cocksucker was born fifty-three years ago, Mother named him Basil. It was the biggest laugh of 1961."

For a moment it looked like Sullivan might grab Ariel by the neck and throttle her. But instead he simply frowned. "All right, enough family history. Your paramour knows too much already. One way or another, he has to die. So let's get on with it." He turned to Marlowe. "Take out one of his eyes. The left one."

Marlowe held up his hand. His nails were filthy. "Should I use my fingers, Sully?"

"Nay, that would be uncouth. Find a stick."

The Rifleman obediently lowered his gaze and started searching the area at the base of the big pine tree. He combed the soil and pine needles, picking up fallen branches to see if they were suitable. Meanwhile, John shivered on the ground. He wasn't afraid of dying. He was ready to die. But he was terrified of being mutilated. He knew that at some point he'd break down and start screaming. He'd howl and weep and beg for his life while Sullivan made jokes and Marlowe guffawed. And the worst part was that Ariel would see the whole thing.

Marlowe finally found a stick he liked. He snapped it in two and chose the piece with the sharper end. Then, before John could resist, another Rifleman knelt beside him and pinned his arms to the ground. John was shivering violently now. He was going to break very soon. Sullivan stood a couple of yards away, observing everything with great interest. Ariel sat in the dirt nearby, her face buried in her hands.

Marlowe bent over John, pointing the stick at his face. But then he hesitated. He stood up straight and looked over his shoulder at Sullivan. "Which eye did you say, Sully? The right?"

Sullivan shook his head. "Nay, the left. Damn it, can't you remember any—"

Before he could finish the sentence, Ariel pivoted on the ground and punched the back of his knee. It was a vicious blow, with plenty of momentum behind it. Sullivan let out a gasp as his knee buckled. Then, as he fell forward, Ariel climbed on his back and reached around to claw his eyes.

Marlowe shouted, "Sully!" and dropped his stick, but as he rushed toward Sullivan a gunshot broke the hush of the pine forest. Marlowe shrieked and spun around, clutching his shoulder. At first John assumed that Ariel had grabbed a gun and started shooting, but she was busy raking Sullivan's face with her fingernails. Then there was a second gunshot. The bullet smashed into the skull of the Rifleman who'd pinned John to the ground. The man's head jerked to the side and spouted blood as he crumpled.

Then the woods exploded with gunfire. The barrage came from deeper within the forest, behind the pine trees to John's right, and it struck down three more Riflemen, killing them where they stood. The rest of Sullivan's men scrambled for cover, diving behind tree trunks and rock piles and thickets. Within seconds they pulled out their carbines and returned fire, but their shots were wild and random because they couldn't see their attackers. Meanwhile, Sullivan flung Ariel off his back and retreated with his men, hurtling over a fallen trunk and disappearing in the undergrowth. Marlowe followed him, staggering.

While the bullets whizzed overhead, Ariel crawled over to John, dragging her useless legs behind her. "Don't get up," she warned. "Stay low and follow me."

Although John was bewildered, he didn't ask any questions. His gratitude and relief were so strong he would've followed her anywhere. His broken ribs flared in agony as he rolled over onto his stomach, but he didn't make a sound. Then he and Ariel scuttled on their elbows through the dirt, heading for the trees that the unseen attackers hid behind.

Soon the gunfire ebbed. Sullivan and his men were running through the woods, heading back to the highway by the lakeshore. After a few more seconds John heard the distant roar of half a dozen motorcycle engines. The roar grew louder as the diminished band of Riflemen revved their bikes and raced off. Then the noise gradually faded, and the forest fell silent again.

When John looked up he saw an Amish man step out from behind one of the pine trees. He wore a broad-brimmed straw hat and a long-sleeved white shirt without any buttons. A pair of suspenders held up his pants. He was tall and powerfully built and had a thick reddish beard, but no mustache. John recalled what Ariel had said about the residents of Haven, how they disguised themselves as Amish to avoid scrutiny from the local authorities. But this particular man's disguise was marred by the fact that he carried an M4 carbine. He approached them cautiously, holding his gun at the ready. "Lily?" he called. "Are you injured, milady?"

Ariel nodded. "I can't walk but I'm in no immediate danger. I'm very glad to see you, Conroy."

The man pointed his rifle at John. "Who is this outsider? Did Sullivan bring him here?"

"Nay, I did. He's a friend. How many guardsmen are with you?"

He whistled. Four more men in Amish garb emerged from hiding, each carrying either an assault rifle or a pistol. "We were on patrol near Flower Creek, two miles to the north," Conroy said. "We spied the flare, so we hastened here to investigate."

Ariel turned to John and smiled. "I owe you an apology. Bringing the flare gun was a good idea." She sat upright, resting her back against a nearby pine.

John was surprised to see the small, leather-bound notebook in her lap. He pointed at it. "You got it back?"

"I pulled it out of the pocket of his jacket while I was scratching the bastard's face." Her smile broadened. "Pretty clever, eh?"

"Lily!" Conroy stared at her, dumbounded. "He knows about your Treasure?"

"I told you, cuz, he's a friend. Over the past two days he's saved my life many times."

Conroy turned to John and looked at him carefully. "I've seen this outsider's face before. In our files. Is this your paramour?"

Ariel stopped smiling. "Aye, he is. What of it?"

Conroy's face reddened. "I need to speak with you privately, milady."

Ariel took a deep breath. Then she nodded at Conroy, who approached the pine tree and crouched beside her. They spoke in whispers that became more urgent and agitated as the conversation went on. After a couple of minutes Ariel's face had reddened just as much as Conroy's. They exchanged a few more heated whispers, and then Conroy stood up and went to talk with the other guards. At the same time, Ariel looked at John. Her eyes were glassy.

"My cousins are going to take us to Haven." She spoke haltingly now, her voice tense. "But they have to bind your hands."

"You mean, tie me up?"

She nodded. "I had to tell him what you know. About Haven. And our family. I had no choice."

John's throat tightened. "Wait a second. What's going to happen when we get to Haven?"

"You must appear before the Council of Elders. Your fate is in their hands now." Her voice cracked. "I'm sorry, John. I'm so, so sorry."

Conroy returned with two of his men. One of them pointed a pistol at John's head. The other held a length of rope.

PART II
HAVEN

ELEVEN

John marched through the woods with his hands tied behind his back. The guardsmen from Haven made no allowances for his broken nose and ribs. They trained their pistols at his head and kept him moving.

The trail twisted through the forest, climbing over knolls and descending into ravines. It would've been a grueling hike even if he wasn't injured. John panted from the effort, his chest aching with every breath, but he didn't complain. Keeping his face rigid, he stared at the back of Ariel's head, which bobbed behind Conroy's. The guard carried her piggyback, cradling her broken legs against his hips while she gripped his muscular shoulders. John focused on her long, swaying red hair and felt a surge of anger. She'd handed him over, turned him in. Once they reached Haven, the Elders would kill him. He was guilty of the crime of knowing too much.

The sheer ingratitude of it, that's what he couldn't get over. He'd saved Ariel's life, and this was how she repaid him! She said she'd had no choice, but John didn't believe it. Did she really have to reveal that he knew her family's secret? Couldn't she have left out that detail when she explained the situation to Conroy? But no, she had to tell him everything. She had to follow her damn oath to the letter.

After a while he shifted his gaze from Ariel to her cousins. The two guardsmen behind him, the ones who carried the pistols, were young men with bright red hair and sparse beards. Conroy and the two other guards were older, their long beards flecked with gray. Except for their Amish clothing and facial hair, they looked a lot like Sullivan's men. Clearly, there'd been a split among the men in Ariel's family, with some leaving Haven to follow Sullivan and the rest remaining loyal to the Elders. John still didn't know what had caused the split, but he could see its effects in the way the men treated Ariel. Whereas the Riflemen had looked at her with undisguised hatred, the guards from Haven treated her with respect. Although Conroy had scolded her earlier, now he showed great deference, constantly checking to see if she was comfortable as he carried her through the forest. Meanwhile, the other guards sneaked glances at her as if she were a celebrity. No, more than a celebrity—there was genuine awe in their faces, and some fear as well. They looked at her as if she were a goddess, a temperamental deity who'd hurl a lightning bolt at them if the mood struck her.

John frowned. Ariel wasn't a goddess. But maybe she wasn't human, either. *Three hundred and seventy-three years.* Could anyone stay human after living for so long? Maybe that was why she'd handed him over to Conroy. John was less than a tenth of her age. Even if she cared for him, it didn't matter. When balanced against her eternal family, how could his fate be important?

After a solid hour of walking, Conroy called for a ten-minute break. They stopped at a small clearing, a rough circle of weeds and mud surrounded by the pines. Conroy crouched by one of the trees and Ariel slid off his back. She looked over her shoulder and stared at John for a moment, her face pale and unreadable. Then Conroy ordered the two younger guards to escort John to the other side of the clearing, as far as possible from Ariel.

Grabbing him by the elbows, the guards found a relatively dry patch of ground and lowered him to a sitting position. The movement jarred his broken ribs, and he let out a gasp. The guard on his left, who had a sharp chin and wire-rim glasses, looked at him gravely. "Are you in pain?"

John shook his head. "Nah, I'm feeling great. Never better."

The guard pulled an army-surplus canteen from his backpack and unscrewed the cap. "Tilt your head back. You need to drink."

John wanted to refuse as a matter of principle, but he was too thirsty. He tilted his head back and opened his mouth, letting the guard pour the water onto his tongue. It tasted horrible, like moldy bread. John spat it out. "What the hell? You trying to poison me?"

"Nay, it's medicine," said the guard on his right. This one had thick reddish eyebrows. "To ease the pain in your chest and the swelling in your nose."

John eyed both of them warily. He remembered the herbal potion Ariel had made and how quickly it had healed her bullet wounds. But he was suspicious. "What's the point of giving me medicine if you're just gonna kill me once we get to Haven?"

The guards exchanged glances, and then the sharp-chinned one spoke. "We aren't brutes, sir. We take no pleasure in watching you suffer."

"Well, that's good to know." John grimaced, feeling another stab of pain in his rib cage. "All right, I'll drink it. Might as well be comfortable in my last hours."

He opened his mouth again and forced himself to swallow the potion. When he was finished, the guard capped the canteen. "Now rest and conserve your strength, paramour. We still have miles to walk."

The guards holstered their pistols but kept watching him carefully. Up close, they looked even younger, in their late teens or early twenties. John decided to start a conversation with the boys. They might tell him something useful. "By the way, you don't have to call me paramour. My name is John Rogers. I'd shake your hands, but mine are tied up at the moment."

It was a bad joke, and neither of the guards smiled. But the sharp-chinned one tipped his straw hat. "Gower Fury is my name." He pointed at the other guard. "And this fellow is Archibald."

Gower? Archibald? Although the men of Haven weren't eternally youthful like the women, their names and speech patterns seemed to come from a different century. "Excuse me if this sounds rude," John said, "but you guys have a very old-fashioned way of talking."

Gower shrugged. "This is the way we speak in Haven. We learned our grammar from our mothers and grandmothers, who spoke this way in England before they came to America. Only the Rangers speak as you do, and only when they're undertaking their assignments."

"Rangers?"

"They're the ones who are allowed to venture outside Haven to perform the tasks assigned by the Council of Elders. Very few of us are granted this privilege. You must undergo years of training as a guardsman before the council will let you become a Ranger." Gower pointed at himself, smiling proudly. "I'm in training now."

John thought of Hal and Richard, the men who'd accompanied Ariel in New York. He wondered if anyone at Haven knew they were dead. "So the Rangers go with the women when they're meeting their paramours?"

Gower nodded. "That's one of the assignments, but there are many others. The Rangers gather information about the state of the world. They also participate in our scientific investigations and oversee our financial interests."

"Financial interests?"

"Aye, our family has made many discreet investments in the outside world. The Rangers operate the holding companies, which buy and sell—"

"Hold, Gower." The guard named Archibald, the one with the thick eyebrows, rested his hand on the other's shoulder. "You say too much."

The look on his face was so serious, John had to laugh. "You're kidding, right? Once we get to Haven, I'm dead. Who am I gonna tell your secrets to?"

Archibald shook his head. "Our task is to guard you, not talk to you."

"Just tell me one thing, okay? What's Ariel's task? What does she do for Haven?"

The guardsmen exchanged glances again. Then Gower stared at Ariel, who was drinking from a canteen on the other side of the clearing. "She's a Ranger, our very best. The Elders have sent her on many important assignments, starting more than three hundred years ago." He gazed at her for a few more seconds, then blushed as he turned back to John. "I'm jealous of you, sir. Although your current situation is unfortunate, at least you had the chance to be her paramour. It must've been a great gift."

The kid was smitten with her, no doubt about it. John wondered how many other men at Haven felt this way about Ariel. For all he knew, she might even have a husband there. "What does she do at Haven when she's not on assignment?"

"Oh, many things. But her greatest passion is for science. She oversees the experiments in our botanical and genetic laboratories. She's accumulated so much knowledge over the years that her contributions are indispensable."

"And, uh, is she married? You do have marriages at Haven, right?"

Archibald laughed, slapping his hand against his thigh. "Look at him! Gower, I believe this man loves her almost as much as you do!"

Gower glared at him, and so did John. Archibald was a real jerk. "Stop being an asshole," John warned. "I just asked a question."

The asshole sneered. "And it's not our place to answer it. You should pose your question to milady. Assuming, that is, you get a final opportunity to talk with her."

That put an end to the conversation. John stared at the ground for several minutes, refusing to look at either Ariel or the guards. Then Conroy said it was time to start moving again, and they resumed their march through the forest.

The next few miles on the trail were just as rugged as the ones before, but John found the going a little easier now. His chest didn't hurt as much, and his nose had stopped throbbing. The herbal potion was working as advertised.

He was still anxious, though. He kept thinking of the Council of Elders and the fate that awaited him. He needed to distract himself, to change the subject of his thoughts. If he was going to die a few hours from now, he wanted to think of only comforting things. So as he marched through the woods he focused on the only truly happy time in his life, the years when he worked with Father Murphy. He pictured the old priest striding down the forest trail, dressed in his usual outfit—jeans, flannel shirt, construction boots. The guy never wore his clerical collar. He said it made him look like a clown.

It was easy to imagine Father Murphy striding beside him, because that's how they'd spent most of their working hours, walking together down the streets of Kensington. Every evening they'd visit the busiest street corners and try to persuade the younger kids to go home to their mothers. Talking to the older boys—the fifteen- and sixteen-year-olds— was usually a waste of time because they'd already committed themselves to the drug business, but the younger ones still had a chance of getting out. Sometimes John would simply grab the boys and drag them to the youth center at St. Anne's Church. Because he'd worked the corners himself he knew how to argue with the kids. Father Murphy let him do most of the talking, and John got better and better at the job as time went on.

When he wasn't working for the Anti-Gang Project, he took classes at the community college, trying to make up for all the years he'd pissed away. That was where he met Carol, a pretty, studious accounting major from South Philly. She was suspicious of him at first—she could tell he was from the streets. But he invited her to a church supper at St. Anne's, and all her suspicions vanished once she saw him with Father Murphy and the kids. A few weeks later she left her parents' house and moved into John's apartment on Somerset Street. She got pregnant soon afterward, and John was ecstatic. Just before she started to show, they got married at St. Anne's, with Father Murphy performing the honors. Ivy was born six months later.

The next five years passed quickly. John saved some money, got his bachelor's degree in social work, and changed hundreds of diapers. Carol stayed home with the baby, but after a while she grew restless. She wanted to move to a better neighborhood before Ivy started kindergarten. John, though, hated the idea of leaving Kensington. The Anti-Gang Project had become a crusade for him, an all-consuming struggle. Salazar, John's old rival in the Disciples, had taken over all the drug crews in the area, and his boys harassed John whenever they could. The animosity between the two men was growing, and John felt that moving out of the neighborhood would be like backing down from the fight. His attitude made Carol furious; she said he cared more about a bunch of gangbangers than his own daughter. Even Father Murphy worried that John was becoming obsessed. "You're doing a lot of good, son," he used to say. "And the Lord will surely reward you for your good deeds in heaven. But I have to warn you: In this world, no good deed goes unpunished."

At the time, John thought this was one of the old priest's jokes. But it was true. The good get punished. The innocent get punished.

After the shooting Carol couldn't forgive him. As soon as Ivy's funeral was over, she moved out of their apartment and returned to South Philly. Meanwhile, John bought a gun on the street, an old SIG Sauer semiautomatic. He'd been fast asleep when the bastards had fired at the windows of his apartment, so he couldn't identify Ivy's murderers, couldn't testify against them in court. But he knew who did it. He knew *exactly* who they were. He went looking for Salazar and his boys, searching every corner in the neighborhood, ready to send them to hell.

He never got his revenge, though. Justice was done, but he didn't get any satisfaction from it. In the end, John was left with almost nothing. Just a child-size bed and an old wooden bureau, full of tiny pink clothes.

Now his vision blurred as he recalled the neat piles of shirts and pants. His foot slipped on a wet rock in the middle of the trail and he nearly fell on his face. *This was a mistake*, he thought as he struggled to stay on his feet. *I was supposed to focus on happy memories.* And here was the most embarrassing part, the revelation that made him cringe: he hadn't learned a damn thing from the tragedy. He was still doing good deeds and getting punished for it.

In this world, no good deed goes unpunished.

If he got the chance, he'd ask the Elders to put those words on his tombstone.

After another hour they finally emerged from the pine forest. The trail ran down a grassy slope to a broad plain of farmland. About a hundred yards ahead was a long chain-link fence that stretched at least a mile to the east and west. On the other side of the fence were fields of cornstalks, nearly ready for harvest, and wide pastures dotted with grazing cattle. Way off in the distance John spotted a large red barn, a gray silo, and half a dozen modest houses arranged in a circle. It looked like a small farming community, with room for thirty or forty people at the most.

This wasn't what he'd expected. He'd assumed Haven would be more densely populated. Curious, he stared at the guards, who turned their heads this way and that, on the lookout for strangers. Conroy's men had stowed their weapons in their backpacks, but they couldn't hide John or Ariel, neither of whom looked Amish. No one else was in sight, though, so Conroy waved the guardsmen forward. They marched down the trail to the fence, which was at least twelve feet high and topped with concertina wire. Just outside the fence was a deep drainage ditch that surrounded the farm like a moat.

They headed for a narrow wooden walkway that crossed the ditch. On the other side was a gate in the fence, locked with a heavy chain. Another bearded man in Amish garb stood behind the gate, waiting patiently. He called out, "How now, Conroy?" and unlocked the gate as they approached.

Conroy, who still carried Ariel on his back, answered him with a nod. Then they marched through the gate and into the farm, following a path that ran between two cornfields.

The barn and the farmhouses were still half a mile away, but soon they came to an outbuilding, a simple shed with cinder-block walls and a rusty metal roof. The guard named Archibald stepped forward and used a key to unlock the shed's door. John grew nervous as they filed into the structure, which was the size of a two-car garage and completely dark inside. *What the hell are we doing here? Is this where they're going to kill me?* Then he saw Archibald touch a glowing keypad next to a door at the far end of the room. The guard pressed a sequence of numbers, and a moment later the door slid open. The space beyond the door was a brightly lit square, about six feet across. It was an elevator.

Archibald went in first, and then the other guards nudged John inside. Conroy pressed another sequence of numbers on a keypad inside the elevator, and the door slowly closed. The space was so crowded that Ariel, clinging to Conroy's back, was only a couple of feet from John. But she didn't look at him. She stared straight ahead. The elevator started to descend.

John couldn't tell how far down they went, but it was at least half a minute before the elevator stopped. As the door opened he heard a sudden blizzard of sounds, a chorus of footsteps and laughter and voices, both male and female, echoing off granite walls and a highly polished floor. To his astonishment, he saw a large room that looked like the lobby of a skyscraper. A marble fountain, carved in the shape of a tree, stood in the center of the room, spurting gouts of water that arced from the sculpture's trunk and splashed against the stone branches. About thirty men and women stood around the fountain, gathered in small groups, chatting like office workers on their lunch break. But their conversations sputtered to a halt as the guards exited the elevator. Everyone stopped to look at Ariel and John.

He stared back at them. All the men in the room, young and old, were dressed like the guards, in Amish-style clothing and beards. The women, in contrast, wore a bewildering variety of garments. Some wore dowdy, black, floor-length dresses, while others wore extravagant, brightly colored gowns. Still others were in modern dress: pantsuits, T-shirts, sweater sets, miniskirts. All the women were young, and all had red hair and green eyes, but they didn't look alike. Some were fat, some were thin, some were tall, some were short. Some were plain, and some were almost as beautiful as Ariel. The overall effect was bizarre. John felt like he'd just walked into a costume party.

The crowd parted to make way for the guards. Conroy took the lead, and all eyes in the room fixed on the woman he carried, focusing first on Ariel's injured legs and then on her desolate face. It was difficult to read their reactions—some people seemed sympathetic, but most seemed confused. Then Conroy passed by and everyone shifted their attention to John, looking him up and down. Their reactions to him were crystal clear: they glowered in outrage. He had no right to be here.

The guards turned to the right and passed through a doorway to an even larger space, an immense cavern with walls of rough stone and a rocky ceiling that arched a hundred feet overhead. It was a natural cavern that the people of Haven had obviously modified for their own use, building structures and terraces and pathways within the chamber and installing elevators that connected it to the surface. To his left John saw a pair of concrete structures, each five stories high, that resembled office buildings. To his right was an industrial-looking building with many crisscrossing pipes that extended across the cavern and delved into its floor. Fixed to the cavern's walls were powerful arc lamps that flooded the space with bluish light. Dozens of men and women strolled along the pathways, moving from one building to another.

Gower walked beside him on a pathway that ran the length of the cavern. Conroy and Archibald were just a few yards ahead, but the chamber hummed with so much mechanical background noise that they were out of earshot. John decided to risk asking Gower a question. "This place is amazing. How many people live down here?"

The young man grinned. He seemed pleased by John's interest. "Ah, let me see. I believe there are almost one thousand nine hundred Furies in Haven at the moment. I'm not counting Sullivan's Riflemen in that number, nor the Rangers who are currently on assignment."

"My God, that's incredible."

Gower nodded. "Our family has grown considerably. When the Elders came to America, there were only twelve people in their party."

"Wait a second, when was this?"

"They arrived in Boston in 1646. But they didn't stay there. They began searching beyond the colonies for a place where they could live unnoticed."

"Beyond the colonies? What do you mean?"

"They left New England and came to the Great Lakes, which were just starting to be explored. The Elders discovered this cavern during their wanderings and decided to locate their farm near its entrance. Everyone lived aboveground at first, because the area was a true wilderness then. The only people nearby were a few Ojibway clans."

Ojibway. That was the name of the ferryboat he and Ariel had hijacked. "That's an Indian tribe, right?"

"The Elders had an excellent relationship with them. The Ojibway left us alone and we did the same. But in the 1800s the white settlers flooded into Michigan, and there was a danger they'd become too curious about our community. The Elders recognized that if they wanted to keep their secrets, they had to make themselves inconspicuous. They had to hide their growing family."

"Is that when they started building all this stuff underground?"

"Aye, they built the first dwellings in the cavern then. Later on, they added larger structures for our libraries and laboratories and machine shops. Nowadays we need only a few dozen people to remain aboveground to work the farm, but most of us go outside at least once a week to get exercise and fresh air."

"And you pretend to be Amish whenever you're on the farm?"

He nodded. "It's a suitable disguise for us because Amish communities keep to themselves and have little contact with the outside world. If we run into any outsiders when we're on patrol, we shy away from them and speak with each other in the German dialect that the Amish use. Our chain-link fence is a bit unusual for an Amish farm, but our neighbors understand that we value our privacy."

John thought of the fenced-off cornfields he'd walked past just a few minutes ago. "And you need the fence because you're also guarding the entrance to the cavern. Which is big enough that you can hide a whole city from the world."

"That's not all." Gower pointed at the industrial building with all the pipes. "This cavern is geologically active. The churning of the earth below us produces heat, and our geothermal plant uses the heat to generate electricity. We don't need to be connected to the state's power lines, so we appear to be similar to other Amish communities, which traditionally don't use electricity from public—"

Gower's voice had been rising as they spoke, and Archibald overheard him. Scowling, he looked over his shoulder at Gower, who immediately stopped talking. Archibald scowled at John as well, for good measure, then faced forward.

The pathway led to a large building at the very center of the cavern. Constructed from massive blocks of gray stone, the building was shaped like a pyramid, rising so high that its point nearly touched the cavern's ceiling. The entrance was triangular, and the stone walls were inscribed with the same runes John had seen in Ariel's notebooks. The guardsmen opened a pair of heavy bronze doors and then marched down a long, dark hallway. As soon as the doors closed behind them, all the mechanical background noise ceased. Except for their rapid footsteps, the hallway was silent. Then another pair of doors suddenly opened in front of them and they entered a huge, grand room with a white marble floor. *This must be it*, John thought. *This must be the council chambers of the Elders of Haven.*

John had to blink a few times until his eyes adjusted to the light, which was much brighter here than in the cavern. He noticed that the room had an odd shape: the floor was square, but the walls were triangular. They leaned inward to form a pyramidal space that mirrored the overall shape of the building. Each wall was covered with a mural, a gorgeously colored painting of muscular men and beautiful women in old-fashioned dress. But as John looked closer he noticed something disturbing. The men in these murals were slaughtering the women. In one painting, a mob used torches to light a pile of wood under a woman tied to a stake. In another, a priest looped a hangman's rope around the neck of a teenage girl. In the third mural, an executioner swung an ax at a woman sprawled on the chopping block; in the fourth, a woman with a millstone around her neck sank beneath the waves while the men onshore pointed at her.

It took John a second to figure it out. These were pictures of the genocide that Ariel had described, the mass killings that swept across Europe four hundred years ago. *The massacre of the witches.* The images were so shocking that John just stood there, mouth agape, while the guards marched ahead. Gower had to tap his shoulder to get him moving again.

The council chambers were laid out like a courtroom, with a judge's bench on a dais at the front of the room and a central aisle running between several rows of seats for the spectators. The bench was empty except for an elderly man with a long white beard, who stood at the left end of the dais. Conroy hurried down the aisle until he reached the front row, and then, with an exhausted grunt, he lowered Ariel into one of the seats. Gower and John followed them to the front of the room, but Gower didn't allow John to sit. He had to stand between the front row of seats and the dais.

Meanwhile, the old man with the long beard shuffled toward Conroy. The two of them conferred in whispers for a fairly long time, maybe half a minute. Then the geezer turned around and went through a doorway to another room. John guessed he was the Elders' bailiff, the guy who ushered people in and out of the chambers. And sure enough, the old man reappeared about a minute later, leading three red-haired women toward the bench.

Because John stood so close to the dais, he got a good look at the three Elders. The first in line was short and pinkish and fat. She wore a silky green dress that showed off her ample breasts, which bulged and wobbled just below the plunging neckline. The woman behind her, in contrast, was tall and thin and wore a long-sleeved, high-collared, jet-black dress that covered nearly all of her very pale skin. She seemed ghostly, weightless, so insubstantial that a light breeze would blow her to pieces, and she stared straight ahead as if in a trance. But it was the third woman who really caught John's attention. She was small but athletic, with strong, sinewy arms and long, fiery hair. Even before she sat down in the central seat behind the bench, John knew this had to be Chief Elder Elizabeth Fury, Ariel's mother. The resemblance was striking. You could've almost mistaken mother for daughter, if not for one crucial difference. Elizabeth's left eye socket was empty. A thick ribbon of scar tissue ran down her forehead to the empty socket, then continued across her left cheek to her jawline.

John winced and turned away from her, looking instead at the short, buxom Elder. But now he noticed that this woman had deformities too— one of her ears was mangled, and she was limping as she took her seat to the left of Elizabeth. And when he focused on the pale, thin Elder seated to Elizabeth's right, he observed that one of her hands was actually a wooden prosthesis. He remembered what Sullivan had said about the Elders: all of them were more than five hundred years old, and Elizabeth was more than a thousand. Although they didn't age, they weren't immortal. They could be cut and bruised and broken and burned, and though they could treat themselves with powerful herbal medicines, some of their wounds would never heal. When he studied the women more carefully, they didn't seem young at all.

Once they were seated, Elizabeth fixed her gaze on John. She didn't look at Ariel, even though her daughter sat less than ten feet away and was clearly injured. The Chief Elder's lone eye, green and wary, shone on him like a spotlight. Her face was surprisingly emotionless. Unlike the other residents of Haven, she didn't seem outraged by John's presence. Instead, she seemed calm and businesslike, coolly determined to get to the bottom of the matter. After several seconds she turned to Conroy.

"I'm ready to hear your report, Master of the Guardsmen." Elizabeth's voice was different from Ariel's—deeper, harder. She pointed at the white-bearded bailiff, who stood at attention in the corner of the room. "Old Sam says you encountered my son as well as my daughter?"

Conroy approached the bench and bowed in her direction. "That's correct, milady. It pains me to report this, but Basil was torturing—"

"Nay, don't call him by that name." She shook her head. "He no longer has the right to it. Call him by the name he's taken."

"Aye, milady." Conroy bowed again. "Sullivan was torturing Lily and her paramour when we came upon them. It seemed clear that he intended to murder them, so I gave the order to fire. We slew four of the Riflemen, but your son escaped with the others."

Elizabeth's face was still impassive but John got the sense that she was struggling to rein in her emotions. She took a deep breath and turned to Ariel. "Are you all right, child?" Her voice softened. "How badly did he hurt you?"

Ariel bit her lower lip. She, too, seemed to be striving to maintain her composure. "The worst injury is to my legs. The Riflemen shot me during the first ambush, in Brooklyn two nights ago. I assume you saw the media reports about the incident? There must've been stories on television and in the newspapers."

Her mother nodded. "The news reports mentioned the name of your hotel and the fact that none of the victims of the shootings could be identified. We deduced that Sullivan had attacked you."

The buxom Elder sitting to Elizabeth's left leaned forward. John noticed, to his surprise, that her plump chin was quivering. "And what of *my* sons?" she asked. "Did either of them survive?"

Ariel shook her head. "I'm sorry, Aunt Margaret. Hal and Richard died while defending me. They were badly outnumbered, but they fought valiantly to the end. Their actions brought great honor to the Ranger Corps."

For a moment it looked like Margaret would start crying. But instead she pressed her lips together and pointed at Ariel. "And what have you brought back from your assignment?" She wasn't really pointing at Ariel, John realized. Her finger was aimed at the small leather-bound notebook resting in Ariel's lap. "Do you have the information we requested from Caño Dorado?"

Ariel held the notebook above her head. "Everything is here. Sullivan tried to take my Treasure, but he was unsuccessful."

"Well, what were the results of the experiments? Did Mariela find the catalyst?"

"Auntie, please. You know the agreement we made. This information was entrusted to me alone."

"I don't need all the details, girl!" Margaret's face reddened. "I'd just like to know if the results were worth the sacrifice of my sons!"

"Enough." Elizabeth raised her hand for quiet. "Sister, we can discuss this at a later time. Right now we have a more pressing matter to consider." She pointed at John but kept her lone eye fixed on Ariel. "Lily, what happened between you and your paramour? Do you realize how unnatural this is, to have an outsider standing before our council?"

Elizabeth's contempt was so obvious, it made John grimace. Feeling a surge of adrenaline, he strained against the rope that tied his hands behind his back, but he couldn't loosen it. "You think I wanted to come here?" he shouted. "You really think—"

"Silence!" The command came from Old Sam, the white-bearded bailiff, whose voice was unexpectedly loud. "If you utter another word, we'll gag you!"

John didn't care. They were going to kill him anyway, so what was the point of obeying? He was just about to tell the whole Council of Elders to go fuck themselves when Ariel turned his way and gave him a pleading look, mouthing the word "stop." Then she turned back to Elizabeth.

"Mother, it's Sullivan's fault. He broke his oath and revealed our secret because he wanted to hurt me. It was part of his torture."

"You're jumping ahead, child. Before we get to that part, I'd like to know why you brought your paramour with you to Michigan."

"I didn't bring him. He brought me. And his name is John, if you please." She gave her mother a pointed look. "John drove me to Michigan because I had no other way of getting here. Hal and Richard were dead, and both my legs were broken."

"Why didn't you communicate with us? We could've dispatched another team of Rangers to assist you."

Ariel frowned. "Sullivan is intercepting our communications. If I'd sent out a call for help, his men would've found me."

Elizabeth frowned too, her expression mirroring her daughter's. "And what makes you think our communications lines aren't secure?"

"How did Sullivan find us in Brooklyn? How did he know our plans so thoroughly?" Ariel furrowed her brow. She was getting agitated. "We have to face the facts. Sullivan has spies in Haven. Someone is betraying us."

The council chambers fell silent. Still frowning, Elizabeth shook her head. She clearly didn't agree with Ariel. The Elder named Margaret seemed less skeptical; a worried look appeared on her face and she shifted nervously in her chair, which creaked under her weight. It was impossible to say what the third Elder thought—the pale, ghostly woman was still staring straight ahead, her expression unchanged since she entered the room.

After a few seconds Elizabeth waved her hand in a dismissive gesture. "That's another matter we can discuss later. I'd like to keep the focus on your paramour, Lily. I still don't understand why you sought his help. You have more experience than anyone else in the Ranger Corps. Couldn't you have found a way to return to Haven on your own?"

"I was bleeding to death, Mother." She raised her voice in exasperation. "John rescued me from Sullivan's men and bandaged my wounds. The Riflemen were pursuing us, so we had no choice but to keep moving."

"Didn't you consider the consequences of involving an outsider in your plans? Even with Sullivan at your heels, you should've realized how dangerous this was."

"Of course I saw the danger. But the alternatives were worse. If I'd tried to fend for myself, the Riflemen would've captured me, and all the information from Caño Dorado would've fallen into Sullivan's hands." Ariel raised the notebook again, waving it in the air. "So I made the best of the situation. I didn't lie to John, but I didn't reveal any information forbidden to outsiders. I was planning to part ways with him before we reached the gates of Haven. As long as he didn't know our secret, I could let him return to Philadelphia. It was an acceptable risk."

"Aye, but look at the result." The Chief Elder pointed again at John. "Sullivan may be at fault, but your actions made it possible."

Ariel nodded. "Agreed. But no blame whatsoever should fall on John. He did nothing to deserve any punishment, Mother. From the start he only wanted to help me."

It was a good speech, John thought. In addition to all her other talents,

Ariel would've made a pretty decent lawyer. And her arguments seemed to have an effect on the Elders, judging from their expressions and body language. Elizabeth had stopped frowning. She pursed her lips as she stared at her daughter, her lone eye glistening. Margaret leaned back in her chair, as if deep in thought, and crossed her arms under her bosom. And for the first time, the ghostly Elder appeared to show some interest in the proceedings. The pale, thin woman turned her head ever so slightly and stared directly at John. Her face was absolutely still and her gaze was unnerving. John felt like an insect under a magnifying glass.

After a long pause, Elizabeth let out a sigh. "This is disturbing news, Lily. Your brother's hatred is beginning to overwhelm his sanity."

"Beginning? I think not. Sullivan lost touch with his sanity long ago."

"Nay, his rebellion was logical, at least at the start. He wanted something we weren't willing to give, so he took up arms against us. It was a grisly choice, but perfectly rational. But breaking his oath? Revealing our secret to outsiders? That endangers his band of Riflemen just as much as it threatens Haven."

"Again, I agree with you. But I don't understand what—"

"Mark my words, child. If he breaks his oath once, he'll break it again. And the oath is all that stands between us and destruction." Elizabeth made a chopping motion with her right hand. Then she turned to her left and stared grimly at Margaret. "Sister, do you remember the Burning Times in Germany? The bonfires at Trier?"

Margaret shuddered. John could actually see her trembling. Her plump body shivered within the tight green dress. She scowled at Elizabeth. "How can you ask such a question? Of course I remember."

"I remember it, too. The summer of 1587. When we lost Gabriele and Trude and Juliane and Grandmother." Elizabeth raised her arm and pointed at the mural on the opposite wall. "Lest we forget, it's pictured right there. The burning of Grandmother Annika, who screamed in Ancient Persian as her skin turned black. I saw it myself, just before we left Trier and fled to England." She stared at the painting for several seconds, then turned back to her daughter. "Let me ask you a question, Lily. Do you really think it couldn't happen again?"

Ariel took a deep breath. "You know my opinion on this subject. We've discussed it many times. If we take the proper precautions beforehand, I think we can safely begin the process of revealing our—"

"You think humanity has grown more civilized? You think they've given up all their murderous habits?"

"Nay, but—"

"How many genocides have taken place in just the past century?" Elizabeth's expression turned fierce. The long, ribbonlike scar on her face seemed to darken. "The Armenians, the Jews, the Bosnians, the Rwandans, they all thought they lived in a civilized world."

"Mother, please listen. We can't stay hidden forever. At some point we have to trust them."

"Who should we trust? The Americans? The same people who slaughtered the Ojibway and all the other tribes?" Elizabeth was shouting now. Her words echoed against the murals on all four walls of the chamber. "Nay, we can't do that. For the sake of our family, we must uphold our oath, which has protected us ever since we came to this country. We must track down Sullivan and punish him for his transgressions. By violating our most sacred law, he put all our lives at risk. For this reason we must execute him." Her voice quavered when pronouncing the word *execute,* but her fierce expression remained unchanged. "And unfortunately, we must also execute your paramour, Lily. It's the only way to ensure he won't spread our secret."

John wasn't surprised. He'd recognized from the start that Elizabeth Fury wasn't the compromising type. Before she'd even started questioning Ariel, he'd resigned himself to the prospect of a death sentence. And to tell the truth, he wasn't even angry anymore. The Elders had nothing against him personally. They would've done the same to anyone in his situation. But he *was* a little disappointed by Ariel's reaction to the verdict. He'd expected her to raise her voice and start shouting objections, like the good lawyer she was, but instead she just sat there in the front row, biting her lower lip and furrowing her brow. When she finally spoke, her voice was barely above a whisper.

"You'll put him to death even though he's innocent? Even though he saved the life of your only daughter?"

Elizabeth nodded. "His guilt or innocence doesn't matter. I'd condemn him even if he were Jesus of Nazareth. I can't spare one life if it threatens the lives of all two thousand of us."

"And is this the decision of the entire council?" Ariel stared at her aunt Margaret. "Are all the Elders in agreement?"

Margaret looked uncomfortable, but in the end she nodded. "I abide by the Chief Elder's decision."

Then Ariel turned to the third Elder, the ghostly woman sitting to Elizabeth's right. "And you, Aunt Cordelia? Do you also consent?"

Cordelia didn't seem to hear her. She kept staring blankly at John, her face as white as milk.

Elizabeth leaned toward her sister. "Delia? Are you paying attention?"

A few more seconds passed. Cordelia sat very still, resting her wooden left hand on her right forearm. Finally, she opened her mouth to speak. "I have a question for you, John. Do you have a wife or children?"

Her voice startled him. It was slow and breathy, the voice of a seductress. "Uh, no," he answered.

"Any living relatives? Mother, father, siblings, cousins?"

He shook his head. He had no idea why she was asking these questions. "I never knew my father. My mother is dead, and I never met any of her relatives. She hated her family."

"What about friends, co-workers? Is there anyone in Philadelphia you feel especially close to?"

Once again he shook his head. It was embarrassing to admit, but he was basically alone in the world. Maybe that was why the thought of dying didn't bother him so much. He had so little to lose.

His answers seemed to satisfy Cordelia. She turned to her sisters, slowly pivoting her pale face. "I see an alternative to executing the paramour. He can stay in Haven."

Elizabeth frowned. "You mean keep him as our prisoner? For the rest of his life?"

"Nay, not a prisoner. He can join our community. He doesn't have any strong ties to his old life, so he can start a new one here."

Elizabeth said nothing, but Margaret chuckled. Her breasts heaved against the neckline of her dress, threatening to pop right out. "You're saying we should *adopt* this outsider? Take him in like a stray dog?"

Cordelia shrugged. "Why not? He's clearly a capable young man. And we've lost so many of our young men to Sullivan."

"I think it's a brilliant idea," Ariel interjected. She grinned from ear to ear, beaming in triumph. John got the sense that Cordelia's suggestion was no accident. Somehow or other, Ariel had arranged it. She flashed her broad grin at her aunt, and Cordelia smiled in return. Then Ariel looked at John and her face turned serious. "I have to warn you, it won't be easy.

You'll need to leave everything behind. No contact whatsoever with any-one you once knew. And you'll need to learn our ways and follow our laws." She locked eyes with him as she delivered her warnings. She was sending him a message: Just say yes. "So, John, what do you think? Are you willing to try it?"

"Yes," he said. He suspected that Ariel wanted him to answer immedi-ately, before the other Elders could raise any objections.

"Excellent," Ariel replied. "And I volunteer to oversee your training. I'll assess your talents and find a suitable place for you here." Smiling again, she turned to her mother. "Would this plan be acceptable?"

Elizabeth didn't respond right away. Instead, she let out a weary grunt and stared at her daughter. Meanwhile, Margaret shifted in her chair again and Cordelia returned to her blank-faced trance, gazing straight ahead at nothing. John had the feeling that the Council of Elders made decisions by consensus, and that Ariel had outmaneuvered her mother. But Elizabeth didn't seem to be angry. Her scarred face had gone slack. She just looked tired.

"Are you sure about this, Lily?" she finally asked. "It's a risky experi-ment. I don't need to remind you what happened the last time we tried it."

Ariel stopped smiling. "That was long ago. I'm wiser now."

"I hope so, child. I truly do." She shook her head. "I'll give you three days to work with your paramour. Then the council will analyze his prog-ress to see if he will fit into our community." Grunting again, she rose to her feet. At the same time, she pointed at the notebook in Ariel's lap. "And I expect you to continue working on your other experiments as well. Don't let your paramour distract you from your primary assignment."

Margaret and Cordelia also rose from their seats, automatically follow-ing their sister as she left the judge's bench and descended from the dais. Old Sam the bailiff stepped toward the exit and held the door open for the Elders as they filed out of the chambers. Before Elizabeth left the room, though, she looked over her shoulder and glanced at John one more time. She narrowed her lone eye. The look wasn't friendly.

TWELVE

Sullivan stopped his Harley in front of a ramshackle barn on Maple Road, five miles south of Sault Sainte Marie. It was another cold night on the Upper Peninsula, so cold that an unseasonable frost had carpeted the ground a few hours before dawn. When Sullivan shut down his bike's engine and switched off the headlamp, all he could see at first was the moonlight glinting off the ice. After a couple of seconds, though, his eyes adjusted to the darkness and he saw a gleaming black Chevrolet Suburban parked in the weeds about fifty feet away. Although this farm had been abandoned more than a decade ago and the barn looked like it was ready to collapse, the structure wasn't empty. Judging from the footprints Sullivan spied in the frost, at least four men were inside.

He got off his motorcycle and headed for the barn door. He wasn't carrying his Mauser tonight. He planned to rely on his powers of persuasion instead. Sullivan had a talent for convincing other men to serve his ends. Using his wits and charisma he'd already assembled an army of nearly two hundred Riflemen. Although Haven's guardsmen had dealt him a blow yesterday—he should've brought more men with him when he confronted Ariel and her paramour—the setback would be temporary. He was going to shelve his old plans and pursue a bolder strategy. And this strategy required forging an alliance.

As soon as he slid the door open, someone inside the barn turned on a flashlight and aimed it at his face. At the same time, someone else shouted, "Freeze!" and a third person cocked a shotgun. But Sullivan wasn't worried. He smiled at the men as he raised his hands in the air.

"And a good fucking evening to you, too." He changed his voice, switching to the accent and idioms of twenty-first-century America.

"Don't move a fucking muscle, Van." This voice belonged to FBI Special Agent Mike Larson, who stood between the man with the flashlight and the one with the shotgun. "Are you armed?"

"What the fuck do you think? Of course not."

"Well, we're gonna search you anyway. Just stand still."

The man with the flashlight handed it to Larson, then stepped forward and started patting Sullivan down. Both he and the man with the shotgun wore the same kind of ugly gray suit that Larson did, so they were probably FBI agents too, lower-ranking officers whom Larson had brought along for protection. The agent reached under Sullivan's bomber jacket and slapped his ribs and waist, then bent over to pat down his legs. Sullivan felt an urge to smash the cur's head, but he clenched his hands and suppressed it. As he peered into the darkness he spotted the fourth man on their team, who had short, graying hair and an anxious expression on his face. This man looked less professional than the others. He stood several feet behind Larson, deliberately staying in the background, and kept his hands in the pockets of his green windbreaker.

Once the agent completed his search, he grunted, "He's clean," and returned to his partners. Then Agent Larson stepped forward, shining the flashlight in Sullivan's eyes. "What happened to your face, Van? Looks like you got a few scratches there."

It took some effort, but Sullivan managed to keep smiling. Hatred of Ariel flared in his chest. "I had a little trouble with one of my bitches," he replied. "You know how it is."

"Really? You sure about that?" Larson gave him a skeptical look. "I heard that you and your boys were busy yesterday. There was an incident on Mackinac Island."

Sullivan shook his head. "Never been there. That's the place with the fudge, right?"

"Yeah, it's a friendly, peaceful place. So peaceful there's only half a dozen cops on the whole island. You can imagine their surprise when a bunch of thugs in black leather jackets showed up at the White Star Ferry docks and started shooting."

"Wow, that's fucked up. Who were they shooting at?"

Larson frowned. "Funny you should ask. The White Star Ferry has a surveillance camera on the wharf, and it took a picture of the guy. It was the drug dealer from Philadelphia who drives the Kia with the vanity plates. John fucking Rogers. The same guy we were looking for at the goddamn checkpoint on the bridge." He moved a step closer to Sullivan. "You were playing games with me, weren't you? You wanted to get rid of Rogers, but you couldn't find him. So you decided to ask the feds for a little help. You ratted out Rogers and his meth business to get us to put pressure on him. After we set up the checkpoint, you put your own boys on Mackinac Island, because you knew Rogers wasn't stupid enough to take the bridge. You were using us to trap him."

"Whoa, I don't know what you're—"

"I don't like games, Van. You're in a hell of a lot of trouble now. While your boys were chasing Rogers, the asshole hijacked a goddamn ferryboat and beached it on the shore of Lake Huron. The picture of the boat is gonna be on the front page of every newspaper in the fucking state today. We're talking some serious shit here, and you're buried up to your neck in it. Do you have any idea how long I could put you away for this?"

The agent stood right in front of him, trying his best to intimidate. This was a stupid tactical move on Larson's part. With one quick lunge Sullivan could put the man in a headlock. The agent with the shotgun wouldn't fire for fear of hitting his boss, and in the next instant Sullivan could grab Larson's pistol and eliminate all four of them. He'd been a Ranger for thirty years before he started his rebellion, and close-quarters combat was one of his specialties. But this wasn't the time for combat. It was time to be clever.

"So why don't you arrest me?" he asked. "Why are we talking in this fucking barn instead of the police station?" He didn't wait for Larson to answer. "It's because you don't have any evidence against me. The cops didn't catch the shooters on Mackinac Island, did they?"

Larson grimaced. "Don't worry, we'll find them."

"No, you won't. And you won't find Rogers, either. Not without my help, at least. And I bet you still want to find him, probably more than ever. Now that he's in all the newspapers, you better fucking catch the asshole, right?"

The agent raised his eyebrows. "So you know where Rogers is?"

"Look, I'll be honest with you. I hate the fucker. Some of the John Does he killed in Brooklyn were friends of mine. And it's true, I needed some help to track him down. But I wasn't bullshitting you about his meth connections. Rogers is a major player. His supplier is one of the biggest methamphetamine labs in the country."

Sullivan paused, enjoying the moment. He was toying with Larson, pulling his strings. The agent was already convinced that Rogers was a killer and a drug dealer, thanks to the evidence Sullivan had planted in the junkie's house and Rogers's apartment. The next step was obvious.

"So where is this lab?" Larson asked.

"You're in luck. It's near a town called Pickford, less than twenty miles from here. And Rogers is there right now."

"And why should I believe any of this? How do I know you're not playing games with me again?"

Sullivan reached into the pocket of his bomber jacket and pulled out a small digital camera. "The meth lab's in the middle of a giant, fenced-off farm. It's the perfect place to conceal the operation. A couple of days ago I posted one of my boys near the farm's gate, in a hidden spot in the woods, so he could monitor who was going in and out." He turned on the camera and displayed an image on its screen, the only image stored on the camera's chip. "He took this photo twelve hours ago."

Larson grabbed the camera and enlarged the image. It was a picture of seven people, five of whom seemed to be Amish men. The tallest and huskiest—Conroy Fury, Master of the Guardsmen and one of Sullivan's least favorite cousins—carried Ariel on his back. The only man without a beard was John Rogers, who stood in the middle of the group, just his head and shoulders visible.

Larson stared openmouthed at the photo. "What the fuck's going on? Are those guys Amish?"

"Yeah, their farm's on Route 129. The past few years have been tough for farming, and they needed to find another way to make some cash. So they got into the meth business. They let Rogers and a bunch of other assholes build an underground lab beneath one of their barns. A really, really big lab."

"Amish farmers making meth? Are you fucking serious?"

Sullivan shrugged. "The money's good. They don't use the drug them-selves, it's only for outsiders. So in their eyes, I guess that makes it okay."

The agent shook his head as he stared at the camera's screen. Then he looked over his shoulder and gestured at the man standing behind him, the nervous one in the green windbreaker. "Uh, Captain Dunn? Can you take a look at this?"

The man came forward and Larson handed him the camera. Sullivan noticed that the man's windbreaker had the words WHITE STAR FERRY printed on the chest. This was the captain of the ferryboat that Ariel and her paramour had hijacked. He studied the camera's screen for a few sec-onds, then pointed at the display. "That's him, all right," he said. "That's the one who took the *Ojibway.* And that's the young lady who helped him. Except she was disguised as an *old* lady when I saw her."

Larson said, "Okay, thanks," and Captain Dunn retreated to the back of the barn. Then the FBI agent turned back to Sullivan. "You know any-thing about this woman? Is she Rogers's girlfriend?"

For once Sullivan didn't have to lie. "Yes, she is. And she's making a big mistake."

Larson took one last look at the photo, then ejected the camera chip. "You mind if I borrow this? I think I'll pay a visit to that farm on Route 129." He slipped the chip into his pocket and returned the camera to Sul-livan. "I'll ask the longbeards why they're hanging out with a drug dealer from Philly. If they're smart, they'll give him up. If not, we'll just have to sit tight and watch them."

Sullivan frowned. Larson's strategy didn't sound promising. "You sure that's the best way to do it? You might scare him off."

The agent seemed amused. He put his hands on his hips. "You got a better idea, Van?"

"Yeah, I do. Send in a SWAT team and raid the farm. It would be the biggest drug bust in the fucking history of the state."

Larson laughed. "I wish it were that simple. But unfortunately we need a search warrant. And we don't have enough evidence to convince a judge to give us one."

"What if I could get the evidence for you?"

A hungry look flickered in Larson's eyes. The agent was ambitious. That was his weak point. He was willing to disregard his doubts because he wanted Sullivan to be right. "And how would you do that?"

"Just give me a few hours. I'll figure something out."

Larson spread his arms wide, like a priest offering a blessing. "Hey, I won't stop you. We both want the same thing, right?"

Sullivan nodded, although he couldn't imagine anything further from the truth. The FBI agent wanted a promotion. He wanted the governor of Michigan to pin a medal to his chest for arresting the man who'd hijacked the *Ojibway*. What Sullivan wanted, on the other hand, was much grander. He was going to change the world, turn it upside down. And the key to achieving his goal was a chemical formula that had been translated into ancient runes and inscribed in the pages of Ariel's Treasure. For a few minutes yesterday he'd held the formula in his hands, only to see it snatched away by his bitch of a sister. But he would get it back soon. The Elders of Haven would gladly surrender it to him once they realized what the alternative was.

He smiled once more at Larson. Even though they wanted different things, they could still work together. "Nice doing business with you." Sullivan turned to leave the barn. "I'll be in touch."

THIRTEEN

John's room was a luxurious prison cell. He lay on a queen-size feather bed with silk sheets and goose-down pillows. The walls were decorated with paintings in magnificent gilt frames, the kind you usually see only in art museums. Next to the bed were a mahogany night table and a gorgeous antique grandfather clock. But the room had no windows and the door was locked.

According to the clock, it was 10:00 A.M. When John awoke an hour ago he'd found a breakfast tray on the night table—scrambled eggs, bacon, toast, all of it delicious—but no one had come to his room since then to pick up the dirty dishes. As he lay in bed he carefully surveyed the walls and paintings, looking for a hidden surveillance camera. His room was in the same pyramidal building as the Elders' council chambers, and he wondered if Elizabeth Fury was watching him right now, monitoring the outsider who'd dared to come to Haven.

Finally, he heard a knock on the door. "Can I come in?" It was Ariel's voice.

John hesitated before answering. He was still angry at her for turning him in. But she'd also won him a reprieve. She'd convinced the Elders not to execute him, at least not right away. He supposed he ought to thank her. "I gotta warn you, I'm naked," he said. "Someone stole my clothes while I was sleeping."

"We washed them," she replied from the other side of the door. "Now I'm bringing them back. Just get under the covers."

He tossed a satiny blanket over himself as Ariel unlocked the door and opened it. To his surprise, she was on her feet. She wasn't walking normally yet—she hobbled on a pair of crutches, wincing as she entered the room—but she wasn't helpless, either. "Holy shit," he marveled. "Your bones are healed already?"

"Not quite." With a grunt and a final stride she reached his bed. She wore jeans and sneakers and a plain white blouse. "But I'm making progress. Fury women heal quickly, that's part of our genetic inheritance. I've also taken more of our herbal medicines, and you've seen what they can do. How are *you* feeling?"

John massaged his ribs under the blanket. Conroy's men had given him another dose of the moldy water last night before he went to bed, and now his chest felt much better. When he touched his nose, there was almost no pain at all. "You're right, you got some good medicine here. The food ain't bad, either."

Nodding, Ariel dropped a brown-paper bag on his bed. "Here are your clothes. I'll turn around while you get dressed."

Technically, there was no need for her to turn away. She'd already seen him naked. But now the emotional distance between them was so great, it was like looking at a stranger. John stared at her back as he opened the bag and found his pants and underwear. All he felt was bitterness. "Wow, laundry service too. This place has everything. It'd be perfect if it weren't for the locked doors."

"The Elders insisted on that." Her voice was cool and even. "You'll have to earn their trust."

"And what about you? Do *you* trust me?"

"I know you're not stupid. You're smart enough to realize you can't escape Haven. You don't know the codes for the exits."

He put on his underwear, then stepped into his pants. "But that's not the same thing as trust, is it?"

Her back stiffened. She started to turn around, but then stopped herself. "I understand. You're upset that you didn't have a choice in this matter. And I'm upset, too. I didn't want this to happen."

"Right, right. But you were bound by your oath." He zipped up his pants and reached for his shirt. "That was more important."

"Things are different here, John. In your world, the most important thing is personal freedom. That's the philosophy of the whole country, the American way. But here in Haven we see ourselves as servants of the community. Our duties are more important than our freedom. We all work toward a common goal."

He grew impatient as he buttoned his shirt. Ariel was spouting platitudes. He wanted more than that. "Really? So what's your goal?"

"Remember what I said when I met you? In that bar in New York City?" Now she turned around. Her eyes startled him, they were so avid. "Our goal is to turn ourselves into angels and turn the earth into paradise. So we can bring God into the world."

John remembered. That's what made him fall for her that night, what she'd said about God. At the time he'd assumed she was speaking figuratively, waxing poetic. But now he wasn't so sure. "I don't get it. How can you—"

"Put on your shoes. I'm going to take you upstairs."

"Upstairs?"

"To Aunt Cordelia's office. Where she sees the future."

Ariel took him on a roundabout route, guiding him along the zigzagging corridors of the building, which was called the Pyramid, naturally enough. As John had guessed, the building was Haven's command center and communications hub. First, they walked down the hallways of the ground floor and passed enormous rooms full of computer servers and fiber-optic lines. Then they took an elevator to the library on the second floor, where they walked past bookcases holding thousands of rare and ancient manuscripts. Then they ascended to the third and fourth floors, which held the offices of Haven's government, the hundreds of people who carried out the orders of the Council of Elders.

The great majority of the workers they passed in the corridors were women. The few men they saw wore Amish clothes and stared curiously at John as he walked by. The women, in contrast, mostly ignored him, averting their eyes. The news of his arrival must've spread throughout Haven by now, and fewer people seemed shocked by his presence.

He sidled closer to Ariel, who was moving amazingly fast for someone on crutches. "There's more women than men here," he noted. "I guess that's because the women don't die, right?"

She frowned. "First of all, our women *do* die. Staying young isn't the same thing as being immortal."

"Okay, okay, let me rephrase it. You *rarely* die."

"That's not true, either. Until a few hundred years ago the average life-time of a Fury woman was only twice as long as a man's. They didn't age, but they died in plagues, they died while giving birth. Because we can keep bearing children as long as we live, childbirth was our number-one killer."

"Wait, I thought your mother was a thousand years old. How did she live so long?"

"She avoided having babies. Besides Basil and me, she had only one child, a girl named Lavender. She died in infancy eight hundred years ago."

"Okay, but things must've changed a lot in the past hundred years, right? I mean, no one dies from plagues or childbirth anymore."

Ariel nodded. "It's true, our death rate is very low now. All we have to worry about are accidents and homicides. But our birth rate is also low. Procreation can be a challenge when all your men are infertile and you have to seduce strangers under difficult circumstances." She looked John in the eye, as if to remind him of their own difficulties. "And we have other problems too. The extra gene in our DNA affects pregnancy as well as aging. Our bodies will reject any fetus that doesn't have the extra gene in one of its X chromosomes. Because we mate with outsiders who lack that gene, at least half of our pregnancies end in miscarriages."

She seemed at ease talking about genetics. John remembered what Gower had said about Ariel, how her greatest passion was for science. "So you go to all that trouble to find a paramour, and most of the time it doesn't even work?"

"Exactly. About fifty years ago many of our women started using donor sperm to become pregnant, and that's certainly easier. But some of us are uncomfortable with that method. We want to at least see the men who will father our children."

Her voice quavered. She was thinking again of her own attempt to get pregnant. John decided to steer the conversation back to generalities. "Okay, your birth rate is low and the death rate of your women is very low. So if your men die at a normal rate, eventually you're gonna have a lot more women than men, right?" He gestured at the dozens of women striding in and out of the offices along the corridor. Only a handful of men were among them.

Ariel sighed. "Yes, there's an imbalance. And it's getting worse. Right now we have seventeen hundred women and four hundred men, but almost half of our men have left Haven to join Sullivan." She stared at the women in the hallway, some of whom nodded a greeting at her before marching past. "Sometimes I wonder if the imbalance is partially to blame for the rebellion. Maybe our men felt diminished as they became a smaller portion of our community. They're still an important part of the Guard and the Ranger Corps, and we rely on them to work the farmland aboveground, but there aren't many men in leadership positions in Haven."

"Didn't you say that the men rebelled because they were getting impatient? Because you weren't working fast enough on a new kind of medicine?"

Before she could respond they reached the end of the corridor. In front of them was another elevator, with a glowing keypad on the wall beside it. Ariel tapped the keys, opening the door, and they stepped inside. "Aunt Delia's office is in the capstone, the very top of the Pyramid." The door closed and the elevator lurched upward. "After we talk to her, I'll try to answer all your questions."

When the door opened John saw a room full of computer screens. Dozens of flat-screen monitors covered the sloping, triangular walls, which converged at a point directly overhead. Some of the screens showed familiar things that John recognized immediately: a weather report, a CNN broadcast, a scrolling list of share prices on the New York Stock Exchange. Other screens displayed video feeds from overseas, news reports in Chinese and Spanish and Arabic. Still others showed digital maps of the world, with various regions highlighted in cold blue or flaming red. In the center of the room was a circular desk holding half a dozen keyboards, and next to it were three office chairs on rolling casters. Elder Cordelia Fury sat in one of the chairs, her wooden left hand resting on the desk, her flesh-and-blood right hand poised over a keyboard. She wore the same long-sleeved, ankle-length black dress she'd worn in the council chambers, and her face also looked the same: pale and vacant. But instead of staring into space, now she gazed at the largest screen in the room, a jumbo-size monitor on the opposite wall. It displayed the text of what looked like a scholarly article. The title at the top of the page was *Oxford Journal of Archaeology*.

Ariel hobbled into the room. "I did as you asked, Auntie. I brought my paramour."

Cordelia didn't turn her head, but her pale lips curved into a smile. "One moment, child. I'm reading a new study of an archaeological site in southeastern Turkey. Please, take a seat. I'll be done soon."

Rolling her eyes, Ariel led John toward the circular desk. She sat down in the unoccupied chair to the right of Cordelia, and John sat in the one to her left. He glanced at Cordelia's wooden hand, which rested on its side. He noticed that the wood was a little too dark to be lifelike, and there was a small carving of a butterfly etched on one of the knuckles.

As they waited for Cordelia to finish reading, John listened to the jumble of audio from the various news reports playing on the screens overhead. With all the cacophony in the room, he couldn't imagine how Cordelia could concentrate on anything, and yet she seemed content. Ariel, though, was getting annoyed. She furrowed her brow and lowered her eyebrows as the minutes passed. Finally, she let out an exasperated groan. "Auntie, you said you wished to speak to John."

Cordelia kept reading. After a few seconds, though, she raised her wooden hand and pointed its stiff fingers at the screen. "These archaeologists claim that a Stone Age tribe occupied the site in Turkey approximately twenty thousand years ago. According to our oldest Treasures, our family originated in the same region, near the Euphrates River. This site may be one of their first dwellings."

Ariel shook her head. "You said you had important matters to discuss, Auntie."

"Aye, and this is one of them. We can't predict the future without understanding the past. How many times have I told you that, child?"

"Many, many times. But—"

"Just imagine it." Cordelia's smile broadened as she stared at the screen. "Somewhere on the grassy plains near the Euphrates, a random mutation occurred inside one of the egg cells of a Stone Age tribeswoman. A section of DNA in the cell's X chromosome flipped from one configuration to another, and the new pattern was passed down to the tribeswoman's daughter. And look at all the wonders that came into the world from that tiny molecular rearrangement!"

"You're right, Auntie, 'tis astounding. But time is running short this morning. Mother gave us only three days to prepare John for—"

"Then let us begin his education." She lowered her left hand, returning it to her lap, and with her right hand she tapped the ENTER key on the keyboard in front of her. "If he is to live the rest of his days in Haven, he must learn our history."

All the monitors in the room suddenly went black. A moment later the screens flashed back to life, each displaying the same kind of runes John had seen in Ariel's notebook. The angular symbols scrolled upward on every screen, slowly at first and then more rapidly. It was like watching a strange, disorienting blizzard, where the snowflakes streamed upward instead of down. It made John dizzy.

"This is Aric," Cordelia said. "The world's first written language. It was developed by our ancestors twelve thousand years ago, long before the Egyptians and Sumerians invented scripts for their own languages." She raised her wooden hand again and pointed at the largest monitor. "Those runes are from the very oldest Treasure in our records, which was written by my great-great-great-great-grandmother. Her name was Umma, and she was a remarkable woman. According to her Treasure, she birthed one hundred and ninety-six children and lived for more than three thousand years."

John looked askance. One hundred and ninety-six kids? That couldn't be right. "And you believe it?"

For a moment he thought he might've insulted Cordelia, but instead she smiled again. "Well said, John. A good historian questions everything. Because the world is full of lies." She tapped another key on her keyboard, enlarging the runes on the jumbo-size screen. "But Umma's Treasure is believable because it's so meticulous. She recorded the births and deaths in her tribe, year after year. She realized there was something special in her blood that preserved her youth, something she'd inherited from her mother and passed on to her daughters, but not to her sons. Unfortunately, the vast majority of her children didn't live as long as she did. More than a hundred of them died before the age of five."

Ariel squirmed in her chair, bored and impatient. She obviously knew this story, John thought. She must've learned it when she was a little girl, way back in the seventeenth century. But John was fascinated. "Why did so many of Umma's kids die?"

"They were a tribe of nomadic hunter-gatherers. In times of plenty, children were born. When there were harsh winters or droughts, the children starved. This was a fact of life for all people on earth twelve thousand years ago. What made Umma unique was that she decided to change this fact." Cordelia tapped yet another key on the keyboard, which highlighted some of the runes on the monitor, coloring them yellow. "These runes describe a species of wild emmer wheat that grew in southeastern Turkey. For hundreds of years Umma collected varieties of the wild plant and crossbred them. She sought to develop a hardy grain that could feed her family in good times and bad. And after nearly a millennium of effort, she succeeded. Other tribes in the area started planting her wheat. It became the first farm crop in the Fertile Crescent. Then it spread to Egypt."

Once again, John was skeptical. "She invented farming?"

"It would've happened sooner or later, mind you. But Umma sped the process. Because she lived for so long, she could take on tasks that required generations to complete. And she used her accumulated knowledge to lead her people wisely. What's more, she recognized that this was her life's purpose. This was the reason why she and the other women in her family had been given the gift of everlasting youth." Cordelia highlighted another set of runes on the screen. "She wrote this promise in her Treasure. The best translation is, 'We must turn the desert into a garden. We must turn the earth into paradise. Then God will be born.'"

John had heard this quote before, of course. Those were the same words Ariel had spoken. He turned to her, and she grinned. She seemed pleased that Cordelia was finally getting to the point. "And Umma's daughters inherited this promise," Ariel said. "They sought to change the world for the better, in large ways and small. Some of them focused on inventing useful devices, such as the ox-drawn plow. Others traveled to distant lands and became oracles or priestesses. They tried to alter the course of history, steering the world's emperors and pharaohs toward peace, not war."

"They weren't always successful," Cordelia added. "And very often they were persecuted and murdered. Our grandmothers were expert in many of the sciences, particularly medicine and botany, but the common people of the ancient world didn't understand science. They believed we were practicing magic. They called us sorceresses and witches."

Ariel grimaced. "Please don't say that word, Auntie. I've told John never to use it."

For the first time Cordelia turned away from her screens. She looked at John with fervent green eyes. "Our family migrated many times to stay ahead of our persecutors. We escaped the Persian Empire by fleeing to Italy. And when the Roman Empire grew strong we settled in northern Europe, out of reach of the emperor's legions. After Rome fell, we blended in with the Frankish and Germanic tribes that had just swept into Europe." She moved her chair a bit closer to John's. The casters squeaked as they rolled across the floor. "The medieval period was our golden age. We hid in plain sight, dwelling in the small villages of France and Germany. Our grandmothers found husbands among their neighbors, men who were willing to keep our secret. When their husbands grew old and died, the women and their children moved on to another village and started again. And all the while, our Elders governed the family, meeting once a year on a hilltop in the Black Forest. They continued our scientific investigations and our attempts to better the world."

Ariel leaned toward her aunt. "Don't forget to mention your own contributions. Tell John about your travels to the Near East. How you became an adviser to Saladin and helped him defeat the Crusaders."

Cordelia nodded. "Aye, the Crusaders had to be defeated. They were horrible people."

She frowned at the memory but said nothing more. Ariel waited a moment, then shook her head, incredulous. "That's all you have to say about it?"

"Saladin was a genius. All the credit should be his. I merely informed him of the vulnerabilities of Richard the Lion Heart, who was an arrogant brute." Cordelia kept frowning. She was clearly upset. "In those days Europe was full of brutes like him, sadistic kings and princes who would commit any atrocity to stay in power. When I returned to France I saw the first portents of the coming disaster. The princes and churchmen were slaughtering the Jews and the Cathar heretics. I should've realized that we would be next. But I was too busy with my other interests, my painting and poetry and natural philosophy. When the massacres started, we were completely unprepared."

"Auntie, please. You can't blame yourself for—"

"My own suffering was minimal. I had no daughters or sons." She raised her wooden hand and held it at eye level. "All I lost was my left hand, lopped off by a raving priest with an ax. But our family was nearly annihilated. At the start of the fifteenth century there were three thousand of us, spread across western and central Europe. By the time we departed for America, only twelve of us were left."

The room fell silent. Ariel lowered her head and stared at the floor. John thought of the murals he'd seen in the council chambers, the paintings of women dying in bonfires and on the gallows. The massacres were ancient history for the rest of the world, but they were still raw, traumatic memories for the Elders. Which explained why they lived in an underground cavern and vowed to execute anyone who learned their secrets.

The runes were still scrolling upward on the screens overhead. After several seconds Cordelia lowered her wooden hand and turned her attention back to her keyboard. With a tap of a key she removed the runes from the monitors, which went back to displaying the crazy assortment of maps and news broadcasts. Then she looked at John again. "So do you understand now why I sit here every day, surveying this pageant of facts and images? I'm trying to observe the world from every angle, to see all its trends and movements and upheavals. I have the Internet to assist me now, but in years past I pursued the same goal by reading every newspaper and book I could get my hands on. Because we can't afford to be caught unprepared again. We need to see the world clearly so we can predict the future."

John nodded. He did understand. "So have you been successful? Have you ever predicted something before it happened?"

"I can't predict the minor events of history. I can't say which candidate will win a presidential election or which corporation will earn the biggest profits. But if I look hard enough I can see the outlines of the major events that are coming. Like wars and revolutions."

"Tell him about Germany, Auntie." Ariel's face was sober. "You predicted the world wars long before they happened."

"Aye, child, but that wasn't difficult. Anyone could see that Europe still seethed with brutality. And though we'd left those dangers behind when we came to America, I knew the brutes might eventually follow us here. So we took steps to make sure there was a counterbalancing force, a mighty nation on this continent that could oppose the madmen who were sure to rise to power in Germany and Russia."

"Wait a second." John was having a little trouble absorbing all this. "You took steps? What do you mean?"

"We encouraged the revolt of the American colonies and the founding of the United States. But that wasn't my doing. The Elders gave that assignment to the Ranger Corps." With a look of pride on her face, Cordelia pointed at Ariel. "And my niece played a very prominent role."

John stared at her. He was flabbergasted. "Okay, what did you do?"

Ariel scowled. Ignoring his question, she looked at her watch, then turned to Cordelia. "We're on a very tight schedule, Auntie. Is there anything else you wanted to tell John?"

She shook her head. "Nay, I suppose that's enough for today. We'll have more time to talk if the council allows him to join our community."

"Mother seems resolutely opposed to the idea. Is there any chance you can speak to her about this?"

Cordelia let out a long sigh. "I'm afraid I might do more harm than good. Elizabeth and I agree on very little these days. If I take up this issue with her, it might stiffen her opposition. And Margaret will go along with her, of course. She always does." She pursed her lips in distaste. "It might be better if you approached Elizabeth yourself, child. Try to convince her that this is a necessary step."

"Oh, I'm so tired of arguing with her!" Ariel's voice rose and her face reddened. "She has charted our course and refuses to veer from it. Tell me, Auntie, when did she become so obstinate?"

"Now, now. Your mother doesn't respond well to heated argument. I suggest that you wait until your emotions have cooled before you take up the matter with her." Cordelia gave her a stern look of warning. Then she turned to John. "I'm glad we had this opportunity to talk. After Lily was granted permission to choose a paramour, I showed her the stories about you that appeared on the Internet three years ago. I never thought I'd get the chance to meet you in person, but now that I have I'd like to extend my deepest sympathies. There's nothing worse than losing a daughter."

John's stomach burned. It felt like someone had dropped a hot coal in his guts. But he shouldn't have been so startled. If Cordelia kept a constant watch over the world, alert to every eddy in the flow of history, then it wasn't so surprising that she'd come across the news accounts of what had happened to Ivy. The story made national headlines after John released his statement to the newspapers.

He swallowed hard, trying to douse the burning sensation in his stomach. "Thank you," he whispered.

"You're a brave man," Cordelia added. "And I hope we can count on your bravery. I hope you'll agree to help us."

Now he was confused. "Help you? I thought—"

"Listen to me, John," Ariel interjected. She seemed a little upset that her aunt had brought up this subject before she could. "We're trying to save your life by persuading the council to let you stay in Haven. And the surest way to accomplish this is to prove your worth to the Elders. As it so happens, there's a task you can perform for us. If it goes well, my mother and Aunt Margaret will see your arrival here as a stroke of good fortune. They'll be better disposed to accept you into our community."

John was still confused. He had no idea what Ariel had in mind. "What are you talking about? What's the task?"

She rose to her feet, propping the crutches under her arms. "We're going downstairs now. To the laboratories. I'm going to show you our Fountain of Youth."

FOURTEEN

Archibald was annoyed at Gower. At times like these he couldn't even bear to look at the fool. As they conducted their morning patrol outside Haven's fence, combing the woods and fields to see if any Riflemen lurked nearby, Gower jabbered about the events of the day before. The lovesick dolt had been pining for Lily since he was a teenager but had never spoken a word to the woman. He'd joined the Guardsmen and started training for the Ranger Corps in the hope that he'd someday have a conversation with her, and although he still hadn't achieved this goal he felt he was making progress now. He'd helped to save Lily's life, and he'd conversed with her paramour. Gower was too kindhearted to be jealous of the outsider; instead, he praised the man's obvious intelligence. Archibald didn't know whether to laugh or weep.

They were nearing the end of their patrol, weaving through the forest toward Haven's southern gate, when Gower uttered his most ridiculous statement yet. "I've made a resolution, cuz," he said. "I'm going to approach the paramour and offer him my friendship."

Now Archibald laughed. He couldn't stop himself. "Well, you better do it soon. The man will be dead by Tuesday."

"Nay, didn't you hear what the council decided? Lily will find a place for him in Haven."

"That place will be in our crypt. I not only heard what the council decided, I saw the look on the Chief Elder's face after they made the decision. She doesn't like the outsider. At the end of the three days, she'll order his execution."

Gower thought this over, scratching the tufts of reddish hair that grew under his chin. His beard was the ugliest in all of Michigan. "I hope you're wrong. Lily would be bereft to see him die."

"Aye, but it might work to your advantage. You could go to Lily and console her. Tell her how highly you thought of her paramour. How his death was such a great loss to the community, and so on and so forth. With this strategy you might wriggle your way into her bed."

The fool kept scratching his scraggly beard. Finally, he shook his head. "Nay, I couldn't do it. She'd see right through me. Lily is uncommonly perceptive."

"Perhaps you should set your sights on a less discerning woman then. Seduction is impossible without deception. I've given you this advice many times before, if you recall."

Gower frowned. He resented any suggestion that his affections were misplaced. "I wonder about the value of your advice. Tell me, how much good has it done for *you*?"

Archibald was surprised. His kindhearted cousin had managed to wound him. But that wasn't terribly hard to do. Archibald's failures in the romantic arena were glaring. "Even the wisest farmer can't plant seeds in stony ground. And the hearts of Haven's women are stony indeed."

Gower's face was blank. The metaphor seemed to puzzle him. "Plant seeds? Are you speaking of impregnation?"

"Nay, but that's part of the problem, is it not? Perhaps if we could impregnate our women, they'd treat us with greater respect. As it is, they'll employ us as servants but not accept us as husbands."

"You're exaggerating, cuz. You know very well that my mother had a husband."

"He died twenty years ago. Why hasn't she taken another?"

"She says she's still mourning. She loved him very much." Gower looked up and gazed at the high branches of the pine trees. "And you know how busy my mother has been since she was chosen to run the geothermal plant."

"Just think for a moment. The women of Haven outnumber the men by more than four to one. We're such a scarce commodity, one would expect them to be fighting over us. But instead, only a tenth of the women take husbands, leaving half of the men without partners. Why is that?"

"Pardon, can you repeat those fractions? This is a baffling equation, cuz."

"Let me put it another way. Let's assume that ten or twenty years from now your mother finally finishes mourning her last husband. If I were to propose marriage to her then, do you think she would accept?"

Gower let out a guffaw. It was so loud it echoed against the tree trunks. "I should think not. You're my companion, not hers. She's known you since you were a child."

"Exactly. You've made my point. The women see us as children. Even the younger women, the ones our own age, don't look at us as equals. They focus their romantic fantasies on their paramours and give us only sisterly or motherly attention."

Archibald was serious, but Gower still seemed amused. Grinning, he wagged his finger. "Your outlook is too dark, Archie. There are many happy couples in Haven. It's true, some of us have to work hard to find a partner. But from what I hear, it's no different in the outside world. I'm sure the men there have their own troubles."

By this point they'd reached the edge of the woods. Haven's southern gate stood a hundred yards away, manned by that lummox Old Prentice, who waved when he saw them. Gower waved back, then turned to Archibald. "Do you have any plans for your off-duty hours today? I was considering a visit to the gymnasium."

Archibald shook his head. Haven's gymnasium was one of his least favorite places. It stank like an old sock. "I'd rather stay outside. I'm feeling a little foggy this morning. I need to clear my head."

"Ah, that explains your dark mood. Shall I see you at dinner, cuz?"

"Aye, see you then."

He watched Gower walk to the gate, which Old Prentice unlocked and opened. Then Archibald retreated into the woods. He headed southwest, taking a disused, overgrown trail that meandered between the pine trees.

As he followed the trail he struggled to tame his ferocious thoughts. His mood was dark indeed, colored by the foulness of yesterday's events. But the thing that angered him most wasn't the firefight with Sullivan's men or the encounter with the paramour. It was the revelation that Hal and Richard were dead. Mind you, he'd never been fond of the twins. On the contrary, he'd rather hated them. They were conceited twits who'd always received deferential treatment because their mother was an Elder. But they were also excellent Rangers, two of the best fighters in the whole Corps, and Archibald had grudgingly admired their skills. The fact that they'd given their lives to defend Lily—the ice princess of Haven—seemed a travesty, a horrible joke.

He walked faster, wiping the sweat from his brow. He knew he shouldn't be so shocked. Sacrifice was one of their family's founding principles. Haven's women used their centuries of wisdom to better the world, and the men used their superior strength to defend the women. Although this arrangement was sometimes unfair, giving women most of the power in their society, the nature of their biology demanded it. But the family's rules were based on the assumption that their biology was unchangeable, a fixed truth written inside each of their cells, and now this assumption was no longer valid. The study of genetics—in Haven's laboratories and the outside world's—had advanced tremendously over the past few decades. Now it was possible to peer inside the body's microscopic machinery, to see the molecular cogs that carry out the chromosomes' commands. And scientists could use this knowledge to tinker with the machine.

That was the impetus behind Sullivan's rebellion. Haven's researchers had discovered the mechanism behind the women's eternal youth and glimpsed a way to extend this biochemical miracle to the men. But when Sullivan and his followers demanded that the council pursue this research without delay, the Elders decided instead to proceed with their customary caution. So Sullivan escaped Haven along with two hundred other men, who took most of the weaponry from the community's arsenal and stole ten million dollars' worth of gold bars from the family's vault.

Archibald had known that the rebellion was coming. A week before the mass escape, Sullivan had tried to recruit him to the cause. The man was gifted with a silver tongue and made a persuasive case. He promised to refrain from violence. His aim, he said, was to exert pressure on the Elders, not to murder anyone. But Archibald saw through his lies. He recognized that Sullivan had no scruples whatsoever and that the rebellion would kill more Furies than anything since the Burning Times. And Archibald couldn't take up arms against his mother and sisters. It was unthinkable.

At the same time, though, he didn't warn the Elders about Sullivan's plans. There was a part of Archibald that wanted the rebellion to succeed. He wanted to live on equal terms with Haven's women. He was tired of cowering in the shadows of his mother—Grace Fury was a deputy to the Chief Elder—and his nine sisters, who also worked for the council. His mother, who was honest to a fault, once admitted to Archibald that she could never love him as much as she loved her daughters. "I'm sorry, Archie," she'd said. "But my sons die too swiftly. I can't give you my whole heart if I know it's going to be broken so soon."

He stopped for a moment to catch his breath. Leaning against a massive tree trunk, he tried to imagine what would happen if Sullivan's rebellion succeeded. He envisioned a future where any man in Haven could become a council deputy, or maybe even an Elder. With only a few well-chosen changes to their biochemistry, Haven's men could live just as long as the women, and the family's sons would be loved just as much as the daughters. It was a wonderful vision, strange and exhilarating. Although Archibald still recoiled from Sullivan's brutality and the prospect of violence, he'd come to believe this was a future worth fighting for.

He was about to resume walking when he heard a twig snap somewhere off to his left. Turning in that direction, he saw two men in motorcycle jackets coming toward him. They were a study in contrasts—one was young and short and wiry, the other was middle-aged and built like a gladiator. Archibald recognized both of them. The younger one was Percy Fury, a vicious fellow who was kicked out of the Guard a few years ago for aiming a gun at one of his fellow trainees. The older one was Sullivan.

Both men held pistols and kept them pointed at Archibald as they approached. Fear constricted his throat, but he knew enough not to draw his own gun from the holster under his shirt. Sullivan and Percy were better marksmen than he could ever hope to be. Instead, Archibald casually doffed his hat and smiled. The key to dealing with these brutes was to show no trepidation at all. "Good morrow, gentlemen," he said. "I'm surprised to see you here. Didn't we agree at our last encounter to meet at the old quarry? That's where I was headed this morning."

Neither man uttered a word. Percy, who carried a backpack over his shoulder, walked right up to him and without so much as a "by your leave" stuck his hand inside Archibald's shirt and removed the gun from his holster. Then he took a step backward, allowing Sullivan to come near. The chief of the rebellion smiled in greeting, then slammed his fist into Archibald's stomach.

In agony, Archibald slumped to the ground, his back sliding against the rough bark of the pine tree. The pain was blinding, but the fear was worse. They were going to kill him. "Mercy!" he gasped. "What . . . have I done?"

Sullivan was still smiling. "It's not so much what you did, but what you failed to do." He bent over, bringing his face close to Archibald's. "Before Conroy opened fire on me yesterday, why didn't you shoot the cur?"

"You asked me to be your eyes and ears. You said nothing about—"

Sullivan punched him again, this time hitting Archibald above his left ear. Although his eyes were closed, he saw a burst of white light behind his eyelids, a signal of distress from his jarred brain. He felt dizzy and nauseous and terrified, as if he were falling from a great height. When he opened his eyes he lay faceup on the ground, and the pine branches whirled in green circles above him. Sullivan's voice rang in his head, loud and scolding. "You said you wished to help us, Archibald. But when you found yourself in a situation where you could offer some assistance, you did nothing. I'm waiting for an explanation."

His vision darkened. He bit the inside of his cheek to keep himself from losing consciousness. *I have to say something,* Archibald thought. *I have to plead for my life.* "I . . . I was frightened. And I'm not a good shot. I wouldn't have hit Conroy. I would've only given myself away."

"You should've made an attempt. At the very least it would've surprised Conroy and slowed him down." Sullivan loomed over him. The brute's head was at the center of the whirling pine branches. "I'm beginning to wonder about your loyalty, Archibald. Whose side are you on?"

"I want . . . I want the rebellion to succeed."

"And we were on the brink of success yesterday. I held the prize in my hands, the chemical formula that so many good men have sacrificed their lives for. But because of your inaction, Conroy's attack frustrated our plans."

Archibald started weeping. *It's no use,* he thought. *The madman is going to execute me no matter what I say.* "Please . . . please forgive me. I didn't know . . ."

Above the noise of his own sobs he heard Percy cackling. The little idiot had taken out his camera and was taking pictures of the scene. Percy was perhaps the most odious of all the Riflemen, a monkeylike spy who lurked in the woods outside Haven and photographed everyone who entered and exited the community. Archibald fervently hoped that Sullivan would perform the execution himself and not assign the task to this underling. That would be the ultimate indignity.

After several seconds Sullivan bent lower, his pistol in hand. Archibald breathed a sigh of relief. *He's going to do it himself.*

"Given the circumstances, I think it's fair to say that the failure is your fault." Sullivan pressed the muzzle of his gun against Archibald's forehead. "Don't you agree?"

Archibald closed his eyes and nodded.

"And because it's your fault, you owe me a debt. Now you're obligated to carry out certain tasks for me, so you can make up for your mistakes. Agreed?"

Archibald's attention was so focused on the cold steel pressed against his brow that it took him a few seconds to absorb what Sullivan had said. Confused, he opened his eyes. "What? You want me to—"

"Aye, I'm giving you another chance." Sullivan stood up straight and returned the pistol to the holster under his jacket. "You're going to deliver a package for me. You shouldn't have any trouble smuggling it into Haven because you know all the entrance codes. Once you've brought it inside, another associate of mine will assist you. Several people inside Haven have been kind enough to offer me their services."

He extended his right arm toward Percy, who unslung his backpack from his shoulder and handed it to Sullivan. Meanwhile, Archibald struggled to sit upright. He was elated to be alive, but still dizzy and confused. "A package?"

Sullivan carefully lowered the backpack into Archibald's lap. It was heavy, at least twenty pounds. "Open it up and take a look. But mind that you don't jostle the thing. It's rather delicate."

Obediently, Archibald gripped the backpack's zipper and opened it. Inside was a contraption fashioned from two steel pipes, each about a foot long and three inches in diameter. The pipes were bound together with black electrical tape. Attached to the contraption was a small radio with a silver antenna and half a dozen wires that ran into holes drilled into the pipes. Although Archibald had little knowledge of electronics or engineering, he saw right away that the package was a bomb.

His stomach heaved. He was going to vomit. "Nay, I can't." He swallowed hard and pushed back the bile that was rising in his throat. "I can't do it."

Sullivan smiled again. "But you're obligated. Remember?"

"I'd rather die." Amid his nausea, Archibald felt a spark of courage. "Shoot me instead. Right this instant."

"Now, now. If you perform your task correctly, the bomb won't hurt anyone. It will merely cause some damage to Haven's mechanical systems."

"And what purpose will that serve?"

Sullivan stopped smiling. "Don't question me, whoreson. I'll tell you what you need to know and nothing more. And if you betray us, I'll flay your skin with my fingernails. Your death will be longer and more painful than the paramour's."

He bent his fingers, turning his hands into claws. His nails were long and jagged and filthy. Archibald's courage faded as he stared at them. He couldn't fight Sullivan. The man was too strong.

Sullivan waited until this truth sank in. Then he pointed at the device inside the backpack. "I'm going to tell you how it works. Listen carefully."

FIFTEEN

Haven's laboratories occupied a space carved out of the floor of the cavern, directly beneath the Pyramid. John's stomach flip-flopped as he and Ariel rapidly descended in the elevator.

He sneaked a glance at her while she looked up at the digital display that showed the floor numbers ticking downward. He was glad that she wore modern clothes instead of the old-fashioned dresses that her aunt Cordelia preferred. Although Ariel's jeans and blouse were plain, they showed off her figure well. She'd obviously spent enough time in the outside world to know how people dressed these days. Her long red hair was tied in a ponytail, exposing the back of her neck, which was shiny with sweat. She must be exhausted from limping along on her crutches, he thought.

Or maybe she was anxious. John was anxious, too. They had plenty of things to be worried about.

The elevator door opened and they stepped into a long, brightly lit hallway with a tiled floor and immaculate white walls. The hallway was empty but not silent. The fluorescent lights buzzed and the ventilation system thrummed. There were sturdy steel doors on either side of the hall, and as John walked behind Ariel he saw a small plaque on every door, giving the name of each laboratory they passed: MICROBIOLOGY, NEU-ROSCIENCE, COMPUTER MODELING, PLANT BIOLOGY. They kept going until they reached the end of the hallway, where there was a door marked MO-LECULAR GENETICS. Unlike the other labs, this one had a keypad next to the door. Ariel tapped a sequence of keys, unlocking the door, and then led John inside. "Welcome to my home," she said. "When I'm in Haven, I spend nearly all my time here."

The room was large, at least thirty feet across. Three lab tables ran the length of the room, each with its own sink and cabinets and refrigerator. Each table also held a computer, a microscope, a rack full of test tubes, and several bulky pieces of equipment that John couldn't identify. But what really caught his attention were the shelves lining the walls. All together, they held hundreds of laboratory flasks, each marked with a white label and filled with several ounces of liquid. Some of the liquids were colored and some were cloudy, but most were clear. It was a veritable forest of chemicals.

John let out an appreciative whistle. "Wow, this is impressive. How many people work here?"

Ariel turned on the lights and hobbled toward the table at the center of the room. "I usually have six assistants. But right now I'm working alone." She sat down in the chair in front of the computer. Setting her crutches aside, she pointed at the chair next to hers. "Come on, sit down. I'm going to explain this as best as I can."

As John sat in the chair, Ariel turned on her computer and typed in a password. Then she clicked on an icon shaped like a fountain—specifically, the marble fountain carved in the form of a tree, the one John had seen when he entered Haven the day before. After a few seconds, an odd grid appeared on the screen:

	X^F	X
X	$X^F X$	~~XX~~
Y	$X^F Y$	~~XY~~

"Okay," she started, "this is something that geneticists call a Punnett square. This particular square shows all the combinations of the sex chromosomes that can arise from the mating of a Fury woman and an ordinary XY man. In a Fury woman, one of the two X chromosomes has an extra gene, which we call the Fountain gene. Named after the Fountain of Youth, naturally. So we label one of the X chromosomes as X^F."

John studied the grid. It seemed easy enough to understand. If you mixed and matched the chromosomes from the parents, there were four possible combinations. "Why are the XX and XY combinations crossed out?"

"Remember I told you that a Fury woman's body will reject any fetus that doesn't have the extra gene? So, the XX and XY babies will never be born."

He nodded, remembering. "Right, that's why your birth rate is so low."

"That's one of the effects of the Fountain gene. It produces a special kind of protein that radically changes our biochemistry. It's called an activator protein because it activates other genes that are normally dormant."

Now John was starting to lose her. "Uh, slow down. What do you mean?"

"The body has a complex system for switching genes on and off. In an ordinary female embryo, for instance, one of the X chromosomes is deactivated about a week after conception. But the protein produced by the Fountain gene blocks the shutdown process. It not only stops the deactivation of its own gene, it prevents other genes from getting switched off when the embryonic and fetal stages are over."

The explanation didn't help. John was bewildered. But he didn't need to understand everything. Just the basics. "And then what happens? What's the upshot?"

"The activated genes produce their own special proteins, which enhance the body's ability to repair cellular damage, especially damage to the DNA strands. In a female with the X^F chromosome, the cells repair themselves so efficiently that they don't accumulate biochemical waste or mangled DNA. That means our organs don't deteriorate, and we don't get any cancerous growths. After our bodies are fully grown, they stay in equilibrium. In other words, we don't age."

"All because of one little gene? Seems miraculous doesn't it?"

"No, there's an explanation. All the species in the animal kingdom evolved from single-cell organisms that could divide forever without damage, like amoebas. But somewhere along the line, probably between one and two billion years ago, some of the organisms lost that ability. A random mutation split the Fountain gene in two and moved the halves to opposite ends of the chromosome it was on." Ariel made a karate-chop motion, miming the breakage of the gene. "The fractured gene couldn't produce the activator protein anymore, so the mutation stopped the antiaging effect. But it also raised the organism's reproduction rate. And because having lots of descendants is more important to the survival of the species than everlasting youth, the mutated organisms eventually dominated the planet. They gave rise to all the animals we see today."

John's head was spinning. "Okay, okay, so—"

"Then twenty thousand years ago there was another mutation, this one occurring within an egg cell of one of my distant ancestors." Ariel couldn't stop talking, she was too impassioned. Her face flushed and her eyes blazed. "The mutation rearranged the cell's X chromosome, bringing the two halves of the Fountain gene back together and restoring its ability to produce the antiaging protein. After this egg cell was fertilized and developed into a baby girl, the Fountain gene filled her body with the protein, which kept her eternally young after she reached sexual maturity."

"And that was the first Fury? Your great-great-great-grandmother?"

"Correct. Believe it or not, a human's biochemistry is roughly similar to an amoeba's, so the restoration of the antiaging effect isn't so surprising. The Fountain gene causes some odd side effects in humans, though. It's linked to another gene that gives us green eyes and red hair." Smiling, she tugged at her ponytail. "Also, our teeth never stop regenerating. New teeth are always forming in our jaws and pushing out the old ones. And that's a good thing, because otherwise we'd suffer from centuries of tooth decay."

He recalled the baby tooth Gabe Rodriguez had found in Ariel's mouth while stitching up her bullet wounds. It had puzzled the hell out of Gabe, but now it made sense. John pointed at the computer screen, specifically at the part of the Punnett square that was marked $X^F Y$. "But what about your men?" he asked. "They inherit the Fountain gene too. Why don't they get the antiaging effect?"

Ariel's face turned serious. "Here's where it gets complicated. Although the X chromosome has been pretty stable over the course of evolution, the Y has changed a lot because it mutates frequently. One of the newer genes on the Y produces a different kind of activator protein, which triggers the development of human sperm and a few other cellular processes that are essential to male fertility. Unfortunately, this protein also interferes with the one produced by the Fountain gene. Whenever the two proteins come near each other, they merge into a useless clump. Because both proteins are immobilized, neither one can do its job. That's why our men age normally but never become fertile. Although they inherit the Fountain gene, they show none of its effects except the green eyes and red hair."

John nodded. He was starting to get the gist of what Ariel was saying. Mother Nature had given her family a gift, but there were some strings attached. "When did you figure all this out? A long time ago, or just recently?"

Ariel made a sweeping gesture, pointing at all the lab tables in the room. "Our family has a long tradition of scientific research. My grandmothers discovered the rules of heredity hundreds of years ago by experimenting with plant hybrids. But we also keep abreast of research in the outside world. When scientists in the international Human Genome Project mapped the full chemical sequence of human DNA a decade ago, we realized we could use this information to identify the gene on the X chromosome that makes us unique." She grinned with pride. "We identified the Fountain gene five years ago. A year later we identified the Upstart gene, the one on the Y chromosome that works at cross-purposes with Fountain. Then we started the effort to isolate the activator proteins produced by the genes. I had to recruit more assistants to work on the project, because by that point we were under pressure from our men."

"Pressure? What do you mean?"

"Both the young men and the old were anxious to see progress. Because the young wished to father children, they hoped we'd learn how to disable the Fountain gene or its protein. With Fountain out of the way, the Upstart gene could make them fertile. But the older men wanted the opposite. They hoped we'd discover how to shut down Upstart, so their Fountain genes could stop them from aging." Ariel turned away from the lab table and pointed at the hundreds of flasks on the shelves. "You see all those chemicals? Those are the drugs we tested, trying to see if they inhibited either Fountain or Upstart. Unfortunately, none of them worked. Although a few of the compounds shut down Upstart, they weren't safe. They also turned off dozens of crucial genes on other chromosomes, which would be fatal."

She stared at the crowded shelves, slowly turning her head from left to right. Instead of continuing the story, she remained silent for a long while, biting her lower lip and averting her eyes. John sensed she had more to say but dreaded telling the next part. He leaned toward her. "What happened then?"

Ariel took a deep breath. "About two years ago I decided to conduct a test. Our lab had hundreds of blood and tissue samples from Fury women. Because the Fountain gene is in all our cells, I knew those samples would contain the gene's protein. I wondered what would happen if I extracted the protein from that tissue and injected it into a Fury male. If the man's cells were literally *flooded* with Fountain proteins, I hypothesized that Upstart wouldn't be able to block them all. Maybe enough of the Fountain proteins would escape immobilization and trigger the antiaging effect. It was a radical idea, but I knew that scientists in the outside world were using a similar technique to fight tumors. The crucial step is binding the protein to molecules that can carry it from the bloodstream into the cells."

"And who was the subject for this test?"

She paused before answering. "Sullivan volunteered. This was before the rebellion, obviously. He and I had been on bad terms for many years, but I decided not to let our history get in the way."

John knew that "bad terms" was a hell of an understatement. He'd witnessed Sullivan thrashing Ariel. And he remembered what the bastard had said during the beating, how he'd railed about killing any man who came near her. It was clear that sometime in the past, maybe years and years ago, Sullivan had desired his half sister and Ariel had rejected him. But John wasn't going to bring up this subject now. "So did the test work?" he asked.

"Yes, Sullivan stopped aging. But only temporarily."

She fell silent again. John waited several seconds, but she didn't say anything else. "I don't get it," he said. "What went wrong?"

She frowned. "The treatment worked, but it required a huge amount of Fountain protein. I extracted the stuff from nearly all of our tissue samples, and even then I had only enough to treat Sullivan for a week. He stopped aging for seven days—I could see the changes in his cellular activity—but then it resumed when we ran out of the protein. At first I thought I could get more by culturing big batches of Fury cells, or using recombinant technology to insert the Fountain gene into other cells. But Fury cells don't grow well in the lab, and the protein is tricky to produce any other way. We just couldn't make enough."

"So what did you do?"

"I kept at it. Maybe you didn't notice this, but I can be pretty damn stubborn. It occurred to me that the cellular processes triggered by Fountain are similar to what goes on inside every human fetus during its development. So I guessed that some of the proteins in a fetus would be similar to the Fountain protein. As it turned out, we had some fetal tissue samples in our lab. One of our Rangers had collected them from a hospital in Detroit several years ago because we were doing a study on birth defects. When I analyzed the samples I discovered I was right. The fetal tissue was full of an activator protein that was very similar to Fountain's. And there was a chemical reaction that could transform the fetal protein into Fountain protein. All I needed to do was find a catalyst, a special enzyme to trigger the reaction."

John winced. He pulled away from her, shifting in his chair. The memory of the specimen jar had come back to him. Once again he stood in the woods of Valley Forge National Park and stared at the tiny brown hand floating in the yellow liquid. He shook his head to dispel the memory. He was angry at Ariel now. "Jesus, that's horrible. Didn't you realize what you were doing?"

He expected her to get angry, too. He thought she'd furiously defend herself. But instead she simply nodded. "Yes, at that point I saw what could happen. Once we had the catalyst, we'd need fetuses to supply the protein. At least ten thousand fetuses a year for a few hundred men. It was an ethical nightmare. So I told the Council of Elders I couldn't continue doing this research."

"How did they react?"

"They agreed with me, but not because they had ethical concerns. Mother was worried about the practical consequences. The only source for so much fetal tissue would be the outside world's abortion clinics. Every year they send hundreds of thousands of fetuses to medical-waste companies for disposal. A good number of those fetuses, maybe fifty thousand, would be large enough for our purposes. But even if we could secretly obtain some of those aborted fetuses, we couldn't keep the arrangements secret for very long. The outsiders would eventually discover what we were doing. So the council instructed me to go back to my lab and start over." She lowered her head and gazed at the floor. "At first I was relieved. I felt like a weight had been lifted from my shoulders. Then a week later, Sullivan and his friends escaped from Haven."

John's anger subsided. As he stared at Ariel's disconsolate face he saw how guilty she felt. She'd opened a Pandora's box. She felt responsible for the rebellion. "And then Sullivan's men decided to collect some fetuses on their own?"

Ariel kept her eyes on the floor. "They're bribing someone who works for one of the medical-waste firms. So far they've managed to keep it quiet. They've hidden the fetal tissue in our caches. A few of Sullivan's men previously worked in our labs, so they know how to extract the fetal protein from the tissue. But they can't turn the fetal protein into Fountain without the catalyst. They have to know the catalyst's chemical formula before they can produce the antiaging remedy." She shook her head. "Mother was frantic when she learned what they were doing. It was exactly what she'd feared. Can you imagine what would happen if an outsider discovered that our family was grinding up fetuses to produce medicine? The reaction would be catastrophic. It would be the sixteenth century all over again."

John could imagine it. People would be outraged and horrified. Maybe they wouldn't burn or lynch the Furies, but they'd certainly want to. First, the police would round up and interrogate Sullivan's men. Then they'd raid Haven and arrest everyone else. "You're right," he said. "It wouldn't be pretty."

"The Elders had no choice but to start negotiating with Sullivan. Mother sent him messages, begging him to come back to Haven. She promised to devote all our resources to discovering a better way to produce the Fountain protein. At the same time, she ordered me to find the formula for the catalyst. She thought we could use it to produce a small amount of Fountain from the XX and XY fetuses that our women miscarry. We could also make regular blood donations and extract Fountain from that supply. All together, we might be able to collect enough protein to treat the oldest of our men until we came up with a better solution."

"How did Sullivan respond?"

"He said it was a good start. He refused to return to Haven, but he agreed to stop attacking our Rangers while we worked on the catalyst. But I didn't trust him. My half brother is as devious as a crow. I knew he'd use his spies to watch our labs. So I contacted Mariela, the chief of our Caño Dorado outpost, and told her to do the catalyst work there."

John had heard the name of the outpost before. Sullivan had mentioned it, and so had Ariel's Aunt Margaret. "Caño Dorado? Where the hell is that?"

"It's not in one location. It's a floating outpost, literally. The researchers travel from place to place in the Amazon River basin, searching for undiscovered plants and analyzing their properties. They go up and down the Amazon and its tributaries, carrying their lab equipment in skiffs and canoes. Sometimes they're in Brazil, sometimes Peru or Colombia or Bolivia. And no one in Haven knows where they are, except me."

"Why you?"

"They're loyal to me. Mariela and all five of her assistants worked in my lab at one time or another. And they're all women. That's why I could trust them with the task of finding the formula for the catalyst. Sullivan couldn't spy on them."

"But he figured out a plan for getting the formula, didn't he? By attacking you in New York?"

Ariel finally raised her head and looked him in the eye. "Mariela took great pains to keep the formula secret. When she was ready to deliver it to me, she hired a courier, a professional who usually transports diamonds for international gem brokers. She traveled to Panama to meet him and wrote the formula in runes so the man wouldn't understand it. But Sullivan discovered that Hal and Richard and I were going to meet the courier in New York, at Grand Central Station. So he ordered his men to follow us to the rendezvous, but they didn't attack us there."

"Because Grand Central was too public?"

"Exactly. The Riflemen followed us and waited until we reached the hotel in Brooklyn. They knew I'd be more vulnerable there." She moved closer to John, leaning forward in her chair. "But they didn't count on you, John. You did much more than save my life. If Sullivan had taken the formula, he would've used the catalyst on every fetus he could get his hands on. And he would've stayed on this risky course until he destroyed all of us." She moved still closer. "So I'm grateful. You saved my family. Maybe the Council of Elders doesn't appreciate it, but I do."

Her face was just inches away. She was so close he could feel the warmth of her breath on his cheeks. He wanted to kiss her, and he had a strong feeling that Ariel wanted it, too. But John held himself back. Ariel had explained a lot of things, but she'd left out something important. "And now you want me to help you again? To prove my worth to the Elders?"

She nodded, keeping her eyes locked on his. "I'm trying to come up with my own plan. Trying to figure out a way to neutralize Sullivan without killing all his followers. But first I need some information from you."

She lowered her gaze, staring at his chest. "Well, to be more precise, I need some information from your body."

"My body?"

"I'd like to see how you react to the Fountain protein. I've tested it on Fury men, but never on an outsider."

John was surprised. His passionate feelings for Ariel swiftly dissipated. "What are you trying to find out?"

"I want to know how much protein is required to trigger the antiaging effects in your cells. You have the Upstart gene on your Y chromosome, but you don't have the Fountain gene on your X. So I'm guessing you'd need more protein than the average Fury male would, because you don't have any natural sources in your body. But it's hard to say exactly how much more you'd need."

Her tone of voice had changed. She was speaking so clinically now. John hated the sound of it. "And how will this information help you?"

"I'm not sure yet. But it could be useful."

This answer was unsatisfying. He looked at her carefully. "No, you're up to something. You're wondering what would happen if people in the outside world learned about your Fountain of Youth. Because if they hear it exists, they're all going to want it. Am I right?"

She gave a noncommittal shrug. "Maybe so. But you're jumping ahead. Right now I just want to collect some data. So will you help me?"

John backed away from her and rose to his feet. It wasn't that he didn't trust Ariel. He just didn't like being used this way. He started pacing back and forth, moving between the lab table and the shelves full of flasks. "This protein you want to inject into me, does it come from fetuses?"

"No, it comes from us, the Fury women. At my request, the Council of Elders ordered every woman in Haven to donate a pint of blood." She pointed at the refrigerator at the other end of the lab table. "Some of the donated blood is already in there. I'm going to extract the Fountain protein from that supply. It'll be enough to stop a male Fury from aging for about ten days. But I don't know how it'll affect you."

"How will you know if it works? Can you tell if I've stopped aging?"

"I'll take cell samples from various parts of your body. I'll look at them under the microscope and analyze their chemical composition. Fountain halts aging by accelerating the rate of cellular repair, and there's a distinctive chemical marker that'll show the rate. I should be able to tell if it's working in a day or two."

"Will there be any side effects? Anything dangerous? If Fountain counteracts the Upstart protein, won't it make me infertile?"

"Just temporarily. It'll probably lower your sperm count for a few days, but then you'll return to normal. There shouldn't be any side effects other than that."

John stopped pacing. He stood in front of the shelves, looking at the laboratory flasks instead of Ariel. He noticed she hadn't reminded him that his cooperation might help sway the Elders. Maybe she knew he didn't need a reminder. Or maybe she sensed that he didn't care how the council ruled on his case. Whether he lived or died wasn't important. His decision would be based on something else altogether.

He turned around and walked back to Ariel. A few long strands of red hair had escaped from her ponytail and hung in front of her pale forehead. Even though she was three hundred and seventy-three years old, she was still the most beautiful woman he'd ever seen. He'd sacrificed everything to help this woman, throwing away his whole past life in the process. How could he say no to her now?

He stopped in front of her chair. "When do you want to start this experiment? Today?"

"No, tomorrow morning. I need some time to purify enough protein."

"Okay, I'll do it. Just don't poison me, all right?"

In response, she jumped out of her seat and wrapped her arms around him. She clung to his shoulders, keeping her weight off her healing legs, and pressed her lips against his. After a moment of stunned paralysis, he gripped her waist and closed his eyes. Her lips tasted of salt and oranges. Just like before, when John had kissed her in that hotel room in Brooklyn, he felt like he was falling. The laboratory and everything in it disappeared, all the hundreds of flasks whirling out of sight.

The kiss went on and on. Then Ariel pulled back and smiled at him. "Thank you, John," she said. "Once again I'm in your debt."

The look on her face was so intoxicating that John leaned forward to kiss her again. But she let go of him and fell back to her chair.

"Sorry, not now. I have to get to work." She slid her chair to the other end of the lab table and opened the door to the refrigerator. Inside was a stack of pint-size plastic bags, each filled with dark red blood. "Conroy will be your escort for the afternoon. He should be waiting for you now by the elevator."

John frowned, unable to hide his disappointment. "I'd rather stay here."

She shook her head. "You have more to learn about Haven. Conroy will show you our recycling system and the geothermal plant."

Ariel reached into the refrigerator and pulled out one of the plastic bags. John waited a few seconds, then headed for the door. Before he got there, though, she called out to him. "Don't get the wrong idea."

He looked over his shoulder at her. "About what?"

"About why I kissed you. I wasn't rewarding you for saying yes. I did it because I wanted to."

She smiled at him again before turning away.

SIXTEEN

Agent Larson had met plenty of asshole bureaucrats during his sixteen years at the bureau, but for sheer plodding pomposity it was hard to beat Kent Halstead, deputy secretary of the Homeland Security Department. The silver-haired, impeccably dressed Washington official had been assigned to lead the search for John Rogers, but so far he hadn't brought much urgency to the task. After flying by chartered jet from D.C. to the Upper Peninsula, Halstead had spent most of his first day setting up his command post in the federal office building in Sault Sainte Marie, the largest town close to Mackinac Island. Finally, at 6:00 P.M. he summoned Larson to his new office and requested an update on the investigation.

Larson sat in an uncomfortable chair while Halstead studied three photographs spread across his desk. The first photo, which had appeared on the front page of the *Detroit Free Press* that morning, showed the *Ojibway* beached in a marsh just north of the Les Cheneaux islands. The second was the surveillance-camera shot of John Rogers on the White Star Ferry pier, and the third was the image retrieved from Van's camera chip. Halstead spent the most time staring at this last photograph. He scrutinized it from every angle, first squinting at Rogers's caramel-colored face and then examining the bearded Amish men beside him.

"Where was this photo taken?" he asked.

Larson knew how to handle bureaucrats like Halstead. The most important thing was to speak with utmost confidence. "According to my informant, it was taken just south of the Amish farm near Pickford."

"Is there any corroborating evidence for this? Does the photo have a GPS tag?"

"No, sir, unfortunately it doesn't."

Halstead tapped the photo with his index finger. "What about the people next to Rogers in this picture? Have you identified any of them?"

"Not yet, sir. When we visited the farm this afternoon, the men we spoke to claimed they didn't recognize any of the suspects. But I believe they were lying. There's a strong family resemblance between the men we saw on the farm and the men in this photo. Notice their reddish hair and beards. It's likely that the whole clan is involved in the drug operation."

The deputy secretary tilted his head and narrowed his eyes. It was an ugly, irritating, skeptical expression. "And what about the woman in the photo? Is she part of the clan too? She has red hair but she doesn't look Amish. No bonnet on her head, at least."

"My informant says she's Rogers's girlfriend. I'm guessing Rogers met her while doing business with her family. He must've persuaded her to give up some of the Amish traditions."

Halstead narrowed his eyes further. "You believe the Amish men let one of their daughters hook up with a meth dealer?"

Larson was starting to really hate this guy. He was the kind of bureaucrat who moved up in the ranks by shooting down everyone else. "Rogers is a violent character. He has a long association with one of the Disciples gangs in Philadelphia. His Amish partners are probably afraid of him."

"But according to the reports from the Philadelphia police, Rogers gave up the gang life." Halstead reached into the pocket of his expensive suit and pulled out a piece of paper covered with scribbled notes. "Yes, here it is. He left the Disciples back in 2004 and started working for an antigang project run by one of the local churches. And in 2011 his five-year-old daughter was killed in a drive-by shooting. A very sad story."

"Yes, sir, I saw those reports, too. But that church project shut down three years ago and Rogers has been unemployed ever since. We know he's back in the drug business because the Philadelphia police found a stash of methamphetamine in his apartment. And we have reason to believe he recently murdered one of his customers. The police also found Rogers's fingerprints on a knife that was used to kill a junkie in that city."

The deputy secretary still looked skeptical. His eyes were shit-brown slits. "But how do we know that the Amish are in business with Rogers? Besides the statements from your informant, do you have any evidence that there's actually a meth lab on that farm? What did you see when you visited the place?"

"Their security measures are suspiciously excessive. They have a twelve-foot-high fence surrounding the entire property, and a deep trench just outside the fence that would stop any vehicle from crashing through it. And the men refused to let us inspect their barns or farmhouses. They said it would be a violation of their privacy."

"Well, the Amish *are* very private, aren't they?" Halstead's voice had a sarcastic tone. "And the Mackinac County Sheriff told me that this is one of the oldest Amish communities in the Midwest. I find it hard to believe that they've suddenly started making methamphetamine, no matter how bad the farm economy is."

Larson shifted in his chair. He wanted to beat the crap out of this blueblood bastard. But instead he clenched his jaw and leaned across Halstead's desk. "I've done some checking around, sir. Even for the Amish, these people are reclusive. They have no contact whatsoever with the other Amish communities in the state. And they've made some unusual purchases over the years. I talked with some of the local companies that have done business with the farm. They say the community often buys big loads of building materials—pipes and cement and wire and steel beams. And yet there's no sign of new construction on the farm." He paused a moment to let these facts sink in. "The only logical conclusion is that they've built something underground. My informant says the meth lab beneath the farm is huge. And they're constantly expanding it."

Halstead raised his eyebrows. For the first time he seemed to be taking Larson seriously. But then he shook his head. "Sorry, but I'm not convinced. Your evidence isn't solid enough. And if you can't convince me, I doubt you'll find a judge who'll grant you a search warrant. We're talking about a religious community here. We can't set foot on that farm unless we're absolutely sure."

"Sir, I don't need a warrant yet." Larson looked the bastard in the eye.

"I just need some help with my surveillance efforts. I've positioned several agents just outside the fence, but they can't observe all the activity on the farm because it's so big. The farmhouses at the center of the property are more than half a mile from the fence, and my agents' view is obstructed by the cornfields and outbuildings." He leaned a little farther across the desk. "What I need is an aerial view of the farm, preferably from a high-altitude surveillance aircraft. I assume the Homeland Security Department has that capability?"

The deputy secretary gave him a cagey look. "Are you referring to our drone aircraft? The MQ-9 Reaper?"

Larson nodded. "I know your department uses them to keep an eye on the Canadian border. I'd like you to divert one of the Reapers a little farther south so it can observe the Amish farm. It needs to be in position by noon tomorrow."

"Why then?"

"My informant called me earlier this afternoon and said a significant event would occur on the farm at that time. He didn't specify the exact nature of this event, but he said we could collect evidence of criminal activity if we had aerial surveillance in place."

Halstead furrowed his brow. He seemed confused. "What do you think he means? Is he talking about a drug transaction? Is someone coming to the farm to purchase methamphetamine?"

"Possibly. I believe he was deliberately vague because he didn't want to incriminate himself. But his tips have always proved good in the past. And I know the cameras on those Reapers can take some pretty detailed pictures. With any luck, we'll observe something that'll convince a judge to issue the search warrant. Then we can raid the farm and arrest Rogers."

The deputy secretary lowered his head and studied the photos on his desk again. "And you're sure that Rogers will be there?"

"My agents are watching everyone that comes and goes. If he tries to leave the farm, we'll see it."

Halstead didn't say anything for a while. He just stared at the photos, his brow still furrowed, obviously trying to come to a decision. But Larson already knew what the bureaucrat would do. His superiors had ordered him to find John Rogers. It was a hijacking case, and Homeland Security took that kind of thing very seriously. And there was political pressure too. Tourism was important to northern Michigan, and Rogers had instigated a gunfight in one of the state's most beloved tourist spots. The governor's office wouldn't be happy until the man was either dead or in jail.

"All right," Halstead finally said. "I'll make the arrangements. You'll get your drone."

SEVENTEEN

After a phenomenally boring tour of the recycling system, the water treatment facility, and the geothermal plant, Conroy led John to one of Haven's mess halls for dinner. It was essentially a cafeteria, located on the top floor of a glass-fronted building near the center of the cavern. But it was much larger and fancier than any cafeteria John had ever seen.

He sat at a long table of beautiful dark wood, polished to a high shine by centuries of use. The meals were served on antique china plates, probably imported from England during the colonial days, and the food was excellent: thick rare steaks, sweet warm corn bread, and fresh vegetables from the farm above the cavern. The only problem was that John had no company. Conroy sat at the same table but several feet away. Although he kept a watchful eye on John as he ate, he didn't say a word. The Master of the Guardsmen was dutiful and humorless.

While John carved up his steak he surveyed the diners at the other tables. Most were female. There were four or five women for every man. What's more, the sexes didn't mingle. The men sat alone or in small groups, eating their meals in silence. With their long beards and Amish clothes, they looked gruff and depressed. The women, in contrast, gathered in large, boisterous parties. They told jokes and laughed and flounced in their long gowns. The largest group was about twenty feet to John's left. At least two dozen women sat around an enormous oval table loaded with wine bottles and goblets. Among them was Elder Margaret Fury, who sat quietly at the edge of the party. She didn't join in the laughter or conversation. Dressed in a crimson gown, she sipped wine from her goblet, alone in the midst of the crowd. John stared at her until she caught him looking. She shot him an ugly look, and he quickly turned away.

There were couples sitting at smaller tables here and there, but most were pairs of women. John saw only three mixed couples, and in each case the man appeared to be much older than the woman. They looked like fathers and daughters rather than husbands and wives. He watched one of the women cut a steak into small pieces for a man who seemed to be in his nineties. She looked like she was twenty-two, like all the other women in the room. John wondered how old she really was.

As he gazed at them, someone yelled, "How now, John!" behind him. He looked over his shoulder and saw Gower, one of the guards who'd escorted him through the woods yesterday. The young man's face was sweaty and cheerful behind his ragged red beard. He strode toward John's table, holding in each hand a pewter tankard topped with foam. "I've brought a peace offering!" he shouted. He set one of the tankards on the table beside John's plate. "You need some drink to quaff with your meat!"

It was beer. Some of the foam slid down the side of the tankard. "Uh, thank you," John said.

Several feet to his right, Conroy frowned mightily at Gower, but the younger guardsman didn't seem to notice. He'd clearly had a few beers already. He pointed at the chair beside John's. "May I join you, sir? I've had my supper but I'm not ready for bed yet."

John shrugged. "Sure, why not?"

With a huge smile, Gower pulled out the chair and sat down. Then he lifted his own tankard high in the air. "To your health, John Rogers! May the Council of Elders rule in your favor and welcome you into the bosom of our family!"

"I'll drink to that." John picked up his tankard and clanked it against Gower's. "Cheers."

Gower needed no encouragement. He tilted his tankard and drank greedily. John followed suit but stopped at once. The beer was different. It was rich and smoky and bittersweet. He took a big gulp, smiling as he swallowed. It was the best beer he'd ever tasted. "Wow. This is great."

"You like our ale?" Gower wiped his mouth on the sleeve of his white shirt.

"Yeah, it's fantastic."

"I will convey your compliments to Clarissa, our brewer. She's brewed our ale the same way for three hundred years, but we never seem to tire of it."

John took another gulp. "It sure beats Budweiser."

Gower nodded vigorously. "Aye, I know that name! One of our Rangers brought back a can of Budweiser from his last assignment, and we all took a sip. It was horrid swill! How can you bear to drink it?"

John laughed. It was the first time he'd laughed since coming to Haven. "You get used to it, I guess."

Gower laughed too, very loudly. John glanced at Conroy, who'd turned away from them, scowling at the food on his plate. The guy had a seriously big stick up his ass. At least Gower had a sense of humor.

"Let me ask you a question," John said. He pointed at Gower's shirt and suspenders. "Why do you dress like that even when you're not outside? I mean, you don't have to pretend to be Amish when you're down here, do you?"

Gower thought it over for a moment, taking another drink before answering. "It's a habit, I suppose. And it would be a nuisance to change clothes every time we went outside, don't you agree?"

"The women wear different clothes when they're down here."

"Well, you know how it is." Gower gestured with his tankard at the party of women seated around the oval table. "They like to dress up. Our older women wear dour black dresses, because those were popular in the Puritan times. The women born in the nineteenth century prefer the hoop skirts and such." He leaned closer to John and lowered his voice. "And the youngest ones wear pants or teeny-tiny skirts. I like those the best, don't you?"

John nodded, taking another sip of beer. "But Ariel's one of the older ones, right? And she wears modern clothes."

"Lily is different because she's a Ranger. She's often on assignment in the outside world, so she takes note of the fashions there." His voice grew reverent as he talked about Ariel. "Some of the other women ask her to bring back clothes for them. When she returns to Haven, her bags are full of skirts and shoes."

He laughed again, but John didn't join in this time. He saw Margaret Fury drink the last of her wine and leave the dining room, wobbling and limping. The women who remained at the table started singing a drinking song. It sounded old-fashioned, like something Shakespeare would've sung.

"But it's obvious they're not dressing up to attract men," John noted. "The men and women here, they hardly pay attention to each other."

Gower's face turned serious. "Aye, 'tis troubling. I was discussing this very subject with Archibald this morning. He blames our women, but it's not easy for them, either. Look over there." He pointed at the woman who was feeding small pieces of steak to the ninety-year-old man. "That's my half sister Viola and her husband Oliver. They grew up together and were married when they were both twenty. And now she has to watch him die."

John took a closer look at them. Viola was stunning and Oliver was a wreck. He could barely keep his eyes open while she fed him. "Well, what's the alternative? Would your women rather spend their lives alone?"

"Nay, you have to understand: no one is ever truly alone in Haven. We're a tightly bound family. We do everything together." Gower gestured at the pairs of women scattered across the dining room. "And some women are content to find partners of their own gender. They usually choose someone born close to their own time. It feels more comfortable that way, I suppose."

"What about the men? They partner with each other, too?"

"Aye, certainly. But not all of us." He took another swig of beer and pointed at himself. "Consider me, for example. I am a tragic figure. I pine hopelessly for a woman I've never spoken to."

John could see where this was going. Gower wanted to talk about Ariel. Maybe he wanted some advice on how to approach her. John had no interest in that kind of conversation, so he decided to change the subject. "Would things change if the men didn't age, either? Would that make your situation better?"

Gower hesitated, his eyes darting from side to side. He moved still closer to John and lowered his voice. "Are you speaking of the Fountain remedy that Sullivan is seeking?"

THE FURIES + 169

John nodded. "Ariel told me about it. And about all the problems with it." He lowered his own voice. "But what if there was an easier way to make the medicine? If the men could stop aging, wouldn't they be on more equal terms with the women?"

"That's a difficult question." Gower frowned. "We've lived in this manner for so long, it's hard to imagine different circumstances. And even if the medicine were freely available, I don't know how many men would take advantage of it."

"Wouldn't all of them? Who wouldn't want eternal youth?"

"It's not an unmixed blessing, John." He pointed again at his half sister, who was dabbing her husband's lips with a napkin. "In fact, some of our women detest their longevity. They find the endless prospect so unbearable that they cut their lives short in only their tenth or eleventh decade."

"They commit suicide?"

"Indeed. But that's not the worst of it." Gower tipped back his tankard and finished off his beer. But his intoxication had ebbed. Now he looked grim and sober. "Our oldest women are able to shoulder the burden of the centuries because they dedicate their lives to a higher purpose. Lily is a perfect example of this. She works tirelessly to benefit Haven and to steer the outside world toward a better future. But some women fail to muster that dedication. And then terrible things can happen."

"What do you mean?"

Gower looked down at the table for several seconds, grimacing. Then he turned to Conroy, who was joylessly devouring a lemon tart. "Sir, may I escort the paramour to the privy? Both of us need to relieve ourselves."

Conroy seemed annoyed at the interruption. He scowled and gave a dismissive wave. "Aye, go ahead."

Gower stood up and gripped John's elbow. "Come. I wish to show you something."

He took John to Haven's deepest corner. After leaving the mess hall, they followed a path to the far end of the cavern, where a sulfurous spring flowed out of the rocky ground near the geothermal plant. Warm, greenish water swirled in a bubbling pool and flowed into crevices in the cavern's jagged wall. Carved into the wall near the crevices was an entrance to a tunnel, about ten feet wide and eight feet high. Gower pointed at it. "We're just in time," he said. "The visiting hours are almost over."

John peered into the tunnel. The entrance was dimly lit and the corridor beyond looked deserted. "Visiting hours? Is this a hospital?"

"Aye, it's a hospital. But it's not our primary medical facility." Gower furrowed his brow, searching for the right words. "This hospital is for special cases only."

They stepped into the tunnel. Its floor was paved with big granite blocks, their surfaces worn smooth and glossy, and the walls were decorated with intricate stone carvings of bears and wolves and deer. John was amazed by their beauty. "This place looks old," he noted. "Older than the rest of Haven."

Gower nodded. "When the Furies started dwelling down here, they carved their first underground homes out of the cavern's many tunnels and burrows. It was only later that they built the Pyramid and the other structures on the cavern's floor."

After about ten yards the tunnel curved to the right, leading to a large hushed antechamber with dark stone walls. On the far side of the room were twenty wooden doors, arranged in ten side-by-side pairs. In each pair, the door on the left was marked with the word VIEWING and the door on the right with the word PATIENT. A petite woman in a severe black dress sat behind an antique desk in the middle of the antechamber, guarding access to all the doors. She stared at John for a few seconds, her expression a mix of curiosity and disdain. Then she looked at Gower. Her face, though young and pretty, was as severe as her dress.

"Good evening." Her voice was frosty. "It's been a while, Gower. I haven't seen you in weeks."

Gower's face reddened. He lowered his head, looking sheepish. "I apologize, Constance. My duties with the Guardsmen have kept me away."

"I'm afraid you can't visit Octavia now. It's almost bedtime and I don't want to risk upsetting her at this hour. But you can view her if you wish." Constance pointed at John but kept her eyes on Gower. "This is Lily's paramour, is it not?"

John wasn't surprised by the question. Haven was the size of a small town, so news traveled quickly here. And everyone noticed an unfamiliar face.

"Aye, he's under my watch," Gower replied. This was technically true, although Conroy was probably wondering by now why they were spending so much time in the bathroom.

"May I ask why you've brought the outsider with you?"

Gower shifted his weight from foot to foot, clearly uncomfortable. "It's part of his education in our ways. He must see all of Haven, from top to bottom. Can he join me in the viewing room?"

Constance frowned. "She's your grandmother. Do you truly want him to see her?"

Gower nodded but didn't say anything. Constance kept them waiting for a few more seconds. Then she stood up and led them toward the pair of doors directly behind her desk. She opened the left door, the one marked VIEWING. "I'll give you five minutes. I need to collect the remains of her dinner before turning out the lights. Octavia hasn't been eating well lately."

She held the door open as Gower and John filed into the room. Then she shut it, plunging them into near-darkness. The room was smaller than John expected. It was about the size of a walk-in closet, only eight feet long and four feet wide. It was also empty. There weren't even any chairs. The wall on the left was bare, but the one on the right had a large picture window with tinted glass. After a couple of seconds of bewilderment, John realized it was a one-way mirror. This cramped space was like a viewing room at a police station, a place where cops could watch an inter-rogation or a lineup of suspects without being observed themselves. But when John looked through the tinted glass he saw a padded cell. That, he realized, was the PATIENT room.

He didn't see the patient at first. The room had a low bed, unmade, and on the mattress were two pillows and a heap of tangled sheets and blan-kets. Near the foot of the bed, a tablecloth was spread across the padded floor. The patient's dinner was on the tablecloth, but there were no plates or silverware. Three slices of buttered toast, a sectioned orange, and several small pieces of hamburger meat lay on a washable place mat at the center of the tablecloth. There were also two paper cups, one filled with milk and the other with water. But the meal appeared to be untouched. Octavia, wherever she was, hadn't eaten a bite.

Then John saw the heap of blankets and sheets move across the bed, disturbed by something stirring underneath them. The tangled bedding slid to the side, exposing a tall pale woman in a blue nightgown, lying on her back. She was solidly built, with broad shoulders and wide hips, but her face was like a child's. Her eyes were closed and her bright red hair was long and tousled. She murmured in her sleep, and the sound was amplified by a pair of loudspeakers hanging on the wall above the one-way mirror.

John was startled but managed to stay silent. He turned to Gower and gave him a questioning look, pointing first at the meal on the floor and then at the woman on the bed.

"Don't worry," Gower said. "You can talk here. This room is sound-proofed. She can't hear us, but we can hear her through the speakers."

"That's your grandmother?"

"Aye. My mother was born in Germany almost six hundred years ago, but Grandmother Octavia is much older. In fact, she's the oldest woman in Haven."

"I thought Elizabeth was the oldest. Isn't that why she's the Chief Elder?"

"Nay, my grandmother is a thousand years older. Octavia served on the Council of Elders for three centuries, but after the Burning Times she had to relinquish her seat." Gower frowned. "The massacres were too great a shock for her. She lost all of her daughters except for Claudia, my mother."

"And what—"

Before John could pose the question, the sound of someone knocking on the door boomed out of the loudspeakers. Then he heard the voice of Constance the nurse. "Octavia? I'm coming in."

The tall woman awoke instantly. She leaped out of bed and backed up against the padded wall, moving as far away from the door as possible. Her hands were shaking. "Nay!" she screamed. "Stay out!"

The door opened and Constance stepped into the room. Except now the petite nurse wore a white surgical mask over her face. "Calm yourself, dear. It's just me."

"Murderer! *Murderer!*" Octavia turned her head left and right, frantically looking for an exit.

"Look at me, please." Constance raised her hands above her head. "I bear no weapons. And I'm wearing the mask, as you requested. It's impossible for me to contaminate you."

"Go away, I beg thee! Come no closer!"

Lowering her hands, Constance pointed at the untouched meal on the floor. "You know you can't go on like this. If you want to live, you have to eat."

Octavia went into a crouch, sliding down to the floor. Then she buried her face in her hands and started to weep. "Oh, I'm dying, I'm dying." Her voice was lower now, muffled. "You're trying to poison me. You want me dead."

"Please, dear, listen to reason. Don't you remember what I did when I delivered your dinner? I ate a piece of your meat and a section of your orange. Now do I look poisoned to you?"

"You want me dead. You want me dead."

The poor woman cried softly. She curled her body into a tight ball and shook with sobs. She repeated "You want me dead" several more times, and then she started babbling something John couldn't make out. After a while he realized she was speaking a foreign language. He couldn't understand the words, but their sound was familiar.

Constance let out a sigh. She knelt on the padded floor and began cleaning up the untouched dinner.

Gower turned to John. Seeing his grandmother in this state had clearly upset him, but he kept his voice steady. "Octavia went mad a century ago. Her fear of death grew so strong, it warped her mind."

John was confused. "Why is she afraid? She's going to stay young forever."

"Aye, but she can still die in an accident. The chance of that happening in any year is less than one in a thousand, but because Octavia has lived for more than two thousand years, she fears that the odds have turned against her. So she never leaves her room, never handles anything sharp. And she constantly worries about poison."

"And you say she's been like this for a hundred years?"

"Sometimes she's a little better, and oftentimes she's worse. She refuses to eat until she makes herself sick. Then the nurses have to sedate her and feed her intravenously. This happens month after month, in a nightmarish cycle. And Octavia isn't the only one who suffers from this malady. There are nine other women in this hospital who have similar afflictions. Most of them are over the age of three hundred, but the madness can strike women as young as a hundred and fifty."

By this point Constance had finished cleaning up. She looked again at Octavia, still curled up on the floor. Then she left the room.

At the same time, John took a step away from the one-way mirror. He was anxious to get out of there. "I'm sorry about your grandmother," he told Gower. "And I see your point. I wouldn't want to live like that."

"Nor I." Gower let out a long whoosh of breath and turned toward the door. "Eternal youth can all too easily become eternal suffering."

As they headed out of the room, John could still hear Octavia babbling. It suddenly occurred to him why her foreign words sounded familiar.

John had heard them before, in South Philly of all places. On the street corners where the aging wiseguys bullshitted with each other in their native tongue. "Is she speaking Italian?" he asked.

Gower shook his head. "Nay, not Italian. But your guess is close. She's speaking her first language, Latin."

"Latin?"

"She was born during the reign of Octavius, the first Roman emperor. That's who she was named after."

Then Gower opened the door and they left the viewing room.

On their way back to the mess hall John spotted Archibald, the other young guardsman who'd escorted him through the woods to Haven. He was striding across the cavern's floor in the opposite direction, with a backpack slung over his shoulder. Gower called out to him, but Archibald didn't stop. He turned away from them and took a different path, heading for the geothermal plant.

Conroy was furious by the time they returned to the dining room. Gower invented a rather complicated excuse, saying that one of the toilets in the bathroom had overflowed, forcing him to take John to his quarters so they could clean their soiled shoes, but Conroy didn't want to hear it. He took custody of John and immediately escorted him back to his luxurious prison cell. When Conroy opened the door to the room, though, he froze in the doorway, his hand on the knob. Sitting on the freshly made bed was Elder Margaret Fury. She sat on the edge of the mattress with her hands in her lap and the folds of her crimson gown carefully draped over her legs. She looked regal, as if she were posing for an official portrait.

"Milady!" Conroy exclaimed. "What are you doing here?"

There was no reaction on Margaret's pale, plump face. She sat absolutely still. "I need to have a private talk with Lily's paramour. Could you please stand outside the door until we're finished?"

The Adam's apple in Conroy's throat bobbed up and down. He was clearly flustered, but he couldn't find any reason to protest. "Aye, milady," he muttered. "Please call for me if you require my help." He ushered John into the room, then retreated as gracefully as he could, shutting the door as he left.

Margaret relaxed a bit. She took a deep breath, and her bosom heaved within the bodice of her gown. "Come closer, John. I can barely see you over there."

John stepped toward the bed, stopping about a yard away. He needed to be careful. This was one of the three women who held his fate in their hands. "What do you want to talk about?"

"How was your first day in Haven? Did Lily take you to see Cordelia?"

He nodded. "Yeah, it was interesting. Like a history lesson."

"Our sister Delia is like a faucet. Most of the time she's closed tight and nothing comes out of her. But if she deigns to open up, 'tis like a deluge." Margaret looked up at him and smiled, but it was a cunning smile, full of strategy. "And what of the laboratories? Did Lily take you to see them, too?"

"Just her own lab. Molecular genetics, I think it was called."

"I don't know if you realize it, but that was a rare privilege. Lily has become intensely secretive about her work. She's banished all her assistants from her laboratory and put a lock on the door for good measure." She grimaced for an instant, then smiled again. "I assume she explained her research to you? The development of the catalyst that will produce Fountain protein from fetal tissue?"

John's guard went up. He had to be especially careful now. "Yeah, she talked about that stuff, but I'm not big on science. I didn't really get it."

Margaret raised an eyebrow. Her smile hardened. "Let's not play games with each other, John. You're a smart man, and I think you know how fraught our situation is. This is the most serious threat our family has faced since coming to America. So I won't tolerate any lies."

"Whoa, hold on." John held out his hands like a traffic cop. "First of all, I'm not lying. Second, I—"

"Did you know that the guardsmen on our farm received a visit today from the Federal Bureau of Investigation? A special agent named Michael Larson showed them your photograph. Our guardsmen denied any knowledge of you, of course, but the agent is sure to come back. I suspect that Sullivan is whispering in his ear. He's used similar tactics in the past few months, encouraging the local constables to pursue our Rangers and guardsmen."

John took a step backward. This was disturbing news. "Why are they looking for me? Because of the ferryboat?"

She nodded. "Aye, that incident has become the chief topic of the state's newspapers. This investigation puts us in a difficult position. The federal agents are already outside our fence, watching as much of the farm as they can. We want them to leave, but we can't simply hand you over to the FBI. Once you're in their custody, you'll tell them everything you know about us. So we have only one reasonable option, which is to kill you and place your corpse so far from Haven that no one will connect the two. It's the only way we can avoid further scrutiny."

He clenched his hands. She was threatening him. "So why haven't you killed me yet? I'm sure Conroy would be happy to do the job."

"Oh, it's definitely under consideration. But my sister Elizabeth and I are prudent leaders. Before we take any irreversible steps, we need to determine if you could be useful to us in other ways. That's why I came to see you tonight."

"And is that why you're asking about Ariel's research? You want me to spy on her?"

"Now that Lily knows the formula for the catalyst, it's her duty to share it with the council. But she has refused to do so. Because she leads our research efforts she feels entitled to keep this information from us. Elizabeth and I have tried to reason with her since she returned to Haven yesterday, but Cordelia has taken Lily's side, and the girl has supporters among the researchers and Rangers." Margaret frowned. "So we've been forced to consider other measures."

John studied her carefully. She was hiding something, no doubt about it. "Why do you want the formula so badly?"

Her frown deepened. A pair of vertical lines appeared above the bridge of her nose. "I'm not going to explain our reasons to you, paramour. All you need to know is that your life hangs in the balance. Elizabeth and I control the council. We can overrule Cordelia and order your execution."

"Do you want the formula so you can hand it over to Sullivan?" He mentioned this possibility only because he couldn't think of anything else. "Are you going to surrender to him?"

"Surrender?" Margaret's voice fell so low he could barely hear it.

"Yeah, maybe you've decided to give in to his demands. Maybe you think working with him is less dangerous than fighting him."

Margaret slowly rose from the bed. Wincing, she limped toward John and pointed a trembling finger at his face. "That bastard just killed two of my sons. You saw it happen, you saw his men slaughter Hal and Richard. Do you think I could ever work with such a man?"

"I don't—"

"He murdered one of my daughters as well. Three of my girls served in the Rangers, in the Transport squadron that flies our researchers to the tropics. Six months ago Sullivan's men ambushed their plane at the St. Ignace airfield. They fired their carbines at the aircraft, then rode off on their motorcycles. My Veronica was unhurt, but the Riflemen wounded my Gwendolyn. And they shot my Gilda in the heart."

Her whole body shook with anger now, quivering inside her crimson gown. But John was angry, too. He was tired of being threatened. "Look, I'm sorry about what happened to you, but I had nothing to do with it. The only reason I'm here is because I wanted to help Ariel. She's the one I care about, so I'm not gonna start spying on her."

Margaret scowled, scrunching her plump cheeks. "How long were you in bed with her before Sullivan attacked? Ten minutes? Five? And you value those minutes more than your life?"

John forced himself to remain calm. He wasn't going to give her the satisfaction of seeing him fly off the handle. He smiled and leaned forward, lowering his face until it was only a few inches from hers. "We have a saying in Philadelphia: I think you've mistaken me for someone who gives a shit."

Her green eyes flashed hatred. For a second he thought she was going to haul off and slug him. But instead she pulled away from him and sneered. "Then you're a fool. And so is your little harlot. You'll both be in Hades before the week is over." She abruptly turned toward the door. "Conroy! I'm ready!"

The guardsman opened the door instantly, as if he'd been clutching the knob ever since he closed it. Margaret marched out of the room without looking back. Then Conroy slammed the door shut and locked John inside.

EIGHTEEN

Archibald crouched beside a massive pipe rising from the floor of the geo-thermal plant. This section of the plant was usually deserted at night, and he was hidden by the crisscrossing maze of smaller pipes that surrounded the massive vertical one. But he was still terrified that someone would see him.

Getting down on his hands and knees, he rapped his knuckles on the linoleum floor tiles around the base of the pipe, which was more than five feet in diameter. He crawled around the thing twice but couldn't find the loose tile that Sullivan had assured him would be there. Sweat streamed down his neck and soaked the back of his shirt. Waves of heat radiated from the pipe, warming the floor so much it scorched his palms. He could hardly think because of all the noise coming from within the pipe, the thunderous gushing of high-pressure steam.

He couldn't do this. He was starting to panic. He closed his eyes and tried to calm himself by picturing something pleasant, but all he could see were Sullivan's fingernails, caked with filth.

Archibald took a deep breath. Pushing Sullivan out of his mind, he opened his eyes and stared at the gray pipe in front of him. He didn't know all the technical details of the geothermal plant, but he had a basic understanding. He was looking at the uppermost part of the main intake pipe, which descended six thousand feet below Haven. In those crystalline depths, a plume of magma extended from beneath the earth's crust and heated an underground reservoir, creating vast pockets of steam. The intake pipe was like a long chimney, allowing the steam to surge upward. After its mile-long ascent, the rushing vapor turned the turbines of the geothermal plant, generating enough power to light a city. Then the plant's machinery cooled and condensed the steam, turning it back to water. Some of this water was used for Haven's needs, but most was injected back into the depths of the earth. Because the water cycled back and forth between Haven and the deep reservoir, the entire operation was invisible from aboveground. But Archibald was going to break that seamless cycle.

Feeling a bit calmer, he resumed his inspection of the floor. After another minute he finally discovered the loose tile and pried it up, exposing a foot-deep hole adjacent to the pipe. He didn't know who'd dug the hole—Sullivan wouldn't reveal the names of his other spies—but the fellow had done an admirable job. The device in Archibald's backpack fit the hidden space perfectly. He set the device's timer and put the tile back into place. Then he grabbed his empty backpack, crawled out of the maze of pipes, and walked away. It was that simple.

But as he strode past the machinery in the turbine room and headed for the exit, he began to panic again. There were other things Sullivan had refused to tell him. Archibald didn't know how powerful the explosive device was, or how much damage it would cause. If people were working in that section of the plant when the device exploded, would they be injured? Or killed? He had no idea. His anxiety intensified, tightening his throat and twisting his stomach. And then, just as he left the turbine room and approached the pair of swinging doors at the plant's exit, he heard footsteps behind him. He glanced over his shoulder and saw Claudia Fury—Gower's mother, the director of the geothermal plant! She was less than six feet away.

He thought about running, but what good would that do? If she called for the guards, they'd apprehend him before he could escape from Haven. No, it would be better to feign innocence. If Claudia asked him why he'd come to the plant, he'd simply give her a good reason. Earlier that evening, in fact, he'd prepared several believable excuses. But at the moment he couldn't recall any of them. Panic had erased everything in his head. He stopped in his tracks, frantically trying to remember.

Then Claudia walked right past. She didn't even look at him. She stepped through the swinging exit doors and turned left, briskly striding away. Archibald hung back for a few seconds, then followed her outside. She was heading for the old asylum at the far end of the cavern, where the madwomen lived. In all likelihood, she was going to see Octavia, her mother. Although visiting hours were long over, the nurses made exceptions for high officials like Claudia.

Archibald frowned. He should've been relieved but instead he was furious. The stupid woman hadn't noticed him. Of if she had, she'd immediately dismissed him as inconsequential. Like most of Haven's women, she either ignored the community's men or treated them as servants. They were too short-lived to be taken seriously.

He stared at Claudia until she entered the asylum. *Your world is about to change, woman*, he thought. *And it will happen at exactly noon tomorrow.*

NINETEEN

John was back in Ariel's laboratory the next morning, lying on a gurney she'd parked beside one of the lab tables. He lay faceup with his shirt unbuttoned and watched her scurry from one table to another, collecting everything she needed for the test. She didn't need to use her crutches anymore. She wasn't even limping. Her legs appeared to be fully healed.

After she readied all her equipment, she hooked him up to an EKG machine so she could monitor his heart rate. While she connected the machine's wiring to half a dozen suction cups pressed to John's chest, he told her about his conversation with Margaret Fury the night before. To his surprise, Ariel seemed unconcerned about Margaret's threats. She rolled her eyes when John mentioned the "little harlot" comment.

"Margaret is hardly one to talk. She has five daughters in Haven and another two serving in the Rangers." She positioned another suction cup on his breastbone and pressed it down firmly. "And she would've had far more if she hadn't joined the council. Our Elders are forbidden from venturing outside Haven to seek paramours."

John was puzzled. "Then how did Margaret give birth to Hal and Richard?"

"She used artificial insemination. One of her daughters in the Rangers obtained some donor sperm from a fertility clinic and brought it back to Haven." Ariel stuck the last suction cup on John's chest, then turned on the EKG machine. "Mother also used donor sperm to become pregnant with Basil. Frankly, that's one of the reasons why I refused to consider artificial insemination for myself." She frowned, probably thinking of Sullivan again. Then the screen on the electrocardiograph came to life, displaying a green line that spiked with each of John's heartbeats. She cheered up as she looked at it. "There, you're all set. Now I'll know if Fountain puts any stress on your metabolism."

She stepped toward the lab table and picked up a vial full of yellowish fluid. This was the Fountain protein she'd painstakingly extracted from the pints of blood donated by Haven's women. John squirmed a bit as she opened the vial and dipped the needle of a syringe into the fluid. He felt an urge to change the subject. "Can we get back to Margaret for a second? I don't think you're taking her seriously enough. She really hates you."

Ariel kept her eyes on the syringe. She pulled up the plunger, slowly drawing the yellowish fluid into the tube. "That's nothing new. Margaret's been sniping at me for over a hundred years."

"She said you'd be dead within a week. I think that's a little more serious than 'sniping.'"

"How is she going to kill me? She doesn't even know how to fire a gun." Ariel shook her head. "You have to understand, John, we've been having the same arguments for centuries. For the past two hundred years I've told Mother and Margaret that our family needs to become more democratic. But they don't want to change. They think we're in a never-ending war with the outside world, so we have to run our community under martial law, forever."

"But now you really *are* at war. You're in a civil war against Sullivan, and the Elders are getting desperate. At least that's the way it looks to me."

She finished filling the syringe. Holding it with the needle pointed upward, she flicked her index finger against the tube and pushed the plunger a tiny fraction to remove any bubbles from the fluid. Then she stepped toward John. "You're right, this is a crisis. And Mother wants to control everything, including the formula for the catalyst, because that's the way she always handled crises in the past." Ariel leaned over his gurney and gently tapped the underside of his forearm, searching for a suitable vein. "But a crisis can also be an opportunity. If we handle the situation carefully enough, we can take a step forward. Our family may finally be able to emerge from hiding."

Lifting her chin, she stopped inspecting the veins in his forearm and looked him in the eye. Her cheeks were flushed, pinkish at the center. She was breathing fast, as if she were winded from talking too much. And her eyes were wild with hope. Their irises were a brighter green than John remembered, shining like crystals under the lab's fluorescent lights.

Then she lowered her head and slipped the needle into one of his veins.

She pushed the plunger into the syringe, ever so slowly. John felt a burning sensation in the crook of his arm and then a cool swelling as the yellowish fluid flowed into him. Ariel narrowed her eyes and opened her mouth, her whole body focused on the task, and the silence in the lab was so absolute that John could hear her breath whistling between her parted lips.

It took her almost half a minute to complete the injection. Then she removed the needle from his arm and set the empty syringe on the lab table. "Just relax now. Your circulatory system will distribute the protein to all of your cells. When I injected Sullivan, he said he felt no effects at all during the first half hour. But he could've been lying, of course."

John still felt the coolness in his arm but it was starting to fade. While Ariel turned to the EKG machine and stared at the spiking green line, he took a deep breath and lay back on the gurney. It was impossible to relax, though. His mind was racing. "So you're planning to reveal the existence of Haven?"

She grabbed a nearby chair and moved it next to the gurney. Then she sat down beside him. "Let's talk about something else, all right?"

"But that's why you're doing this test on me, isn't it? You want to know if Fountain will stop outsiders from aging. That's the first question people will ask after they learn about your family, and you want to be able to answer it."

Ariel took a deep breath. "It's true, I want to be ready. Right now, though, I'm just laying the groundwork. It may take decades to convince the Council of Elders to take this step. Mother and Margaret are opposed to even discussing the idea." She leaned closer to him. "But please, John, let's drop the subject for now. This conversation is raising your heart rate and interfering with the experiment. The body releases hormones in response to stress, and they can have significant effects on your metabo-lism. So let's talk about something that's cheerful and stress-free."

"Stress-free?" John frowned. "You want to talk about the weather?"

"No, that wouldn't be very interesting. The weather in Haven is always the same. How about sports? Do you like baseball?"

"Seriously? You follow baseball?"

"Well, not so much now. But about ninety years ago I got very inter-ested in it. I had to go to New York several times in the 1920s because Cordelia had predicted an economic depression, and I was assigned to sell some of our family's financial interests. And whenever I went there I tried to catch a Yankees game so I could watch Ruth and Gehrig play."

He looked at her carefully. "You're joking, right?"

"Not at all. They were marvelous. I saw Gehrig hit a three-run homer in the second game of the 1928 World Series. It was a big, big hit. The ball landed in the centerfield bleachers."

She wasn't joking. She'd been there. John tried to picture her in the stands of Yankee Stadium, in the background of one of those herky-jerky, black-and-white newsreels from nearly a century ago. Then he remembered what Cordelia Fury had said about Ariel's past. "What about farther back? Didn't Cordelia say you helped America win the Revolutionary War?"

Ariel rolled her eyes again. "I love Aunt Delia, but sometimes she exag-gerates. I provided some assistance to the Continental Army during the Battle of Brooklyn. And immediately afterwards."

"I didn't even know there was a battle in Brooklyn."

"I was thinking of it the other night, actually, when we were in Bush-wick. Most of the fighting took place just a few miles away. In the area where Prospect Park and Green-Wood Cemetery are now."

"So were you in the infantry? Firing a musket?"

She laughed. It was nice to hear her laugh again. John remembered the first time he'd heard that high, sweet chord of delight, when Ariel stepped into the bar in Greenwich Village. "No, those guns were awful. Every time you pulled the trigger you expected the thing to blow up in your hands." She shook her head. "I stayed away from the front lines. I worked as a washerwoman instead."

"A washerwoman? Don't tell me you cleaned General Washington's clothes."

"No, I worked for General Howe. He commanded the British army that was ordered to defeat Washington and occupy New York. After they landed in Staten Island, the general's aide-de-camp hired some local women to launder the uniforms of the top officers. I slipped into the work crew."

John smiled. He clasped his hands behind his head and started to relax. This was fascinating. "Okay, let me guess. You put itching powder in the general's underwear."

"Believe me, I thought about it. Howe was an arrogant fool. But I kept my head down and spent a lot of time in the officers' tents, shining their boots while they talked strategy. After a few weeks I learned that Howe was planning to outflank the Continental Army by sending the British troops through Brooklyn. So I stole a rowboat and went to Manhattan to warn General Washington."

"And that saved the day? We won the war because you tipped him off?"

Ariel made a face. "I'm amazed that you know so little of your country's history, John. Are the schools in Philadelphia that bad?"

"I don't know. I stopping going to school after seventh grade."

"All right, I'll try to fill the gaps in your education. The Battle of Brooklyn was a disaster for the Americans. It almost ended the Revolution."

"What went wrong?" John thought it over for a second. "Washington didn't believe you?"

"Exactly. He received me politely enough and listened to my report, but he was convinced that the British maneuvers in Brooklyn were a diversion. He thought the main attack would target Manhattan. So he kept most of his troops there and sent only a few thousand men across the East River." She scowled. "It was stupid. He was already outnumbered, and then he split his army in two. Howe shattered the Americans in Brooklyn and sent them running back to the river. When I saw Washington again in Brooklyn Heights, he was panic-stricken. He had no idea what to do."

"Wait a second. You saw him again?"

"I had more information for him. Howe, like the fool he was, had decided to halt his advance. That gave Washington some breathing room. He was thinking of making a stand at Brooklyn Heights, but I told him to load his men onto every available boat and retreat to Manhattan. And this time, thank heaven, he took my advice."

John stared at her, amazed. She was telling the story as if it had happened yesterday. "It must've been a real kick in the pants for him, taking advice from a washerwoman."

"Yes, but at heart he was a humble man. He learned from his mistakes.

After Brooklyn, he became a master at retreat. He launched raids to harass the British, but he hid his army in the hills and avoided open battle with Howe. That's how he won the war." She smiled at the memory. "I saw him one more time, at Valley Forge, and he gave me a bright yellow petticoat as a present. It was lovely."

Ariel tilted her head slightly and stared into space. She seemed to be lost in a pleasant reverie. Then she turned back to John and scrutinized his body, her eyes roving across his face and torso. "How do you feel now? Are you dizzy? Nauseous?"

John shook his head. "I feel fine." He sat up and flexed his arms and legs. "No changes so far."

"It's still early. It'll take a while for the Fountain protein to enter your cells. And the first proteins that pass through the cell membranes will be immobilized by the proteins produced by your Upstart gene. The cellular concentration of Fountain has to rise above a critical level before it can have any effect. We may have to wait another ten or twenty minutes." She glanced at the clock on the wall, which said it was ten minutes before noon. Then she placed a hand on John's shoulder. "In the meantime, you better lie down. You might get light-headed, and I don't want you to fall off the gurney."

Gently but firmly, she pushed him down. Her hand was warm. She kept it on his shoulder even after he was lying down flat. John wanted her to keep it there. He smiled at her. "I don't think Cordelia was exaggerating. You did help us win the war. I mean, who knows what would've happened if you hadn't knocked some sense into Washington? We could all be English colonists still."

But she didn't smile back at him. Her face turned serious. "It had to be done. Cordelia was insistent. And history proved her right only a century and a half later. If it wasn't for the United States, the Nazis would've defeated England and Russia, and the Japanese Empire would've conquered all of Asia. The whole world would've descended into nightmare." She lifted her hand from John's shoulder. "But there was a price to be paid. A very high price."

"What do you mean?"

"We knew that the new country would devastate the Native Americans. They'd already been ravaged by plagues and war before the Revolution, but they still had a chance to recover. And the English were trying to help them by discouraging the colonists from settling west of the Appala chians. Over time, the Native American tribes could've unified and established their own nation in the western half of the continent. But once the United States became independent, the tribes were doomed. They were crushed by your westward expansion."

John looked askance. "So what are you saying? You prevented one catastrophe but couldn't stop the other?"

She nodded. "The trouble is, we can't steer history like a car. All we can do is nudge it a little, and sometimes there are no good options." She raised her hands in a gesture of helplessness. "And do you know what made it worse? Even back then, I knew the value of what we were going to lose. Before the Revolution, I'd spent more than a hundred years learning about the Native American tribes. I made many friends among the Ojibway when I was growing up in Haven in the 1600s."

"Gower said your family didn't have much contact with the Ojibway. He said they left you alone, and you did the same."

"Well, it's true, that was our official policy. But I was a very impetuous youngster, and Mother couldn't stop me from leaving Haven. This was when we lived aboveground and used the cavern only for storing our Treasures. There were just a few dozen Furies then."

"And you were the only white people in the area?"

"No, there were some French traders and missionaries in St. Ignace and Sault Sainte Marie. We stayed away from both outposts, but the French had brought smallpox to North America, and soon the Ojibway were dying by the hundreds. Our family had already learned how to inoculate ourselves against the disease, and I thought it was our duty to offer this protection to the Ojibway tribes. Mother, though, was dead-set against the idea."

"Why?"

Ariel frowned. "She had the same fears then as she has now. She thought any contact with the outside world would threaten Haven's safety. But several of my cousins sided with me, and we worked out a compromise with Mother. She agreed to let us inoculate the Ojibway as long as we stayed at least two hundred miles away from Haven. We also had to pretend we were French missionaries and nuns, so the Ojibway wouldn't figure out who we were or where we came from." Her frown disappeared. She turned cheerful again. "And that's how the Ranger Corps got started. Our first expedition consisted of four men and five women."

John couldn't help but marvel at all this. He was beginning to see some

of the benefits of eternal youth. Ariel hadn't been confined to the bound-
aries of a single lifetime, the limited set of interests and passions that
could be explored in sixty or seventy years. She'd lived several fascinating
lives, one after another. "It sounds like that's how you got interested in
medicine, too."

"Oh, yes. And we learned just as much from the Ojibway as they did
from us. First we went to the Keweenaw Peninsula, on the southern shore
of Lake Superior. The tribes there had extensive knowledge of medicinal
plants. Then we moved farther west, to Chequamegon Bay. The Ojibway
taught us how to hunt and fish and build birch-bark canoes, so we could
live off the land. We could keep exploring the region and inoculating the
tribes for as long as we wanted to."

"Didn't that worry your mother?"

"Every six months I'd assign a pair of messengers to go back to Haven.
They'd deliver our reports to the council and pick up new supplies and
volunteers." Ariel paused, biting her lip. An uncertain look had appeared
on her face, as if she wasn't sure whether she should continue. She shifted
in her chair. "And every year or so, one of our women would get pregnant, so we'd send her back to Haven with the messengers."

Her cheeks colored. This surprised John. Ariel wasn't the kind of woman
who blushed easily. "They found Ojibway paramours?"

"That was our preferred method during Haven's first century. There
were few Europeans in the area, and most of them were unsavory charac-
ters, either cunning traders or fanatical churchmen. But there were many
Ojibway men."

She said this in a casual way, her voice jaunty and light, but within a
few seconds her face turned a deeper shade of pink. John didn't understand what was going on. Ariel was clearly uncomfortable, and yet she'd
deliberately broached this subject. He could think of only one explanation: she wanted to tell him something personal, but it was so difficult to
say that she had to force herself to do it.

At the same time that he realized this, he had a moment of dizziness.
For an instant the gurney seemed to lurch underneath him. The feeling
lasted for only a fraction of a second, and then he felt fine. It was so brief
he wasn't sure if it was an effect of the Fountain protein or simply a natural jolt of adrenaline. His nerves were in an uproar. Ariel was waiting for
him to ask the obvious question.

He moved a bit closer to her, propping himself up on his elbows. "Did *you* get pregnant, too?"

The muscles in her neck tensed under her skin, but otherwise she didn't move. Her green eyes glistened above her inflamed cheeks. Finally, after ten long seconds, she nodded. "Do you remember what Mother said on the day you came here? Near the end of the meeting in the council chambers?"

John shook his head. Elizabeth Fury had said a lot of things, and he didn't know which one Ariel was referring to.

"She reminded me of the last time I brought a paramour to Haven." Ariel's voice was low but steady. "It was in 1674. His name was Running Cloud. And it didn't end well."

Before John could respond he had another dizzy spell. This one was longer and more intense than the first. The whole laboratory seemed to tilt, and for a second he was amazed that the hundreds of lab flasks didn't slide off the shelves. He felt nauseous as well, and his skin went cold. Ariel looked at him, puzzled, as his head swayed and his mouth fell open. Then she jumped out of her chair.

"John! Are you okay?"

He couldn't answer. The dizziness wasn't subsiding. Ariel grabbed his shoulders and forced him to lie down flat. Her head seemed to wheel above him, lunging across his field of view.

"Listen to me, John! The protein is slowing your circulation. Take rapid, strong breaths, okay? You need to boost your heart rate."

Then he felt the gurney rumble under his back. At first he thought this was another symptom caused by the Fountain protein, but Ariel looked up in surprise at the same time and turned her head to the left and right, scanning the room. She'd felt the rumbling, too. "Mercy!" she cried. "What was that?"

A moment later the lights went out. Then they heard the siren, high-pitched and deafening.

TWENTY

Sullivan stood at the edge of the woods south of Haven, gazing at the farm through a pair of binoculars. It was a gorgeous morning, much warmer than the past few days, and the sky was a perfect, cloudless blue. Marlowe and Percy accompanied him, each man hidden behind a pine tree. Marlowe rubbed his bandaged shoulder and stared at the farm with livid eyes, while Percy pointed his camera at everything in sight, cackling every time he pressed the shutter.

The FBI's surveillance van was about a mile away, parked on the shoulder of the road that ran parallel to Haven's eastern fence. Sullivan adjusted the focus on his binoculars until he could read the logo plastered on the van's side: CHARTER CABLE. The federal agents were posing as cable-TV repairmen. One of them pretended to fix the wiring inside a junction box on a nearby telephone pole. The other agents were inside the van, pointing cameras with powerful zoom lenses at the fenced-off farm. Unfortunately for them, there wasn't much to see. The Elders had laid out the farm in a way that maximized their privacy. The cornfields and hedges and outbuildings at the edge of the property blocked the view of everything at the center. Although the agents could monitor who entered and left the place, they could barely see the farmhouses and barn.

The view from Sullivan's position was equally bad. When he pointed his binoculars at the farmhouses he could see only their redbrick chimneys and wood-shingle roofs. Just beyond them was the barn, and behind that was the barnyard for Haven's sheep and cattle. The barnyard was large, almost four hundred feet wide, and surrounded by twelve-foot-high slat fencing. Like the chain-link fence surrounding the whole property, the barnyard's fence was a little too industrial-looking for an Amish farm, but the Elders had good reason for putting it there. The yard also served as a recreation area for the Furies, and the slat fencing shielded them from view, allowing them to exercise outdoors without pretending to be Amish. You couldn't see them from outside, no matter how powerful your binoculars or camera.

Unless, that is, you were observing the farm from above.

Sullivan tilted his head back and aimed the binoculars at the sky. He wouldn't have been able to spot the drone if he hadn't known which direction it was coming from. The Reaper was only ten yards long, and it was flying at an altitude of 40,000 feet. At that distance, the unmanned aircraft looked like a tiny black cross, several times smaller than a commercial jetliner. It crept across the cloudless sky, cruising overhead at the relatively sluggish speed of two hundred miles per hour. The drone had arrived just in time. When Sullivan checked his watch, he saw it was exactly noon.

He didn't hear the explosion or feel the ground shake. He hadn't expected to. The geothermal plant was almost a mile to the north and five hundred feet underground. Even if the blast had been twice as powerful, he wouldn't have felt it. But he would know very soon whether his device had detonated. He trained his binoculars on a ventilation pipe protruding from the roof of one of the farm's outbuildings. Then he waited.

After half a minute a pale wisp of steam rose from the pipe. The flow rapidly strengthened, gathering force and volume. Within seconds the vapor gushed out of the pipe in a thick, roiling plume. Steam surged out of the other ventilation pipes as well, rising and spreading above every outbuilding and farmhouse. The big white plumes leaned toward the east, pushed by the prevailing winds.

Sullivan smiled. He felt the surge in his own body, a sweet upwelling of triumph. But for the people down below, inside the cavern, the gushing steam was anything but sweet. Because the vapor came from deep within the earth, it was laced with hydrogen sulfide, a gas that forms in underground reservoirs when water dissolves certain minerals. The gas was colorless, foul-smelling, and corrosive.

And highly poisonous.

TWENTY-ONE

John lay helpless on the gurney. He could see Ariel in the feeble glow of the lab's emergency lights, but he couldn't move a muscle. The Fountain protein had immobilized him. He was dizzy and trembling and sick to his stomach, and every inch of his body hurt like crazy.

He felt a flash of pain across his chest as Ariel ripped off the EKG's suction cups. Then she grabbed his gurney at the end where his feet were and wheeled him out of her lab, knocking the door aside. She shoved the gurney down the hallway, running like mad, her face red and contorted. John glimpsed the doors of the other labs speeding past on both sides, and his nausea redoubled. He wanted to die.

At the end of the corridor she pressed the button for the elevator but its power had been cut. Ariel shouted, "Bloody hell!" and turned to a nearby door with an EMERGENCY EXIT sign. She rammed the gurney through the doorway and stopped at the foot of a flight of stairs. Then she grabbed John's legs and draped them over the side of the gurney.

"You have to walk!" she shouted. "We have to go up the stairway!"

John's legs quivered and wobbled beneath him. He could barely stand up, much less walk or climb stairs. He leaned on Ariel as he moved away from the gurney, but she couldn't support his weight. Before they could reach the first step, he fell on top of her and they collapsed in a heap. John's face slapped against the floor, which seemed to tilt like a seesaw. His ears rang, high-pitched and loud. The noise inside his head was even louder than the siren.

Ariel scrambled to her feet and grabbed his right hand. Clasping it tightly, she pulled with all her might. "Get up, John! We have to go!"

He couldn't get up. He was dead weight.

"Damn it!" She bent over and screamed in his face. "That's the evacuation alarm! We have to get to the surface!"

It was getting difficult to think. The Fountain protein was messing with his mind. He imagined that the alarm was sounding inside his body. His cells were burning. They were exploding, one by one. "I can't," he muttered. "I—"

"Yes, you can!"

Her voice knifed through him. It pierced his skin and slipped into his Fountain-clogged bloodstream. With an enormous effort of will, he raised his right hand and placed it on the first step, palm down. Then he dragged his body forward and started crawling up the stairs.

The first flight of steps was agony. His calves and thigh muscles were on fire. Ariel helped him along, bending over him and hooking her right arm under his left. But the second flight was easier. His nausea and dizziness began to subside. At the foot of the third flight he was able to reach for the railing and stand up. As the pain in his muscles eased he started taking the steps two at a time. Ariel shouted, "Good! Keep going!" and his heart pumped faster. A burst of new energy spread to his arms and legs.

John felt almost normal by the time they reached the top of the stairway. He saw another door with an EMERGENCY EXIT sign, but he knew they couldn't be at the surface yet. The laboratories were located below the Pyramid. Dashing ahead of Ariel, he opened the door and found himself on the cavern's floor near the base of the Pyramid, which loomed high above them. Battery-operated emergency lights glowed here and there, but most of the cavern was shrouded in darkness.

The sirens were even louder here. Dozens of people ran along the pathways, heading for the exits that led to the farmhouses and barns aboveground. Many of the people carried flashlights and wore gas masks. A few were dressed in bright yellow hazmat suits. The air in the cavern was humid and smelled like rotten eggs.

John grimaced. "Jesus, what happened?"

Ariel rushed past him and turned left, toward the far end of the cavern, where pale clouds of steam billowed between the rocky walls. "Damnation! It's the geothermal plant!" She looked over her shoulder and gave him a fierce look. "Follow the others to the surface! I'll meet you there." Then she sprinted toward the billowing clouds.

John didn't hesitate. He raced after Ariel.

She ran fast, but he kept up with her. He wasn't dizzy anymore. He was fully recovered and then some. After running for about a hundred yards Ariel stopped at a small storage shed next to the pathway. She opened the shed's door, reached inside and pulled out a gas mask. She was about to put it on when she saw John come up behind her. She seemed more resigned than angry. "I had a feeling you'd want to come along. Are you sure you're all right?"

"Don't worry about me. Why is there so much steam?"

"There must've been a break in the intake pipe. The steam is under high pressure, so it's hard to shut down the flow. And there are toxic chemicals mixed with the water vapor. The worst is hydrogen sulfide." Reaching into the shed again, she pulled out another gas mask and handed it to him. "You're going to need one of these."

"How toxic?"

"At low levels it irritates the eyes and throat. At high levels it causes respiratory paralysis. Okay, look at me carefully." She demonstrated how to put on the mask and tighten the straps. John did the same while Ariel watched. Then she removed two more masks from the shed and gave one to him. "Take an extra, in case you find someone who needs it. Follow my lead, all right?"

Then, with one mask over her face and another in her hand, Ariel ran toward the geothermal plant. John followed right behind, sweating like crazy. It was like jogging in a steam room, only hotter and more uncomfortable. Within seconds his clothes were soaked. He had to wipe the condensation off the plastic eyeholes in his mask to see where he was going.

The vapor was so thick they didn't see the plant until they were twenty feet away. As they rushed toward the entrance they nearly collided with someone coming out of the building. It was a tall man wearing a gas mask and carrying a woman in his arms. The woman also wore a mask but appeared to be unconscious. John looked carefully at the man, trying to glimpse the face behind the mask, and realized it was Gower. His eyes were wide and frightened behind the plastic eyeholes.

Ariel pointed at the unconscious woman. "Is that Claudia?" she asked. Her voice, muffled by the gas mask, was barely audible under the wailing sirens.

Gower nodded. "She closed the shutdown valve and then stayed behind to make sure everyone left the plant. But the heat was too much for her. She needs a doctor!"

"So the plant is clear? You're absolutely certain?"

"Aye, she said she checked every room. Now please, I must go!"

"What of the asylum?" Ariel turned and pointed in the direction of the old caves, although they were invisible in the fog. "Has it been cleared too?"

"I don't know!" Gower's eyes widened still further. "You have to go there, Lily! You have to see if Grandmother got out!"

"Aye, I'll go right now. Get your mother to safety."

She slapped Gower's back, pushing him on his way. Then she and John raced to the asylum.

Despite the darkness and vapor, Ariel had no trouble finding the place. After centuries of living in Haven, John thought, she could probably navigate the cavern with her eyes closed. The tunnel that led to the patients' rooms was choked with steam, and the air temperature seemed to rise as they progressed down its length. John felt the heat stinging his arms and the back of his neck. The steam fogged his mask's eyeholes, making it hard to see anything except the emergency lights glowing through the haze.

Then he bumped into someone, a woman, who was staggering down the tunnel in the opposite direction. His heart leaped at first because he thought it was Gower's grandmother, Octavia. But Octavia, he remembered, was tall and solidly built, whereas this woman was petite, even smaller than Ariel. She wore a gas mask but John recognized her right away: it was Constance, the asylum's nurse. She grasped the front of his shirt and clung to him in terror. "Help me! It's too hot! I'm going to faint!"

Ariel gripped the woman's shoulder to get her attention. "Is the asylum clear, Constance? Are all the patients out?"

"I can't find Octavia! She refused to leave her room when the alarm rang and now I can't find her!"

"Calm down, cuz. Could she have left the asylum without you noticing?"

"Nay, impossible! I led the other patients out of the tunnel, then went right back inside to get her. But she's not in her room now! She's not—"

Constance swooned. John grabbed her by the waist to stop her from falling. She wasn't completely unconscious—she muttered and moaned as John held her—but she couldn't stay on her feet, either. Someone would have to help her out of the cavern.

"Take her to the surface," Ariel ordered. "I'll look for Octavia."

John shook his head. "Octavia weighs at least a hundred and fifty pounds. If you find her, you won't be able to drag her out."

"I have to try! I can't just—"

He swung Constance around and draped her limp right arm around Ariel's shoulders. "Take Constance instead. She weighs less than you. I'll find Octavia."

Ariel lurched a bit but held up under Constance's weight. She took a tentative step forward, and the semi-conscious woman stepped with her. It wouldn't be easy, but it looked like she could get Constance out of the cavern. "Okay, you're right," Ariel admitted. "But I'm coming back here as soon as I get her to safety."

"Got it," John said, and then he ran down the tunnel.

Soon he reached the large antechamber with stone walls and wooden doors. Steam swirled in giant eddies here, thick and scorching. The emergency lights were no use, they could barely penetrate the haze, but luckily John remembered where Octavia's room was. Although the heat was turning his arms an ugly boiled red, his mind was clear and his body felt unusually strong. He moved in an unerring line to the door marked PATIENT and burst into the room, yelling *Octavia!* as loudly as he could. The steam was even thicker here, so he used his arms and legs to sweep the room, hoping one of his hands or feet would collide with her. He rushed to the bed and rummaged through the heap of sheets and blankets and pillows, all soaking from the steam. But Octavia wasn't there. Haven's oldest woman was missing.

He dashed out of the room and stood in the middle of the scorching antechamber, trying to think. Should he check the other patients' rooms? Would Octavia have gone into one of those? Maybe Constance was wrong, maybe Octavia had slipped out of the asylum without anyone noticing. She could be anywhere in the cavern. Or maybe someone else had rescued her. Maybe she was safely aboveground now, reunited with her daughter and grandson.

Then another thought occurred to him. He turned around and retraced his steps, heading back to Octavia's room, but this time he opened the door marked VIEWING. He entered the narrow room and walked to the far end. The one-way mirror on the wall showed nothing but dark clouds of roiling vapor, dimly illuminated by the emergency lights.

As he took his fifth step into the room, his foot hit something soft. He knelt on the floor, groping in the darkness, and felt a woman's body lying on its side. First he touched her broad shoulders under her damp nightgown, then her head with its brow resting on the slick floor, then her long hair massed in a tangled wet pile. He didn't need to see her face. He could tell just by touch that it was Octavia.

He fitted his extra gas mask over her face and tightened the straps. Then he slipped his arms under her torso and lifted her, cradling the big-boned woman against his chest. She was even heavier than he'd expected, at least a hundred and seventy pounds, but he had no trouble carrying her. He left the viewing room and hurried out of the antechamber, taking big strides across the stone floor.

Although the heated air had kept Octavia's skin warm, her body was limp. She had no pulse, no heartbeat. She'd probably stopped breathing long before John found her. And yet he ran as fast as he could, carrying her through the tunnel and across the floor of the cavern, as if she were still alive. As if he could still save her.

Haven's main emergency exit led to a trapdoor in the floor of the barn. At least eighteen hundred people had already used this exit by the time John came up the stairs carrying Octavia. The barn, although large, could hold no more than a thousand people; the rest had overflowed into the barn-yard. Dozens of men and women lay on the barn's floor, where the Fury medics treated them for hydrogen sulfide poisoning. Doctors in long black dresses distributed oxygen tanks, connected patients to ventilators, and prepared doses of herbal medicine. But nearly all of them stopped what they were doing and stared at John as he brought in Octavia and rested her on the floor.

He stepped backward while the women crowded around her body. One doctor stripped off Octavia's gas mask and slid a tube down her throat. Another lowered Octavia's nightgown and delivered an injection to her heart. Yet another woman took John aside and treated his burns. She removed his mask and slathered a cooling salve on his arms and the back of his neck. But all the while he kept his eyes on Octavia.

After a few minutes the doctors' frantic activity subsided. One by one, they drifted away and found other patients to attend to. The last remaining medic knelt beside Octavia and placed her hand over the woman's eyes to close them. Then she draped a plain white sheet over the body.

John continued staring at her. He'd suspected that Octavia was dead as soon as he found her, but it was still crushing to see it confirmed. He couldn't help but imagine her final moments in the asylum, hiding from Constance and the other rescuers while the toxic steam swirled all around. She'd grown so terrified of death that its approach had paralyzed her. After two thousand years of dodging its embrace, all she could do was lie on the floor and wait for it to take her.

Many of the other evacuees stared at the corpse too. Although the barn was full to bursting, the place fell strangely quiet. This was clearly a painful blow for the Furies, to lose the oldest member of their family in such an awful way. Several women gazed suspiciously at John, most likely wondering if he'd had something to do with Octavia's death. But a few others—the ones who'd seen John racing across the cavern with her body—looked at him with greater sympathy.

Then someone tapped John's shoulder. He turned around, expecting to see Ariel, but instead it was Archibald, Gower's irritable friend. The man's face was pink and dripping with sweat. He leaned close to John. "You should go outside, to the yard," he whispered. "The women are distraught. Your presence is making it worse."

John nodded. He didn't like it, but Archibald was right. The guy headed for the oversized doorway at the back of the barn, and John followed him outside.

The yard behind the barn was bigger than a football field and surrounded by a high privacy wall. Only about a quarter of the yard was occupied by the sheep and cattle pens. The remainder had been set up as a recreation area, with sections devoted to lawn bowling, croquet, and horseshoes. But no one was playing games or exercising now. Hundreds of evacuees sprawled on the grass, many of them gasping for air or splashing water on their faces. Archibald led John to the far left side of the yard, near the wall, and then halted so suddenly that John almost plowed into him.

Gower was just a few feet ahead. He sat on the lawn beside Claudia, his mother, who'd regained consciousness. He held a cup of water to her lips, encouraging her to drink.

Looking up, Gower saw his friend first. "Archie! Have you heard any news?"

Instead of answering, Archibald pointed at John. When Gower saw John, he scrambled to his feet. His brow was creased and there were dark circles under his eyes. "Did you find Grandmother? Is she safe?"

John shook his head. He'd delivered bad news before, and he knew it was better to do it fast. "I'm very sorry. I found her, but not in time."

Gower didn't react. It was as if he hadn't heard. He stared at John for a few more seconds, then turned back to his friend. "Does he speak aright, Archie? Is she dead?"

Archibald coughed and swallowed hard. " 'Tis . . . 'tis for the best, Gower. You told me so many times . . . how unhappy she was . . ."

His voice trailed off. John looked at him with disdain. What Archibald said was true, but he shouldn't have said it. Gower just stood there, blank-faced and bewildered.

A moment later Ariel came up behind them, striding across the grass. John started to say something, but she mouthed the word "Wait" and walked past him. She went straight to Gower and wrapped her arms around his waist. For an instant he seemed more bewildered than ever. Then he started to weep.

After a few seconds Gower pulled away from Ariel and returned to his mother, who leaned against him and buried her face in her hands. As he consoled her, Ariel went to John and took him aside, moving several feet away from the others. She looked at his burned arms and grimaced. "You must be in pain."

He glanced at the burns, now caked with the glistening salve. He could feel his skin throbbing, but it didn't hurt so much. "I'm fine. How's Constance?"

"She's recovering. Do you realize that you reached the emergency exit before I did? Even while carrying Octavia?"

Ariel sounded angry, as if she were accusing him of something. He didn't understand. "I thought she had a chance. I must've passed you in the haze."

"That was an extraordinary feat of endurance, John. It's not normal."

"What are you trying to—"

He was interrupted by a scream. The source was Claudia, Gower's mother. She stood on wobbling legs and pointed at Archibald. "I saw you last night! What were you doing in the geothermal plant?"

Everyone turned to look at him. Archibald stepped backward in surprise and almost fell. "What? Pardon, Claudia, but I don't—"

"When I left the plant just before midnight I saw you near the exit! Did you tamper with the machinery?"

"Nay, of course not!" He shook his head vigorously.

Claudia moved toward him. Her footing was unsteady, but she kept her hand pointing straight at Archibald's pink face. "Then what were you doing there? You had no business in the plant at that hour of night!"

"Please calm yourself, dear. I was looking for Gower. I wanted to talk to your son, that's all."

Now John stepped forward. He knew that was a lie. "You sure about that? Gower and I also saw you last night, and you weren't interested in talking. When Gower called out to you, you turned away from him."

Archibald sneered, narrowing his eyes. "Mind your place, paramour. That was earlier in the evening, much earlier."

John remembered that the bastard had been carrying a backpack. And after he turned away from Gower, he'd headed for the geothermal plant. John clenched his hands as he recalled the incident. He was starting to get a bad feeling about this.

"What was in your backpack, asshole?" John took another step toward the guy. "It looked pretty heavy."

"This is preposterous!" Archibald stood his ground, but his sneer was fading. "I don't have to explain myself to you!"

Blood rushed to John's head, darkening his vision. "What the hell was in it? Dynamite? A bomb?"

That last question broke Archibald's composure. His mouth opened and his chin quivered. An involuntary, strangled noise came out of his throat, a hopeless yelp. Then he turned to run.

He didn't get very far. John lunged forward and grabbed him by the neck. With a furious roar he shoved Archibald face-first into the grass. He pinned the bastard down and started pounding the back of his skull. Archibald went limp after the first few punches, but John kept thrashing him. His fists were taking orders from a different part of his brain, a part that was mad for vengeance. In the more rational regions of his mind he sensed that people were shouting at him, begging him to stop, but he couldn't. His whole body pulsed with rage.

Then someone standing above him grabbed one of his arms by the elbow. He spun around and reflexively cocked his other arm, ready to bash the face of whoever was trying to stop him. But as he was about to throw the punch he saw it was Ariel. Wide-eyed, she stared at him in disbelief. There was horror in her eyes too, but it was a clinical, fascinated kind of horror, as if she'd just discovered that he suffered from some terrible new disease. "Stop it, John," she whispered. "This isn't you."

His fist hung in the air, frozen, for a couple of seconds. For a moment he wasn't sure if he could bring it back under his control. Then he slowly lowered it and unclenched his hand. He looked down at Archibald, who was writhing on the grass and moaning "Mercy, mercy!" in a guilt-stricken voice. Then John looked at Gower, who was hugging his mother protectively. Finally, he turned back to Ariel. "I don't . . . I don't know what . . ."

"It's Fountain. What else could it be?" Ariel let go of him. "Take deep breaths. You need to wash it out of your system."

He did as she instructed and took several deep breaths. After a little while his vision cleared. Suddenly cold, he started to shiver. "I'm . . . sorry. I didn't . . ."

"I have to get you back to the lab. I didn't expect this at all. Fountain doesn't have these effects on women." She shook her head. "I didn't notice these changes when I tested the protein on Sullivan, but to be honest, I wasn't looking for them. I could've easily missed them."

John shivered harder. He stared at his hands, the swollen knuckles he'd rammed against Archibald's skull. He was afraid of himself, afraid of what was inside him.

Then he heard more shouting. He looked up and saw men and women running across the yard, dashing toward the barn's oversized doorway. For a second he wondered if someone had discovered another bomb. Ariel turned her head this way and that, trying to figure out what was going on, and then she froze. She'd caught sight of her mother. Elizabeth Fury was marching across the yard, scattering everyone in her path.

"Back in the barn!" she yelled. "Get back there right now!"

Elizabeth came straight toward them, striding fast. Her lone eye focused on Archibald. When she got within ten yards of them she pointed at the groaning man on the ground, and then at Gower and Claudia. "Get that guardsman on his feet!" she ordered.

Ariel stepped toward her. "What's going on?"

"Don't just stand there, Lily!" The vertical scar on Elizabeth's face had turned an ugly shade of purple. "Help them carry that guardsman into the barn. We all need to take shelter!"

The Elder's expression was so fierce that John automatically obeyed her. He bent over Archibald and grabbed his ankles while Gower took hold of his arms. But Ariel didn't move. She frowned, her expression equally fierce. "Mother, what—"

"Damn it, girl, look up!" She thrust her hand toward the sky.

John raised his head and looked where she was pointing. Against the swath of deep blue sky was a tiny black cross.

TWENTY-TWO

Agent Larson grinned as the surveillance video from the MQ-9 Reaper streamed across his laptop's screen. The quality of the images was outstanding. The cameras mounted on the drone had been developed to pinpoint terrorists in the mountain villages of Pakistan. Even from an altitude of eight miles, the camera lenses could zoom in on one individual in a crowd, providing enough detail to allow analysts to make an identification. *This is the future of law enforcement,* Larson thought. *Pretty soon the drones will be everywhere.*

Sitting next to him inside the surveillance van was Lieutenant Bob Sims, a U.S. Air Force pilot on loan to the Homeland Security Department. Sims was flying the drone from his own laptop, which was equipped with a joystick and a cable connecting the computer to the powerful antenna on the van's roof. The lieutenant had put the Reaper in a circular holding pattern over the Amish farm. Now he checked the flight path on his laptop's screen and used the joystick to make small course corrections that were radioed to the drone. He also kept the drone's cameras trained on the farm's barnyard.

Large plumes of smoke had been rising from the outbuildings for the past ten minutes. Larson guessed that somehow or other, Van had caused an explosion in the methamphetamine lab beneath the farm. Blowing up a meth lab probably wasn't so difficult; because the drug cookers worked with volatile chemicals, they set off accidental explosions all the time. Although Larson was a bit disturbed by the possibility that his informant had deliberately obliterated the place, he wasn't going to lose any sleep over it. He had little sympathy for meth gangs, Amish or otherwise.

Then they saw the first signs of activity in the barnyard, just as Van had predicted. The surveillance video from the Reaper showed dozens of people running out of the barn and spreading across a grass-covered area. When the drone's cameras zoomed in on the running figures, Larson was surprised to see that most were women. Some wore long, black, Amish-looking dresses, but others wore fancy colorful gowns. He started to wonder if the community was running a prostitution ring as well as a drug operation. But an even bigger surprise was the sheer size of the crowd. After several minutes at least five hundred people had fled from the barn and sprawled on the grass outside. Larson shook his head, unable to figure it out.

And then, after a few more minutes, he got a call on his cell phone. He looked at the caller ID and saw it was his informant. He answered the phone before the second ring. "What the fuck's going on, Van? What's with all the women?"

"Calm down, man. You're gonna give yourself a fucking stroke."

"You said we'd see evidence of a drug operation, but I don't know what the hell I'm looking at. It's like a fucking ballroom-dancing party down there."

"If you just shut the fuck up for a second, I'll show you the evidence. Point the cameras at the far left side of the barnyard."

"Left side? What the fuck do you mean? From what perspective?"

"From the back of the barn. Just look near the yard's southern wall."

Larson repeated the instructions to Lieutenant Sims, who fiddled with the joystick on his computer. The drone shifted its camera until the screen of Larson's laptop showed the area near the wall. About a dozen people were there, most of them on their feet and rushing back to the barn. But one figure in particular caught his attention, a man in Amish clothes lying facedown on the ground. Larson pointed at the screen. "Zoom in on that guy," he told Sims.

The lieutenant increased the magnification. On the screen, two men approached the prone figure and bent over to pick him up. One of them was Amish, but the other man wore normal clothes. He was big too, and his skin was dark. Larson felt a jolt of adrenaline. "No, this guy!" he shouted, pointing at the fucker. "Zoom in on *him!*"

At just that moment the man raised his head, as if he'd somehow over-heard Larson's order. He looked straight at the drone's camera from eight miles below.

It was John fucking Rogers.

TWENTY-THREE

For the next hour John sat in a corner of the barn beside Ariel, Gower, and Claudia. Along with hundreds of other nervous, cranky people, they had to cool their heels on the barn's straw-littered floor, surrounded by hay bales and milking machines and dairy cows that lowed in their stalls.

Conroy and several of his guardsmen took Archibald away, presumably to interrogate him. Elizabeth, meanwhile, rushed to an emergency meeting of the Elders in one of the farmhouses. Ariel was anxious to leave the barn too; she wanted to go down to her lab with John so she could figure out what the Fountain protein was doing to him. But there was still too much hydrogen sulfide in the cavern. Although the flow of steam from the geothermal plant had been shut down and Haven's ventilation fans were flushing out the toxic air as quickly as possible, it would be another hour before anyone could safely go underground.

They sat there without talking. Gower and Claudia didn't even look at John. The mother and son huddled close together, overwhelmed with horror and grief. The revelation that Archibald had sabotaged the geothermal plant and caused Octavia's death was shocking enough, but then they had to watch John pulverize the bastard. Gower and his mother were gentle people, and the savagery of it had upset them. Ariel didn't talk to him either, but after a few minutes she reached out and slipped her hand into his. Without words she was trying to tell him that it wasn't his fault. The problem was in his biochemistry, not his soul. And John tried his best to believe it.

Then Conroy returned to the barn and approached them. His face was grim. "The Council of Elders requests your presence," he said, pointing at John and Ariel. "Come with me."

John assumed the worst. His stomach twisted as he and Ariel stood up. "Is it Archibald? Is he dead?"

"Nay. The traitor is alive and answering our questions. The Elders wish to speak to you about a different matter." He gestured at them impatiently. "Come, make haste."

They followed Conroy to a door that led to a short walkway, which was covered by a canvas awning that blocked any surveillance from above. At the end of the walkway they slipped through the side door of a farmhouse and went downstairs to its basement.

They entered a room that looked like it was used for prayer meetings. Half a dozen benches were lined up on the concrete floor, all facing a wooden table and a lectern. The room had no windows, and the walls were bare except for a couple of framed, hand-stitched samplers, each showing a sentence written in German. John saw the word "Gott" stitched in black thread on the white fabric, so he assumed they were Amish prayers. The farmhouse, he realized, had been carefully decorated to resemble a typical Amish home, just in case it was ever inspected by the authorities. But John suspected that the house, like the barn, had a hidden trapdoor leading to the cavern.

The three Elders—Elizabeth, Margaret, and Cordelia—sat behind the table at the front of the room. Standing beside the table was the elderly, white-bearded bailiff whom the Elders called Old Sam. In his broad-brimmed straw hat and round, wire-rim glasses, he looked just like a geezer from Pennsylvania Dutch country. The Elders were also disguised as Amish now—all three wore plain black dresses and white bonnets. There was even a German Bible on the table to complete the masquerade. The only out-of-place item was a MacBook laptop on the lectern, which had been angled so that its screen faced the Elders sitting at the table.

Conroy escorted John and Ariel across the room. As they approached the table and lectern, John heard a familiar voice coming out of the laptop. All three Elders were staring at the computer with looks of revulsion. When John got close enough he saw Sullivan's face on the screen. He was speaking with the Elders via a wireless video call, standing in front of his own laptop somewhere and facing the machine's camera.

John glanced at Ariel, who stiffened when she saw her half brother on the screen. Judging from the background, he seemed to be deep in the pine woods. A dozen of his Riflemen stood behind him, including Marlowe, the one who'd broken John's nose and ribs. Sullivan's face still bore the scratch marks that Ariel had given him, but he beamed with pleasure when she stepped into view of the laptop's camera. "Ah, sweet sister! I'm delighted that you can join our conversation. And thank you so much for bringing your paramour. Dear me, it looks like his arms have been parboiled. Did you have some trouble getting out of the cavern?"

Before either John or Ariel could respond, Elizabeth leaned across the table and pointed her finger at the screen. "As you can see, we've fulfilled your request. Now proceed with your statement."

Sullivan raised an eyebrow. He looked amused. "Aye, my statement. Well, first let me say how pleased I am that you didn't execute the paramour immediately. I suspect that Lily had something to do with this decision. She's taken quite a shine to the Negro."

"You're trying my patience." Elizabeth furrowed her brow and narrowed her lone eye. "What does this have to do with our present impasse?"

Sullivan kept smiling. "I assure you, Mother, it's quite relevant. Didn't you wonder how I knew the paramour was still alive? It's because he appeared just an hour ago on the surveillance footage that was captured by the drone hovering over the farm. As we speak, the FBI and other federal agencies are examining this footage and preparing a response. I've been told that a team of several dozen armed agents will pay a visit to Haven shortly after eleven o'clock tonight."

Elizabeth didn't say anything at first. She just stared at the laptop's screen, without moving a muscle. Margaret, in contrast, swiveled her head back and forth, her eyes darting between her sister and the laptop. Even Cordelia shifted in her chair, disturbed enough to cast an anxious glance at the Chief Elder. But Elizabeth remained frozen. Her face was like a pale block of stone, and her scar was a reddish crack running down its side.

Finally, she shook her head. "You've broken your oath. You've betrayed your sisters and brothers."

"Nay, just the sisters. My brothers stand with me." Still grinning, he pointed at the Riflemen behind him. "We only want equality, Mother. We used to think it was magic that kept you young, but now we know better, don't we? It's just a protein, an organic molecule. And you have the power to give it to us."

"Do you truly believe this is the way to help your brothers? By exposing us to the American government? By revealing our secrets to bureaucrats and intelligence agents who are still barbaric enough to torture their enemies?" Elizabeth was trembling now, shaking with anger. "Once the federal agents ransack our laboratories, we won't be able to give you anything!"

Sullivan shrugged. "Aye, the consequences will be dire, but you have only yourself to blame. For years we urged you to pursue this research. For decades, Mother. And when the researchers finally succeeded, when they finally identified the Fountain protein, what did you tell us?" He stopped smiling. His face darkened and his green eyes turned murderous. "You said Fountain was too difficult and dangerous to manufacture. You refused us because you were afraid of handling a few aborted fetuses. The slight threat to your safety outweighed all our hopes."

John heard a furious grunt from Ariel. She stepped forward and jabbed her finger at the screen. "Don't change the facts, cur! The threat would be far more than slight. We'd need to process thousands of fetuses every year to make enough Fountain for all our men. It would be impossible to keep the operation secret."

Sullivan turned, aiming his murderous eyes at his sister. "The fetal tissue is not that difficult to obtain. All you need is cash, which our family has in abundance. With the relatively small number of gold bars we took from Haven's vaults, we established the necessary connections with the medical-waste companies that dispose of aborted fetuses. If you had only given us the catalyst to transform the fetal tissue into Fountain, we could've produced as much protein as we needed."

"Fool! I could've developed a better way to synthesize Fountain. I just needed some time to—"

"Aye, you have all the time in the world, but unfortunately we do not. We've waited long enough, sister. We can't—"

"*Silence!*" Elizabeth stood up so forcefully, her chair tipped backward and crashed to the floor behind her. She gave Ariel a baleful look, then turned back to the laptop's screen. "Do you realize that your vindictive acts have doomed all of us? Once the federal agents discover Haven, they won't rest until they know everything. They'll learn about the Riflemen too and all your unsavory connections. Your men will be interrogated and imprisoned, just like us."

Sullivan shook his head. "My actions aren't vindictive. They serve a purpose. After the failure of my last attempt to obtain the catalyst, I decided to pursue a different strategy. But my goal is the same."

"You're speaking in riddles. What's your goal?"

"Haven is doomed, that's true. But our family can escape this catastrophe." Sullivan stepped closer to the camera in his own laptop, somewhere in the woods. His face filled the screen. "You've planned for this day, Mother. I know you have. For centuries you've been obsessed with security. I'm sure at some point you developed a contingency plan that would be put into effect if Haven was discovered."

Elizabeth fell silent again. She folded her arms across her chest as she stood behind the table.

Sullivan nodded, taking her silence as confirmation. "You've placed buried caches all over the country, each filled with currency and weapons and other emergency supplies. Your Rangers operate a transportation network that could disperse our family if it has to flee from Haven. And in all likelihood you've already selected an alternative refuge, a hidden place where the Furies can rebuild their community. I don't know where it is, but for safety's sake it would have to be far away. Beyond the reach of the American authorities, for certain."

Again, Elizabeth said nothing. She had an excellent poker face. Her expression never changed—it was pure, unrelenting ferocity. But John sensed that Sullivan was right. Elizabeth undoubtedly had a backup plan.

"You face only one obstacle," Sullivan continued. "But it's a sizable one. The federal agents have surrounded the farm, and their drone is watching you from above. If you try to escape from Haven, the authorities will arrest you. If some of you manage to slip past them, the drone will reveal where you are. And you have less than ten hours before the agents force the issue by breaking through the fence and searching the premises." He took a step backward, and his face shrunk on the screen. "Your situation is perilous indeed. But fortunately, I'm willing to help you."

Elizabeth let out a mirthless laugh, finally breaking her silence. "And how would you help us, pray tell?"

"As you know, I've assembled a small army, nearly two hundred men trained for combat." He pointed again at the Riflemen standing behind him. "And because of my connections with the authorities, I know the details of their operation—where their agents are stationed, how many are at each post, and so on. My men can launch a surprise attack on their positions. We can neutralize the agents, shut down their communications and disable their drone. That should give you enough time to shepherd the Furies out of Haven and send them on their way to the new refuge you've prepared."

The Chief Elder tilted her head. Now her expression was skeptical. "You think your ragtag soldiers can defeat the American government?"

"We don't have to win this battle. All we need to do is hold them off until you've escaped. Then my men will retreat and melt away in the darkness, dispersing into the countryside like all the other Furies. And we can take steps to discourage the authorities from pursuing us. The most important step is killing Rogers and leaving his body behind at the farm. He's the only one the federal agents are truly interested in finding. They've already identified him as the primary suspect in their criminal investigations, and once they have his body they'll be largely satisfied."

John felt the eyes of everyone in the room fall on him. Margaret Fury stared at him the hardest. If it were up to her, they'd probably murder him on the spot. Elizabeth stared at him too, but not for very long. She kept her focus on Sullivan. "So you're proposing to extricate us from a perilous trap that your own actions have pushed us into. This makes no sense, from a logical standpoint, unless you're going to demand something in return for your help."

Sullivan smiled again. "You're correct, Mother. Luckily for you, our demand is quite reasonable. We want the catalyst. Tell Lily to send the formula to me in an e-mail. And please don't attempt to trick me. As you know, several of my men learned biochemistry from working in Lily's laboratory, and they'll know if she tries to send us an inauthentic formula. As soon as we determine that you've given us the proper catalyst, I'll order my Riflemen to attack the federal agents."

"And how do I know you'll live up to your end of the bargain? After we give you the catalyst, what's your incentive for helping us?"

"Once we receive what we need, the rebellion will be over. We can be allies instead of enemies. After the escape from Haven, we can assist in the relocation of our family. Our great hope is to reconcile with our mothers and sisters and join the new community you establish, wherever it may be."

He tried his best to look sincere, opening his eyes wide and holding out his hands. But Elizabeth frowned at the screen. "That's a wonderful sentiment, but not very convincing."

"Then think about this. If we allow you to be captured, you might feel inclined to tell the authorities everything you know about me and my men. That could make things very difficult for us. Helping you escape serves our own interests."

Elizabeth nodded, still frowning. She stared at the screen for a few more seconds, deep in thought. Then she turned to her sisters, first glancing at Margaret and then at Cordelia. "I believe we'll need some time to discuss the matter."

Sullivan frowned, too. His face reverted to its natural condition, a dark, hateful glare. He seemed relieved that he didn't have to smile anymore. "I'll give you two hours. Either send me the formula by four o'clock this afternoon, or face the Burning Times once more." Then he disconnected the wireless video link and the screen went black.

The silence that followed was so complete that John could hear himself breathing. Ariel bit her lip and muttered, "Bastard." Conroy went to the lectern and closed the laptop, and Old Sam stepped behind the Elders and righted Elizabeth's fallen chair. Then the bailiff shuffled back to his post beside their table.

Elizabeth sat down with a tired sigh. "You were right, Delia," she said, glancing at her sister. "It happened exactly as you said it would."

"Nay, not exactly." Cordelia shook her head. "Your son's crimes have surpassed even my direst predictions."

Margaret leaned across the table. She seemed confused. "How now, what's this? What predictions are you speaking of?"

"Sixty years ago Delia warned me that our men would rise against us. She said it would lead to the destruction of Haven."

"Nay, nay." Cordelia waved her wooden hand in a dismissive gesture. "I merely predicted that the coming advances in genetics and biochemistry would reveal the secret of our everlasting youth. And I surmised that our men would be the first to covet it."

Margaret turned to Elizabeth and gave her an aggrieved look. "You never told me this. Why wasn't this matter brought before the full council?"

"My apologies, sister." The Chief Elder looked down at the table and raised her hands to her forehead. She began massaging her temples. "I saw only one way to forestall Delia's prophecy, and that was to order our women to slay their baby boys. We couldn't do that, of course, so I let the matter drop." Without looking up, she pointed at the closed laptop that had displayed Sullivan's face a minute ago. "And just seven years later I gave birth to that monster."

Neither Margaret nor Cordelia had anything to say in response. Taking advantage of the lull, Ariel approached the Elders' table. She looked directly at her mother. "I won't do it. I won't give Sullivan the formula. And I certainly won't let you murder John." She glanced at him over her shoulder, then turned back to Elizabeth. "Did you know how he got those burns on his arms? He almost killed himself trying to save Octavia."

Elizabeth still didn't look up. She kept rubbing her temples. "Lily, how well do you know your half brother?"

She scowled. "Too well."

"He fell in love with you, did he not? When he was in his twenties?"

Ariel nodded. "And I told him in no uncertain terms never to come near me. Even back then he was a base creature."

"So would you ever trust him? On any matter, large or small?"

"Never." She shook her head firmly. "I'd sooner trust a cobra."

"Then why do you imagine I would feel differently?" Elizabeth stopped massaging her forehead and looked up at her daughter. "I know he's lying. Whether or not we give him the formula for the catalyst, he won't help us. He wouldn't dare attack the federal agents. He was simply hoping we'd be desperate enough to believe him." She curled her lip, disgusted. "But we're not that desperate. We have another option."

Ariel looked at her in surprise. "What do you mean?"

"Sullivan was right. I have a contingency plan. But he didn't guess the extent of it."

Margaret seemed confused again. "Sister! Is there something else you haven't told us?"

"I told no one. I assigned a team of men to do the work a hundred years ago, and I swore them to secrecy."

"What work? What on earth are you talking about?"

Elizabeth leaned back in her chair, and then she did something remarkable. For the first time, John saw the Chief Elder smile. "I ordered them to dig a tunnel."

TWENTY-FOUR

John and Ariel returned to her laboratory as soon as the air in the cavern was breathable, but there was no time to do any more research on the Fountain protein. Although John desperately wanted to know what Fountain was doing to his biochemistry, he'd have to wait for an answer. Ariel was busy downloading the data from her computers and choosing which of her precious chemicals and tissue samples could be saved. John helped her put the selected flasks and petri dishes in sealed cases and miniature battery-operated freezers. In less than an hour they were going to abandon her lab and everything else in Haven.

The researchers in the other laboratories were doing the same thing, packing up the records from centuries of scientific study. In Haven's vaults the workers stacked gold bars onto pallets and stuffed wads of currency into canvas bags. In the arsenal Conroy's guardsmen loaded ammunition into rucksacks. But the most frenzied activity took place on the second floor of the Pyramid, where Haven's library was located. Women in sweat-stained dresses pulled hundreds of Treasures from the shelves and carefully slipped them into fireproof boxes. Other women removed their Treasures from locked drawers in their desks and clutched the leather-bound note-books to their chests as they fled their offices and apartments. From in-side the laboratory John could hear the footsteps of dozens of people running down the corridor, heading for the assembly point that Elizabeth Fury had designated, at the far end of the cavern. He noticed that Ariel kept her own Treasure tucked under her arm as she sat in front of the computer, transferring thousands of gigabytes of data to a handful of flash drives.

By eight o'clock John and Ariel had packed all the cases and freezers into a big black storage trunk, about four feet long and two feet wide, like the trunks that kids bring to summer camp. It was ridiculously heavy, over a hundred pounds, but the trunk had handles at both ends, making it pos-sible for them to carry the thing. Because the geothermal plant was inop-erative and the elevator had no power, they had to haul the trunk up the same stairway they'd climbed a few hours ago, after the explosion. John held the back end of the trunk, bearing most of its weight as they ascended. The Fountain protein was still flowing through his bloodstream, stimu-lating the cells in his muscles and brain, so he had no trouble going up the steps. Ariel, though, was sweating and struggling. In addition to the trunk, she carried a backpack that held her most valuable possessions: her Treasure, her flash drives and a black, foot-long medicine case containing a syringe and nine vials of yellowish fluid. This was the Fountain protein she'd extracted from the blood of Haven's women. Each vial was identical to the one she'd pumped into John.

After they reached the top of the stairway they joined hundreds of Fu-ries rushing across the floor of the cavern. Women poured out of the Pyra-mid, some pushing dollies loaded with boxes, others carrying paintings and sculptures hastily swathed in bubble wrap. A team of guardsmen huddled at the base of the Pyramid and used jackhammers to gouge holes into the structure's stone blocks. Another team drilled holes into the cav-ern's rocky walls, and a third group unspooled enormous lengths of orange cable, which snaked between the cavern's buildings. The men inserted a small gray package into each hole, and then connected the packages with the cable. After a couple of seconds John figured it out: the guardsmen were rigging the cavern with explosives. As soon as Haven was empty, they were going to blow the place sky-high.

The Furies converged at a gap in the cavern's wall, not far from the asy-lum. This gap had previously been hidden by a ten-foot-high frieze with stone carvings of bears and wolves and deer, but an hour ago the guards-men had smashed the relief sculpture with pickaxes, revealing a stone archway behind it. John and Ariel lugged their trunk through the archway and entered a long tunnel dimly illuminated by emergency lights. As John moved deeper inside and his eyes adjusted to the darkness, he saw a line of metallic rectangles stretching into the distance. It was a freight train with a dozen open-top railroad cars and an old-fashioned steam engine at the far end. The train sat on a pair of steel rails that extended as far as the eye could see.

John whistled. "Unbelievable. And no one but your mother knew that this train was parked here?"

"Almost no one." With a groan, Ariel stopped and rested her end of the trunk on the ground. She stretched and shook her right arm, working the kinks out of the muscles. "Mother ordered some work done in this section in the early 1900s, but she told everyone it was a mining operation. And all the men who worked on the tunnel kept it secret until they died."

"How the hell did she get a train in here without anyone noticing?"

"Back in the logging days, there used to be railroad lines all over the Upper Peninsula. Mother must've purchased the engine and freight cars from the Lake Superior line and had them delivered to the other end of the tunnel. Then someone backed the train up until it reached this end."

"How far does the tunnel go?"

"Mother says it ends at the Rudyard Trucking warehouse, which is ten miles west of here. Our family owns the trucking firm, and all the employ-ees are Rangers. They have a fleet of thirty trucks, which the Rangers use for various purposes all over the country. But even they didn't realize there was a train stop below their warehouse." She shook her head as she stared at the railroad cars. "Only Conroy and his chief deputy, Bardolph, were trusted with the secret. They're the ones who kept the train in working order. And Bardolph knows how to drive it."

"So the plan is to shuttle everyone from Haven to the truck warehouse? Then they'll crowd into the trucks, and the Rangers will drive them across the country?"

Ariel nodded. "The trucking company is near an exit on I-75, and the Canadian border is just twenty miles to the north. If the Rangers driving the trucks have the proper paperwork, they can be in Canada in half an hour."

"And where will they go from there?"

"The Elders haven't revealed that information yet. They worry that Sullivan has more spies among our men, and one of them may devise a way to contact the Riflemen."

John peered down the track. The Furies were loading their prize possessions onto the hundred-year-old train, filling the open-top railroad cars with gold and artworks and Treasures. People were climbing into the cars too and finding places to sit next to the trunks and boxes. About fifty feet ahead he spotted a half-empty car that seemed to have room for Ariel's trunk. "Let's put your stuff over there," he said, pointing at the railroad car.

Ariel grasped the handle at her end of the trunk. After a few more seconds of heavy lifting they reached the half-empty train car and passed the trunk to a pair of men standing inside. Then someone shouted, "Lily!" and the name echoed in the dark tunnel. A moment later they saw Conroy running toward them.

The Master of the Guardsmen had an olive-green duffel bag slung over his left shoulder and an assault rifle over his right. Two older guardsmen struggled behind him, weighed down by duffel bags of their own. Both men were panting and red-faced and at least sixty years old. Conroy was panting, too.

"Milady . . . we need . . . your help," he gasped.

"What's wrong, cuz?"

"The Riflemen . . . they're at the fence."

The news wasn't unexpected. Sullivan's deadline had passed four hours ago. By now he surely knew that Ariel wouldn't give up the formula for the catalyst, no matter how much pressure he applied. He also knew that the federal agents would raid the farm by midnight, and once that happened he'd have no chance at all of getting the formula. So his only option was to attack Haven before the agents did. Ariel furrowed her brow, contemplating strategy. "How many men does he have?"

"At least a hundred along the southern fence. And dozens more to the west and north. I've deployed guardsmen behind the outbuildings, but I need more sharpshooters to cover the approaches."

She nodded grimly. "Well, now you have one more." Stepping toward one of the aging guardsmen, she relieved him of his duffel bag. "Are the long guns in here?"

"Aye, the MK-13. That's your favorite, is it not?"

Instead of answering, Ariel turned away from him and headed out of the train tunnel. At the same time, John approached the other exhausted guardsman and offered to take his duffel bag. The man gave him a grateful look, but Conroy scowled. "What are you doing, paramour? You're not coming with us."

Ariel looked over her shoulder. "Let him come. John did ten weeks of basic training with the American army. And he fought well when we were on the ferryboat."

"Ten weeks? That's not very—"

"Don't be a fool, cuz. Let's go."

Conroy kept scowling, but he let John take the duffel bag. Then they followed Ariel out of the tunnel and back to the cavern.

The cavern's floor was even more crowded than it had been five minutes ago. So many Furies streamed toward the tunnel that John started to wonder if all of them could fit in the railcars. The train might have to make two trips to carry everyone to the trucks. And that meant Conroy's guardsmen would have to hold off Sullivan for at least an hour, maybe two.

They ran up a catwalk fixed to the wall of the cavern, then climbed a spiral stairway to the surface. It was longer than the stairway John had used earlier that day to ascend from the cavern to the barn. This one seemed to go on forever, rising past the point where John thought the ground should be. At the top of the steps they found themselves in a dark, circular room about thirty feet across, with a high dome for a ceiling. Spaced at regular intervals along the surrounding wall were several horizontal slits, through which John glimpsed strips of dark purple sky in the final stages of twilight. He stepped closer to one of the slits, and when he looked down he saw the shadowed cornfields and pastures of Haven's farm about a hundred feet below.

The room was at the top of the farm's silo. It had been converted into a sniper's nest. As soon as they entered it, Conroy and the two older guardsmen unzipped the duffel bags and removed several long, sleek rifles. The faces of the tired men turned keen and lively as they loaded the guns and attached night-vision scopes with practiced ease. These guardsmen, John realized, were highly trained and knew their weapons well. They knelt on the floor next to the silo's circular wall and pointed their sniper rifles through the horizontal slits. At the same time, Ariel knelt in front of another slit and loaded her own gun. Then she reached into one of the duffel bags, pulled out a handheld scope, and passed it to John. "You'll be our spotter," she said. "That means you find targets for us." She lay on her stomach and pointed the barrel of her rifle through the slit. "Come down here."

John sprawled on the floor beside her and looked through the spotter scope, which had a night-vision display. He'd seen this kind of display before, during his brief time in the army. It intensified the available light and outlined everything in shades of lurid green. He saw the cornfields again, but now in vivid detail, the tall, ripe stalks crowded in close rows. He saw the cinder-block outbuildings near the edge of the farm and the guardsmen positioned behind them, clutching their carbines and waiting for the attack to begin. And about half a mile away he saw the farm's southern fence, topped with coils of concertina wire, and the pine woods beyond.

"You see that gate in the fence?" Ariel nudged him. "That's twelve o'clock. When you spot a target, call out his position—one o'clock, two o'clock, three o'clock, and so on."

John focused his scope at the edge of the woods. After a few seconds he saw movement, a green blur between the pine trees. Someone who'd been hiding behind one of the tree trunks had darted to another. An instant later he glimpsed someone else raise his head above a pile of stones. "I see Riflemen." Panning the scope from left to right, he saw more of them fidgeting behind the trees. "They're all along the edge of the woods."

Ariel squinted through the scope on her rifle. "I see them, too." She looked over her shoulder at Conroy, who was removing more equipment from the duffel bags. "It's a little strange, cuz, that they haven't attacked yet. It looks like they're waiting for a signal."

Conroy nodded. "The Chief Elder is talking with Sullivan again. Through the wireless video connection." He pulled a long tube out of the bag and began assembling the weapon. "She's pretending to negotiate with him, but in truth she's stalling for time. The evacuation of Haven is taking longer than expected."

Ariel pointed at Conroy's weapon, which was much bulkier than a rifle. It looked more like a rocket launcher. "Is that a Stinger?"

"Aye, to shoot down helicopters. The federal agents may try to fly over our fence." He pointed toward the east. "They've set up a staging area three miles away, but they're not prepared to strike yet. Sullivan is our more immediate concern."

Curious, John turned his spotter scope to the east. Although he didn't see any helicopters, he observed at least a dozen state trooper cars parked in a distant field. He turned back to the south, intending to look for more Riflemen in the woods, but while panning the scope along the southern fence he caught a glimpse of a figure in the grass, about a hundred yards left of the gate. The figure was crawling toward the fence and holding an oversized pair of bolt cutters. "Someone's approaching the fence, eleven o'clock," he told Ariel. "Looks like he wants to cut a hole in it."

She instantly pointed her rifle at the man. "Damnation," she muttered. "It's Harcourt."

"Who? What do you—"

"He was in the Rangers for twenty years before the rebellion. We worked together on dozens of assignments."

The man was fast. Within seconds he reached the drainage ditch just outside the fence and disappeared from view. Then he crawled up the other side of the ditch and started cutting the chain link at the base of the fence. "He's quick with those bolt cutters," John noted. "He'll get through in no time."

Conroy stopped unloading the duffel bags and came up behind them. "Take the shot, milady," he urged. "We can't let him breach the perimeter."

Ariel curled her finger around the rifle's trigger. But she didn't pull it. In the spotter scope John saw the Rifleman snap six more links, making a crescent-shaped tear in the fence.

"Milady!" Conroy raised his voice. "Do your duty!"

She took a deep breath and let it out. Then she fired the rifle.

John saw the impact of the bullet in Harcourt's chest. He fell backward into the ditch, the bolt cutters still in his hands. The gunshot echoed across the farm for a few seconds, then faded away. Then John heard a chorus of enraged shouting, a war cry composed of hundreds of voices. Sullivan's men emerged from the pine woods and rushed forward.

From a distance it looked like pandemonium, but gazing through the spotter scope John could see that the attack was well coordinated. The first line of Riflemen fired a barrage of rocket-propelled grenades, which exploded up and down the length of the fence. The blasts were so bright, they flooded the night-vision display in John's scope, and he had to close his eyes. When he opened them again the fence was wreathed in smoke, and he couldn't see a thing behind it, but he could hear the shouts of the Riflemen and the crackling of automatic weapons fire. After several seconds the smoke began to clear and John aimed his scope at the base of the fence. Sullivan's men were already wriggling through the jagged holes where their grenades had shredded the chain link.

"They're coming through!" he shouted. "Eleven o'clock, twelve, Jesus, the whole fence!"

Ariel and the other snipers started shooting. Tactically, it was an ideal situation for them. Because the fence was half a mile away, it was within range of the sniper rifles but too distant for the Riflemen to return fire with their carbines. And Sullivan's men were easy targets as they scrabbled on their bellies through the holes in the fence. Ariel took her second shot as John peered through his scope, and he saw a man tumble backward into the drainage ditch. Another Rifleman crawled halfway through one of the holes, then shuddered and went limp. Ariel fired again and again, fast and efficient, hitting a new target every few seconds. When John looked up from his scope, though, he noticed she was crying. She didn't make a sound, but her wet cheeks reflected the muzzle flashes from her gun.

After thirty seconds of slaughter Sullivan's men retreated, ducking into the drainage ditch on the other side of the fence. A moment later they lobbed a dozen smoke grenades over the coils of concertina wire. Billows of thick white smoke erupted from the canisters, and soon the fence was hidden again. The snipers kept firing, using memory alone to aim for the holes in the fence, but John saw several Riflemen emerge from the wall of smoke and dive for cover in the cornfields. Within a couple of minutes most of Sullivan's surviving men were inside the fence and advancing on the outbuildings.

Dozens of guardsmen stood at the corners of the outbuildings, alternately firing their assault rifles into the fields and ducking behind the cinder-block walls. They had night-vision scopes too, but they couldn't see the enemy through the rows of cornstalks. After a while it became clear that the Riflemen were outflanking them. When Sullivan's men got close enough to the outbuildings, they threw fragmentation grenades at the defenders. The blasts flashed like supernovas on John's spotter scope, and when the glow faded he saw the corpses of the fallen guardsmen twisted into grotesque shapes.

Ariel tried to aim at the attackers, but there was too much cover and they moved too fast. She pulled back from her rifle's scope and turned to John. "You see anything?" Her voice was frantic. "Any targets at all?"

He shook his head. "All I know is they're getting closer."

"Bloody fucking hell! It doesn't make sense!" She stared into her scope again, grimacing. "We can't see them, but they can see us! How do they know where all our guardsmen are?"

"I don't—"

"It's like they have a fucking map of our defenses!" She looked over her shoulder at Conroy. "Are you monitoring the radio bands, cuz? Could one of the guardsmen be talking to Sullivan, telling him our positions?"

Conroy shook his head. "Only my most trusted men have radios."

"I suspect you've misplaced your trust." She turned back to John. "Use your scope to look at the guardsmen. See if any of them are handling their radios."

With some anxiety John pointed the spotter scope at the defensive positions. He looked at the guardsmen behind the outbuildings, but he didn't know what he'd do if he saw one of them speaking into a radio. He was worried that Ariel would immediately aim her rifle at the guy and execute him. His hands trembled so badly he fumbled the scope, pointing the thing at the sky instead of the ground. And in that instant he saw something, a small flash of green against the vast darkness. A green cross.

John focused on the object. It was the drone, beyond any doubt, but it seemed much larger than it had before. "Look at the sky, ten o'clock." He pointed at the unmanned aircraft. "It looks like it's flying lower now."

Ariel raised her rifle and scanned the sky until she saw it. "It's the Reaper! And you're right, it's only two or three miles up."

"Why did the federal agents lower it? So they can observe their raid on the farm?"

She nodded. "The drone has infrared cameras. They detect heat, so they can see everything in the dark."

"Do you think Sullivan is intercepting the video from the drone's cameras?" John thought of something Sullivan had mentioned during his conversation with the Elders. "He said he could disable the government's drone if he wanted to. So maybe he also has access to its video feed."

She lowered her rifle to the floor and gripped his arm. "That's it! That's how the bastard can see our positions!" She jumped to her feet and turned around to face Conroy. "I'm sorry for doubting your judgment, cuz. Is the Stinger ready?"

"Aye, milady." He bowed his head and then dashed to the other side of the circular room. "I'll open the hatch."

While Ariel picked up the bulky tube of the Stinger and hoisted it to her shoulder, Conroy grasped a handle on the curving wall and began turning it rapidly. John heard the sound of metallic scraping inside the dome on top of the silo. He looked up and saw a steel panel move to the side like a sliding door. The gap widened until it was a huge square, ten feet across, like the opening in the dome of an observatory. But instead of a telescope, Ariel pointed a missile launcher at the sky. She looked through the Stinger's night-vision gun sight, then waved John to her side. "Come here. Help me target the drone."

He stood up and gazed at the sky through his scope, trying to find the drone again. After a few seconds he spotted it. "Okay, it's there, in the lower-right corner of the opening. It's moving to the left."

"Got it." As Ariel pointed the Stinger at the drone and tracked its progress, the launcher emitted a high-pitched tone that grew steadily louder. "The infrared seeker is locked on."

Conroy rushed toward the other snipers in the room and pushed them away from Ariel. "Move to the side! There's going to be a back blast!"

John got out of the way too. Ariel tipped the launcher upward and to the left, compensating for gravity and the drone's velocity. Then she pulled the Stinger's trigger.

A plume of exhaust spewed out of the back end of the launcher as the missile streaked out of the front. The rocket shot upward at incredible speed, zooming in an almost straight line toward the drone. At the last instant it made a course correction and swung into a tight left turn. Then it slammed into the Reaper and exploded.

Conroy shouted, "Huzzah!" as the fireball lit the sky. Ariel lowered the launcher and smiled, watching the flaming pieces of the drone plummet to earth. And then, before John could congratulate her, a much closer explosion rocked the silo. The steel shell of the structure rang with the blast, and everyone in the room fell to the floor.

"Shit!" John was deafened. He could barely hear his own voice. "What the fuck was that?"

"Grenade!" Ariel shouted. "It hit just below us. Conroy, close the hatch!"

Conroy raced back to the other side of the room and turned the handle again. As the hatch slid closed, Ariel scrambled toward the slit. The other snipers did the same and so did John, who was just as anxious to see what was happening outside. He pointed his spotter scope at the ground and saw the guardsmen in full retreat. They'd abandoned the outbuildings and were running back to the barn and farmhouses. Sullivan's men pursued the guardsmen, shrieking their war cries and firing their carbines as they ran. The fields were littered with fallen soldiers from both sides.

Less than two hundred yards away, a pair of Riflemen halted and stood abreast. Moving as one, they raised their grenade launchers to their shoulders. The weapons, John realized, were pointed straight at the silo.

"Watch out!" he shouted, pulling Ariel away from the slit. He threw himself on top of her and covered his ears.

The blasts punctured the steel wall of the silo. John felt the heat on his arms and legs, and bits of shrapnel pinged against his back. When he looked up he saw patches of night sky through jagged holes in the dome. Ariel was unhurt, thank God—she squirmed underneath him, yelling, "Get off me!"—and Conroy lay nearby, stunned but conscious. But the other snipers were dead. They hadn't pulled back far enough before the grenades exploded.

Ariel wriggled free. As soon as she saw what was left of the sniper's nest, she pointed at the spiral stairway and tugged at John's arm. "Let's go, let's go!" she shouted. "We have to get out of here!"

Blood trickled down John's back from the bits of embedded shrapnel, but he didn't feel much pain. The Fountain protein was still doing its job. He stood up and hooked an arm around Conroy's waist, lifting the guardsman to his feet. Then they followed Ariel to the stairway and bounded down the curving steps.

Another explosion shook the silo as they descended. More debris rained on their heads, but they didn't stop. They kept spiraling downward, to the bottom of the silo and then below the surface. Soon they reached the catwalk that ran down the rocky wall of the cavern. Haven was deserted now. John scanned the cavern's floor, still dimly illuminated by the emergency lights, but he didn't see a single person, not even in front of the entrance to the train tunnel. The evacuation had apparently been successful. The Pyramid and the surrounding buildings stood silent and empty, their stone walls laced with skeins of orange cable.

When they reached the bottom of the catwalk, though, the silence was broken by shouting. John turned toward the noise and saw about thirty guardsmen, Haven's surviving defenders. Panicky and exhausted, they'd retreated through the trapdoors in the barn and farmhouses and barreled down the other stairways to the cavern. Conroy swiftly took charge of the men, directing them to the train tunnel. The final straggler was Gower, who was bleeding from a wound on his shoulder but still cradled his assault rifle. He staggered toward Conroy and fell into the older man's arms. Gower opened his mouth, but he was shivering so violently that his words were unintelligible.

"Calm down, lad." Conroy inspected the shoulder wound, which had soaked his shirt with blood but didn't look very deep. "You're not badly hurt."

Gower shook his head. "Behind," he gasped. "They're behind us."

"Sullivan's men? How far behind?"

Before Gower could answer, they heard the Riflemen's war cries echoing down the stairways. Ariel shouted, "Move!" and all four of them raced for cover. They ran along the base of the Pyramid and hid behind its far corner just as Sullivan's men spilled into the cavern. John saw them for the first time without the green shading of the night-vision scope and noticed that their faces were black with camouflage paint. He didn't see Sullivan among them, but he recognized a couple of the men from the torture session in the pine woods. There were about fifty of them in all, not much more than the number of guardsmen, but the Riflemen were mad with rage and bloodlust. They saw the fleeing defenders at the far end of the cavern and rushed pell-mell toward them.

But they didn't see Conroy. The Master of the Guardsmen grabbed Gower's assault rifle, leaned over the stone blocks at the corner of the Pyramid and opened fire on the bastards.

Five of the men in the front ranks collapsed. The others halted, looked around frantically, and turned tail. Conroy downed three more Riflemen before they found cover on the other side of the Pyramid. Then he ducked behind the stone blocks and turned to Ariel. "Go to the tunnel, milady," he ordered. "I'll hold them off till you're safe."

She frowned. "You can't hold them off for long, cuz. There's too many."

"That's true. But I have a surprise for them." He reached into his pants pocket and pulled out a small, square device. It had an extendable antenna and a black button at its center. It looked like a remote control for a garage door.

Ariel paled as she stared at the thing. She grasped Conroy's arm above the elbow. "Nay, you can't trigger it yet! You—"

"Please listen, milady. The explosives will go off in a sequence. First the Pyramid, then the other buildings, then the walls of the cavern. You'll have enough time to reach the tunnel. I'll stay behind to make sure they don't follow you."

"Let me stay here instead of you, cuz." Ariel squeezed his arm. Her eyes were glassy. "You already saved me once. I should return the favor."

"Nay, this is my duty." Conroy shook his head. "But you can repay the debt by giving a message to your mother. Will you do that for me?"

She nodded. A tear slipped from the corner of her eye. Conroy raised his hand to her face and caressed her cheek. Even though he was three hundred years younger than Ariel, he gazed at her as if she were his daughter. "Tell Elizabeth it was an honor to serve her. And tell her I always treasured the gift she gave me."

A sudden hail of bullets struck the stone blocks at the Pyramid's corner. Sullivan's men had regrouped and were preparing to advance. Conroy removed Ariel's hand from his arm, then turned to John and Gower. He pointed at the far end of the cavern, where the other guardsmen were filing into the train tunnel. "Now, go!" he shouted. "Get Lily to safety!"

Conroy turned around, raised his gun, and fired back at the Riflemen. Ariel and Gower just stood there for a moment, unwilling to abandon him. Then John grabbed both of them by the arm and started running toward the tunnel.

They kept their heads low as they ran. A couple of bullets whistled past, but Sullivan's men focused their fire on Conroy. John heard an intensely loud barrage of gunshots behind him, the sound of fifty men strafing the Pyramid, but he didn't turn around, didn't look over his shoulder. He hurtled forward, pulling Ariel and Gower along with him. After half a minute they charged past the geothermal plant and turned toward the tunnel's entrance. Only then did John look back, and he immediately wished he hadn't. Sullivan's men had come around both sides of the Pyramid and trapped Conroy between them. The Master of the Guardsmen convulsed as the bullets slammed into him, but before he fell he raised his left hand, the one that had been holding the remote-control device. An instant later the Pyramid exploded.

The blasts erupted on all four sides of the structure, pulverizing its foundations. Hundreds of stone blocks broke loose from the sloping walls and plummeted to the cavern's floor. The Riflemen had barely enough time to look up before the falling blocks buried them.

Within seconds the Pyramid was a spreading pile of rubble, all its secrets smashed to bits. And while the debris still tumbled and crashed and settled, the explosives in the other buildings began to detonate. The structures collapsed one by one, like dominos falling, starting at one end of the cavern and swiftly progressing to the other. John was only steps away from the tunnel when the shock wave from the blasts almost knocked him over. Gower sank to his knees, but John took one of his arms and Ariel took the other and together they pulled him up. They dragged him into the tunnel just before the geothermal plant exploded, hurling mangled pipes and machinery across the cavern.

Then the explosives in the cavern's walls detonated. This was the final step in the entombment of Haven, obviously intended to guarantee that no one would ever dig up any evidence of the Furies. The blasts cracked the natural pillars and arches that had held up the roof of the cavern. Without those supports, millions of tons of rock and soil began to fall. John and Ariel and Gower were twenty yards inside the tunnel, still sprinting forward, when the cascading rock sealed the entrance they'd just dashed through. Some of the debris spilled into the tunnel, and a cloud of dust buffeted them from behind. The air grew hazy, obscuring the battery-operated emergency lights on the ceiling. John could just barely see the figures of the thirty fleeing guardsmen, about a hundred yards ahead. Aside from them, though, the tunnel was empty. The steel rails stretched into the distance, but there was no train on them.

"Mother of Creation!" Ariel yelled. "They left without us!"

"The train was probably full," John said, coughing from the dust. "Everyone will unload at the other end, and then it'll come back."

"What makes you think—"

She was interrupted by a deep reverberating groan that seemed to come from the bowels of the earth. The floor of the tunnel rumbled and bounced, throwing them off balance. John got the feeling that the planet itself was angry at them. Vast mountains of loosened rock were sliding into the cavern, and the sudden shift of so much mass was destabilizing the whole area. Then they heard a louder, sharper noise just above their heads, and when John looked up he saw cracks forming in the tunnel's concrete ceiling. Within seconds the cracks lengthened and widened. Clods of dirt poured from them, showering the train tracks.

"Run!" John screamed. He grabbed Ariel and Gower again. "The tunnel's collapsing!"

Now they ran faster than ever, because it was worse to be buried alive than to be shot or blown up. They ran through veils of falling dirt, which splashed on their heads and funneled into their clothes. Behind them, the ceiling buckled and gave way, and chunks of concrete dropped into the tunnel along with tons of thudding earth, but they managed to stay a few yards ahead of the collapse. After a minute or so they closed the distance between themselves and the guardsmen, who looked at the three of them in terror. They were caked with dirt, brown from head to toe.

Then John looked beyond the guardsmen and saw a silvery glint at the end of the tunnel. It was the train, coming back for them.

He let go of Ariel and Gower and raced past the guardsmen. He sprinted toward the open-top freight cars at the back of the train, which was moving in reverse at about twenty miles per hour. As he ran he waved his arms to get the attention of the train driver. Ariel had told him the man's name was Bardolph.

"Stop, Bardolph!" he screamed. "Stop!"

After several seconds John heard the screech of the train's brakes. It slowed to a halt just as he came abreast of the last car, but he kept running until he was within earshot of Bardolph, who'd poked his head out of the engine's window to see what was going on.

"Get ready to move forward!" John shouted at him. "I'll give you a signal when everyone's aboard!" Then he turned around and urged the guardsmen to run faster. "Get in the last car! Come on, come on, move it!"

But they needed no encouragement. With the tunnel collapsing in sections just behind them, the guardsmen leaped into the last car. Ariel brought up the rear, helping Gower onto the train, and then John leaped aboard himself and whistled at the driver. "Go, go! Fast as you can!"

It was going to be close. The train was a hundred years old and slow to accelerate. As they crept forward a fissure opened in the ceiling directly overhead, spilling gobs of dirt into the last freight car. Ariel screamed and some of the guardsmen wailed. But then the train gathered speed. Soon they were charging down the tunnel, outracing the collapse. The earth continued to shift and fracture behind them, but the groaning and thudding grew steadily fainter.

The guardsmen got off the train as soon as it reached the western end of the ten-mile-long track. Anxious to leave the tunnel, they hurried out of the freight car and headed for the stairway that Bardolph pointed out to them. John and Ariel were the last to leave the train because they had to steady Gower, who was weak and dizzy from blood loss. Supporting him on both sides, they helped him up the stairs, which led to a trapdoor that had been hidden for decades but now stood wide open. They emerged in an abandoned cellar, moldy from disuse, and then climbed a newer stairway that led to the warehouse of Rudyard Trucking, the transportation business owned and operated by the Ranger Corps.

It was a big building, almost as long as a football field, with a high slanted roof and a raised concrete floor. Running along one whole side of the building was an enormous loading dock where trucks could back up to the raised floor and take on cargo through their rear doors. Judging from the detritus on the floor—discarded boxes, scraps of paper and so on—John guessed that the warehouse had been buzzing with activity not so long ago, but now the great majority of the Furies had departed and only three medium-size trucks were still parked at the dock. The guardsmen who'd come up the stairs just a minute ago had already been assigned a new task, loading the last crates and trunks and boxes onto the waiting trucks. At the center of the warehouse a dozen men and women sat behind a long receiving desk, staring at computer screens and shouting into portable radios. Because they were all dressed in modern clothes—jeans, sneakers, polo shirts, and so on—John assumed they were the Rangers who ran the trucking firm. They were probably monitoring the status of the trucks that had just left. All three of the Elders also sat behind the desk, giving orders and glancing nervously at the screens. Their bailiff, Old Sam, stood dutifully beside them.

One of the Rangers, a tall, slender woman wearing jeans and a backpack, rushed over to John and Ariel and helped them find a place for Gower to lie down. She ripped off his filthy shirt and started to clean his shoulder wound, using sponges and herbal medicines from her pack. Ariel took a moment to check the contents of her own backpack, removing the medicine case and opening it to see if any of the vials of Fountain had been damaged. Then, satisfied that everything was all right, she slung the pack over her shoulder and examined John's back. "You're injured, too. Shrapnel." She looked him in the eye. "You don't feel any pain?"

"Not really," he said, although his wounds *were* starting to hurt now that the danger was past and his adrenaline had subsided. "Well, maybe a little."

Ariel turned to the Ranger medic kneeling beside Gower. "When you're done with the guardsman, treat this man, too."

By that point the Chief Elder had noticed their presence. Elizabeth Fury stepped away from the receiving desk and came toward them, looking Ariel up and down. She bit her lower lip, and for a moment her expression was the same as the one her daughter always wore when she was worried or frightened. But then Elizabeth's face hardened and she narrowed her lone eye. "Where's Conroy?" she asked.

Ariel shook her head. Bits of dirt fell from her hair and sprinkled on the floor. "He saved us all. The Riflemen were right behind us, but he held them off until we could escape the cavern. Then he triggered the explosives. I've never seen a braver end."

The Chief Elder had no reaction. She was good at hiding things, John realized. He waited for Ariel to deliver Conroy's message, but she didn't. Instead, she just stared at her mother. Elizabeth stared back. "Is Sullivan dead, too?"

"Nay, I don't think so. None of us saw him. The cur was too cowardly to take part in the attack. Right now he's probably surveying the ruins of the farm and wondering if we committed mass suicide."

Elizabeth frowned. "He knows us too well to take that idea seriously. He'll start looking for us soon. Fortunately, most of our people have already crossed the border." She nodded at the Rangers working the portable radios. "We're still waiting to hear from two trucks that haven't reached Sault Sainte Marie yet, but the rest are in Canada now."

"And will we go there too?"

"Cordelia will go to Canada to supervise the holding phase. Nearly everyone in the family will disperse across the provinces and find temporary lodgings—rented cabins, hotels, and so on. But you and I and Margaret will go south with the surviving guardsmen."

"South?"

"Aye, we need to prepare our new home. We'll secure the area, then stockpile a sufficient quantity of food, enough for two years. We'll also need to build a power plant." Elizabeth seemed remarkably confident, especially considering the current circumstances. Her faith in her plans was unshakable. "Then our cousins can leave Canada and join us. Not all at once, of course. It may take several months to complete the relocation."

"You're not talking about the southern United States, I presume?"

"Nay, that would be too risky. We have to go into the wilderness again, Lily."

"A wilderness to the south?" Ariel raised an eyebrow. "Are you speaking of South America then? The Amazon basin?"

"Don't be impatient, child." She gave her daughter a scolding look. "I'll tell you the location when the time is ripe."

"Mother, I know more about the Amazon than you do. You've never even been there. You should—"

"Enough." She raised her hand, cutting off discussion. Then she pointed at one of the trucks parked in the loading dock. "You and your paramour will travel in that vehicle. The guardsmen have already loaded your trunk inside. Margaret and I will ride in another truck."

Ariel grimaced. With a frustrated growl, she marched toward the back of the truck and entered its cargo hold. John wanted to follow her, but at that moment the tall medic stepped behind him, lifted his shirt and began tweezering the bits of shrapnel out of his back. The Fountain protein, which had shielded him from so much pain until now, had apparently washed out of his system, and the medic's attentions hurt like hell. And as he stood there, wincing, the Chief Elder gave him a look of contempt. She didn't say a word. She had no interest in talking with him. She just wanted him to know how much she despised him. Once she made her point clear, she turned around and headed back to the team of Rangers.

At least the medic was quick. She soon pulled the last pieces of metal from his skin, sponged away the dried blood, and applied a soothing paste that felt absolutely wonderful. Then he heard an angry cry coming from inside the truck. A second later Ariel stormed out of the cargo hold and stomped toward the receiving desk, heading straight for Margaret Fury.

"Damnable sneak!" she yelled, pointing at her aunt. "You broke the lock on my trunk!"

Margaret opened her mouth wide. "I did no such thing!"

"Don't lie to me, Auntie!" Ariel leaned across the desk and bent over her. "I know you want the formula for the catalyst! You want it so badly you tried to get John to spy on me! And now you've pawed through my belongings like a common thief!"

"Nay, nay!" Margaret rose from her chair, shaking her head fiercely. "I would never dirty my hands by touching your possessions!"

"So what did you do? Get one of your lackeys to perform the deed?"

"This is absurd! First of all, I know very well you'd never put the formula in your trunk." She pointed at Ariel's backpack. "It's in there, is it not? So why would I be so stupid as to—"

"Then who was it?" Ariel looked around the room, breathing hard. "Which one of you is the traitor?"

Elizabeth glared at her. The vertical scar on her face darkened as she stepped toward Ariel. Old Sam stepped toward her too, and so did Cordelia, who raised her wooden hand in a pacifying gesture. "Lily," she said softly, "you must calm yourself, dearest."

John wanted to help her, but he didn't know what to do. He'd never seen Ariel this angry before. He moved forward with the others, trying to catch her eye.

Then, while everyone's attention was fixed on Ariel, Old Sam stepped behind Elizabeth and put her in a choke hold. He hooked his sinewy left arm around her neck, and with his right hand he pulled a pistol from his pants and jammed its muzzle against the side of her head.

"*Stand back!*" he roared. He quickly dragged the Chief Elder across the floor until he stood with his back to the wall. Elizabeth seemed too surprised to resist. She opened her mouth, her lips stretching to form the name "Sam," but no sound came out. She couldn't breathe.

The guardsmen and Rangers were also surprised, but within seconds every one of them pointed an assault rifle at the bailiff. Old Sam responded by tightening the choke hold and making sure that Elizabeth shielded his body. John hadn't noticed until now how tough and wiry the old man was. He didn't even flinch as Elizabeth fought back, scratching his arm and stomping on his feet. He kept his grip on the Chief Elder while facing down all the men aiming their guns at him.

"*I said stand back!*" he bellowed. "If you don't, she dies!"

Elizabeth struggled for breath, her face contorting. After a moment of collective hesitation, the guardsmen and Rangers took a couple of steps backward. Old Sam loosened his hold on the Chief Elder, who took a rasping breath that echoed across the warehouse. Then he looked directly at Ariel. "Take off your backpack, Lily," he ordered. "Drop it on the floor and slide it over to me."

She shook her head. "This is madness. Come to your senses, Sam."

"Nay, I'm no madman. I've fooled all of you for months." He allowed himself a brief smile, then curled his upper lip. "Now give me the backpack."

Ariel narrowed her eyes, returning his look of hatred with one of her own. "So you were Sullivan's informant? The one who told him I was going to New York to get the catalyst?"

He nodded. "And I had every right to do it. Fountain will save my life and many others. Keeping it from us is nothing short of murder." He tightened the choke hold again and Elizabeth squirmed in front of him.

"You've stalled long enough. If you don't give me your pack in the next two seconds, I'll crush your mother's larynx."

Scowling, Ariel took off her backpack, set it down and kicked it across the floor. It came to rest about a yard from Old Sam's feet. "It won't do you any good," she said. "Sullivan is defeated. His Riflemen are dead. Their bodies lie under a mountain of crushed rock."

Very carefully the bailiff extended his foot and toed the backpack closer to himself. "I know Sullivan's plans better than you do. He kept half of his men in reserve, withholding them from the battle. Now I'll contact him and let him know where you are." He turned to the nearest Ranger, one of the men aiming their assault rifles at him. "Give me your radio, Lawrence. You owe nothing to these women."

Lawrence glanced at the portable radio hanging from his belt but kept his rifle pointed at Old Sam. After a couple of seconds he shook his head.

"Don't be a fool!" Old Sam's face reddened. As he grew angrier he flexed the muscles in his left arm, squeezing Elizabeth's throat. She opened her mouth, gagging, and her eyes bulged out of their sockets. Desperate for air, she clawed and yanked at Sam's arm, but he wouldn't let go. And as he throttled Elizabeth, he glared at the Ranger named Lawrence. "Just think for a second, boy! If your mothers and sisters truly cared for you, would they deny you this remedy? Would they allow you to grow old and die even though they possess the cure?"

While Old Sam focused on Lawrence, John quietly stepped forward. Although he was more than ten feet away from the bailiff, he thought he could dare a lunge if he got a little closer. But the old man spotted the movement out of the corner of his eye. He swiftly pivoted, pressing his pistol so forcefully against Elizabeth's temple that her head jerked sideways. "And you're even more of a fool, paramour!" he shouted. "You're fighting to save a woman who was planning to kill you!"

The bailiff was growing more agitated by the second. Spittle flew from his lips as he yelled at John. Meanwhile, Elizabeth was losing consciousness. She let go of the arm that was choking her and hung limply in its embrace. Her lips had turned blue and her tongue lolled out of her mouth. Old Sam must've noticed that she'd stopped struggling, but he didn't seem to care. Even though it made no sense—he'd lose all his leverage if Elizabeth died—he kept on strangling her.

Then Cordelia Fury rushed toward the Ranger named Lawrence and snatched the portable radio from his belt. Before anyone could stop her, she ran to Old Sam with the device in her outstretched hand. She was crying hysterically. "Take it!" she screamed, thrusting the radio at him. "Just don't kill my sister!"

Now it was Old Sam's turn to be surprised. Without thinking, he reached for the radio. At this point John realized that Cordelia had a plan. She'd recognized a simple fact that had somehow eluded everyone else: the bailiff had only two hands. He tried to keep the gun pointed at Elizabeth's head as he reached for the radio, but the half-conscious Chief Elder slipped out of his grasp and began sliding to the floor. He turned away from Cordelia for a moment and grabbed Elizabeth around the waist to stop her from falling. And in that moment Cordelia swung her left arm in an accelerating arc and smacked her wooden hand against Old Sam's head.

Dazed, he staggered backward. As Elizabeth slumped to the floor, groggy and gasping, John saw his chance and lunged. He charged toward Old Sam, crossing the space between them in less than a second. But he was too late. Although the bailiff tottered from the blow to his skull, he stayed on his feet and held on to his pistol. Cordelia hadn't hit him hard enough, and she wasn't ready to hit him again. She stepped to the side, uncertain what to do. Old Sam, shaking off his dizziness, raised his pistol and shot her.

Then John tackled him from behind. The old man hit the floor face-first and the gun fell out of his hand. But John didn't pound him the way he'd pounded Archibald, the other traitor. The Fountain protein wasn't in John's veins anymore, and he didn't feel the insane urge to beat his enemies to a pulp. And Old Sam was out cold anyway, his broken nose leaking blood onto the concrete. So John just grabbed the dropped pistol and pinned the old man to the floor while the Rangers and guardsmen rushed forward. Half of them surrounded the downed bailiff, and the other half ran toward Cordelia.

Ariel was the first to reach her aunt, but she stopped short when she saw the bullet wound. It was in the center of Cordelia's chest, and there was surprisingly little blood on her dress. The bullet had gone straight through her heart, stopping it from beating. John had seen this kind of wound twice before, both times late at night in Kensington. The first time, he was sixteen years old and one of the boys in his corner crew was shot in a drive-by. The second time, it happened to his daughter.

Cordelia was dead, and yet Ariel tried to revive her. She knelt beside her aunt and pressed her palms to the bullet wound and tried to pump

Cordelia's shredded heart back to life. Although everyone knew the effort was futile, no one tried to stop her. She kept pumping her aunt's chest while one of the guardsmen took the pistol away from John and another tied Old Sam's hands behind his back. At the same time, Margaret Fury crouched next to Elizabeth, who'd propped herself up to a sitting position. The Chief Elder was still gasping, and her throat was badly bruised. Margaret rested a hand on her shoulder, but Elizabeth wouldn't look at her. She was staring at Ariel and Cordelia.

"Please, Sister, look at me," Margaret urged. "You must—"

"Nay!" Elizabeth pushed her away and stood up.

"What are you doing? Come back here!"

With sure and steady footsteps Elizabeth marched to the guardsman who'd taken Old Sam's gun from John. She wrested the pistol out of the surprised man's hands, then returned to where the unconscious bailiff lay. Then she bent over Old Sam and shot him twice in the head.

The gunshots echoed against the walls of the warehouse. Elizabeth looked up, and for a moment John thought she was going to shoot him next. But instead she pointed at the trucks parked by the loading dock.

"Move out!" she ordered. "We're leaving *now!*"

TWENTY-FIVE

Agent Larson gazed at the crater that used to be the Amish farm. His task force, which had been preparing for a raid on the underground meth lab, was now engaged in a rescue operation. He and twenty other agents stood at the crater's rim, shining their flashlights at the rubble below. The remnants of the barn and the farmhouses were embedded in a giant mound of soil and cornstalks.

Larson swept his flashlight's beam over the rubble pile, looking for survivors. His agents had already discovered several dozen corpses, but they weren't victims of the cave-in. Most of them appeared to have died from bullet wounds or fragmentation grenades. This evidence was consistent with the earlier reports from the agents in the surveillance van, who'd heard gunshots and explosions at the farm's southern border about an hour ago. Unfortunately, Larson had been slow to respond to the reports because his assault team hadn't yet arrived from Sault Sainte Marie. He and his men didn't reach the farm until after the cave-in.

Now he wondered if he would ever piece together what had happened here. About half of the corpses were dressed in Amish clothes and half in leather boots and motorcycle jackets, which suggested that Van's gang had attacked the farm. But why would he do that if he knew the FBI was going to raid the place in just a few hours? It didn't make sense. And when Larson had tried to call Van to get an explanation, there was no answer, of course.

He switched off his flashlight. *What a fucking mess.* Van's attack must've set off another explosion in the meth lab. But how could it trigger such a big fucking cave-in? The crater was at least a hundred yards wide.

And another thing: Who the hell shot down the drone? The Air Force and the Homeland Security Department were going to be pissed about that.

Larson turned around and walked away from the crater. His career in the bureau was over, that much was certain. His bosses would probably suspend him from duty as soon as they found out what happened. And the truth was, he deserved to be shit-canned. He should've conducted more surveillance of the farm before going ahead with the assault. He'd relied on Van's bullshit stories instead of hard evidence, and he'd obviously overlooked something. He'd missed something important.

He shook his head. *What the hell was it? What did I miss?*

He had no fucking idea.

PART III
FOUNTAIN

TWENTY-SIX

The journey in the truck was miserable. A dozen guardsmen and Rangers crowded the cargo hold, sharing the space with stacks of trunks and boxes. The exhausted men and women sprawled wherever they could, each trying to get some sleep as the truck rumbled down an unseen highway. The cargo hold had no windows or peepholes, and the only light came from a naked bulb dangling from the ceiling. There was no place to wash up or go to the bathroom, either. John smelled so bad, he disgusted even himself.

There was little conversation. No one wanted to talk about the destruction of Haven or the murder of Cordelia. And everyone was careful not to disturb Ariel, who'd shrouded her aunt's body in a canvas tarp and kept vigil over it in the far corner of the cargo hold, hidden behind several stacks of boxes. John wanted to console her, but the others stopped him. For the Furies, mourning was a strictly private affair.

He was just as exhausted as everyone else, so he found a place to lie down and sleep. When he awoke a few hours later he realized that the truck had come to a stop and its rear doors were open. Standing up, he saw a square of night sky and felt a cold breeze. The truck had stopped in a dark field in the middle of nowhere. Maybe Wisconsin, John guessed, judging from how long they'd been driving. Two vans and four large SUVs were parked nearby, and the guardsmen were busy transferring boxes from the truck's cargo hold to the vans and cars. This was a rendezvous point, John realized, a place where the Furies could disperse for greater safety. It was more prudent to travel in half a dozen vehicles than in one.

John needed to take a piss, so he stepped down from the cargo hold and hurried to the edge of the field. After he finished, he turned back to the truck and saw two Rangers holding Cordelia's shrouded corpse. They carried it to one of the vans and placed it inside. Then they got into the van themselves and drove away, presumably to bury her.

The other van drove away too, and so did the SUVs. By the time John returned to the truck, most of the guardsmen and Rangers had departed and only Ariel was left in the cargo hold. She stood near the rear doors, looking up at the stars. John sensed she didn't want to talk yet, so he stood beside her, silent. The sky just above the eastern horizon had started to brighten. It was maybe half an hour before dawn.

After a minute or so, the tall Ranger medic who'd treated John's shrapnel wounds came to the back of the truck and handed him a paper grocery bag. "Here's some food and water," she said. "We still have three hundred miles to go." Then she shut the rear doors, locking John and Ariel inside. Half a minute later the truck's engine restarted and they began moving again. The truck jounced up and down as it crossed the field, but the ride leveled out as soon as they returned to the paved road.

John sat on one of the trunks remaining in the cargo hold and opened the grocery bag. He pulled out two plastic bottles of water and handed one to Ariel. She opened it, took a long drink, then poured the rest of the water on her head. This turned out to be a mistake. The water washed the dirt out of her hair, sending muddy rivulets down her forehead and into her eyes.

"Oh, hell," she muttered, raising her hands to her face. "Hand me another bottle, will you?"

He gave her another bottle of water and a fistful of napkins. She cleaned herself more carefully this time, splashing water on her face and using the napkins to wipe away the dirt. Then she took off her backpack and cleaned her neck as well. John did the same, lifting his shirt to wash his underarms. Afterwards, he smelled a little better—not great, but not putrid, either. Then he looked in the bag to see what else was there. "We got some sandwiches," he reported. "Roast beef and cheddar, it looks like. You want one?"

Ariel shook her head. "No, I'm not hungry. But don't let me stop you."

"I'm not hungry either. I feel a little nauseous, actually. And kind of weak."

She stepped closer and looked him over. "Well, that doesn't surprise me. The Fountain protein put you on a roller-coaster ride." She sat down beside him on the trunk and pressed two fingers to his neck to feel his pulse. "How long did you feel its effects?"

"I definitely felt it in the train tunnel. It was like the world's biggest adrenaline rush. But it faded after that. I started to feel normal again when we reached the warehouse."

She unzipped her backpack and removed her Treasure and a pen. Then she turned to a fresh page in the notebook and started writing in the strange runelike alphabet that was her family's first language. "What about psychological effects? Did you feel any extremes of rage? Any inability to control violent impulses?"

"No, I was lucky. The protein was out of my system by the time I tackled Old Sam."

Ariel frowned at the mention of the traitor's name. Furrowing her brow, she scrawled a few more runes in her Treasure. "I wish I'd had a chance to examine you in my lab. Without any data, all I can do is make guesses. The Fountain protein may have interacted with your other biochemical pathways. Maybe the sudden injection of so much Fountain into your system triggered an overproduction of the Upstart protein to compensate. That might explain why we don't see these effects in women, because they don't have the Upstart gene."

"But why would there be psychological effects?"

"The brain is the most sensitive organ in the body. Any change in biochemistry is bound to influence the signaling among the brain cells. And when their signaling changes, the cells establish new connections."

John squirmed. A disturbing thought had just occurred to him. "Do you think any of the changes in the brain might be permanent?"

She didn't say anything at first, which made him worry even more. She took her time, thinking it over. "In your case, probably not. But I won't risk giving you another dose. The brain is quick to establish new pathways in response to chemical stimuli. Nicotine is the perfect example. The addiction response starts to develop after just a few cigarettes."

"So even though the antiaging effect goes away when you stop taking Fountain, the psychological effects might continue?"

Instead of answering, Ariel looked down at her Treasure. She flipped through the pages until she found one in the middle of the notebook. Then she squinted at the runes. "The only other test subject was Sullivan. I gave him daily injections of the Fountain protein for a week. He didn't report any side effects, so I kept dosing him until I ran out of protein." She looked up from the page. "But now that I think about it, I see he had a reason to lie to me. He wanted us to develop the antiaging treatment as quickly as possible. And he knew we'd have to do additional research if there were any unusual side effects. So in all likelihood he decided not to report them."

She closed the notebook and looked straight ahead, staring at the rear doors of the cargo hold. John leaned closer to her. "You think the protein might've messed with Sullivan's brain? Might've affected him permanently?"

Ariel raised her hand to her forehead, as if trying to calm the thoughts churning behind it. "He was always arrogant and cruel, even as a child. But until he started his rebellion, he never broke any of our laws. Maybe his conscience restrained him. Or maybe fear of punishment." She grimaced. "Something changed, though, after I gave him those injections. He ignored the restraints and acted on his impulses. And maybe Fountain had something to do with that."

She fell silent. Moving mechanically, she put her Treasure back into her pack. Then she removed the medicine case and unlatched it. Inside were the nine vials of Fountain protein, each nestled in foam padding, and the syringe. She rested the case in her lap and stared at the glass vials. There was nothing inside them but thick yellowish liquid, but she examined the stuff intently, narrowing her eyes, as if she could glimpse the microscopic proteins floating in the fluid.

Several seconds passed. Ariel seemed frozen, entranced. John grew nervous. "Look, whatever happened to Sullivan, it wasn't your fault," he argued. "You had no idea this could happen."

She didn't respond. She kept staring at the vials.

"You were trying to help," John added. "You shouldn't blame yourself."

After a few more seconds she let out a long breath and closed the medicine case. She returned it to the backpack and pulled out something else, a small black box. John hadn't noticed it before, perhaps because it was only two inches wide. Ariel held the thing in both hands and opened it. Inside was a gold ring with a jewel-encrusted ornament shaped like a butterfly. The insect's body was a line of six tiny diamonds. Its wings were spotted with rubies and sapphires.

"Aunt Delia made this for me," Ariel said. "She loved butterflies."

"That's right." An image came to John's mind, a recent memory. "There was a butterfly carved on her wooden hand."

"They had great meaning for her. She used to say, 'The flapping of a butterfly's wing on one side of the world can cause a hurricane on the other. That's what makes it so difficult to predict the future.'" Ariel removed the ring from the box and held it up to eye level. Its stones sparkled even in the cargo hold's dim light. "But it has another meaning, at least for me. People are like butterflies. We're lovely and fragile. And in the long run, we're powerless. The wind is stronger than us."

She fell silent again. John, worried she'd go into another trance, pointed at the ring. "It's beautiful. You were close to Cordelia, weren't you?"

She nodded. "Yes, especially when I was young. After every argument with Mother, I ran to Aunt Delia."

"When you say 'young,' what do you mean exactly?" John smiled. "Less than a hundred years old?"

"I mean the seventeenth century, the late 1600s. Mother was especially rigid after we came to America, and I was especially defiant. Delia didn't always take my side, but she stood with me on the most important things. She agreed that it was our duty to inoculate the Ojibway against smallpox. And she stopped Mother from executing Running Cloud after I brought him back to Haven."

John recalled his conversation with Ariel in her laboratory, the one that had ended so abruptly when the evacuation alarm sounded. He'd pushed it out of his mind during the confused hours since then, but now it struck him with its original force. Running Cloud had been Ariel's Ojibway paramour. And he'd gotten her pregnant. "Why did you do that? Bring him back to Haven, I mean?"

She fiddled with the ring in her hand, idly turning and fingering it. "When our family lived in Europe, the women found husbands in the nearby villages. We swore the men to secrecy and they became Furies. But after we came to America, Mother insisted that we live in isolation, so she established the rules for taking paramours. If you wished to become pregnant you had to travel far from Haven to find a man. And as soon as you were with child you had to leave your paramour and return to the family." She frowned. "My cousins and I hated the rules. It was an un-natural way to live."

John nodded. "I have to agree with you there."

"I met Running Cloud while we were inoculating the Ojibway at Chequamegon Bay, about three hundred miles west of Haven. We were posing as French missionaries, but the tribe's chiefs had encountered churchmen before and noticed we were different. We didn't harangue them so much about God, for one thing. For another, we had both men and women in our expedition, and the women were young and looking for partners." She closed her hand on the ring and shook her head in wonder. "I was only thirty-two years old. I was curious and willful and eager to fall in love. And Running Cloud was even younger. Twenty summers, he told me. That's how they measured time, by the number of summers they could remember."

John shifted uncomfortably on the trunk. The tone of Ariel's voice—soft and wistful—made it clear that she still had feelings for Running Cloud, despite the passage of so much time. "So you wanted to defy Elizabeth," he said, trying to change the subject. "You wanted to challenge her rules."

"I just wanted to live with the father of my children, the same way Mother had lived with Arthur, my father. Running Cloud was willing to leave his tribe and join our family. We waited until I was four months preg-nant, and then we canoed the three hundred miles back to Haven. When we arrived I told Mother she had a choice: either kill us or marry us." With a fond smile, she slipped the ring on the fourth finger of her left hand. "While Mother agonized over the decision, Delia made me a wedding ring. Some of my cousins helped her with the metalwork, but she designed it."

Ariel extended her arm and admired the ring on her hand. She was still smiling, but John knew her story wasn't going to be a happy one. She'd already told him, back in her lab, that it hadn't ended well. "How long were you married?" he asked.

"Three years. We built our own house on the family farm, a small cabin thatched with birch bark. Running Cloud finished building it the day before I gave birth to our daughter. She was a happy little girl, always laughing. She loved to walk in the woods." Ariel stopped smiling, just as John had expected. "I thought the three of us would be enough. I thought we could form our own little world. But it wasn't enough for Running Cloud. He missed the world of his ancestors."

"What happened? Did he go back to his tribe?"

"I woke up one morning and he was gone. And so was our daughter."

"Jesus. What did you do?"

"We organized a war party. We had only ten men and twenty women, and Running Cloud's tribe had twice as many warriors. But we had guns, flintlock muskets. Not an accurate long-range weapon, but effective for close-quarters combat." Ariel lowered her head and stared at the floor of the cargo hold. "We reached Chequamegon Bay just two days after Running Cloud did. I convinced Mother to let me try talking to the chiefs first, so she and I walked into the tribe's camp, unarmed, while the rest of our soldiers took positions in the woods. We found the chiefs in the wigwam and presented them with peace offerings, but they threw the gifts in our faces. They called us *Mi'tsha Midé*. That was their word for witches."

"Where was Running Cloud?"

"The chiefs had already killed him. They said we'd corrupted his spirit, so he had to be burned. As soon as I heard this, madness took hold of me. I screamed, 'Where's my daughter?' and charged at them. One of the chiefs lifted an ax, a heavy iron ax we'd given the tribe a few years before when we first made contact with them. But before he could bring it down on my head, Mother stepped in front of me. She knocked the ax handle aside, but the blade hit her face."

John winced. So that was how Elizabeth got her scar and lost her eye.

"Then it was chaos," Ariel continued, still gazing at the floor. "Our soldiers heard the screaming and rushed into the wigwam, firing their muskets. The gunfire terrorized the Ojibway. We slaughtered them as they ran for the woods. Afterwards, we found my daughter in a ditch they used as a trash dump. The chiefs had burned her, too."

Ariel had begun to cry as she told the story. Her tears slipped down her cheeks and nose. One of them dripped from her chin to the floor of the cargo hold. John slid across the trunk, closing the distance between them, and put his arms around her. He felt her trembling. "I'm sorry, Ariel," he murmured. "I'm so, so sorry."

He held her close and gently rubbed her back. She went on crying for a minute or so, her rib cage quivering under his hands. Then she raised her head and rubbed her eyes. The stones in her ring flashed and glittered. "No one challenged Mother's rules after that. She expected me to learn something from the tragedy and become a more dutiful daughter. But the lesson was too harsh. Whenever I saw that scar on her face . . ." Her voice trailed off. Instead of finishing the sentence, she pulled the ring off her finger and returned it to its box. "In the end, I decided to leave Haven for a while. Aunt Delia wanted to know what was happening in Europe, so I volunteered to be her spy. I traveled east to Quebec with a purse full of gold coins and bought passage on a ship heading across the Atlantic." She put the ring box in her backpack and zipped it up. "For the next twenty years I gathered information for Cordelia. I attended parties in the royal palaces in London and Paris. I met King William of England and King Louis of France. I also met Isaac Newton, who was much more interesting. I saw the beginnings of the scientific revolution, and it inspired me. By the time I returned to Haven I was committed to the ideal of bettering the world. I'd found my purpose in life, and it's sustained me ever since." She turned to John and looked him in the eye. "But I'd lost something, too. I didn't seek another paramour. For the next three centuries I had no interest in lovers or children. I lived my life as if I'd outgrown the need for them."

John still held her. She leaned into him, pressing her shoulder against his chest. She wasn't trembling anymore, but her body seemed unusually warm. "So what changed?" he asked. "Why did you walk into that bar in Greenwich Village and pick me up?"

"Because of Sullivan, believe it or not. Or rather, because I was afraid of his rebellion." Ariel gave him a sober look. "I saw how dangerous it was, how it threatened all of us. For the first time it seemed possible that our family could be destroyed. And that thought filled me with an unbearable urgency. Before everything ended, I wanted to have another child. I wanted to sleep with a man again." She allowed herself a smile. "But it couldn't be just any man, of course. Not after I'd waited for so long. So I asked Delia to help me. Although she hadn't ventured outside Haven in hundreds of years, she had information about billions of men in her computers."

John remembered the computer screens in Cordelia's room at the top of the Pyramid. He imagined her scrolling through the vast archives of the Internet until she found the sad story of John's daughter. "And you chose me because we both had daughters who were murdered?"

"No, not just that. I saw something noble in you."

"But I told you, I wasn't noble. I was going to—"

She hushed him by placing her index finger to his lips. "Forget nobility then. I sensed a deep connection between us. Do you know how Mother chose my birth name? She named me Lily because she loved the flower. She named all her children after flowers and other plants."

"Okay, but what does that have to do with—"

"When I had my daughter, I decided to follow Mother's tradition. So I named her Ivy."

John couldn't speak. He was shocked into silence.

Over the next five hours they polished off the roast beef sandwiches and got some more sleep. John found a couple of padded blankets, the kind used to cushion furniture in moving vans, and spread them across the floor of the cargo hold. Ariel was so tired, she drifted off almost as soon as she lay down. He lay next to her and for a while he studied her tranquil face, framed by her tangled locks of red hair. Then he fell asleep, too.

When the truck stopped again and its rear doors opened, brilliant late-morning light flooded the cargo hold. The tall Ranger medic who'd unlatched the doors was silhouetted against the brightness. "Rise and shine," she called out. "We're here."

John sat up and squinted at an utterly flat landscape. Fields of bright yellow wheat stretched to the horizon. He got to his feet and stepped to the edge of the cargo hold, looking for signs of civilization, but there weren't any farmhouses or barns in sight, just acres and acres of cultivated fields. "Where the hell are we?" he asked the medic.

"Western Minnesota," she replied. Then she stepped toward the front of the truck, moving out of sight.

By this point Ariel had awakened. She stretched her arms over her head, then stood up and put on her backpack. Meanwhile, John jumped down from the cargo hold and looked around. On the other side of the truck, at the edge of another wheat field, was a dilapidated trailer resting on cinder blocks. It had dirty beige siding and a rusty screen door and looked like it had been sitting there since the Great Depression. On the roof, though, were several tall antennas and a large satellite dish, and a couple of black SUVs were parked nearby. Just beyond the trailer, a long paved strip ran through the middle of the wheat field, straight as an arrow, for at least half a mile. It was an airstrip.

Ariel climbed down from the truck and stood beside him. "I've been here before. This strip is owned by the Ranger Corps. It's got a nice, long runway."

John looked up and down the strip. "Don't see any planes on it, though."

"They're probably busy elsewhere. The Rangers operate airstrips across the country. And they have a dozen Gulfstreams."

"Gulfstreams? Are those jets?"

She nodded. "They can go four thousand miles nonstop at five hundred miles per hour. And they only cost twenty million each."

"Jesus, where did you Furies get all that money?"

"We've been investing in stocks since the stock market started. Come on, let's see who's in the trailer."

They walked past the Ranger medic, who was checking the oil in the truck engine, and headed for the rusty screen door. Inside, the trailer was bustling. Two women typed on computer keyboards while two others barked orders into portable radios and yet another woman monitored a radar screen. A stern, husky man stood near the doorway, holding an assault rifle. Although he wore jeans and a T-shirt, John could tell he was a guardsman, not a Ranger. The modern clothes didn't fit him well, and his chin was red and nicked because he'd just shaved off his Amish beard. He bowed in front of Ariel, then pointed at the far end of the trailer, where there was a door to a private office. "The Chief Elder awaits you, milady."

"Thank you, Horace," she said, patting his arm. She marched to the door, opened it, and stepped into the office. John followed her and closed the door behind them.

Elizabeth Fury sat at a desk covered with papers, most of which seemed to be maps or satellite photos. She looked up and regarded them with her lone eye. "You're late. I arrived an hour ago."

Frowning, Ariel sat in one of the two folding chairs that faced the desk. "You were in an SUV, Mother. SUVs are faster than trucks."

"Perhaps. I have to admit, it was an exhilarating experience, moving down the road at such a high velocity."

With a start, John realized that Elizabeth had never traveled in a car before. She'd been cooped up in Haven since the seventeenth century. He looked at her in wonder as he sat down in the other folding chair.

The Chief Elder noticed him staring at her. She scowled. "Are you accompanying my child everywhere now?"

"Leave him be, Mother." Ariel leaned forward, resting her elbows on the desk. "What's the status of the dispersal? How many of our people are still in transit?"

Elizabeth reluctantly turned back to her daughter. "Most have found safe accommodations in Canada, either in hotels or rented cabins. They've been instructed to keep their locations secret and communicate with my deputies only through secure channels." She pointed at the door. Her deputies, John guessed, were the women working on the other side of the trailer. "We need to take these precautions because the Riflemen are actively pursuing us."

"So it's true?" Ariel's voice rose. "Some of their fighters survived?"

"Old Sam spoke aright. Sullivan kept several dozen of his men in reserve. After the destruction of Haven he searched the surrounding area, trying to determine how we escaped. Unfortunately, his men caught up with one of our trucks before it reached the Canadian border." She picked up one of the papers on her desk and passed it to Ariel. It was a photograph of a charred truck that had crashed into the pillar of a highway overpass. "According to the local newspapers, witnesses saw several motorcycles speeding away from the scene. Sullivan's men must've used their rocket-propelled grenades."

John craned his neck to get a better look at the newspaper photo. There were bodies on the highway, twisted and blackened. Ariel clenched her hands and let out a hiss. "Were there any survivors?" she asked.

"Nay, we lost everyone in the truck." Elizabeth retrieved the photo and quickly flipped it over on her desk, hiding the gruesome image. "Nineteen women and five men. Including our brewer, Clarissa, and three of her daughters."

"Mother, we need to end this." Ariel pressed her fists against the desktop. "Let me assemble a squadron. Between the Rangers and the remaining guardsmen, we have almost fifty soldiers. We'll find Sullivan's men and finish them off."

Elizabeth shook her head. "You won't defeat them. We lost our best fighters in the defense of Haven, but Sullivan kept his strongest men out of the battle, and he may have as many as a hundred of them. So put the idea out of your mind, child. Our priority now is to establish a permanent refuge and get our family there safely."

"How can we do that if Sullivan is attacking us? He'll track our people down and massacre them before we can—"

"That's why time is of the essence. A Gulfstream is due to arrive here within the hour. You're going to take the jet to South America."

Ariel's eyes widened. "So my guess was correct? Our new refuge is in the Amazon basin?"

Elizabeth reached for one of the maps on her desk. "Aye, it's in southern Colombia, the Caquetá region. A very remote, very unpopulated part of the rain forest." She tapped her finger on an X marked in red pencil on the map. "There's a high ridge in the jungle just south of the Yarí River. A Ranger who was doing botanical research in the area ninety years ago discovered a network of caves at the base of the ridge. He explored the cavern, then plugged and concealed its entrance so that no one else would find it. A year later I arranged the purchase of the site from the Colombian government, along with two thousand acres of surrounding rain forest."

"And this is something else you kept secret? Like the train tunnel?"

"Margaret knows of it. I sent her sons, Hal and Richard, to the site nine months ago after Sullivan started his rebellion. They reported that the cavern was still hidden and still inhabitable. The network of caves is extensive, and one section leads to an underground river that could provide fresh water and hydropower. We'll have enough room and resources to build a new home there."

Ariel bent over the desk and stared at the map. "I know this area, Mother. I never traveled down the Yarí, but I led the Caño Dorado expedition down the Apaporis River twenty years ago." She pointed at a section of the map to the north of the red X. "You're aware of the fighting in that part of Colombia? You've heard of FARC, the Fuerzas Armadas Revolucionarias—"

"Aye, I'm aware of the guerillas. Frankly, the political instability of the area is why I chose it over our other options." Elizabeth pointed at the map, too. "The long war between FARC and the Colombian government has created a no-man's-land in the southern part of the country. The Colombian police and army are afraid to enter the jungle, so we'll be able to establish our refuge without interference from suspicious authorities."

"But the guerillas will be just as suspicious. They work closely with the drug traffickers who smuggle cocaine out of the rain forest. They're bound to notice the movement of our people to the refuge."

"Trust me, child, I've taken all this into consideration. We're going to pose as a community of religious cultists who believe they're being persecuted in the United States. There's a long history of similar communities fleeing to Latin America. If the local bandits object to our presence, we have more than enough currency to buy their favor."

"I don't like it. If we need to pay the criminals, we'll be at their mercy."

"Nay, we won't be vulnerable for long. As soon as we complete the relocation, we'll make our new home impregnable. We'll build a fortified compound around the entrance to the cavern, defended by so many guardsmen that no ragtag band of guerillas will dare challenge us. It'll be easier for everyone to simply leave us alone."

Elizabeth folded her arms across her chest, clearly ready to respond to any further objections. John marveled at how disciplined and organized she was. She'd worked on these relocation plans for nearly a century. It took a special kind of paranoia, he thought, to prepare so thoroughly for disaster.

Ariel, though, still seemed unconvinced. She gave her mother a dubious look. "And how do I fit into the strategy? What's my assignment?"

The Chief Elder picked up another document from her desk. It was a color satellite photograph showing a long yellow line against a solid green background. "This is the airstrip in Caquetá where you'll land. It's close to the Yarí River, but you'll have to go fifteen miles downstream to reach the site of the refuge. I've already radioed Kuikuro, one of my contacts in the area. He's a Huitoto chief, the leader of a tribe that lives in the rain forest. For the past three decades I've paid him a thousand pesos a year to keep watch over our landholdings down there. He and his tribesmen will meet you at the airstrip and guide you down the Yarí in their dugout canoes."

"But what am I supposed to do when I get to the refuge?"

"The site is a mile south of a bend in the Yarí, but I don't want you to go there yet. Your assignment is to build a base camp on the southern bank of the river bend. You'll need to construct temporary shelters and stockpile food for the dozens of Furies who'll join you there over the next few weeks. Kuikuro will help you find tribesmen whom you can hire as laborers. I know you're familiar with the languages of the region. That makes you the best person for the task."

Ariel thought it over for a moment. "I assume I'll have enough money for wages and bribes?"

"We'll load the Gulfstream with gold, dollars, and Colombian pesos. And we'll put three guardsmen on the jet for your protection."

"I want one of them to be John." Ariel pointed at him. "He's proved himself in combat."

Elizabeth scowled again. The sudden movement of her facial muscles tilted her scar a few degrees off vertical. But after a second she nodded. "I know I can't change your mind, so I won't even try. Your aunt Margaret will also accompany you."

"Margaret?" Now Ariel scowled. "Why her?"

"Once our people start arriving at the base camp, they may become overwhelmed by the amount of work that needs to be done. One of the Elders must be there to ensure they'll follow our orders."

"What about you? When will you make the trip?"

"Probably not for several months. I have to stay in contact with everyone, and the communications grid in southern Colombia is spotty, at best." Elizabeth started collecting the papers on her desk, gathering them into a pile. "I'll give you copies of all the maps and satellite photos. And before you leave, I want you to radio the Caño Dorado expedition and instruct them to join us at the base camp. For the duration of this emergency, they'll report directly to me."

Ariel narrowed her eyes. "You have a need for botanical researchers as well?"

"Nay, I don't require their scientific expertise. But they have skiffs and supplies and communications equipment, all of which will be needed at the base camp. I assume you know their current location? Is the expedition anywhere near southern Colombia?"

Her daughter didn't answer. John knew why she was reticent: the members of the Caño Dorado expedition had formulated the catalyst for extracting the Fountain protein from fetal tissue, and until now Ariel had strictly guarded the results of their research. She was obviously nervous about revealing the location of the team, even to her mother. "If I tell you, who else will know?"

"Do you doubt the loyalty of my deputies?"

"Aye, I do. After what happened with Old Sam, I doubt everyone's loyalty."

Elizabeth sighed. She leaned back in her chair and raised her hand to her forehead, and for a moment John saw how desperately tired she was. "You're correct, child. I trusted the man too much. He was so faithful for so many years. I never could've imagined . . ." She stared at the wall as she rubbed her forehead, kneading the skin just below her hairline. "I was the one who should've paid the price for it. Not Cordelia."

Ariel's face was grim. "I don't wish to discuss this right now, Mother. I just want to make sure we don't repeat our mistakes. If another traitor discovers where the expedition is, Sullivan may reach them first and obtain the formula for the catalyst. And the consequences would be even worse than we'd feared."

Elizabeth stopped massaging her forehead. Suddenly alert, she stared at her daughter. "What do you mean?"

"In the past twenty-four hours I've learned that Fountain triggers some disturbing side effects. Because of unexpected biochemical interactions, men injected with the protein seem to lose their ability to curb their violent impulses. The effects may even explain Sullivan's irrational behavior over the past year. If he acquires the catalyst and starts supplying his men with Fountain, they may experience the same effects. Then the Riflemen will truly become an army of monsters."

Elizabeth nodded. Her face seemed to harden as she took in the new information. She sat up straight and narrowed her eyes, her expression mirroring her daughter's. "Then I'll take an oath. I swear by the names of my grandmothers that I won't disclose the location of Caño Dorado. Not to my deputies, not to any of the Rangers, not to a single soul."

Ariel studied her for a few seconds, still reluctant. Then she took the stack of papers from her mother's desk, found another map, and pointed to a sinuous river running across the top. "We're very fortunate. The expedition is in northwestern Brazil, collecting medicinal plants along the Mocó River. That's about four hundred miles downstream from the Yarí, but given the fact that the Amazon basin is two thousand miles across, it could've been a lot worse."

"How long will it take them to reach the base camp?"

"If they run the skiffs at full speed, maybe two days. Luckily, the border between Brazil and southern Colombia is easy to cross. There are hundreds of small waterways that detour the border posts."

"They should get started right away." Elizabeth rose to her feet. "I'll clear out the trailer so you can have some privacy while you radio the orders to the expedition. Is Mariela still in charge of the team's—"

She stopped herself and cocked her head, listening. A moment later John heard a distant roar. It was difficult to hear the noise at first, but it quickly grew louder. He looked up, and so did Ariel. There were no windows in the room, but they gazed at the walls anyway. They both knew what was approaching.

"That's the Gulfstream." Elizabeth pointed at the ceiling. "You'll be in South America by nightfall."

TWENTY-SEVEN

Sullivan stared at a deserted airstrip in northern Wisconsin, just a hundred feet from the rocky shore of Lake Superior. An old trailer sat beside the runway, but his men had already smashed their way inside and found it empty. Now they clustered near their motorcycles, which were parked in an asphalt lot next to the lakeshore. Sullivan had allowed his men a one-hour break, and most of them were sprawled on the gravel beach, snoring away in the sunshine. Dozens of gulls squawked angrily overhead.

This was the second Ranger airstrip they'd raided. The first, near the town of Freda on the Upper Peninsula, had also been deserted. Because Sullivan had been a Ranger for many years, he knew the locations of all their airfields, but there were too many of them. He couldn't visit them all in the hope of finding the Elders. He felt a surge of frustration, raw and overpowering. It was so strong it clouded his vision, blurring the gravel and the gulls and the supine men with the vast gray lake in front of them.

It was nothing, though, compared with the anger he'd felt last night as he stood in the pine woods south of Haven's fence. He knew he'd been

tricked as soon as the ground rumbled under his feet. He'd underesti-
mated his mother's survival instincts. The bitch had devised an escape
from Haven before obliterating the cavern and burying half of his Riflemen. Sullivan ordered his remaining men to search for a tunnel, a hidden
exit they'd somehow missed in their earlier reconnaissance of the area.
Then, on a hunch, he raced to the Rudyard Trucking warehouse. It was
ten miles west of Haven, much farther than he'd thought a tunnel could
reach, but when he arrived he saw right away that a mass exodus had
taken place. Although the warehouse was empty, its floor was spotted
with debris. There were also signs of bloodshed. A couple of fresh red
stains had soaked into the concrete.

Soon afterward, the Riflemen caught up to the last truck heading for
the Canadian border. The attack eased Sullivan's anger for a few minutes
as the truck burned beneath the highway overpass and his men extracted
a few morsels of information from the dying guardsmen. But then he
discovered that one of the corpses in the truck was Old Sam. Worse, he'd
been shot in the head before the attack had even started. The bitches
had eliminated Sullivan's last, best spy. Now he had no one to tell him
what the Elders were doing or where they'd gone.

He clenched his teeth and stared hard at Lake Superior, trying to dis-
solve the blurry mist in his eyes. On the other side of the lake, beyond the
horizon, was the Canadian province of Ontario. That's where most of the
Furies were hiding, scattered and out of reach. But all was not lost. Although
Sullivan couldn't locate the Elders at the moment, he had a good idea where
they were headed. Thanks to his deceased spy, he knew a great deal about
their relocation plans.

Nine months ago Old Sam had informed him of an unusual conversation he'd overheard in the council chambers. Elizabeth had assigned Hal
and Richard to travel to the Caquetá region in southern Colombia. They
were going to investigate a sealed cavern that some long-dead Ranger had
discovered in the 1920s. Old Sam learned the geographic coordinates of
the site and relayed them to Sullivan, who sent two of his own men to the
area. After a few weeks they radioed a message confirming his suspicions: the cavern was Elizabeth's first choice for a new refuge if the Furies
were forced to leave Haven. Sullivan then gave his men a new assignment. Using some of the gold the Riflemen had taken from Haven's vaults,
they made a deal with the FARC guerillas who controlled Caquetá.

His vision suddenly cleared. He could see the waves on the lake's surface and a green buoy at the edge of the bay and a long black freighter far in the distance. And now he knew what he had to do. It was time to get in touch with Comandante Reyes.

TWENTY-EIGHT

It was a long, dull flight. Even though John sat next to Ariel for nearly seven hours, they hardly talked. She was too damn busy.

For the first two hours after the Gulfstream took off, she inspected the contents of the duffel bags Elizabeth had given her. There were fifteen bags in all, stacked in the back of the jet's cabin, behind the five passenger seats. First, Ariel examined the bag holding their carbines and ammunition. Then she inventoried the food rations, clothing, and miscellaneous supplies in the other bags. Then she returned to her seat and spent the next three hours reviewing the details of the mission and poring over the maps and photographs. John looked over her shoulder for a while, then got bored and stared out the window at the Gulf of Mexico and the Caribbean Sea. Finally, just when he thought she'd finished preparing herself, Ariel clasped her seat's armrests, took a deep breath, and closed her eyes. At first he assumed she was taking a nap, but her back was too straight and her face too composed. She appeared to be meditating.

Having nothing better to do, John studied the other passengers. The guardsman named Horace sat in the middle of the cabin, facing John and

Ariel in the rear seats. He was close enough that he and John could have had a conversation, but the man had fallen asleep soon after the flight started. His head tilted to the right and his mouth hung open. John counted seven places on his chin and jaw where he'd cut himself while shaving off his Amish beard. Across the aisle from Horace was another sleeping guardsman, this one named Peter. Both men were big and muscular, but they also seemed a little sluggish and stupid. John would much rather have Ariel at his side in a firefight.

Seated at the front of the cabin, across from the Gulfstream's door, was Elder Margaret Fury. She spent most of the flight leaning forward in her seat, sticking her head into the cockpit so she could talk with the pilot and copilot. They were Margaret's daughters, John had realized right away. Both were short and chubby and had enormous bosoms. He couldn't hear what they were saying, but it was a lively conversation, full of jokes and laughter. This surprised him. Margaret had seemed so mean-spirited every time he'd seen her before.

After another hour John looked out the window again and viewed the continent of South America. They flew over the rugged, snow-capped Andes and the forested foothills on the eastern side of the mountain range. Then the landscape flattened out to a patchwork of farms. As they continued flying southeast the farms grew smaller and scarcer, and then they disappeared altogether and there was nothing below but undisturbed jungle. Several black rivers threaded across the vast green carpet but no towns or highways or railroad tracks were in sight. John was awed and disconcerted. If they fell into that expanse of rain forest, no one would be the wiser.

Then he felt a tap on his arm. Ariel had finished meditating. She nudged him aside and leaned over his seat so she could look out the window, too. "It's beautiful, isn't it?"

"Yeah, I guess. If you like the color green."

"I came here for the first time two hundred years ago, when the people were fighting for independence from Spain. I had some experience with revolutions in North America, so I thought I could help the South Americans, too." She pointed at the jungle below. "The amazing thing is that it hasn't changed. Most of the rain forest still looks the same. That's why I love coming back here."

The sun was descending, and so was the Gulfstream. As they drew nearer to the ground John started to see variations in the landscape, veins of lighter green feeding into the rivers. On closer inspection, the rivers themselves looked like frayed rope, with dozens of thin black strands twisting through the jungle on both sides of the main channel. The black floodwaters flowed everywhere, coursing below the foliage and between the tree trunks, sluicing across the whole region.

The jet flew through a thundercloud and hit a knot of turbulence. John's stomach flip-flopped as the plane rocked up and down. Margaret said something he couldn't hear, and her daughters laughed. Ariel glanced at them, then turned back to John. "Have you noticed the change in Aunt Margaret? She seems happier now, doesn't she?"

"As a matter of fact, I did notice. She hasn't given me the evil eye all day."

"She's always happy when she's with Gwen and Veronica." Ariel glanced at them again. Her face had a wistful look. "I don't particularly like Margaret, but she's a good mother. Some women are better suited for the role than others."

John guessed that Ariel was thinking of her own mother. He'd just recognized another disadvantage of eternal youth: If neither you nor your relatives age, you're stuck with them forever, for better or worse.

"I bet you'd be a good mother, too," John said. "Even better than Margaret."

Ariel shook her head. "I was a mother once. For almost three years. But it was so long ago, I don't even remember whether I was good or bad at it."

"You'd be good at it now. You're older and wiser."

That made her smile. Ariel rested her hand on his shoulder and squeezed it. She kept it there as they looked out the window at the rain forest.

The Gulfstream was quite low now, only a few thousand feet above the jungle. Through scattered gaps in the green canopy John could see the white trunks of the tropical trees rising from the black water. Several miles ahead he saw a patch of higher, drier ground, a rough rectangle of grassland surrounded by the rain forest. And in the center of this patch he spied the yellow line he'd seen before in the satellite photo. It was their destination, the jungle airstrip. The runway was unpaved, just a long strip of dirt with ragged, grassy edges, but it looked golden in the twilight.

Margaret's daughters steered the plane in a wide arc, circling the airstrip as they descended. The field had no control tower, no radar, no lights. Nothing except the dirt runway. John pointed at it. "Not much of an airport."

Ariel nodded. "The strip was made for the drug traffickers. They collect the coca grown in the jungle and turn the leaves into cocaine. Then they load the stuff on small planes and send it north."

"Wasn't that tribesman supposed to meet us here? Kuikuro? I don't see anyone on the ground."

She leaned closer to the window and surveyed the area around the airstrip. "He and his men are probably under the trees. They're going to stay hidden until they're sure we're not traffickers. The drug smugglers will shoot anyone who interferes with their operations, so the tribesmen have to be wary."

"You're sure they're down there?"

"Kuikuro has been faithful to our family for decades. He wouldn't miss this rendezvous."

By this point Margaret had stopped joking with her daughters, so they could concentrate on the landing. The Gulfstream swooped low over the rain forest, on final approach. John looked out the window and saw several herons take flight from the treetops, startled by the roar of the jet engines. The plane seemed to be cruising just a few yards above the foliage. Then they reached the rectangle of grassland and descended to the airstrip. The jet's landing gear bounced against the hard-packed dirt and the Gulfstream rattled like a piggy bank. John squeezed his armrests, convinced they were going to crash. But Gwen and Veronica threw the engines into reverse and managed to slow the plane. Whining and shuddering, it came to rest at the end of the runway, just short of the grass.

Margaret clapped her hands in triumph. "Excellent job, girls!" she crowed. "Your mother is well pleased!"

As soon as the jet stopped moving, Ariel jumped out of her seat and peered through the windows on both sides of the aircraft. She stared at the trees at the edge of the grassy clearing, obviously hoping to see Kuikuro emerge from the jungle. But there was still no sign of him. The sun had just set, and the airstrip was rapidly darkening.

The bumpy landing had awakened Horace and Peter, the sluggish guardsmen. Rising from their seats, they picked up their carbines and turned to Margaret, awaiting her orders. The Elder yawned and stretched her arms wide. "What are you waiting for?" she said. "Go outside and secure the perimeter."

Ariel looked at them nervously. "Do me a favor, Auntie. Tell your daughters not to shut down the engines yet."

Margaret frowned. "We don't want to waste fuel. We only have—"

"Just three minutes. That's all I ask." Ariel quickly unzipped one of the duffel bags and removed an M4 carbine and an ammunition clip. She attached the clip to the rifle and handed it to John. Then she took another rifle out of the bag for herself and loaded it.

John hefted the rifle and switched off the safety. He hadn't held an M4 since his long-ago stint in basic training, but the gun felt familiar in his hands. "We're going to back up the guardsmen?"

She nodded. "It never hurts to be careful. Once you step out of the plane, lie flat on the grass and scan the jungle. The tribesmen usually go shirtless and paint their faces."

Cradling their carbines, they followed the guardsmen to the Gulfstream's door. When it opened, Horace and Peter dashed across the clearing, moving much faster than John had expected. Horace ran toward the trees on the left side of the clearing and Peter headed in the opposite direction. Then both men threw themselves down on the grass and aimed their rifles at the rain forest. John and Ariel did the same thing but stayed close to the plane, each lying prone under one of the wings.

"Kuikuro!" Ariel called. "*Kuikuro!*"

John listened carefully. The jungle thrummed with chatter from its birds and frogs and insects, but he heard no answer to Ariel's call. A swarm of mosquitoes swiftly gathered around him, landing on his head and back and neck. It was already so dark that the rain forest looked like a black, unbroken wall around the clearing. He could just barely make out the figures of the guardsmen, Horace lying in the grass fifty yards to the plane's left and Peter fifty yards to the right.

Then the jungle erupted with gunfire. It came from both sides of the clearing, the tracer rounds flashing in the dark and lancing across the sky. Bullets strafed the grass around Horace, who let out a scream of pain and surprise. Peter returned fire, shooting blindly into the forest, but another round of bullets silenced him. A third barrage struck the Gulfstream, thunking into the jet's wings and fuselage. It all happened so quickly that John never got a chance to fire his gun. Ariel screamed, "Get back in the plane!" and he bolted for the Gulfstream's door, scrambling into the cabin behind her.

As he slammed the door shut, more bullets smashed into the fuselage, shattering some of the windows. Gwen and Veronica cowered in the cockpit while Margaret crouched behind them. Their faces were identical in their terror.

"Can we take off?" Ariel shouted at them.

Gwen raised her head and looked around the cabin. "I think so. The broken windows may slow us down but—"

"Then turn the plane around and get us out of here!"

Margaret's daughters got to work, revving the engines and turning the jet. Their mother looked up at Ariel. "The guardsmen? Are they—"

"Lost."

Keeping her head low, Ariel moved toward the rear of the cabin and thrust the barrel of her carbine through one of the broken windows. John did the same on the other side of the plane. As the Gulfstream turned to face the opposite end of the runway, he saw figures running in front of the black wall of jungle. It was too dark to see their faces, but he noticed they wore combat fatigues and carried assault rifles. They were emerging from the rain forest and racing toward the jet.

"They're coming!" he shouted. "Open fire!"

He aimed at the running men and pulled the carbine's trigger. A burst of automatic fire cut across the clearing, and three of the men fell to the grass. At the same time, the Gulfstream's engines roared to full power and the plane leaped forward, hurtling down the runway. Ariel fired her carbine too, strafing the other side of the clearing as the jet accelerated. Then she pulled away from the window and turned toward the cockpit. "The gunmen are on the airstrip! Gwen, watch—"

Bullets shattered the cockpit window and streaked into the plane. Gwen jerked backward, struck in the head. Her blood sprayed over the instrument panel and controls. Margaret screamed, but Veronica kept her cool, taking over the controls and throttling up the engines. More bullets tore into the Gulfstream's wings, and the jet shuddered as it hit one of the gunmen on the runway. Then the plane lifted off the ground.

They barely cleared the treetops. Veronica struggled with the control column, trying to gain altitude. Margaret reached into the cockpit and pulled Gwen out of the pilot's seat, laying her body on the floor of the cabin, but she screamed again when she saw the wounds to her daughter's head. "Oh, Mother of Creation! Gwen, *Gwen!*"

Ariel dropped her rifle and rushed to the front of the cabin. "Auntie, please—"

"She's dead!" Margaret spun around and flailed at Ariel. "She's dead, you bitch, she's dead, she's dead!"

A tremendous bang shook the fuselage, drowning out Margaret's wails.

Then there was a loud beeping from the cockpit, accompanied by an oddly calm, computer-synthesized voice: *Too low. Terrain. Too low. Terrain.*

"One of the engines is out!" Veronica shouted. "And the other's damaged! She won't climb!"

John's throat tightened as he looked out the window. The Gulfstream was skimming over the dark jungle canopy, less than fifty feet above the trees. He caught a glimpse of something bright at the rear of the plane, and when he looked behind he saw that one of the jet engines was burning. The fire was the brightest thing in the rain forest. He could see its reflection in the black water below the treetops.

Ariel nudged Margaret aside and leaned into the cockpit. "Are you going to ditch?"

"Affirmative." Veronica's voice was high-pitched and frightened. "I'll try to reach the river."

The beeping alarm sounded again. *Too low. Terrain. Too low. Terrain.* While Margaret wept over Gwen's corpse, Ariel ran to John and grabbed his arm, dragging him to the stack of duffel bags at the back of the cabin. "Get in there!" she shouted. "Get on top of the pile!"

"What?"

"Just follow me!" She climbed on top of the bags and wriggled down into the space between them.

John doubted this would work. He never saw a stewardess demonstrate this technique during a flight-safety presentation. But he climbed the pile anyway and squeezed into the dark niche where Ariel lay. Although he couldn't see her so well, he could hear her breathing fast and hard. The duffel bags around them muffled all the other noises, but he could still hear the alarm and the oddly calm voice.

Too low. Terrain. Too—

TWENTY-NINE

Sullivan enjoyed the biggest surprise of his life the next morning.

He and his men were camped at another deserted Ranger airstrip, this one in western Minnesota. They'd arrived the night before and found signs of recent activity—footprints and tire tracks in the mud, a trash can full of shredded documents in the trailer beside the runway—but the Rangers had apparently abandoned the post several hours before the Riflemen got there. Sullivan was convinced that the Chief Elder had been at this airstrip, plotting against him, and he grew enraged when he realized he'd just missed her. His vision blurred again, clouding so much he could hardly see a thing. Shortly before midnight, though, he received a radio message from Comandante Reyes. The rebel commander reported that his guerillas had downed one of the Furies' Gulfstreams, which had crashed into the rain forest near the Yarí River. The good news eased Sullivan's rage. His eyesight cleared, and for a few hours he was able to get some sleep.

And then, at 7:00 A.M., he was awakened by the sound of an aircraft. He rushed out of the trailer and saw a Gulfstream G280 high overhead. The jet slowly circled the airstrip, as if its pilot were studying the ground and deciding whether it was safe to land. Anyone with eyes could see that the strip was occupied by Riflemen—several dozen Harley-Davidsons were parked in the field beside the runway—so Sullivan fully expected the plane to go away. But instead the Gulfstream descended.

His men gathered along the runway and surrounded the jet as soon as it came to a stop. The pilot shut down the engines, and a few seconds later the door to the cabin opened. The first to step out of the plane was Grace Fury, first cousin to Elizabeth. She was a deputy to the Chief Elder and the most fecund woman in the whole family. Over the past five hundred years she'd borne seventeen daughters, nine of whom were still alive. She'd also given birth to nineteen sons, all deceased except for the latest one, Archibald, Sullivan's unfortunate spy. Grace wore a black, long-sleeved, ankle-length dress, a style she'd adopted back in the sixteenth century. Sullivan hated her almost as much as he hated his mother.

Right behind Grace was Claudia, also a cousin to Elizabeth, who formerly ran the geothermal plant that Archibald had sabotaged. She was accompanied by her son Gower, who wore a bandage on his shoulder and an angry scowl on his face. Bringing up the rear were the Gulfstream's pilot and copilot, both of whom happened to be granddaughters of Grace. No one in the group seemed frightened or nervous, even though Sullivan's men pointed a dozen rifles at them. On the contrary, they seemed defiant and determined. They were full of grim purpose.

Grace Fury crossed the runway and approached Sullivan. His men stopped her and checked her for weapons, patting down the slim body beneath the black dress. She endured the inspection, silent and unsmiling. Once his men gave the all clear, Sullivan stepped toward her. He could barely contain his curiosity. *What the hell was she doing here?*

Grinning, he bowed before her in an elaborate, mocking fashion. "Greetings, milady! Thou art more lovely than a summer's day, and more temperate. Thou art the very embodiment of temperance."

Her upper lip twitched, but other than that she didn't respond to his taunts.

"I'm delighted you came to visit," he continued. "May I ask how your son Archibald is faring? I do hope your sisters don't punish him too severely. He's a good lad at heart."

"Archibald is dead." Grace's voice was low and hoarse. "While riding in our truck convoy yesterday he grabbed a pistol from one of the guardsmen and shot himself."

Sullivan gave her a look of exaggerated sympathy. "Oh, this must be a terrible blow for you, milady. And I suppose it's my fault, is it not? I feel just awful about this."

"Cordelia is dead too. And so are Margaret and Lily. And Lily's paramour as well. You have much to celebrate."

He did indeed. He felt a surge of joy in his chest. "Were they all in the Gulfstream that went down in Colombia? I suppose you received their distress signals before the jet crashed?"

"Aye, and we heard the calls for help radioed by our friend Kuikuro. Did you know that your Colombian allies slaughtered him and everyone else in his village?"

Sullivan shrugged. "What can I say? We're paying the guerillas well, so they're eager to please."

Grace's lip twitched again. She was trying hard to conceal her emotions, but her contempt was too strong. "Let me explain our reasons for coming here. The Chief Elder has chosen new leaders for our family to replace the ones you murdered. Claudia and I are now members of the council."

"Congratulations, milady. I'm sure this is a dream come true for you. But where is my mother? Why isn't she here as well?"

"We've been ordered to take you to her. In this Gulfstream."

Sullivan looked askance. "Do you take me for a fool? I'm not going anywhere without my Riflemen."

"You can bring as many of your men as will fit on the plane."

"But Mother will have a larger number of fighters at her side. I believe I've killed most of your guardsmen, but surely a few dozen have survived."

"We've chosen a meeting place that will be to your advantage. If you're still worried that we're planning to trick you, you can keep me here as a hostage, and Claudia, too. That will guarantee your safety. Elizabeth wouldn't forfeit our lives just to eliminate a scoundrel such as you."

It was intriguing, Sullivan had to admit. But he remained suspicious. "And what's the purpose of this meeting, pray tell?"

Grace's throat bobbed. She was swallowing hard, tamping down her disdain. "Elizabeth wants an end to this war. She has a proposal for you."

THIRTY

It was only much later—after they'd clambered out of the wreckage of the Gulfstream and waded through miles of waist-deep swamp and found a hiding place at the foot of an enormous kapok tree—that John understood how he and Ariel had survived. She explained the reasons in a sober voice as they huddled on the ground between the kapok's giant roots, which stretched from the trunk in five-foot-high tentacles that hid them from view. They'd slept for a few hours in the shelter of this massive root system, and now Ariel reached into her backpack and pulled out a handful of the military-style rations she'd salvaged from the duffel bags in the Gulfstream. The rations looked like granola bars, each wrapped in clear plastic.

"The first reason is that we had an excellent pilot. Veronica did a good job of controlling our descent." Ariel examined the ration, trying to see what was inside the wrapper. The sun had come up half an hour ago, and early-morning light filtered into the rain forest. "A damn good job, considering what she had to work with. That jet had a hundred bullet holes in it."

John nodded. "I'm still amazed she got it off the ground."

"She did everything right. If she'd had a few more seconds, we would've made it to the river. We would've cleared the trees and made a soft landing in the water." Ariel shook her head. "That's what hurts so much. She came so damn close."

Fixing her eyes on the ration, Ariel started to unwrap it, but after a couple of seconds she stopped and stared at the ground. John guessed she was remembering what they'd seen after the crash, after they'd crawled out of the Gulfstream's severed tail, which had broken off from the rest of the aircraft and wedged into the mud and black water of the swamp. All around them, smaller pieces of the jet were scattered across the jungle. Torn sections of the wings hung in the tree branches. One of the engines poked out of the fetid water, its upper section still burning. And there were body parts too. Margaret and her daughters had been crushed and mangled.

"But why did we survive and the others—"

"The tail's the safest part of any aircraft. It stayed in one piece while the rest of the fuselage broke apart. The duffel bags also helped, by cushioning the impact. And the rest of it was luck, just pure dumb luck. Without it, we'd be dead, too."

She shook her head again, slow and mournful. John was a bit surprised by the depth of her grief. He knew Ariel hadn't liked her Aunt Margaret very much. In fact, the two women had seemed to despise each other. But now that Margaret was dead, Ariel seemed almost as distraught as she'd been after the death of Cordelia, the aunt she'd loved. John wondered if the extreme longevity of the Fury women intensified their bonds. Maybe Ariel's feelings for her aunts were so powerful because they'd lived together for so long.

She finally took a deep breath and looked up. She stared at the ration in her hand, as if trying to remember what she was going to do with it. Then she gave it to John. "Here, try this one. I think it's peanut butter."

He took a bite. It was brown and starchy and tasted more like licorice than peanut butter, but he ate it anyway. He was too hungry to be choosy. "So who attacked us last night? It wasn't Sullivan's men, was it?"

"No, they were FARC guerillas. But it wasn't a coincidence that they showed up at the airstrip just as we landed. They must be working for Sullivan. He must've paid them to ambush us. He knew we were heading for the new refuge on the Yarí River, and he didn't want us to get there."

"Do you think the guerillas will come looking for us? Now that it's morning, they'll probably investigate the crash site."

Ariel shrugged. "It all depends on how competent they are. If they have good tracking skills, they might be able to tell that we left the site. We probably broke a few branches when we waded through the swamp, and a good tracker could follow the trail." She examined another ration, holding it up to the light. "But if these guerillas aren't native to the area, they won't go very deep into the jungle. It's a dangerous place if you don't know what you're doing."

"Yeah, I already figured that out." He held up his arms, which were dotted with insect bites. "When we were going through the swamp last night I heard something splashing in the water. Something big and heavy."

"I heard it, too." She unwrapped her ration and started eating. "It was either an anaconda or a caiman."

"Caiman? That's like a crocodile, right?"

"They rarely attack people, but when they do it's usually fatal. They're fast and big, up to twenty feet long." She took a bite out of the starchy brown bar in her hand. At the same time, she turned her other hand in a circle, pointing at the kapok tree and the area around it. "That's why we didn't stop last night until we found some high ground. I wanted to get away from the caimans and piranhas."

John raised his head and peered over the kapok's massive roots. The tree dominated a smallish hill that rose above the jungle's floodwaters. They stood on an island in the rain forest, a patch of dry land surrounded by swamp. They'd have to return to the black water if they wanted to go anywhere. "So what's our next step? If Sullivan knows about the refuge, it doesn't make sense to go there, does it?"

"No, I'm sure the guerillas are already at the bend in the Yarí. Sullivan probably told them to slaughter any Furies who arrive."

"Maybe we should head in the opposite direction then? Go up the river instead of down?"

"That would be the smartest move if we only had ourselves to worry about. But I'm concerned about my cousins in the Caño Dorado expedition. Mother ordered them to go to the refuge as quickly as possible. Although she probably realizes by now that Sullivan's allies shot down our plane, she may not be able to send a warning to Mariela. The expedition is traveling through an area that has no radio towers."

He knew Ariel well enough to guess what she was planning. "And you think *we* should try to warn them? Convince the expedition to turn around before they run into the guerillas?"

She nodded. "I think we can intercept them, but it won't be easy. We're ten miles upstream from the refuge, and Caño Dorado is still hundreds of miles downstream. If the guerillas are lying in wait at the bend in the river, we'll have to maneuver around them somehow." She turned toward the rising sun. Somewhere in that direction, behind the thick green curtains of foliage, was the Yarí. "What we really need is a canoe. A dugout canoe, the kind the Amazon tribesmen use. Then we could slip past Sullivan's allies by navigating the channels that run parallel to the river."

John frowned. He didn't like this plan. He understood that Ariel was trying to protect her cousins, but he wished that just this once she'd think about her own safety. "I don't know. It sounds kind of dicey."

"We're not completely defenseless, you know." She picked up her carbine and pointed at John's. They'd carried the rifles all the way from the crash site, holding them above the floodwaters as they'd waded through the swamp. "And I know the rain forest pretty well, maybe better than the guerillas do."

He didn't know what to say. If he argued that they shouldn't risk it, she might accuse him of cowardice. And, in a way, she'd be right. He was afraid of losing her. He didn't want to risk Ariel's life to save someone else's. "Two carbines won't make much of a difference. If the guerillas spot us, we're dead. End of story."

"But if Mariela and the—"

"Look, I don't care about Mariela. I care about *you*."

Ariel put down her rifle and looked at him. Her expression wasn't angry or accusatory. On the contrary, she seemed choked up, overcome by emotion. She bit her lower lip and leaned toward him. "Okay, I understand," she whispered. "You're worried about me. You don't want me to get hurt."

"I'm just wondering if it's worth—"

"Oh, John, I wish we didn't have to do this. I wish we could disappear, just you and me."

She grasped his hand, and he choked up, too. The sadness in her voice was palpable. Ariel was resigned to her fate. She would never abandon her family, no matter how much she wanted to. Even in the face of certain doom, she'd stand by them. But John took some consolation in the fact that Ariel wished things could be different. She knew how strongly he felt about her, and she returned those feelings. If she weren't so damn loyal to her family, they could've been happy.

They sat there for a long while, holding hands and not talking. Then

Ariel let go of him and reached into her backpack again. "I thought of something that might help us. Before we go wading through a swamp full of caimans, I might be able to draw the animals away from us." She pulled out the medicine case holding the syringe and the nine vials of Fountain protein. "But I haven't tested the idea yet."

John felt uneasy. "Wait a second. You want to inject me again?"

"No, no, this is a different kind of test." She opened the case and removed one of the vials of yellowish fluid from its slot in the foam padding. Then she rose to her feet and surveyed the area around the kapok tree. "Okay, the coast is clear. Come on, this way."

He stood up and followed Ariel as she left their hiding place at the foot of the kapok. They walked down the smallish hill, weaving between the trees that crowded the slope and being careful not to disturb the ant nests that clung to the lowest branches. In a couple of minutes they reached the water-line where the swamp lapped the hillside. Trees poked out of the floodwa-ters here, their trunks rising to great heights and their branches fanning out overhead to form the jungle canopy. Thousands of leaves floated on the water, which was the color of strong tea. John couldn't see anything below the surface.

Ariel halted at the water's edge. Then she pulled the stopper from the vial she was holding. "Remember I told you, back in Haven, that we modi-fied the Fountain protein so it could enter cells by passing through their membranes? Well, that means the protein can also pass through other thin membranes, such as the skin of fish and other aquatic animals. If you added the concentrated fluid to a warm pool or pond, the protein mole-cules would diffuse through the water and seep into the animals' bodies."

"You mean you wouldn't have to inject it into their bloodstreams?"

"No, the protein would go directly to their cells. And that would make Fountain's effects more intense and immediate."

Holding her arm over the swamp, Ariel tilted the vial and poured its contents into the black water. The protein formed a bright yellow blot on the surface that quickly faded as it spread outward and downward. She watched the stuff disperse into the floodwaters for about twenty seconds. Then she took several steps backward, moving up the slope. "Step away from the water, John. I don't know exactly what will happen now, but I have a hypothesis."

"Really? What—"

It was like an explosion. Dozens of creatures started thrashing in the swamp, spraying water and mud in every direction. As John leaped up the slope he saw a fantastically long snake raise its head to the surface and open its mouth wide. It was an anaconda, thick and black, and it was in distress. Several piranhas had sunk their teeth into the snake's skin and now they hung like medals on its coiling body. The anaconda writhed in the water, shaking off the clinging fish, but more of them attacked the snake, tearing into its flesh. Then an even larger reptile shot out of the water, a shiny black caiman with greenish eyes and a corrugated hide. The caiman opened its enormous jaw and snapped it shut on the snake's coils, biting the anaconda in two. Its death throes made the water boil, and the piranhas razored into its remains. Meanwhile, the caiman swam to the water's edge, clacking its jaw and hunting for its next victim.

John sprinted farther up the hill. Ariel ran beside him, looking over her shoulder at the feeding frenzy she'd triggered. They didn't stop until they stood fifty feet up the slope, safely out of range of the maddened animals. John's heart hammered against his sternum. "Jesus!" he gasped. "What the hell happened?"

"My hypothesis was correct." Ariel's voice was calm and clinical. "Fountain has similar effects on a broad range of species. The protein stimulates the animals' metabolism and alters their behavior."

"You mean it drives them crazy." Panting, John pointed at the roiling floodwaters below. "So how is this going to make it easier for us to wade across the swamp? You just made it a hundred times more dangerous."

Ariel shook her head. "The protein's effects should fade after a few minutes. It hits the animals fast, but it leaves their bodies fast, too."

"But now there's a huge dead snake in the water, and who knows how many piranhas feeding on it. Every predator in the whole damn rain forest is going to swim over here."

"That's what I'm counting on. We're not going to wade through this part of the swamp, John. We're going in the opposite direction." She pointed at the slope on the other side of the kapok tree. "The water over there will be empty of predators, because they're all going to come here."

Ariel smiled, clearly proud of herself for thinking of such a clever trick, But John was still worried. The sight of the enraged caiman had unnerved him. "Are you sure about this? The last thing we need is a drug-crazed crocodile chasing us."

She nodded. "All we have to do is wait ten minutes. The protein will be completely dissipated by then."

John looked again at the swamp. Although all the animals had returned to the depths, the surface of the black water still heaved and rippled. "Let's give it thirty minutes, okay? Just to be on the safe side."

Later that morning they learned what had happened to Kuikuro. As they hiked across another stretch of high ground—a forested ridge that overlooked the north bank of the Yarí River—John spotted a break in the trees and caught a whiff of something burned and rancid. He gave a hand signal to Ariel, who raised her carbine and crept forward, careful not to make a sound. They skulked to the edge of a clearing that contained four large piles of smoldering wood. On closer inspection it became clear that the piles had formerly been thatch-roofed huts that the guerillas had torched the day before. Surrounding each charred hut were several blackened corpses.

Ariel glowered as she squinted through her rifle's gun sights. The guerillas were long gone, but John thought she might start shooting anyway, firing into the air out of sheer rage. Instead, she scrutinized the ruins of Kuikuro's village, looking for any evidence—footprints, bullet shells, cigarette butts—that could tell her something about their adversaries. As she studied the ground she spied a heap of palm fronds in the shadows just beyond the clearing's edge. Stepping toward it, she tossed some of the fronds aside and uncovered a long dark slab of tropical wood, beautifully carved and sanded. It was a dugout canoe. Kuikuro and his tribesmen had hidden it so well that the guerillas had missed it.

Ariel stared at the thing for several seconds. Then she tilted her head back and looked up at the sky. "Thank you, Mother," she whispered.

The canoe made all the difference in the world. After they put it in the water they could navigate the rain forest. They could drift with the current down the narrow channels that ran alongside the Yarí. They could paddle across the marshes and thickly wooded swamps, concealed by all the vegetation around them. And they could float silently past the guerilla sentries who were keeping watch over the Yarí's main channel. For the next nine hours they moved like ghosts through the forest, making good time as they drifted to the east. By evening they were uncertain exactly where they were, but Ariel felt sure they'd passed the bend in the river where Sullivan's allies lay in wait.

They paddled in the darkness for six more hours, trying to put as much distance as possible between themselves and the guerillas. Then a quarter moon rose above the trees, and as they steered the canoe into a new channel they glimpsed a wooden structure up ahead, shining in the moonlight. It was a simple square hut resting on poles sunk into the swamp. It had a plank floor and a thatched roof, but no walls. And it was empty, deserted. Except for a few fallen leaves, the hut's floor was bare.

John was puzzled. There were no other structures nearby. The hut was entirely surrounded by jungle. "What the hell is this?" he whispered.

Ariel, who sat at the front of the dugout, looked over her shoulder. "It's an Amazonian motel."

"What?"

"Some of the tribesmen are nomadic. They move from place to place across the rain forest, depending on how high the floodwaters are. One of the local tribes uses this hut during the rainy season, I bet. But it's unoccupied the rest of the year."

"You think we can stop here for a few minutes? Because I really need to get out of this canoe."

Ariel nodded. "Sure, let's tie up. Just don't expect any room service."

They tied the canoe to one of the poles and climbed into the hut. John sprawled across the plank floor, delighted to get a chance to stretch his cramping legs. Meanwhile, Ariel opened her backpack and inspected their remaining supplies. Paddling the canoe had been hard work, and they'd already eaten more than half of their rations. Staring at her face in the moonlight, John could tell she was worried. They had no idea how much farther they'd have to travel downriver before they'd reach the Caño Dorado expedition. They might have to go hungry if they didn't rendezvous with Mariela by tomorrow night.

In the end Ariel decided they should split one of the rations for dinner. She broke the bar in two and gave John the bigger piece. They ate in silence, mostly because they were so tired. John was dying to close his eyes, even if it was only for half an hour. He was going to suggest that they take a quick nap before moving on, but Ariel spoke first.

"I'm sorry, John," she said. "I haven't been fair to you."

"Fair?" He didn't know what she meant. "Are you talking about the rations?"

She shook her head. "You've done so much for me. You've helped me at every turn. And what have I done for you?"

"Well, let me think about it." He smiled. "I've never been to a foreign country before. That's something."

"John, please. I'm serious."

"So am I. You've made my life more interesting. Ever since I met you, my life has been interesting as hell. A little terrifying too, but that's all part of the package, right?"

He was trying to make her smile, but it wasn't working. Her face was sad and knowing, like the face of a doctor who's about to deliver some bad news. She looked him in the eye. "You know what I thought the first time I saw you? In that bar in Greenwich Village? I said to myself, 'This man is unhappy. He's been unhappy for a long time.'"

John nodded. He couldn't deny it. He wondered, though, why Ariel wanted to talk about this now. "Were you surprised? You'd already seen all the news stories on the Internet. You knew what happened to my daughter."

"To be honest, I was mystified. From the very beginning, I could tell you were hiding something. Something that wasn't in any of the stories I'd read. And you're still hiding it."

He frowned. "Wait a minute. Whatever secrets I was hiding, they were nothing compared with yours."

"Agreed. But I've told you all my secrets. You know everything about me. Or at least all the important things."

"And now you want to know everything about *me*? So we'll be even?"

"No, that's not the reason. I thought talking about it might help you. But if it's just going to make you upset . . ."

Her voice trailed off. She turned away from him and gazed at the black wall of surrounding jungle. Then she raised her head and stared at the quarter moon. The silver light bathed her face.

John's heart softened as he looked at her. He recognized that Ariel's intentions were good. She wanted him to share his past with her because she thought it would ease his unhappiness. And maybe she was right, maybe it would help. So why was he fighting it? Why did it frighten him so much?

He cleared his throat. This was going to be hard. "Okay. You know about Salazar, right? He was mentioned in all the news stories."

She turned back to him. Her eyes gleamed in the moonlight. "He was the gang leader who ordered the drive-by shooting that killed your daughter."

"We grew up on the same street in Kensington. Miguel Salazar was his full name. He was a year younger than me." John grimaced. He didn't like to think about the bastard. "Even as a kid, he was scary. He never smiled, never laughed. I once tried joking with him and he threw a brick at me. In other words, he was perfect for the drug business."

"Both of you were in the same gang when you were teenagers, right? That's what the news articles said."

"But I left the Disciples, and Salazar stayed. I started working with Father Murphy's Anti-Gang Project, trying to steer kids away from the drug crews. Salazar preferred recruiting the younger kids, the twelve- and thirteen-year-olds, because they were more impressionable. And he demanded total obedience. If any of his kids stepped out of line, Salazar would beat him with a hammer. So he hated the Anti-Gang Project. It threatened his control."

"Is that why he ordered the shooting?"

John nodded. "I don't know if he was trying to kill me or just send a message. But it didn't matter. His boys drove down our street at two in the morning and strafed our apartment. They blew out the windows of the living room. Then they fired at Ivy's bedroom."

This was the most difficult part, remembering the moment when he'd rushed into Ivy's room. The shattered window, the glass on the floor. The constellation of bullet holes in the newly painted walls. Ivy slept with so many blankets heaped on top of her than John couldn't tell at first whether she'd been hit. But he knew, he already knew. She was a light sleeper. She would've woken up if she'd been able to.

Ariel came toward him, edging across the hut's plank floor. But she didn't say a word, and John was grateful for her silence. It gave him the strength to continue.

"I lost my mind. That's the only way to describe it. Carol, my wife, she ran into the bedroom too and started screaming, but I didn't even look at her. I ran downstairs and looked up and down the street. The car was long gone, but that didn't stop me. I started racing across the neighborhood, trying to find Salazar." John closed his eyes. It was a little less painful that way. "I went to the police, but they couldn't do a thing. They didn't even try to find any witnesses who saw the car. When it comes to gang shootings, there are no witnesses in Kensington. No one will say anything against the Disciples." He shut his eyes tighter. He wasn't in the rain forest anymore. He was back in Philadelphia. "This will tell you how insane I was. When I went to Ivy's funeral the next day I had a gun tucked in the back of my pants. A forty-caliber SIG Sauer semiautomatic that I'd bought on the street for two hundred dollars. Just in case I spotted one of Salazar's boys on the way to the cemetery. I was going to kill them all. Every last goddamn one of them."

He felt Ariel's hand on his upper arm. She gripped it gently, massaging his biceps. At the same time, she leaned close and touched her forehead to his. He could feel her warm breath on his cheeks.

"What stopped you?" she whispered.

He opened his eyes. Ariel's face was so near, he couldn't see her very well. He hesitated, nervous about how she'd react to the rest of the story. Then he forced himself to continue. "Father Murphy conducted the burial service. Afterwards he took me aside and said, 'Give me the gun.' He knew what I was planning to do. He could see it in my face. He even tried to reach behind me and pull the gun out of my pants. But I wouldn't let him. I said, 'Father, I love you, but right now you better stay out of my fucking way.'"

"But he didn't, did he?"

"No, he didn't give up. He was the stubbornest man I've ever known. Everyone else had already left the cemetery, but we were still out there by the open grave, shouting at each other. Finally he said, 'Just give me the gun for twenty-four hours. Then I'll give it back and you can do whatever the hell you want with it.' And I said fine, okay, because I was tired of arguing with him and I knew I could buy another gun anyway. Then he made me promise two things, that I'd go to Saint Anne's Church that afternoon and that I'd never tell anyone I'd given him the gun." John frowned. "That should've made me suspicious. But I wasn't thinking straight. I wasn't thinking at all."

Ariel shifted her head to the side, bringing her lips close to his ear. Her long hair brushed against his jaw. "What happened?"

"I kept my promise. I went to the rectory at Saint Anne's. Father Murphy wasn't there, but some of the old ladies in the congregation tried to console me. They held my hands and prayed and tried to make me eat a sandwich. I sat there for a couple of hours, dead to the world. I didn't want to go home because I knew Carol was in the apartment, packing her things. She blamed me for Ivy's murder, so she was moving out. She couldn't stand to spend another minute with me." He clenched his hands and winced. "And then I heard sirens, a whole bunch of them. A few minutes later someone burst into the rectory and yelled, 'Father Murphy's been shot! He's dead, he's murdered!'"

Ariel let out a soft "oh" of pain.

"I ran out of the church and rushed toward the sirens. They'd found his body in the basement of an abandoned row house. Just a few feet away were the bodies of Salazar and two of his boys. They'd all been shot in the head with forty-caliber bullets."

She tightened her grip on John's arm. "Your SIG Sauer was forty caliber."

"The cops couldn't find the gun. Their best guess was that another gang attacked the Disciples while they were having a sit-down with Father Murphy. He was just an innocent victim who got caught in the crossfire. It was a plausible story, and there was no evidence to dispute it." He shook his head. "But I'll tell you what really happened. Father Murphy killed Salazar and his boys. Then he shot himself. When the other Disciples rushed to the scene, they grabbed the gun and dumped it in the river. They didn't want anyone to know that a seventy-five-year-old priest had just iced their captain."

"Mercy." Ariel bit her lip. "He killed them to save you."

John was crying now. "He knew he couldn't stop me from going after Salazar. And that I'd probably wind up dead or in jail for the rest of my life. So he did the job himself. And he sent me to the rectory to make sure I had an alibi." His throat tightened, and he let out a sob. "But here's the worst part. Father Murphy believed in heaven and hell. So he didn't just sacrifice his life for me. He sentenced himself to eternal punishment. He gave up God Himself for me."

"Oh, John." She wrapped her arms around his waist and held him tight.

He was sobbing freely now, like a child. It would've been humiliating if anyone else were holding him, but Ariel knew what to do. Keeping her lips close to his ear, she murmured, "Hush, baby, hush. It's all right, it's okay." At the same time, she rubbed his back, making circular "there, there" motions between his shoulder blades. It was simple, commonsense consolation, but it worked. Ariel understood and forgave him. *She's good at this*, he thought. *It's yet another of her talents.*

John stopped crying after a minute or so. He felt weak and shaky, but also relieved. He hadn't realized until now how much his secret had burdened him. Grateful, he nuzzled his head against Ariel's shoulder, luxuriating in her embrace. "You were right," he whispered. "I feel better now."

"I'm glad." She patted his back. "But you haven't finished the story yet. Tell me how it got into the newspapers."

"Well, gang murders in Philly are pretty common, but this one made the news because of the priest connection. A reporter at the *Inquirer* called me after he heard that I worked with Father Murphy, and he got excited when I told him what had happened to Ivy. He asked if I was glad that Salazar was dead. So I gave him a quote, and the next day it was on the front page." He shrugged. "And you know the rest, right?"

Ariel pulled back, holding him at arm's length so she could look him in the eye. "Yes, I know the rest. In fact, I know the quote by heart." She took a deep breath. " 'No, I'm not glad. Every death is a tragedy. My little girl is in heaven now, looking down at all of us, and I know she's not happy with what she's seeing.' "

He opened his mouth in surprise. "My God. You memorized it."

"It's a good one." She smiled. "And I should know. I've heard a lot of quotes over the past four hundred years."

John smiled back at her. Then he leaned forward and kissed her. He couldn't help it.

It was a good, long kiss. He hooked his arms around Ariel's shoulders and pulled her close. She opened her mouth, warm and eager, and the tip of her tongue touched his. She smelled of salt and sweat and the black water of the rain forest. Her lips had the licorice taste of the ration they'd shared.

He didn't want to stop. He couldn't get enough of her. After a while he slipped his hands under her shirt and caressed her back, feeling her smooth skin and all the bony knobs underneath. Ariel shivered and grasped the back of his neck, kneading the muscles there. Then she pulled up his shirt and touched his nipple, moving her index finger in slow circles around it. Soon he was in a frenzy, out of control, like the animals that had churned the floodwaters after tasting the Fountain protein. He tore off Ariel's shirt and unclasped her bra. Then she unbuckled his belt and unzipped his trousers. It was a mutual frenzy, a shared madness. While Ariel wrenched off his pants and boxer shorts, he slid his hands into her jeans and gripped the waistband of her panties. Within seconds they were both naked, their bodies shining in the moonlight.

John lay on his back on the plank floor. Ariel hovered over him, her knees on either side of his waist. She stretched her hand toward him and touched his cheek, stroking it gently. Then she gripped his erection and angled it upward, pressing its tip between her labia. Leaning forward and lowering her hips, she guided him inside her, slowly engulfing him.

The moon was above her left shoulder and its light silhouetted her. John could see the outline of her body and her long, gorgeous hair, but the rest was dark, a mystery. He grasped her waist as she rocked up and down, and though he could barely see her face he knew she was smiling at him. She laughed and ran her hands through her hair. Then she let out a moan and cupped her breasts, holding one in each hand.

She was unashamed, unafraid. Rocking faster, she let go of her breasts and reached down to her crotch. She rubbed her clitoris with her middle finger, jiggling it rapidly as he moved in and out of her. She moaned again, louder this time. "Oh, John. Oh, sweetness."

Behind her voice he heard all the noises of the jungle, the nighttime chorus of frogs and birds and insects. The noises rang in his head, steady and loud, like the thumping of his blood in his ears and the slick, rhythmic smack of their bodies. He thought he'd have to shout if he wanted Ariel to hear him. When he spoke, though, his words came out in a whisper. "I love you, Ariel. I want to be with you forever."

She heard him. She arched her back and groaned with pleasure, grinding her crotch against his. Her head tilted backward, catching the moonlight, and for a moment he could see her eternally young face. She'd squeezed her eyes shut and opened her mouth wide. It was a silent scream, ecstatic and beautiful. John could see the wave of pleasure coursing through her, making her tremble, and a second later he felt it rush through his own body. He writhed beneath her on the plank floor, pumping madly.

For an instant, the universe was theirs. All of creation whirled around them.

They fell asleep afterwards, which was a mistake. When they awoke three hours later, half a dozen men in olive-green fatigues loomed over them. The guerillas stood around them in a circle on the hut's plank floor. The pale light of dawn reflected off the barrels of their assault rifles.

John felt a surge of adrenaline and despair. He tightened his hold on Ariel, who stiffened in his arms. Her eyes darted toward the corner of the hut where they'd stashed their carbines, but the guerillas had already grabbed the guns and Ariel's backpack as well.

The biggest man, a monster with tree-trunk arms and a face spotted with grotesque pimples, said something in Spanish, and the others laughed. John understood Spanish pretty well—half his friends in Kensington had been Latino—so he knew the guerilla had just made a comment about Ariel's ass. She'd put on her T-shirt and panties before falling asleep, but not her jeans. John sat up and pointed a finger at the big, pimpled bastard. "*No seas ojete,*" he warned.

The men laughed again. The big one, who wore a bright red bandanna, stepped forward and poked his rifle into John's ribs. "You don't have to curse me in Spanish, señor," he said. "You can call me an asshole in English, if you like."

"Listen, we're Americans. If you fuck with us, you'll be in deep—"

"No, no, please. Don't waste your breath. I'm not impressed that you're American." He waved his hand dismissively, then gave an order in Spanish to his men.

Two of the guerillas grasped John's arms and lifted him to his feet. Then one of them pulled a rope out of his pocket and began tying John's hands behind his back. His guts roiled as he felt the rope around his wrists. "Look, you're messing with the wrong people. I don't know who you guys are, but—"

"I'll tell you exactly who we are. My name is Comandante Reyes. I'm the man who shot down your expensive airplane. But the truth is, I'm glad you survived. I'll get paid twice as much for bringing you back alive."

Another guerilla stood behind Ariel and tied her hands together. She kept her eyes on Reyes, studying the man. After a few seconds she curled her lip in disgust. "Let me guess. The man who's paying you is named Sullivan?"

"*Sí,* Señor Sullivan." The commander smiled. He seemed genuinely pleased that Ariel had guessed right. "He says he's your brother. And he's anxious to see you."

"He's here? In Caquetá?"

Reyes nodded. "*Sí, sí.* And someone else from your family is here, too. Your sister, I think."

"Sister? I don't have a sister."

"No? That's strange. She looks just like you." Leaning toward Ariel, he closed his left eye and pointed at it. "But she's missing one eye. You sure you don't know her?"

THIRTY-ONE

First, the guerillas got on the radio and reported to their headquarters camp, describing in rapid Spanish what they'd found. Then they loaded John and Ariel into their skiff. They put John in the back of the boat and Ariel in the front, keeping them separated and well guarded. Then the men began poling the skiff down the shallow channel in the rain forest, using long sticks with pronged ends to push the boat through the black water. This, John realized, was how the guerillas managed to sneak up on them. Except for an occasional splash, the skiff moved silently across the swamp.

It was slow going, though, because the boat was big and hard to maneuver. After about thirty minutes they reached a wider channel, deep enough to allow them to use the skiff's outboard motor. They lowered the propeller into the water and started the engine. The boat shot forward, and soon they were speeding across the floodwaters. After another half hour they reached the main channel of the Yarí and headed upriver. About three miles ahead, the Yarí turned sharply to the right. That was their destination, John thought, the river bend. Elizabeth had said it was just a mile away from the Furies' new refuge.

As they approached the bend, John noticed that the local geography was a little unusual. A long, curving peninsula extended from the Yarí's south bank, first stretching north toward the middle of the river and then turning back south, like a fishhook. Between the tip of the peninsula and the south bank was a narrow, shallow strait, maybe five feet deep and sixty feet wide. The skiff slowed as it passed through the strait and entered a wide oval lagoon enclosed by the fishhook-shaped peninsula. Five other motorized skiffs were beached at the far end of the lagoon, and on the high ground beyond them were six large canvas tents. More guerillas in green fatigues milled around the tents, cleaning their rifles or eating breakfast around the campfire. John counted twenty-three men in all. A few of them waved at the boat, and Comandante Reyes waved back. Reyes, John observed, now wore Ariel's backpack.

The guerillas landed the skiff on the riverbank in front of the tents. Two of the men hauled John out of the boat and poked their rifles into his back, ordering him to march in front of them. He looked over his shoulder and saw Ariel following them, flanked by another pair of guards. He thought the guerillas would stop at the tents, but instead they marched right past the camp, following a dirt trail that led into the rain forest.

Reyes and several other men walked alongside them, cradling their rifles. John got a bad feeling as they entered the shade of the jungle canopy. At any moment he expected the comandante to halt their forced march and order his men to form a firing squad. John tried to reassure himself—if Reyes wanted to execute them, he reasoned, the man would've done it as soon as he'd found them—but the fear stayed with him. He pulled his arms, tugging at the rope that bound his wrists behind his back. There was no give at all. He was helpless.

The trail was straight and new. The bushes and branches on either side were freshly cut, hacked by machetes sometime in the past forty-eight hours. The trail also sloped steadily upward. After ten minutes or so, John grew winded from the climb. When he looked over his shoulder again he saw that they'd ascended at least two hundred feet. The Yarí River sparkled in the distance behind them, visible through the gaps in the trees. They were mounting a massive knob in the middle of the rain forest, a lonely hill that was the highest point for hundreds of miles around. John craned his neck, gazing at the vast green carpet surrounding them. Then the guards poked him in the back again and ordered him to walk faster.

After another ten minutes the trail leveled off and started to slope downward. They descended into a crater at the top of the hill, a dark, densely wooded bowl. The trail narrowed to less than the width of a man, and the guerillas had to use their machetes to lop off the encroaching branches. Then they reached what appeared to be a dead end. The trail led to a sheer stone ridge at the rim of the bowl, rising fifty feet above the forest floor. There was no path going around the ridge, and it was too steep to climb. But at the base of the stone wall John spied a dark crevice, an entrance to a cavern. Shards of fractured rock lay nearby, scattered in the brush. These shards, John realized, were the debris from an explosion. Very recently someone had used a stick of dynamite to reopen the cavern's sealed entrance.

Prodded by the guerillas, John squeezed through the crevice. The cavern was so dark he couldn't see anything at first, but after a few seconds he glimpsed a beam of light from a Coleman lantern. He headed for it, walking slowly. As his eyes adjusted to the dark he started to comprehend the cavern's dimensions. Although the rocky ceiling in this part of the cave was only twenty feet overhead, the cavern's floor sloped downward toward an immense lower chamber, as large as a football stadium. John stopped in his tracks, amazed. The guerillas stopped too, conferring with one another in Spanish, and that gave Ariel a chance to walk up beside him. She peered into the depths of the cavern and sniffed the air.

"Not bad," she said. "It's almost as big as Haven."

"Yeah, plenty big." He edged closer to her and lowered his voice. "Do you think we should make a run for it?"

She looked askance. "You want to run through a pitch-black cave with our hands tied behind our backs?"

"I'm just—"

"Keep moving, *Americanos*." Reyes nudged them from behind. "Your countrymen are waiting."

As John resumed walking he saw several figures in the light from the Coleman lamp. Two of them sat on a low, flat outcrop that rose about a yard above the floor of the cavern like a granite platform. Nine others stood behind the outcrop, arrayed in a rough semicircle. The standing figures were Riflemen. John couldn't see their faces—they stood too far from the lantern—but he noticed the light gleaming on their carbines and leather boots. As he neared the outcrop, though, he recognized the seated figures, whose faces were lit from below by the lantern at their feet. The one on the left was Sullivan. He reclined on the stone ledge, propping himself on his elbows and spreading his legs wide. The one on the right was Elizabeth Fury, who sat with her back perfectly straight.

Sullivan was still dressed like a biker, in the same filthy bomber jacket he'd worn in Michigan. He put on a look of mock surprise, opening his mouth and raising his eyebrows, as John and Ariel came near. "Hark! Who approaches? Can I believe my eyes? Is it Lily and her paramour, arisen from the dead?"

Comandante Reyes stepped forward. "You see, Señor Sullivan? I told the truth when I gave my report over the radio. They're not even injured. They fell out of the sky and landed in God's hands."

"God's hands? I think not. Our family doesn't believe in God." Sullivan squinted at Reyes. "How did you find them?"

"They were stupid. They fell asleep in one of the tribesmen's huts. That's why we patrol the huts every morning, because people are stupid."

"So true, so true. But you're a clever fellow, Reyes, and you'll be well compensated for your cleverness. Now could you and your comrades step outside for a moment?" Sullivan pointed at the distant shaft of sunlight coming through the cavern's entrance. "I have to discuss some family business with my sister."

"No problem, señor." Reyes cheerfully took off Ariel's backpack and dropped it at Sullivan's feet. "I'll just leave this with you." Then he turned around and led his men out of the cavern.

Meanwhile, Ariel glared at Sullivan. John had never seen her so angry. Even in the dim light from the lantern, her eyes flashed with indignation. Straining against the rope that bound her hands behind her back, Ariel rushed toward her half brother. But she stopped at the last minute, just three feet in front of him, and aimed all her rage at Elizabeth instead. "What on earth have you done, Mother? How can you sit next to this viper?"

The Chief Elder remained still. Her long black dress blended in with the outcrop, but her scarred face glowed in the lamplight. Rather than look at her daughter, she stared at the jagged wall of the cavern. "I had to end the war, Lily. Too many of us were dying. We've just finished negotiating the terms of a truce."

"A truce or a surrender?" Ariel's voice was thick with contempt. "Did you agree to give him the formula for the catalyst?"

Elizabeth nodded. "After we learned that your plane went down, I flew to Brazil to rendezvous with the Caño Dorado expedition. And yes, I ordered

Mariela to hand over the formula. Then Basil and I arranged to meet here so we could settle our differences. I went up the Yarí with the expedition while Basil and nine of his men traveled in one of our Gulfstreams to the Caquetá airstrip."

"You've gone back to calling him Basil?" Ariel glanced at Sullivan, who was following their argument with a grin on his face. "I thought you said he'd given up the right to that name."

"Basil, Sullivan, it doesn't matter." Elizabeth waved her hand in a dismissive gesture. She was still staring at the cavern's wall. "I determined that the risks of continuing the war were greater than the risks of letting our men use the catalyst to produce the Fountain protein."

"Mother, don't you remember the numbers involved? To make enough Fountain to stop all the men from aging, they'd need an enormous amount of fetal tissue. They'd have to collect thousands of pounds of aborted fetuses *every month*."

Elizabeth finally turned to look at her daughter. Her lone eye glittered. "The numbers have changed, child. Our family now has half as many men as it had a week ago. Nearly a hundred guardsmen died in the battle of Haven, and the Riflemen lost a similar number. It's an appalling tragedy, but it does ease the task of procuring the fetal tissue."

Sullivan suddenly sat upright. His grin widened, as if he'd just had a wonderful idea. "May I add a point, miladies? The relocation to this new refuge will also work in our favor. The Colombian authorities are afraid to step foot in this part of the country. We can take advantage of the smuggling routes and make deals with every abortionist on the continent. The government isn't even likely to notice."

Ariel turned to face him, practically snarling. "Abysmal fool! Fountain alters your brain chemistry! It'll poison you!"

"Oh, really?" Sullivan put on another look of amused surprise. "The protein gives eternal youth to our women, and yet it poisons our men? Does that seem logical to you?"

"Aye, because of the interactions with your Y chromosome! You felt the side effects yourself when I injected you with Fountain, but you failed to report them. You were so damn eager to get the protein, you didn't tell me about the problems."

He stopped grinning. "There were no problems. Quite the contrary. Fountain made me stronger. That's the real reason why you don't want us to have it."

Now John stepped forward. He couldn't stay silent any longer. "Ariel's right. I took just one dose of the protein and it screwed up my head."

Sullivan let out a mirthless laugh. "Shut your mouth, paramour."

John didn't look at him. He addressed the nine Riflemen standing behind Sullivan and Elizabeth. Those were the people he needed to convince. "It's true, the protein makes you feel stronger. But it also makes you angrier, more violent. I was out of control."

Sullivan looked over his shoulder at his men. He realized what John was trying to do. "Can you believe the gall of this outsider? First he fucks the only daughter of our Chief Elder. Then he persuades her to give him the remedy that was meant for us. And then he tells us that we shouldn't take it ourselves."

"Don't you see what's going on?" John pointed at Sullivan. "Fountain damaged his brain. He can't control his impulses. He's already killed half the men he led into rebellion, and now—"

"*Silence!*" Sullivan jumped off the outcrop. John assumed the man was going to pummel him, and he braced himself for the first blow. But instead Sullivan knelt on the cavern's floor and unzipped Ariel's backpack. He reached into the bag and tossed aside the first few items he found— flash drives, rations, ammunition clips. Then he pulled out the medicine case and unlatched it. He shouted, "Aha!" as he stared at the syringe and the eight remaining vials of Fountain. Holding up the case so his men could see it, he pointed at the empty slot in the foam padding where the ninth vial had rested.

"You see? One of the vials is missing. The paramour is still taking the protein. It's too dangerous for us, but not for him, apparently."

Ariel shook her head. "Nay, you don't—"

"I'll show you how dangerous it is." Still facing his men, Sullivan removed the syringe and one of the vials from the case. He pulled the stopper off the vial and drew the yellowish fluid into the syringe. Then, without any hesitation, he jammed the needle into the crook of his arm and injected Fountain into the vein.

The Riflemen murmured. Although John couldn't see their faces, he knew they were watching carefully. Sullivan placed the empty syringe back in the case and closed it. He took a deep breath and paced in front of the outcrop, swinging his arms. He smiled at Elizabeth, who was still sitting rigidly on the ledge, and gave Ariel a lascivious smirk. Then he lunged forward and socked John in the stomach, throwing all his weight into the punch.

The blow staggered him. John doubled over, gasping for breath. But somehow, thank Jesus, he managed to stay on his feet.

Sullivan turned back to his men. "There, that felt good. In fact, I've never felt better. As you can see, Fountain doesn't hurt me. The only one hurting is this wretch."

He punctuated the sentence by smashing his fist into John's face. This time John tumbled sideways to the cavern's floor, his left shoulder smacking painfully against the hard stone. His ears rang and the whole cavern seemed to revolve around him, the Coleman lantern swinging crazily. Amid the maelstrom he saw Ariel rush toward him, her eyes wide and her mouth open and her forehead creased in fear. Before she could reach him, though, Sullivan grabbed her by the waist and threw her in the opposite direction. She slid across the floor and came to rest near the outcrop, at her mother's feet.

Elizabeth Fury stood up. Even in his nauseous, disoriented state, John could see how enraged she was. The scar on her face had become a thick dark line. She stepped between her daughter and son and pointed a trembling finger at Sullivan. "Remember our agreement, Basil! No harm comes to Lily! You're forbidden to touch her!"

"I apologize, milady." Grinning again, he bowed in front of his mother. "I don't know what came over me. I must've succumbed to the influence of that pernicious protein."

The Riflemen laughed in the background, but Elizabeth grew angrier. "Don't jest with me, varlet! If you break your promise, our truce is over!"

By this point, Ariel had lifted her head from the floor and sat up. She wasn't hurt, but with her hands tied behind her back it was a struggle for her to stand up. Elizabeth bent over her, offering to help, but Ariel scowled. "This makes no sense, Mother. Before we left Haven you told me that Sullivan couldn't be trusted. So what makes you think he'll keep his word now?"

"Believe me, our truce isn't based on trust. The Riflemen have spent all the gold they stole from our vaults, and now they're in dire need. The catalyst is useless to them without the money to acquire the fetal tissue. And I still control our family's financial assets." Elizabeth gave her son a pointed look. "If Basil and his men abide by the terms of the truce, I'll give them a yearly income that will meet their needs. If not, they'll get nothing. This arrangement will keep the peace between us."

"Nay, he'll trick you." Ariel shook her head. "He'll figure out a way."

Sullivan wagged his finger at her. "Ah, such lack of faith. When did you become such a cynic, Sister? Frankly, I think your paramour has had a bad influence on you. We need to do something about that." Tapping his finger against his chin, as if in deep thought, Sullivan stepped toward John, who was still too dizzy to sit up. "By the way, under the terms of the truce, I decide what happens to this outsider. Although I can't touch you, Sister, I'm free to do whatever I like with him."

"What?" On her feet now, Ariel turned to her mother. "Is this true?'

Elizabeth nodded. "I'm afraid so. Basil was insistent on this point."

John clenched his jaw and bit the inside of his cheek, doing everything he could to dispel the fog in his head. His situation wasn't good. Elizabeth had used him as a bargaining chip in her negotiations with Sullivan, and now the madman was going to kill him. His throat tightened, but not because he was afraid. He felt an unbearable sadness. He hated the thought that he'd never spend another night with Ariel.

He lifted his head, suddenly desperate just to look at her. But she was focused on Sullivan. Her face reddened and her eyebrows skewed in anger. "Nay! I'll stop you!"

Sullivan snapped his fingers. "Percy, Giles."

Two of his men stepped forward, emerging from the darkness, and flanked Ariel. Sullivan gave her a scolding look. "Sister, you should know better. I can't let you interfere with my plans. We'll have to put you under guard. You can join Mariela and your other cousins from the Caño Dorado expedition. They also objected to the truce that Mother and I negotiated. They're in one of the cavern's lower recesses at the moment. My men had to tie them up, unfortunately."

The Riflemen grabbed Ariel's bound arms. She struggled in their grasp, twisting and squirming. "Mother! You're going to let them do this?"

Elizabeth didn't answer her. She turned to her son instead. "Don't drag this out, Basil."

"Of course not." Sullivan snapped his fingers again, and two more Riflemen stepped out of the darkness and headed for John. "We'll take care of the paramour immediately."

John looked up at the two men approaching him. One of them had a bandage on his shoulder and a tattoo of a spiderweb on his face. It was Marlowe, the man who'd tortured him once before. The prick smiled, clearly delighted to get a second chance.

"We got a surprise for you," he muttered, bending low so that no one would overhear. "I hope you like ants."

THIRTY-TWO

Fifteen minutes later they left the cavern and returned to the bend in the Yarí River. It was a grim procession through the rain forest led by Sullivan, Elizabeth, and Comandante Reyes. The guerillas and Riflemen trailed behind, pointing their guns at John, Ariel, and the six women from the Caño Dorado expedition, all of whom marched with their hands tied behind their backs. John trudged a few yards behind Ariel and Mariela, the expedition's leader, who was remarkably tall, almost six and a half feet. She was also remarkably combative. As she walked down the trail she cursed Sullivan's men, using some of the foulest language John had ever heard. The Riflemen retaliated by jabbing their carbines into her back, but that only made her curse louder. Finally, Ariel shook her head and whispered something to Mariela, who fell silent at once. Then Ariel glanced over her shoulder at John and managed an anxious smile. She was trying to give him some hope, but she clearly had none herself.

When they reached the river they turned away from the guerillas' tents and the half-dozen beached skiffs, at least two of which must've been taken from the Caño Dorado women. Instead, they headed for the fishhook-shaped peninsula that curved along the Yarí's south bank. For most of its length, the peninsula was just a strip of mud and reeds, so narrow in places that they had to march single file. To John's left was the main channel of the river, flowing swiftly east, and to his right was the lagoon that the peninsula encircled. Its black surface swarmed with dragonflies and water striders. Every so often a fish splashed near the riverbank, disappearing before John could get a good look at it. He reminded himself that the world was beautiful, that it had existed for millions of years before he was born and would endure long after he was gone. But the beauty of the rain forest failed to comfort him. He closed his eyes and pictured Ariel's body in the moonlight. He didn't want to die.

As they rounded the peninsula's quarter-mile curve John noticed a bustle of activity near the tents on the other side of the lagoon. Laughing and shouting, the guerillas streamed out of their camp and raced to catch up to Comandante Reyes. No one wanted to be left behind. All twenty-three of Reyes's men joined the back of the procession, their faces rapt and eager and focused on John. They were looking forward to this unexpected bit of entertainment, and he was the star attraction.

At its tip the peninsula widened to a round, wooded knoll, about fifty feet across. The knoll rose a few yards above the water level, and a cluster of trees grew on top of it. The tallest was a kapok that stood at the very southernmost point of the peninsula. Its massive branches stretched over the shallow strait that separated the peninsula's tip from the Yarí's southern bank. As they neared the kapok John was surprised to see a pair of men squatting in the mud between the tree and the water. They were Amazon tribesmen, wearing nothing but loincloths, their chests and faces painted with black squiggles and lightning bolts. Both men hunched over a pile of bright green leaves, which they were tearing into strips and weaving into some kind of basket. For a moment John thought this encounter was accidental, but it soon became clear that the tribesmen were part of the show. The guerillas let out a whoop of delight when they saw the pair.

The procession halted in the shade of the kapok and Sullivan strode toward the base of the tree. He still wore his bomber jacket, which seemed an insane thing to do in the jungle's midday heat, but he wasn't sweating. He looked cool and comfortable and perversely cheerful. When he reached the kapok he bent over and picked up a long, straight stick from the ground. He swung the thing like a sword, slicing the air out of sheer exuberance. Then he poked its tip into a mound of brown soil between the kapok's roots.

"Ladies and gentlemen," he shouted, loud enough for everyone to hear. "I'd like to introduce you to my good friend, *Paraponera clavata*. More commonly known as the bullet ant."

He pulled the stick out of the mound and moved closer to his audience. John saw an unusually big ant scurrying down the stick. It was at least an inch long and looked like a wingless black wasp, with oversized mandibles and a pointed abdomen. The ant sped toward the hand that held the stick, but before it could get there Sullivan grabbed the stick's other end instead.

"It's called the bullet ant because of its sting," he added. "Paraponera's sting is more painful than any other insect's. As painful as a bullet hitting the flesh." Sullivan walked past his Riflemen and their prisoners, giving everyone a chance to look at the insect. Then he stepped toward the pair of tribesmen squatting in the mud. "It's such a nasty creature, one might assume that the local people would steer well clear of it. But the inhabitants of the Amazon have devised an initiation ritual in which young men deliberately endure the stings to prove how tough they are." He jabbed the stick at one of the tribesmen. "Show them."

The man seemed terrified of Sullivan. With trembling hands, he picked up the basket he and his companion had woven and showed it to the crowd. It wasn't actually a basket, John realized. It was more like a sack, about the size of a large purse, and it was threaded with the wriggling bodies of dozens of bullet ants. The insects had been wedged between the tightly woven leaves, with their heads and thoraxes protruding from the outside of the sack and their pointed abdomens twisting within. The sight of it alone was bad enough, but the ants also made shrill noises as they struggled, a clicking, shrieking chorus.

Now John was afraid. His stomach heaved as he stared at the inside of the sack, laced with all the squirming stingers. It was the mouth of hell.

"I've modified the ritual a bit," Sullivan continued. "Traditionally, the young men put their hands inside glove-sized sacks. They pass the initiation if they can endure ten minutes of stinging. Afterwards, their hands are paralyzed for several days. But I wanted something a little more dramatic." He stepped directly in front of John and held the stick below his nose. The bullet ant scurried past, a few inches away. "I ordered the natives to make a bigger sack for you, paramour. We're going to put it over your head."

Two of Sullivan's men stepped behind John's back and grabbed his arms to steady him. Sullivan threw away his stick and gingerly grasped the sack from the tribesman, and at that moment the guerillas let out a joyful roar. Their screams of excitement made John's stomach heave again. His knees shook and his skin went cold. Then he heard a higher-pitched scream, frightening but familiar, and he knew it was Ariel. He couldn't hear what she was saying, couldn't make out the words, but he told himself it didn't matter. *She cares about you. She loves you. Just focus on that.*

Sullivan turned the sack upside down and held it in the air above John's head. The shrill clicking of the bullet ants grew louder. He could hear them rustling between the woven leaves, waving their stingers up and down, striving with all their might to free themselves and attack their enemy. He squeezed his eyes and mouth shut as Sullivan lowered the sack. For Ariel's sake, he would try to be strong.

The first sting was to his scalp, just above his left ear. Sullivan was right: it felt like someone had just shot him in the head. The pain exploded in the left side of his skull, and he involuntarily jerked his head in the opposite direction. An instant later he felt the stings on the right side, on his ear and cheek and temple, like lead slugs slamming into him. He kept his eyes closed as the ants stung him again and again. The bullets hit him from all directions, drilling into his skin and muscle and bone.

His knees buckled, but the Riflemen propped him up. He felt like he was floating on a sea of pain. He listened for Ariel again, but he couldn't hear anything above the shrieking of the ants. He wanted to tell her something important, something he'd forgotten to say before. He reached for her in the darkness, stretching his arms. She stood far away, in a blooming garden, hundreds of years in the future. She was in Paradise, leaning over a cradle. God had just been born.

Remember me, Ariel. Remember me.

Cool water poured over his chest and arms. John lay on his back in the mud, drenched and shivering. He could hear the water splashing over his face too, but he couldn't feel it. Everything above his neck was throbbing with pain. He felt as if he'd just pulled his head out of an oven.

He tried to open his eyes. His cheeks and forehead were swollen, but he managed to pry his eyelids apart. He saw a bright hazy swath of sky and a man standing over him with a bucket in his hands. This, obviously, was the man who'd just splashed water on his face to revive him. Although John's vision was blurry, he could make out the spiderweb tattoo on the man's face.

Marlowe smiled. "That was just the warm-up, asshole. There's more to come." Then he rejoined the other Riflemen standing in the shade of the kapok.

John squinted at them, even though it hurt like a son of a bitch. They were still pointing their carbines at Mariela and the other women from Caño Dorado, but he didn't see Ariel among them. With a fierce grunt he craned his neck, trying to see behind them. Comandante Reyes and his guerillas were lined up along the edge of the lagoon, eager for more midday entertainment, and Elizabeth stood on the other side of the knoll, staring at the Yarí's main channel, her face resolutely turned away from the sadistic spectacle. But he couldn't find Ariel. Then, just as desperation started to overwhelm him, he heard her voice. "I'm over here, John."

He turned his head, shuddering in agony, and saw her standing ten feet away, with Sullivan behind her. He gripped her hair with one hand and held the sack of bullet ants in the other. His expression had changed sometime in the past few minutes, while John lay unconscious. He no longer seemed comfortable or cheerful. His lips were pulled back from his teeth and he was sweating freely in his bomber jacket. His cheek twitched as he looked down at John. "Your face looks like porridge, paramour. Not even my slut of a sister would want to kiss you now."

John strained at the rope binding his wrists, but it was as tight as ever. Bracing himself for more pain, he pursed his lips. "Why . . . haven't you . . . killed me yet?"

"It's very simple. I'm going to break you before I kill you."

"No." His skull flared as he shook it. "You won't."

"Not with physical pain, no. It's a useful tool, but it only goes so far. Emotional pain is the best way to destroy someone's soul." Sullivan shook the sack of bullet ants, raising the volume of their shrieks. "I'm going to put this over Lily's head now. That will be interesting, won't it?"

John felt a jolt of alarm. He sat up, his head bursting, and struggled to his feet. Marlowe grabbed him before he could take a step toward Sullivan, and the Rifleman named Percy smacked him with the butt of his carbine. At the same time, though, Elizabeth came striding toward them, her long black dress dragging through the mud. Although her head had been turned away from them, she'd clearly been paying attention. She glared at her son, her hands clenched.

"Enough of this, Basil! Just execute the man and have done with it!"

Sullivan grimaced. His cheek twitched again as he narrowed his eyes. "Don't tell me what to do."

"I won't tolerate any more threats to Lily! Let go of her this instant!"

Instead, Sullivan yanked on Ariel's hair and pulled her backward. "She needs to be punished. You did a poor job of disciplining her, Mother. I'm going to teach her to be obedient."

"I said *let go of her!*" Elizabeth jumped toward him and knocked the sack of bullet ants out of his hand.

Pandemonium erupted. The woven sack hit the ground and broke apart. Some of the leaves came loose, freeing the ants, which swarmed over Sullivan's boots and up his legs. With a scream, he let go of Ariel and ran toward the water, stamping his feet and slapping his pants to shake off the insects. Meanwhile, Elizabeth slipped her hand under the neckline of her dress and removed a pocketknife hidden in her bra. Pulling out the blade, she cut the rope binding Ariel's hands. Then she brandished the knife at the five Riflemen who'd raised their carbines and surrounded her and Ariel. "Stand back!" she yelled. "Leave us be!"

The Riflemen kept their distance, unwilling to act without further orders. Sullivan swiftly recovered from his scare, but his face had turned bright red in humiliation. He stomped toward the circle of Riflemen and the two women at its center. "That was stupid," he hissed. "Very stupid."

"Let us go in peace!" Elizabeth yelled. "You can keep the refuge and all the surrounding property. We'll help you relocate the rest of your men and provide you with all the gold you need."

"I don't need your help." He sneered at her. "You're useless to me now."

"You won't survive in this jungle without our money. You'll need food and medicine and construction materials. And you'll need to keep paying your guerillas if you want their protection."

Sullivan shook his head. Then he reached into his bomber jacket and pulled a pistol out of his shoulder holster. It was a Mauser, a sinister-looking, old-fashioned gun, like something a Nazi spy might carry in a World War II movie. "I'm tired of your advice, Mother. And I'm sick of hearing your voice."

Elizabeth widened her lone eye. She brandished her knife again. "Don't be a fool! If I don't return safely to my cousins, you'll get nothing from us! You'll rot here!"

"We can earn our own money. I have a plan."

"It's not as easy as you think. Do you realize how long it took our family to build up its wealth?"

"There's a quicker way. We're going to sell Fountain protein to the highest bidder."

She gave him an incredulous look. "What?"

"Eternal youth is a valuable commodity. The billionaires in America and Europe and China will pay us handsomely for it."

"So you plan to reveal the existence of Fountain? And its antiaging effects?"

"Only to a select few individuals. The people who can afford to pay us."

"Stop and think for a moment, Basil. Once you reveal this secret, it'll spread like wildfire."

"Not necessarily. Not if we're careful."

"It doesn't matter how careful you are. You can't control the—"

"I already told you, I don't need your advice!" Sneering again, he pointed the gun at her chest. "Your day is done, Mother. Your reign is over. This is the dawn of a new age, the Age of the Immortals. And I'm going to be its master."

Elizabeth didn't respond at first. She cocked her head and stared at her son in disbelief for several seconds. Then she started laughing. She lowered her knife and raised her other hand to her mouth, trying to suppress her laughter, but she couldn't stop herself. "Dear Mother of Creation, you can't be serious. You—"

Sullivan leaped forward, lightning fast, and ripped the knife out of his mother's hand. Then he pressed his pistol to her chest and fired.

Elizabeth's death changed everything. As John watched the Chief Elder fall, his fear was so great he nearly collapsed, too. He knew there was no one to stop Sullivan from hurting Ariel now. Although John had resigned himself to his own fate, he was horrified by the thought of Ariel in pain. Sullivan knew this, knew how much it would tear John apart, so he was sure to keep hurting her for hours, torturing and maiming her in front of everyone on the muddy riverbank. And in the end, Sullivan would kill her. He'd force John to watch the light go out of her eyes.

Ariel knelt beside Elizabeth's body, her hands slick with her mother's blood. She was crying silently, staring straight ahead as the tears trickled down her face. John tried to go to her, but Marlowe and Percy held him back. Although everyone there was gazing at Elizabeth's corpse, the sight seemed to have a special fascination for the Riflemen. They must've felt like they'd just witnessed the death of a god. The men gazed at Ariel too, looking for signs that she was afraid, but she gave them nothing but that blank, paralyzed stare. John realized she was doing the same thing he'd done. She was resigning herself to her fate.

John let out an anguished cry and struggled with Marlowe and Percy, twisting in their grasp. Sullivan was right: this agony was worse than the pain in his head and face. He couldn't let them kill Ariel! If she died, who would plant the garden? Who would turn the earth into Paradise?

Meanwhile, Sullivan paced back and forth along the riverbank, still gripping the Mauser in his right hand. He seemed more agitated than ever. His eyes were bloodshot and his neck was shiny with sweat. He avoided looking at his mother's body and stared at the ground instead, specifically at the ruined sack that had formerly held the bullet ants. Finally, he turned to the pair of Amazon tribesmen, who were still squatting in the mud a few yards away.

"Get me another one!" he shouted, pointing at the sack as he strode toward the tribesmen. When they looked at him in confusion, he bent over and slapped the nearest one in the face. Then Sullivan pointed at the tents on the other side of the lagoon. "Do it now! Before I shoot you!"

Cowering, the tribesmen slunk away and ran down the length of the peninsula. Sullivan watched them go, then turned to Reyes. "I apologize for the delay, Comandante. There will be a brief intermission while we wait for our native friends to prepare the second act."

Reyes chuckled. "It will be a long wait, señor. Those men won't return."

"What do you mean?"

"They're going back to their village. I think you frightened them."

Scowling, Sullivan raised his Mauser and aimed it at the fleeing men. But they were too far away, and after a moment he lowered the gun. His hands were trembling. With great difficulty, he slipped the pistol back into his shoulder holster. "Heathen knaves," he muttered. "They're more like apes than men."

"Señor, may I ask a question?" Reyes stepped forward and pointed at the six women from the Caño Dorado expedition. "Are you planning to kill these girls, too?"

Sullivan looked confused. He probably hadn't thought that far ahead. "They're my sister's allies, so they bear no love for me. If given a chance, they wouldn't hesitate to slit my throat. Killing them would be the safest option, I suspect."

"But they're such beautiful young girls." Reyes stepped toward Mariela and reached for her long red hair. He laughed as she twisted away and cursed him in Spanish. "It seems such a shame."

The guerillas behind Reyes murmured their agreement. The men nodded and nudged one another and slapped their rifles. The Riflemen showed some interest too. Marlowe and the others stared hungrily at their cousins. The fact that the women were sweaty and bedraggled and had their hands tied behind their backs seemed to make no difference.

After a few more seconds Sullivan grinned. A look of astonishment appeared on his face, as if he couldn't believe he hadn't thought of this idea himself. He nodded rapidly, sweat dripping from his hair. "You're right, we shouldn't kill them yet." He turned to Marlowe. "Bring my sister over here."

Marlowe let go of John and stepped toward Ariel, who still knelt beside her mother. She didn't resist as he pulled her up and dragged her to Sullivan. John winced as she walked by without even glancing at him. She was resigned, defeated. Her face was blank because she'd withdrawn her soul to the farthest corner of herself. The Riflemen could do whatever they liked with her, and she wouldn't feel anything.

Sullivan positioned himself so that John could see what he was doing. As Marlowe stood behind Ariel and took hold of her arms, Sullivan reached into one of the pockets of his bomber jacket and pulled out the knife he'd taken from his mother. Very slowly, he pulled out the blade and held it in front of Ariel's face. At the same time he glanced over his shoulder at John. "Watch carefully, paramour. You might learn something."

He gripped the collar of Ariel's shirt and pulled it toward him. The fabric stretched in front of her and strained against the back of her neck, but she didn't react. Her face was as expressionless as a mannequin's. Then Sullivan lowered the blade to the collar and began cutting downward. The tip of the knife sawed back and forth, less than an inch from her throat.

John's stomach twisted. He could hardly breathe. He wanted to throttle

Sullivan, to strangle the bastard, to grab the knife out of his hands and stab him in the heart. But John knew it was hopeless. He might be able to wrench himself out of Percy's grip, but what would he do then, with his hands tied behind his back?

Sullivan cut halfway down Ariel's shirt. Then he stopped, hands trembling, and stared at the lace cups of her bra. His hands shook so violently he could barely hold on to the knife. He closed his eyes for a few seconds, as if trying to control the tremors through sheer force of will. Marlowe leaned forward, still pinioning Ariel's arms, and asked, "You okay, Sully?" Nodding, he answered, "Yes, yes, of course!" But then he dropped the knife and stepped away from her.

"Keep her here," he barked at Marlowe. "I'll be back in a moment."

While the Riflemen looked on curiously, Sullivan stepped toward the water's edge, facing the shallow strait that separated the peninsula from the mainland. His back was turned, but John saw him reach into the pockets of his jacket. From his left pocket he removed a syringe. From his right he pulled out one of the vials of Fountain.

A light went on in John's head. Now he knew why Sullivan insisted on wearing that heavy jacket in the rain forest. He needed the jacket so he could stash the syringe and vials in its pockets, and he needed to keep the protein close at hand because he was addicted to it. He probably got hooked before he started his rebellion, when Ariel tested Fountain on him. After the protein ran out, he must've gone into withdrawal, but he'd obviously craved the stuff ever since. He'd given himself an injection only an hour ago inside the cavern, and now he already needed another. And as Sullivan stood there at the edge of the river, pulling the stopper from the vial with trembling hands, John saw what had to be done. It was the only way.

With a ferocious twist he freed himself from Percy's grasp and started running toward Sullivan. The bastard was trying to hold the vial steady so he could dip the syringe's needle into the yellow fluid, and he was so intently focused on this task he didn't hear John coming. Marlowe yelled, "Hey!" and lunged to intercept him, but at the same time he let go of Ariel. She spun around and kicked Marlowe in the crotch, stopping him cold. Running past them, John lowered his shoulder like a linebacker and plowed into Sullivan, knocking him face-first into the river. The Fountain protein spilled out of the vial and spread across the water in a yellow smear.

Luckily, John kept his footing on the river's muddy bottom. Because his hands were tied behind his back, he would've had a hard time getting back upright if he'd fallen. He felt an urge to stomp on Sullivan's neck and pin him underwater, but he didn't have the time. Instead he left the bastard behind and waded as fast as he could across the strait. The water deepened as he reached the middle of the channel and soon it was up to his shoulders. He sloshed frantically forward, taking huge strides. Then he heard Sullivan's furious voice behind him.

"Go after him! I want him alive!"

Within seconds John climbed out of the water and up the muddy bank on the other side of the strait. He didn't stop until he reached the high ground, twenty feet from the water's edge, and when he turned around he saw thirty men coming after him. Sullivan had picked himself up and ordered the Riflemen and guerillas to wade across the strait. Now everyone was in the water except for Marlowe and Comandante Reyes, who stayed behind to guard Ariel and the six women from Caño Dorado. While Sullivan paced along the riverbank, screaming orders at his men, Marlowe and Reyes stared across the strait at John. They were probably wondering why he just stood there instead of running into the rain forest. Taking advantage of their inattention, Ariel quickly bent over to pick up the pocketknife that Sullivan had dropped in the mud. Then she turned to Mariela and gave her a hand signal. A moment later all the women took a couple of steps backward, stealthily moving away from the water's edge.

Most of the men were wading through the deepest part of the channel when the piranhas struck. One of the guerillas thrashed in the water, shrieking in Spanish. Then two of his comrades joined in, flailing their arms as they struggled to return to the riverbank. Soon the water began to roil around the men and there was a frenzy of splashing. The Fountain protein had spread to the depths of the channel, its molecules seeping through the skin of the fish and inflaming their primitive brains. Then John caught a glimpse of a long black snake, thicker than a fire hose, coiling around the terrified waders. One of the men disappeared, his head pulled under the water. Then another man vanished. Then another.

There were screams in English too, from the Riflemen in the strait. The maddened piranhas swarmed thickly around the men, jabbing and biting and jumping out of the water. John spotted Percy splashing back toward the peninsula, but when he was just ten feet away from the riverbank he stumbled. As soon as he hit the water the piranhas surrounded him, tearing off chunks of flesh every time they struck his body.

John stepped farther away from the riverbank. So many men were dying in the strait that a bright red stain spread across the black water. He saw the piranhas feeding on another fallen Rifleman. He saw an anaconda drag another guerilla below the surface. And then he looked across the channel and saw Sullivan standing in the mud near the water's edge, gazing in dismay at the slaughter. For a moment John actually felt sorry for the man. Then Sullivan spotted him, and John could see the rage in his face, even from a hundred feet away. Although Sullivan couldn't have guessed the cause of this catastrophe, he definitely sensed that John was behind it. He reached into his jacket again, pulled out his Mauser and fired.

John hit the dirt and the bullet whizzed overhead. Sullivan fired again, and this time the shot came closer. John scuttled backward, trying to find some cover, but he was on open ground, with no trees or bushes or tall grass nearby. On the other side of the strait Sullivan stepped closer to the water and held his arm steady, tilting his head slightly as he looked at John through the Mauser's gun sights. But before he could pull the trigger, the river at his feet erupted in spray and a huge glistening reptile rocketed toward him. A black caiman, at least fifteen feet long, lunged out of the water and clamped its massive jaw around Sullivan's legs.

He screamed as the caiman's teeth sank into his calves. The reptile pulled his feet out from under him and he fell backward into the mud of the riverbank, dropping his gun. Then the caiman snapped its jaw to get a better grip on Sullivan's legs and started crawling backwards, pulling him into the river.

He would've disappeared under the water if not for Marlowe. The Rifleman sprinted forward and grabbed Sullivan's right arm. "I got you, Sully!" he yelled. "I got you!" He dug his heels into the mud of the riverbank and leaned backward, trying to pull Sullivan out of the caiman's mouth. At the same time, he looked over his shoulder at Comandante Reyes. "Help me, damn it!"

Reyes reluctantly came forward and grabbed Sullivan's left arm. He and Marlowe pulled together, but the caiman didn't let go. It snapped its jaws again, fastening its teeth on Sullivan's thighs. Meanwhile, Ariel saw her chance and gave Mariela another hand signal. An instant later all the women turned around and ran toward the trees at the top of the knoll. John felt a burst of relief as he watched them. Then he started running too, heading toward the place where the peninsula branched off from the mainland.

As he ran he kept his eyes on the other side of the strait. He saw the caiman shake its head fiercely and heard Sullivan shriek as the flesh tore off his thigh bones. Comandante Reyes lost his grip on Sullivan's left arm and tumbled into the mud. Marlowe kept his hold on the right arm, but the caiman was stronger. It crawled backward, pulling steadily on its prey and dragging Marlowe closer to the water's edge. *"Sully!"* he screamed, his face red and frantic. *"Hang on, Sully!"*

Then Marlowe spotted the Mauser lying in the mud. While holding on to Sullivan with one hand, he picked up the gun with the other and fired at the caiman's back. The first two shots seemed to have no effect, but after the third shot the caiman twisted angrily. It snapped its jaw once more and gave a final tug on Sullivan's legs, pulling something loose. Then it retreated into the river while Marlowe dragged his unconscious boss away from the water. Sullivan's left leg, severed at the knee, spewed blood over the riverbank. Reyes, who'd retreated to higher ground, knelt in the mud and vomited.

John turned away from them and kept running. He couldn't watch anymore. He had to get back to Ariel and make sure she was safe. For obvious reasons, he couldn't wade back across the strait to the tip of the peninsula. He had to take the long way around the lagoon.

Soon he reached the canvas tents of the guerilla camp, which was empty and silent. All the guerillas were in the water, either dead or dying. As John ran past the camp, though, someone burst out of the last tent with a knife in his hand. The man lunged at him, fast as the caiman, and grabbed John's arms from behind. Then he used the knife to cut the rope binding his hands. John looked over his shoulder and saw it was one of the Amazon tribesmen, the one Sullivan had slapped. Bowing his head in respect, the man pointed inside the tent he'd just come out of. Leaning against its central pole were three AK-47 rifles.

John darted into the tent and grabbed all three guns. By the time he came back outside, the tribesman had vanished into the rain forest. John offered his silent thanks, then charged toward the peninsula.

The lagoon was still frothing as he ran along the strip of land surrounding it. Corpses bobbed and drifted this way and that, nudged by the schools of piranha feeding on them. He hoped to hell that Ariel and her friends had stayed away from the water. As he approached the wooded knoll near the tip of the peninsula he saw two prone bodies lying at the water's edge, half-eaten corpses that had drifted onto the riverbank. Then he saw a third body farther away from the water, but this one was alive. Comandante Reyes lay facedown in the dirt, his arms and torso slashed in several places and his shirt soaked with blood. Ariel bent over him, holding the pocketknife to his throat, while Mariela tied his hands behind his back using the same rope that had formerly bound his prisoners. The other women crouched in the brush nearby.

Their heads turned as John came near. Ariel spun around, ready to attack, her tear-streaked face contorted in anger. Then she recognized him. Her mouth opened but no words came out. She dropped the knife and ran into his arms.

It was a brief embrace, though. After two and a half seconds she took one of John's assault rifles and handed another to Mariela. "We still have to deal with Marlowe," she said. "He's on the other side of the trees, and he has the Mauser. I heard him fire a shot a minute ago." Raising her rifle she headed for the tip of the peninsula. John and Mariela followed her while the other women remained hidden in the brush.

The three of them crept silently under the knoll's trees. When they reached the kapok they took cover behind the trunk and peered around it. Both Sullivan and Marlowe lay faceup on the riverbank, halfway between the kapok and the water's edge. Sullivan's face was as white as paper. He'd died in the mud, bleeding out from his severed leg and the other wounds from the caiman attack. Marlowe was dead too, but he hadn't been killed by any of the jungle's animals. The ground under his head was saturated with blood and his right hand still clutched the Mauser. He'd shot himself in the mouth.

John stepped out from behind the kapok and approached the corpses. He saw nothing in Sullivan's face. The man looked empty, deflated. But Marlowe had clearly died in despair. He'd lost his master, his reason for being. He couldn't fight anymore and he couldn't surrender. He couldn't go on.

In that moment John knew the rebellion was over.

EPILOGUE

The rainy season in the Amazon was particularly bad the next year. In April the Yarí rose so high that it inundated the south bank at the bend in the river. The floodwaters swamped the peninsula and the area where the guerilla camp once stood. But by that point the tents had been taken down and carted away. The Furies had already moved to the network of caves that honeycombed Monte Mariposa, the tall hill south of the river.

The relocation had gone more smoothly than anyone could've imagined. Ariel had led the effort from the very first day, organizing the women from the Caño Dorado expedition as they took over the guerilla camp and turned it into their headquarters. She inventoried their supplies and set up a rotation for guard duty. Then she retrieved the expedition's radio equipment and reestablished contact with the Furies in North America. Over the next few days Ariel worked like a demon, and John started to worry about her. He wondered if she was working so hard just to stop herself from thinking about her mother and Cordelia. Then it occurred to him that the opposite might be true. Ariel, he suspected, wanted to honor the loved ones she'd lost. By preparing her family's new home, she was carrying out the last assignment Elizabeth had given her before they left for South America. And when Ariel needed to select a code name for the refuge, she chose Mariposa—Spanish for butterfly, Cordelia's favorite symbol.

The first order of business was deciding what to do with Comandante Reyes. Mariela and a few of the other women argued in favor of executing him, but Ariel overruled them. Reyes was still in shock, traumatized by the slaughter in the lagoon, and Ariel realized he could do a useful service for the Furies. Before she released him she described the horrible way he would die if he ever returned to the Yarí River. When Reyes rejoined his comrades in the FARC insurgency, he told stories of a family of *brujas* in the jungle who could summon caimans and anacondas to attack their enemies. As a result, the guerillas kept their distance from the Furies' refuge, and the Yarí became the most peaceful river in Colombia.

The second task was extending an olive branch to the remaining Riflemen. Ariel opened negotiations with the men in western Minnesota who were holding Grace, Claudia, and Gower as hostages. She told them what had happened to Sullivan. She gave them the details about the Fountain protein, explaining how it would addict and poison them. And she promised full amnesty to all who laid down their arms. The Riflemen didn't respond to the offer right away. There was a fair amount of hemming and hawing. But in the end they accepted her terms. The men were leaderless, penniless, and on the run from the law. Although the FBI had suspended Agent Larson, the bureau was still investigating the strange incidents in northern Michigan and still on the lookout for the Riflemen. They had no choice but to return to their mothers and sisters.

Then Ariel organized the gradual migration of eighteen hundred Furies from Canada to Colombia. Over the next six months they came in groups of ten to twenty, flying on commercial jets from Toronto to Bogotá. Pretending to be tourists visiting southern Colombia, they traveled by chartered bus to San Vincente del Caguán, where they boarded the skiffs that carried them downriver. And they brought supplies with them: food, medicine, laptops, and a whole lot of money. Once they arrived at the bend in the Yarí, Ariel put them to work. They made the cavern inhabitable and built water wheels for generating electricity. They constructed new laboratories underground, and a new library as well, and began the process of transferring their Treasures to it. In the deepest chamber of the cavern they built a crypt for Elizabeth and all the other Furies who'd died. Ariel made special arrangements to exhume Cordelia's body from her hastily dug grave in Wisconsin and bring it to South America.

Outside the entrance to the cavern the Furies cleared the trees and brush that had filled the huge bowl at the summit of Monte Mariposa. Then they divided the fertile land into sloping fields and planted corn, beans, manioc, and yucca. They also built a compound of huts above-ground, at the very center of the bowl, enough to house a few dozen people. To the outside world, they would pose as a New Age commune, a bunch of hippies from the United States and Canada who'd decided to establish their own utopia in the Colombian rain forest. Ariel liked this disguise much better than the Amish one. She enjoyed wearing the peasant blouses and tie-dyed skirts that were part of the subterfuge.

Although the Chief Elder was now Grace Fury, who'd automatically ascended to the position after Elizabeth's death, many of the Furies started to believe that their true leader was Ariel. She was involved in every aspect of the relocation, and she was more likable than either Grace or Claudia, the other council member. After a few months Grace felt compelled to recognize Ariel's contributions by offering her the third seat on the Council of Elders. Ariel accepted the offer but insisted on two conditions. First, she convinced Grace to make the council an elected body within five years. Second, she received permission to marry John Rogers.

John did all kinds of work during the construction of the refuge—carpentry, welding, stonecutting, cooking—but the job he loved the most, strangely enough, was farming. He got a big kick out of planting the seeds and watching the crops grow. And his favorite partner to work with was Gower, who'd had enough of being a guardsman and wanted to give agriculture a try. In the evenings the two of them would work side by side, weeding the rows of bean plants and chatting about baseball. John was trying to get Gower interested in the sport. Sometimes Ariel would join them and talk about watching Lou Gehrig and Bob Meusel play, and Gower would become thoroughly confused about which players were alive and which weren't.

On the last evening of April, though, John was working alone in the bean field when Ariel stepped out of the cavern to join him. She walked slowly along the edge of the field, then turned and made her way down the aisle of dirt between two bean rows. She wore a skirt tie-dyed with gorgeous starbursts, explosions of yellow and orange and red, and a loose peasant blouse that stretched expansively over her swollen belly and enlarged breasts. She was seven months' pregnant and still getting used to walking with the extra weight. When she reached John she took his hand and they walked together across the field, heading up the slope that led to the rim of the bowl. They liked to sit on a stone ledge at the rim and watch the sun set over the rain forest below.

As they walked, Ariel placed John's hand on her belly. "Jaunui's been kicking a lot today. And stepping on my bladder too. I've been running to the bathroom every five minutes."

John pressed his hand flat against her blouse and waited for a kick. Jaunui—which was the word for water in the language of the local tribes— wasn't really the baby's name. It was just a nickname they were using until the child was born. They didn't know yet if the baby was a boy or a girl.

Ariel frowned. "Wouldn't you know it, now it stopped. Every time I get up, Jaunui takes a break. But as soon as I sit down and try to work, it starts up again."

"Well, that makes sense. When you're walking, you're rocking the baby to sleep."

"I'm telling you, I don't remember so much kicking the last time I was pregnant."

John chuckled. "That was three hundred and forty years ago. How can you remember anything from back then?"

"Oh, hush. I wish you could get pregnant. Then you'd know what I'm going through."

They walked on in silence. John sensed that something was bothering Ariel, something besides the baby's kicks. Now that the relocation was mostly complete, she'd started looking for other challenges to take on, and one of them was inheriting her aunt Cordelia's role as the family's prophetess. She'd already set up a satellite dish so she and her cousins could access the Internet, and now she spent a few hours each day scanning the world's news so she could see where things were headed. Unfortunately, the news was bad more often than it was good.

"Okay, what happened?" John asked. "Another nuclear test in North Korea?"

She shook her head. "No, not yet. It's just a million other things. In

Africa, in China, in the Middle East. And nothing's going right. There's so much work to do, I don't even know where to start."

He draped his arm around her shoulders and squeezed. "Don't worry. You'll figure it out."

"The situation is getting worse, not better. It's going to take hundreds of years to turn things around."

"But that's okay. You got all the time in the world, right?"

She stopped walking and looked at him. It was true, she had more than enough time ahead of her, a long golden trail stretching to the horizon. But he didn't. That's what was bothering her. "I'm sorry, John," she whispered. "Let's talk about something else."

He smiled. They were very near the stone ledge at the rim, but instead of heading for it he turned Ariel around and pointed at the fields they'd planted inside the bowl. "Look what we've done," he said. "We've made our own garden. It's not Paradise, but it's enough for me." Then he pointed in the other direction, at the vast carpet of rain forest surrounding Monte Mariposa. "And this is for you. You're going to turn the whole world into a garden. And maybe Jaunui will help you."

Ariel started crying. John touched her cheek and wiped away a tear with his thumb. Then he led her to the stone ledge and they sat down to watch the sun set. The fiery circle was just about to touch the green carpet.

"There's only one thing I feel bad about," John observed. "I'd like to see God being born. You know, with the manger and the farm animals and the three wise men and all."

Ariel laughed through her tears. "It may not happen exactly that way, you know."

"Do me a favor. When you see Him, give Him my regards, will you?"

"Of course. I think She'll enjoy hearing about you."

Then John kissed her, and the sun sank below the horizon.

AUTHOR'S NOTE

I got the idea for *The Furies* from one of my son's term papers for middle school. He was reading about the Salem witch trials, and during the course of his research he came across a fact that startled me: the witch hunt in the Massachusetts Bay colony was just one episode in a long, terrible series of massacres. During the sixteenth and seventeenth centuries, witch-hunters in Germany, France, Switzerland, and Great Britain killed thousands of people. In the late 1500s, for example, 368 accused witches were burned to death in a campaign begun by the Archbishop of Trier in Germany. The great majority of the victims were women. Two villages in the area were left with only one woman each.

Historians have struggled to explain the causes of the mass hysteria and slaughter. Some have noted that the period of the witch hunts roughly coincided with destabilizing events such as the Protestant Reformation, the Counter-Reformation, and the rise of nation-states. In the midst of chaos, local authorities may have sought to bolster their control by encouraging the persecution of the least powerful members of society. But this argument isn't entirely convincing. It doesn't explain why the churchmen and secular leaders focused the public's hostility on witchcraft in particular, or why the persecution was so brutal.

I decided to invent another explanation. I imagined the Furies, a large, secretive family living in Western Europe at the time of the witch hunts. Although they dwelled side by side with other villagers, the Furies had their own history and customs. The family was led by its women, who shared an idealistic, pre-Christian philosophy. The Furies also shared a genetic distinction, a hereditary trait that made them the target of their neighbors' fear and hatred. The markers of this trait were red hair and green eyes, which were considered the signs of a witch in premodern times.

As in my previous novels, I've tried to incorporate real-world scientific ideas and technologies into the book. The descriptions of gene expression, evolutionary biology, and therapeutic proteins are based on the latest research in those fields. I'm grateful for the encouragement and support from my colleagues at *Scientific American*. I'd also like to thank my agent, Dan Lazar of Writers House, and my editor, Peter Joseph of Thomas Dunne Books/St. Martin's Press. And thank you, Lisa, for giving me the love story that I've retold here.